"GET OUT!"

No one moved though I yelled my loudest. I hit the back of the crowd and began to shove my way through. Pushing through the last row of Robin's band, I *almost* scrambled out of the cave. Four flying–saucer–like vehicles stood in the compound in front of the cave. Over a hundred men and women stood around them. Most wore some sort of formfitting white body armor. Suddenly a loud roar, sounding like the whine of a jet engine, filled the sky. Another flying saucer platform swooped down and landed in a cloud of dust and swirling leaves. And Joan of Arc was now by my side. Reaching over her shoulder, she pulled her sword from its scabbard and pointed to the enemy who was forming a skirmish line in front of our cave.

"We have them where we want them," she said, sounding satisfied.

I looked over at her. Her eyes were wide and wild. She was not only a loon, but suicidal as well. Our attackers were carrying weapons that ran the gamut from primitive looking spears to cannonlike devices which could probably bring down the entire mountain.

We were Dead . . .

QUAD WORLD

Robert A. Metzger

A ROC BOOK

ROC
Published by the Penguin Group
Penguin Books USA Inc., 375 Hudson Street,
New York, New York 10014, U.S.A.
Penguin Books Ltd, 27 Wrights Lane,
London W8 5TZ, England
Penguin Books Australia Ltd, Ringwood,
Victoria, Australia
Penguin Books Canada Ltd, 2801 John Street,
Markham, Ontario, Canada L3R 1B4
Penguin Books (N.Z.) Ltd, 182-190 Wairau Road,
Auckland 10, New Zealand

Penguin Books Ltd, Registered Offices:
Harmondsworth, Middlesex, England

First published by Roc, an imprint of New American Library,
a division of Penguin Books USA Inc.

First Printing, November, 1991
10 9 8 7 6 5 4 3 2 1

RoC Roc is a trademark of New American Library,
a division of Penguin Books USA Inc.

Printed in the United States of America

To my family

I would like to acknowledge both Charlie Ryan and Richard Curtis who gave a new writer a chance, and Andre Norton and Robert Heinlein who opened up a ten-year-old's imagination.

Contents

Prologue 11

CHAPTER 1
Welcome 17

CHAPTER 2
Tom 31

CHAPTER 3
Robin and the Fair Joan 42

CHAPTER 4
Cardinal Bonaparte 58

CHAPTER 5
Joe Average and Vlad Junior 74

CHAPTER 6
Anna, Jesus Christ, and Sir Basil 91

CHAPTER 7
Escape 105

CHAPTER 8
Tartan the Barbarian 124

CHAPTER 9
Revenge 141

CHAPTER 10
The King and Necro Ned 161

CHAPTER 11
God, the Supreme, and Loki Too 176

CHAPTER 12
On the Threshold of Hell 194

CHAPTER 13
Memories of Hell 208

CHAPTER 14
Behind the Mask 226

CHAPTER 15
Colin Wood 242

CHAPTER 16
The Pearly Gates 256

CHAPTER 17
Colin Junior in Bruinland 271

CHAPTER 18
Truth and Consequences 286

CHAPTER 19
Full Circle 300

CHAPTER 20
Next Day 316

Prologue

Dummar Aircraft Co, Research Lab
Malibu, California
July 10, 1990—Tuesday, 8:29 A.M.
Walnut Conference Room

Opening the conference room door and stepping in from the fluorescent brightness of the hallway, I walked into the shadow-filled room. Running my hand along the wall I flicked on the lights and walked directly over to the room's bay window. Perched high in the hills, the lab had an unbroken view of ten miles of California coastline. Breakers rolled in, crashing against the sea wall that protected the multi-million-dollar beach homes of the Malibu Colony. Far out beyond the white water, out where the sea glimmered gold and orange, one lone surfer bobbed in the swell.

Ting ting ting . . .

I flicked off my watch's alarm and tossed the folder that had been tucked under my arm onto the conference room's table. It slid several feet before coming to rest on the high-gloss lacquer surface. The Silicon Integrated Circuits lab status meeting was permanently fixed in time and space: always held in the Walnut Conference Room and always called for eight-thirty on a Tuesday morning. Same station, same time, and unfortunately usually the same, meaningless problems discussed.

Sitting, I switched on the overhead projector that

was sunk into the tabletop. Behind me, a projector screen dropped from the ceiling and covered the bay window. I slipped my first transparency onto the overhead, looked over my shoulder, and twiddled with the focus knob until I got some minimal level of crispness. Leaning back in the Naugahyde chair, I propped my feet up onto the corner of the table. Since I'd never been able to start the meeting before eight-forty, I had at least eight minutes to kill. I stared at my feet.

My brown leather wingtips looked like shit. I'd bought them over three years ago when I had first gotten this job, wore them every day to work, and had never bothered to shine them—not once. Shining shoes was a waste of time. It didn't get one more circuit pushed through the lab or a single line completed for a *Journal of Applied Physics* paper. Normally I would not even waste the time considering the state of my shoes, but they had degraded to such an extent that it was obvious that their days were numbered. The fact that a great deal of the stitching no longer seemed to remain, and that my brown socks poked through between leather uppers and plastic soles, implied that they were on the verge of total disintegration. That mattered. My only other shoes were a pair of currently gray, but at one time white, tennis shoes. If I wore those to work I'd offend the sensibilities of the three-piece-suit crowd. In the good old days, before I had been put in charge of the Integrated Circuits lab, I would have simply considered that an added bonus. But no longer. I had become politically astute. When I pitched a program to the suits, or needed more hands in the lab, things like footwear, color-coordinated ties, and buttoned-down collars, seemed to mean more to the bean-counters that ran this company than the actual technical content of my request. There was no escaping it, I'd have to get a new pair of shoes. An image filled my head. I saw myself squirming through a mall, choked full of people who were incapable of taking more than two shuffling steps forward without halting directly in my path, or even worse, pinning me up against the window of a frozen yogurt parlor, holding me captive, and then exposing me to detailed discussions that revolved around the merits of pink versus purple hair, or the grim details of stuffing a forty-two-inch ass into a thirty-six-inch pair of jeans. My stomach tightened in a knot. Suddenly my shoes didn't look quite so disgusting. With a little luck, I could probably get another few weeks out of them. Maybe, just maybe.

The conference room door snapped open and images of fat asses, new wingtips, and frozen yogurt on a stick vanished. Kent Cooper lurched in. He held a styrofoam cup in each hand. Half falling and half sitting, he seemed to collapse in a chair at the far end of the table. He blew on one of his coffees and then took a quick sip. He grimaced and his eyes narrowed to slits. Apparently the cafeteria was maintaining its high level of culinary excellence.

He looked like hell, and I doubted that even two cups' worth of caffeine would make any real difference. His new baby had been home for almost a month now, and judging by his appearance his body had not yet adjusted to that organic alarm clock firing at not quite periodic two-hour intervals.

"Morning," he said to me, grinning as he always did.

I just grinned back at him. In many ways I found him quite remarkable, but on mornings when he looked like this I was in flat-out awe of him. He and his wife had survived two years with their first kid and, apparently having so enjoyed the pain, suffering, and sleep-deprivation associated with the process, had opted for a second. It was just one of the many amazing facets of his masochistic personality.

"Tube three has a crack in its hydrogen injector, and I had to kill it last night," I said by way of casual converstation.

He nodded, but didn't look up. He seemed to be intently studying something floating in one of his coffees. So I left him alone and let him contemplate whatever it was he saw in his coffee.

I could suddenly hear an argument in the hallway.

The door eased open, then closed without anybody's having entered. It opened again and a leg popped in, but a body didn't follow. I recognized that perfectly polished penny loafer digging into the shag carpet. I shook my head, trying to rattle my brain. I seemed to be suffering from a shoe fetish today.

"If I don't get twenty gallons per minute of deionized water flow through those back hoods, we'll be eating silicon wafers like they were potato chips," said Jack Behnke as he hung out into the hallway. "And those chips go for eight bucks a pop."

"Have to redesign everything to do that," said some distant voice.

"Not my problem," said Behnke, sounding somewhat happy about the pain he was inflicting. "I speced the requirements, and you guys signed up for it."

"We're out of money," said the distant voice, now starting to sound panicked.

I laughed quietly to myself. Behnke was obviously talking to someone from plant facilities. It was the one department at Malibu that seemed to have the unique ability to not only spend all their allocated funds before a job was completed, but on many occasions the money would evaporate to nothing before they had so much as laid a single length of pipe, or even opened up a tool box.

"It has to be completed before first shift tomorrow morning," said Behnke. He walked quickly into the conference room and slammed the door behind him before anyone could tell him why that request was impossible to meet. Jogging around the end of the table, he jumped into a chair next to Cooper. His knit tie flew up and disappeared over his shoulder. "That entire department is brain-dead," he said as he smiled. Behnke possessed a dazzling set of white teeth. The tips of his over-large canines seemed to twinkle. I think his teeth maintained their high luster because of the large number of asses that he continually chewed on.

The door banged open.

I glanced up at the clock. It was eight-forty.

Behnke shut up.

Techs and the rest of the staff engineers walked in.

I gave Behnke a smile that he returned. Cooper, Behnke, and myself were a team. Between us we could say anything, and most often did. But it never went beyond *us*. The environment at Dummar was far too political for loose lips.

"I want to be out of here by nine," I said as people slowly found their seats. In actuality, I would have liked to have never been here at all. Nothing was ever really accomplished in a meeting. The real decisions were made while scurrying down a hallway or while standing captive with a section head in front of a urinal. But management was of the mindset that progress and output had a direct correlation with the number of meetings held. Actually, I tended to agree with that. But where they saw a positive correlation I saw a negative one. But mine was not to reason why, mine was but to work and die.

Several had not yet seated themselves, but I wasn't about to waste any more time. Pulling a pen from my top pocket, I pointed at the first line on my overhead transparency.

"I want to prioritize the circuit lots that are about to hit the nitride deposition tube, so we can open a time slot to take it down for cleaning. It's flaking so badly now that it's going to start affecting chip yields."

I looked up, getting ready for the barrage I knew was about to come. Everyone was going to demand that their project deserved Number One Priority.

Nobody spoke.

Nobody moved.

The room had suddenly taken on a sick green tint, and something buzzed in my ears. I didn't seem to be breathing.

I tried to speak, but my lips wouldn't move.

I didn't have long to consider the strangeness of all this. The room went black.

And I knew what'd happened.

There wasn't the slightest doubt in my mind.

I had just dropped dead at the start of the eight-thirty Tuesday Silicon Integrated Circuits meeting.

Unbelievable. Deaths in the workplace always peak on Monday mornings and Thursday afternoons. That was a scientific fact.

I had no right to be dying on a Tuesday morning.

CHAPTER 1

Welcome

I wondered what had gotten me. Thirty-four-year-olds who didn't smoke or drink weren't supposed to drop dead. My heart was good, and my blood pressure a respectable 78/115. I shouldn't have died, and especially not on a Tuesday. I didn't even have a will. But of course, it wasn't as if I had actually needed one. There hadn't been anyone to leave anything to. My folks had died almost fifteen years earlier when a drunk in a Cadillac, who couldn't tell right from left, had made it almost a mile on the wrong side of the Santa Monica Freeway before he caught my parents' little Toyota head-on. There were no relatives. I was single, and didn't really have what one could call friends. I had acquaintances, people to say hello to while racing down the hallway, or someone to share a cafeteria bench with while trying to down a greaseburger and a Coke.

There wasn't anyone crying at my tombstone. Hell, I doubted that there even *was* a tombstone. I was probably planted in the far corner of a ten-acre patch of green in some place like Van Nuys or Mission Hills. I'd be right out there at the intersection of row 876 and column 239. Beneath smoggy skies, and within earshot of a freeway, a little brass marker in the overgrown grass would mark my eternal resting spot:

JOHN SMITH
BORN MAY 21, 1956
DIED JULY 10, 1990

My estate, including the life insurance that the company insisted I carry, was probably worth a couple of hundred grand. Every last dime of that would go to the State. My legacy to mankind would probably be the funding of twenty yards of sewer line on the outskirts of Barstow. Thousands would be indebted to me whenever they flushed.

I coughed.

My lungs were congested, full of liquid.

Very strange. Dead men shouldn't be coughing, and they certainly shouldn't be worrying about congested lungs. My head pounded as if I'd just caught a speeding two-by-four above the eyes. I felt feverish and my joints throbbed. It felt an awful lot like the flu.

Flu?

Being dead was certainly bad enough, but to also be subjected to the flu was adding insult to injury. My throat was dry, and I couldn't swallow past what felt like some large glob of mucus. What I really needed was a drink of water. A beer would have gone down just great.

I opened my eyes.

I was seated in a soft chair, with my elbows propped up on the table in front of me. I was in a room in which the walls were covered with walnut paneling. A mental clutch, buried somewhere deep beneath my frontal lobes, popped into first gear.

I was in the Walnut Conference Room.

I was not dead.

My joints were on fire. Bending forward, I let my head rest against the tabletop. The lacquered wood felt cool. Sweat dripped down my face, gathering at the tip of my nose in large fat drops, until they fell, splattering into the carpet.

I wasn't dead, but I was as sick as the proverbial dog. Hell, any dog that felt this bad would simply have curled up and died.

That didn't sound like such a bad idea.

I must have been hit with one of those new-and-improved mutated flu strains that had floated in from some Third World germ factory. Right now I was probably eyeball-deep in viral nucleic acids courtesy of Katmandu, or some damn swamp in southwest Cameroon. Coughing something up from deep in my lungs, I sloshed it around my mouth for a few seconds and then spit it out beneath the table. The janitors would just have to earn their money this week.

If I had been sick enough to have passed out, it made absolutely no sense that I was still in the Walnut Conference Room. My comatose butt should have been hauled down to Malibu Emergency. Right now, some beefy nurse named Gretchen should have been sternly telling me that if I didn't quiet down and keep the thermometer tucked under my tongue, she'd happily find another place to stick it.

Sitting up quickly, I watched the room tilt from side to side. I stood, and the joints in the small of my back popped. It sounded like corks exploding from champagne bottles. The conference room was dark—much darker than when I had first awakened. I glanced up, trying to ignore the stabbing pains in my neck. The fluorescents were dead, with one entire bank dangling down, having crashed through the overhead grillwork. Ceiling tiles littered the far end of the conference room table.

Someone's ass in plant facilities would fry for this.

Walking slowly, and taking shuffling steps so I wouldn't find myself facedown in the dusty shag carpet, I moved toward the window.

A bloated orange sun sat on the horizon. The ocean was gray. I leaned against the window and, shivering, listened to the buzzing insects that seemed to fill my ears. The last sliver of sun quickly vanished beneath the water.

I blinked, squeezing my eyelids tight, trying to force my pupils to dilate. It was dark, far too dark. Staring down the black coastline, I couldn't see a single light. Those multi-million-dollar beach homes, filled with movie stars and Vid preachers, usually blazed as if lit with searchlights.

A power outage.

That had to be it. No power—no lights. I nodded to myself, banging my head against the window. That was the answer. I had the flu, and there had been some sort of monstrous power outage. I could rest now. It all made sense. I stared out into the dark.

Think you moron!

The voice echoed in the back of my head.

The Pacific Coast Highway should be a sea of cars. Cars have headlights and taillights.

I smiled. Of course. The answer was obvious. The road must be closed. There had probably been another damn rock slide that had shut down all four lanes. Suddenly all the pieces came together. There must have been an earthquake. Just as the flu had nailed me and I had passed out, an earthquake had hit. It had knocked the power out and rock slides had closed the highway. It even explained the state of the conference room.

What timing. I never got sick. But the day some killer flu snuck up on me and kicked me square in the ass had to be the same day that "the big one" hit.

Carefully walking back to the table, I dropped into a chair. I would wait until someone returned for me. Wrapping my arms around my chest, and trying not to cough, I closed my eyes.

Pzzzzt!

Reflexes tossed me out of the chair and threw me onto the floor. Rolling on my shoulder, and feeling no pain, I came to my feet. My body was crouched low, my hands reaching forward, and my fingers flexing. I felt the wall at my back.

Lights were on.

Sparks shot out from the wiring of the dangling bank of fluorescents. The arcing and hissing wiring had been what had startled me.

Standing, I could feel that my head was almost clear. For the first time since waking, I was able to take a deep breath without my lungs burning. Smoke began to drift down from somewhere in the ceiling. Trotting over, totally amazed at how well I was feeling, I went toward the door and ran my hand along the wall in the direction of the light switch. If I killed the power, it might just stop whatever was smoking in the ceiling.

The light switch by the door was gone.

Every Tuesday morning for the past three years I had flicked on that light switch.

I suddenly felt dizzy.

"Where's the goddamned light switch?" I leaned against the wall, feeling hot and flushed. The fever was on me again.

"Light request?" asked a sweet, feminine-sounding voice.

I turned, still leaning against the wall. The room was empty. That was a bad sign, a hell of a bad sign. I was hearing voices.

"Light request?" asked the voice again.

I then realized that the voice was coming from somewhere above me. I looked up, peering through the thickening smoke that was drifting down. *A speaker grille.* Someone from the Central Security Station must have been listening in on the conference room. She might have control over the power.

"Kill the lights!" I shouted.

The room was thrown into darkness.

The door was practically at my back. Fumbling, I searched for the doorknob, grabbed it, and pushed the door open.

I stumbled out and leaned against a wall in a hallway that I'd never seen before. The wall at my back was soft and warm, nothing like the hard steel-sheet walls that should have been there.

Obviously, I had not been in the Walnut Conference Room. The missing light switch should have told me that, but this flu was scrambling my brain. After I had passed out they must have taken me to some other room.

I stared down the long hallway.

The labs were not all that large. I had never seen this hallway, or come across anything that even resembled these strange walls. I turned my head, looking down the opposite direction. It was identical, and just as featureless as the other end of the hallway had been.

Not quite.

Almost sunk into the wall, and colored in the same cream color, was what looked like a phone. Hugging the wall, and dragging my cheek along its warm surface, I worked my way toward it. Grabbing it, I popped it from the wall. A remote. No cord. I looked at it closely. No buttons, no dial, no nothing. Desperate, I put the receiver up to my ear. It was dead. There was no dial tone—not even a hiss.

"Shit!" I said into the phone.

"No one of that name is listed in the directory," said the same voice that I had heard in the conference room. "Are you trying to reach an outside party?" she asked.

I took a deep breath, that is, as deeply as someone could breathe who felt like they had a quart of slime filling each lung.

"What's happened around here?" I asked. I leaned my forehead against the wall and closed my eyes.

"Can you be more specific?" she asked.

In that instant, I realized that she had to be one of the many morons from the Plant Facilities Department. We had just had an earthquake that had probably flattened Los Angeles and she didn't seem to have noticed it.

"The *big* quake," I said cynically. "Can you remember back to a few hours ago, when your ass was being bounced around your office?"

"Define big?" she asked.

I reopened my eyes, pulled the phone away from my ear and stared at it, then pushed it back up against the side of my face. "Larger than 5.0 on the Richter scale," I said with a surprising degree of calmness.

"The last quake of that magnitude or larger occurred 854 days ago, measuring 5.8, and was centered on the Paso Robles fault."

I just shook my head. Then I realized that she must be in shock. A ceiling tile had probably smacked her on the head and she was still woozy. That had to be it. She was suffering from a concussion.

"Let me speak to someone else," I said.

"There is no one else," she answered.

I was getting mad now. I needed a doctor, and didn't have time to play games with a delirious woman. "Am I supposed to believe that there is no one else in this entire building?"

"The man responsible for the reactivation of system lighting has just entered the building."

Now I was getting somewhere. The damn building must have been evacuated and somehow, in all the confusion, I had gotten left behind. I'd be tearing someone a new asshole when I found the idiot responsible for that slipup.

"How can I get to him?" I asked.

"Simply follow the red arrow," she said.

Red arrow. She was a certifiable loon. This hallway was one unbroken, cream-colored tunnel. "What red arrow?" I snapped at her.

"The one below your left foot," she said.

Like an idiot, I looked down at my feet. Like an even bigger idiot, I lifted up my left foot.

I damn near dropped the phone.

Where my foot had just been there was now a red arrow. It was somehow beneath the floor, or possibly even within it. It pulsed on and off in about one-second intervals.

I felt sick. Things gurgled deep in my gut.

Somehow the phone was back up to my ear. "I don't understand," I said in an almost inarticulate mumble.

"When you hang up the phone the arrow will lead you to the man who has just entered the building. I suggest that you do this while the lights remain on. As a result of the large power drain from systems activation earlier this day, there has not been sufficient time to recharge. I estimate less than five minutes of lighting remain."

I nodded stupidly at the phone for a second, then hung it up. The instant it hit its cradle the arrow flitted across the floor and pulsed its way down the hallway. It got about six feet in front of me and then halted.

I shuffled a few steps in its direction, then stopped.

It pulsed a few more feet down the hallway, then stopped.

When I caught up with it, it made a turn at the first corridor intersection it encountered. I followed. It traveled down another long, featureless hallway, then turned a corner and lead me into a dead-ended hallway. The arrow pulsed momentarily at a blank wall, then vanished.

The wall I faced hissed, and then detached itself, quickly sliding into the section of wall next to it. I looked down at the floor, beyond where the wall had been, expecting to see the arrow, but it was still gone.

I looked up, saw something, and then looked right back down at the floor. My fever must have been a lot higher than I had imagined. There was no doubt about it, I was delirious.

I looked back up. What I had thought I had seen was still there. *He* stood at the end of this new hallway. I had hoped that *he* would have vanished in a puff of smoke, or perhaps dribbled into the floor. No such luck. It was amazing what my delirious brain was capable of generating. The guy was completely decked out in a space suit. However, it was not one of those form-fitting white NASA jobs, but an aluminum-foil special that sprouted a wild array of coat-hanger antennas. His left arm had been replaced with some sort of manipulator that looked a hell of a lot like a lobster claw. He wore a leather belt with two holsters, one of which held a pearl-handled pistol and the other what had to be his ray gun. This guy looked like a refugee from a fifties sci-fi flick that had been shot over a weekend in someone's basement. All that was missing to make him the perfect alien invader was the bubble space helmet. Instead, he wore a red beret.

I watched him reach his right hand over his shoulder and tug at something that must have been strapped to his back. Moving so quickly that he seemed to blur, that *something* was now in his hand. Colored a dull gray, it looked like a toaster—two slices. He pointed it at my head.

Something finally leaked through to my brain. That

voice that had earlier echoed in the back of my head now told me that I was about to receive something much more lethal than a faceful of toasted raisin bread.

His fingers seemed to have melted into the toaster's dull aluminum sides.

"Good night!" he screamed in a screechy voice.

I wanted to jump, to find cover, but there was no place to hide. The corridor at my back didn't turn a corner for at least fifty feet.

I just stood there. If killed in this nightmare, I hoped that I'd simply wake up.

The tendons flexed in the exposed parts of his hands.

I squinted, gritted my teeth, then closed my eyes. I wondered if I'd feel anything when my brain was splattered against the cream-colored walls. For just an instant, an image of someone from Plant Facilities wiping down the red-stained walls filled my head.

Something tickled deep inside of my head.

I opened my eyes.

His hands were flexing convulsively.

"Crash hard!" he screamed. "The Supreme wills it!"

Every time his hands flexed that same something tickled inside of my head.

"Shielded," he said, while sneering at me. He reslung the toaster across his back and pulled his ray gun from its holster. The gun's tip shimmered a deep purple.

It was one thing to take it like a man, and accept your fate when faced with the prospect of being raisin-breaded to death by a toaster, but it's something totally different when you're threatened by a loon in a spacesuit who's waving a ray gun. Blind instinct finally took over.

I turned and ran.

"Stop!" he screamed.

Once I started moving it was going to take a hell of a lot more than the screech of a NASA-induced nightmare to slow me down. I seemed to eat up the hallway. Never had I run so fast. My head cleared, my lungs sucked down air, and before I would have thought it possible I'd started my turn into the hallway corner, dropping down to all fours as I did in order to increase traction.

Fzzzt!

Hot air fanned the side of my face.

With the added incentive of ray-gun blasts I was certain that I'd practically fly down the next hallway.

Wrong.

My hands grabbed the wall just as I rounded the corner. And I mean *grabbed.* My fingers bit into the soft wall and sank almost knuckle-deep. I shredded a five-foot length of the cream-colored material before I came to a stop. It seemed to turn to goo in my hands, and I threw the now slimy stuff onto the floor where it hit with a wet-sounding smack. I crept slowly back toward the corner I had just rounded.

And I didn't have the slightest idea why I was doing this. Inside I was screaming, demanding that my body turn tail and run down the hallway. I was getting no response. My body continued to creep up to the corner. I had no idea why I was doing this. Something else was apparently calling the shots—something that was going to get me killed in this nightmare.

The spaceman's galvanized lobster claw jutted from around the corner. I wanted to crawl into the wall, but my body had other plans. My right hand grabbed the claw, and instead of trying to push it aside pulled it straight toward my chest. I wanted to close my eyes, but no such luck. I was staring directly into the spaceman's now startled face. Pulling him toward me had thrown him off-balance and he was now falling, with that claw hand leading the way.,

I'd be skewered for sure.

Then, at a speed that I would not have believed possible, I sidestepped like a matador skirting around a bull. This move sent him sailing down the hallway, but apparently my body did not consider that sufficient. My left hand shot up for his face—palm open. I caught him square in the nose. I could feel things break, almost shatter. With a final flick of my wrist, my hand pushed his splintered nose up into his brain. Suddenly looking extremely limp, he flew past me.

I turned.

I was back in charge. Whatever had been running my body by remote control was gone. I collapsed to the floor.

Then I looked over at the spaceman. It appeared as if he had been kneeling, perhaps praying, and then had simply fallen over, landing flat on his face. His ass was still propped up, pointing straight at me.

I had just killed a man.

My only experience with fighting had been in the fourth grade. The result of that encounter had been two black eyes, six stitches, and a cracked rib. All mine.

The spaceman wheezed.

I scrambled down the hallway on all fours, moving like a scuttling crab. I only stopped when my head smashed into a wall and I fell back on my butt.

He had to be dead. I'd felt him die.

Sweat dripped down my face and my vision began to tunnel. I told myself that all I had heard was trapped air in his lungs gurgling up through his throat. That explanation didn't seem to reassure me.

Then, without the slightest warning, my stomach exploded. I didn't even have time to get to my knees, but threw up in my lap. My already bruised throat burned, and my nose stung as stuff backed up through my nostrils. One explosive burst was all there was. Putrid green slime ran down the front of my shirt and dribbled over my pants. The stuff that now covered my clothes had absolutely no resemblance to the waffles and eggs I had eaten for breakfast.

Standing, I felt the muscles in my legs start to twitch, and my left knee turned to jelly. Again I was on the floor and again I tried to stand, this time almost crawling up the wall. I locked my knees and took several deep breaths.

Somehow, I did not faint.

Mercifully, he had not moved. He was dead, there was no doubt about that. I hoped.

"Shit!" I managed to scream, just as I launched myself from the wall I was leaning on, bounced off the opposite wall, and once again hit the floor. I had seen something—several somethings—move.

Pushing my way up the wall, this time only sitting, I looked at the dead man. He was still dead, but things continued to move.

The claw that had been his right hand had detached itself and was now crawling across the floor. As I watched, it jerked and spasmed, and a small cloud of smoke quickly engulfed it. Little puffs of blue smoke were also rising from his ray gun.

Something else was moving. Where I had ripped off a large patch of wall covering and thrown the goo to the floor, the torn wall had almost repaired itself. It wasn't that the wall had simply closed the rip. No, by comparison that would have been far too easy. The goo that I had tossed onto the floor had almost vanished. Only a small pile of the stuff remained. The rest of it was undulating in a narrow line, like a long column of ants marching single file, working its way up the wall to fill in the gouge. As I watched, the pile on the floor grew smaller and smaller and eventually vanished. There was not the slightest indication that the wall covering had ever been ripped out.

I just closed my eyes and banged the back of my head against the wall. I shivered. Again I could feel my face flush and my lungs clog. A stabbing pain sliced through my chest with each breath.

Before I even opened my eyes I'd stood, in one quick jerk. Opening my eyes, I ignored the fact that the hallway had taken on a green tint and was listing back and forth like a boat in a hurricane. I went down to the end of the hallway and pulled a phone out of the wall.

"Get me out of here!" I screamed into it.

"Specify the destination," the female voice said sweetly.

I could handle no more of this. "Get that damn red arrow back here, and take me outside of this building by way of the nearest exit!"

At my feet the red arrow appeared again, then darted

down the hallway in the direction of the spaceman. I dropped the phone and stumbled forward. Nothing was left of his smoking possessions but little piles of gray goo. Not a weapon left. Not quite. The pearl-handled pistol hadn't melted.

Bending over, and risking fainting, I tugged at his belt buckle. My fingers felt almost boneless, as if made of rubber. After I'd tugged at leather and brass, from all possible angles, the buckle finally popped open. Standing, I leaned against the wall for support, planted the toe of my black boot in his side, and pushing, rolled him over.

A small little piece of myself, detached and hiding somewhere deep in the back of my brain, wondered about the black boots that I now seemed to be wearing. I had never owned a black pair of boots. God, how I suddenly missed those familiar, ratty brown wingtips. Those old shoes seemed a world and a lifetime away.

My hands, which seemed to be controlling themselves, strapped the gun belt around my waist, managing to rebuckle it on only the fifth or sixth attempt. The red arrow still pulsed, seeming to patiently be waiting for me. I shuffled forward, my feet not so much walking as scraping against the floor with each step I took. Down hallways, through door panels, past twists and turns, I wandered for what felt like hours. It was probably only minutes.

I stared down at thick brown carpeting. I looked up. It was the lobby—the lobby at Dummar. That big polished obsidian block that made up the guard's desk filled the adjacent wall. In front of me, across the lobby, stood the front doors.

Walking, even though my feet seemed to catch in the thick carpet, I worked my way into the center of the lobby. I tried to show my badge at the guard's desk but I no longer seemed to have a badge. No problem. Dummar Research Labs no longer seemed to have a guard. I didn't have to lean on a door to get it open. One was already propped open, probably courtesy of my dead friend from outer space.

Outside.

It was a warm Malibu summer night. In the distance, surf pounded. That was wrong. The beach was at least a mile down the hill. The background buzz of Los Angeles, twenty miles away, always drowned out the sounds of the ocean.

But apparently, no longer.

Starlight lit the night.

I walked. First I shuffled over concrete, then packed dirt and weeds, and finally through chaparral and gravel. Loose rock crunched under my boots.

One more step and I could rest. One more step and I'd be safe. I took that one more step. There was no ground beneath my boot. I fell, sliding down in a torrent of rock and dead brush.

I came to a bone-crunching stop.

On my back, I watched the stars flash across the sky. North, south, east, and west they raced. The stars produced only feeble light, but holding up my hand I could see every bloody scratch that covered it. More than just starlight lit the night. I twisted around, as rocks tore at the skin on my back.

There it was, far to the north, almost over the rim of the canyon I had just slid into. A large, glowing number blazed in the sky: 27.

I felt myself smile. How nice, I thought. The night sky is numbered. What a wonderful place this is.

Rolling onto my belly, I crawled.

Darkness came.

CHAPTER 2

Tom

My mouth felt as if I had been chewing on gravel and wood chips. I kept my eyes closed, not yet willing to risk opening them, hoping that when I did I'd be looking up at the white paneled ceiling of a hospital room. Except for the debris that seemed to fill my mouth I felt far better than I had any right to. Taking a deep breath, I was able to completely fill my lungs without invisible steak knives stabbing me in the back. I had no headache, and my joints didn't throb. Whatever virus had gotten ahold of me, it seemed I'd finally fought it off.

Shifting ever so slightly, I expected to hear the crackle of starched cotton sheets, but it sounded more like shifting gravel.

Oh God.

My hands were palms up, held closely by my sides. Turning my right hand slowly over, I tried to grab a handful of cotton sheet. I didn't have to look, I could feel it. My hand was full of pebbles and dirt. Sucking down a deep breath I held it, then opened my eyes.

Above my head, visible in a gray light, I could see a cracked concrete ceiling that was only a few feet above me. Dried spindly roots, thick with spider webs, poked through the shattered concrete.

Please let me sleep, I begged.

Something invisible seemed to reach into my brain and squeeze. My body tensed. I willed it to relax, but my arms turned and my hands opened. I felt my palms press into the gravel.

Don't move! I screamed to myself.

I felt myself sit up.

Again, something else seemed to have taken control of me.

"Hi," said a deep voice.

My body didn't so much as twitch, even though I thought the shock of hearing that voice was going to melt down my brain. My body continued to sit up, and I felt something cold and firm in my right hand.

The pistol.

I was pointing it squarely at the chest of someone who sat in front of me. He sat at the entrance of what looked like a drainage pipe. Bright light from outside framed him in a golden halo.

"Hi," said the man in front of me once again.

My index finger squeezed down.

I could not kill again. I refused. I absolutely refused. My finger continued to squeeze. My extended arm shook.

"Hi," he said for the third time.

Please, I begged. *This man is no threat.*

My hand slammed down into the gravel. I dropped the gun. That invisible something that had been in my head vanished, and I was in control again.

The man scrambled toward the pipe entrance, seemed to decide that he couldn't reach it, then dropped down, trying to hug the inside of the cement pipe.

"Hi," he whispered in a squeaking voice.

He was now in the shadows, no longer just a silhouette.

He wore no red beret. Whoever, or whatever he was, at least he wore no red beret. Barefoot, and wearing what looked like the remnants of a blue jumpsuit, he smiled at me with a wide, stupid-looking grin. He clutched a large bundle of rags to his chest. It was only then that I noticed his hands. They looked as if they had been dyed red. I didn't like the look of that. It was too reminiscent of a red beret.

I opened my mouth to ask him who he was.

"Urmph . . ." I mumbled in a cracked whisper.

My throat was bruised, swollen and dried. It felt as if I had swallowed a bottle of furniture polish and then let it dry on the inside of my throat. I tried to force down some spit but there was nothing to force down.

The man moved, and reached out toward me. He held out a silver-colored flask. It looked about quart-sized, and when he shook it something inside sloshed.

I almost tore off several of his fingers as I pulled it from his hands. It looked like a standard canteen that you'd find in some army surplus store, but where it narrowed down at its neck it didn't have a cap. It was a single piece of continuous metal.

I looked up at him and shook the canteen.

He just smiled.

Holding the canteen in front of my lips I upended it, then shook it, showing him that nothing was coming out.

He continued to smile.

I was damn near dying of thirst. I shook the canteen a few more times out of sheer frustration, then tossed it at him. Deftly catching it, he put the canteen's neck up to his lips. His Adam's apple bobbed up and down and a thin stream of water dribbled from the corners of his mouth.

I felt my eyebrows arch. It was impossible.

Reaching for the canteen, I pulled it from his mouth. It was still upended, but nothing poured out. The top surface was still a solid, unbroken piece of metal.

With his sleeve, he wiped the water from his chin.

Wrapping my lips around the neck of the canteen, I upended it. Water, cool and unbelievably refreshing, poured into my mouth and trickled down my throat. Only after I'd almost completely emptied it did I stick my tongue into its neck, trying to feel the release mechanism. I could stuff my tongue almost a half an inch into the canteen, but all I felt was smooth metal. Pulling it from my mouth, I could see that the top of the neck was once again a solid, smooth surface.

I shook the canteen in his direction. "How does that work?" I asked. It hurt my throat to talk, but at least I could now.

He only smiled. His eyes looked blank.

Shrugging, I tossed the canteen back toward him. He caught it and stuffed it inside his bundle of rags. I had much larger mysteries to deal with than trick canteens. If the canteen's operation was too complicated a question for him, I'd keep it simple. "What's your name?" I asked.

The smile slowly faded from his face. His eyes narrowed, and he clenched his jaw. His lips moved slowly, then twitched. He said nothing. Reaching up with one hand he rubbed his mouth, then tugged at a lock of long blond hair that hung over his right eye.

It looked as if he was going to start crying.

He squirmed, then began to smack the sides of the pipe with the palms of his hands. His face turned red, and he suddenly wrapped both hands around his throat. It looked like he was strangling himself.

"Tom!" he screamed. Then, almost instantly, the smile returned to his face. He dropped his hands into the dirt.

I wasn't sure exactly what was wrong with him, but I was fairly certain that he wouldn't be answering too many of my questions. Sticking out one of my legs, I began to prod him with the tip of my boot. Before he went into some sort of convulsive fit I wanted to get out of this pipe. He seemed to understand, and quickly backed out. I crawled out after him.

I had to shield my eyes, the sun being so dazzlingly bright. Tom sat in the dirt about a dozen feet from me, tossing a pebble from hand to hand. A stupid-looking grin still filled his face.

Leaning against the drainage pipe, I looked around. I was about halfway down a narrow draw. Far below me I could hear the sound of rushing water. That had to be Malibu Creek. Above and behind me I could see the path of broken brush and ripped-out weeds where I'd slid down the side of the hill last night.

After I'd killed the spaceman.

I dropped to the ground, my suddenly rubbery legs collapsing beneath me. I looked up into the crisp blue sky, then stared down at the back of my right hand. It was *my* hand. It didn't wobble, didn't shimmer, or have any ghostly appearance. I wasn't dead, and this wasn't any delirious dream. Things were too crisp and far too clear.

This was real. And it was insane.

"What the hell happened to me?" I shouted over at Tom.

Looking up, he smiled, then quickly returned to tossing the pebble from hand to hand.

I breathed deep, then blew the air out through my clenched teeth. *Relax*, I told myself. I wasn't hurt, didn't seem to be sick any longer, and judging by the familiar surroundings I was in Malibu Canyon.

I took a quick glance around, just to reassure myself of that. I looked up along the entire lip of the canyon. It was familiar in shape, looking like the same wall of rock that I'd seen countless times on my drive into work, but something was different. Something hovered above it. Bright red, it hung motionless up in the sky. It was what I'd seen last night: 27.

At first I thought it was written in wispy smoke, but the edges of the two numbers were crisp and far too sharply defined. It had been there last night and was still there this morning. It couldn't be made of smoke.

"Tom!" I called out to him.

He dropped his pebble, stood, and walked over to me. He grinned as if he knew some hilarious secret. Perhaps he did.

I pointed toward the numbers.

His gaze followed the direction of my pointing finger. Looking into his eyes, I could tell that he saw it. I wasn't imagining it, unless of course I was also imagining him.

"What is it?" I asked, not really expecting an answer but still hoping for one.

"God," he said quickly and simply.

I turned and looked at him. "What is it?" I asked again.

He continued to look into the sky. "God," he said without the slightest hesitation.

I shook my head. Asking him his name had caused

him to choke himself, but asking him about numbers in the sky didn't seem to faze him. His answer made absolutely no sense to me, but he seemed pretty damn definite about it.

"God?" I said.

Smiling, he nodded.

I'd had enough of this. Talking to him was getting me absolutely nowhere. The answers I needed were back at Dummar. Turning, I walked up the draw, kicking at dead brush and rocks, and began to crawl up the side of the hill. Tom scrambled up beside me. I was about to tell him to stop but saw no reason why I should. He continued to grin at me. If he had been a dog his tail would have been wagging, pounding at the ground.

I felt really good, better than I had any right to. It was still early morning, but the summer sun was hot and sweat ran down my face. My damp arms became dirt-streaked. I was working hard but breathing easy. The muscles of my forearms looked corded and rock-hard. I hadn't realized I was in this good shape. Hitting the gym a couple of times a week hadn't exactly been a part of my standard schedule. My only real exercise had been giving the candy machine a swift kick when my Mars Bar got hung up inside of it.

Nearing the top, in a final burst of speed, I leapt up, trying to jump up onto the plateau. But all I managed to do was to get my leg caught on something, fall flat on my face, and then get the wind knocked out of me.

Pulling down a breath I looked over my shoulder, back down the side of the hill, to see what had caught me. Tom held on to a handful of my pant leg. That perpetual grin of his was gone. Not letting go of my pants, he slowly crawled up beside me. Only then did he let go. He then moved another half foot above me and peered over the top of the hill. Reaching back down he tugged at my shoulder, pulling me up.

I slowly crawled forward.

At first I didn't even recognize it. Then I saw a familiar low-slung building nestled into the side of an adjacent hill. It was Dummar Labs. But it was a lot more than just that. Yesterday morning when I had driven into work, Dummar had been two buildings and a half-dozen small parking lots. This morning the parking lots were gone, and in their place stood buildings I had never seen before. They were big buildings, almost ten stories tall, made of what looked like gray smoked glass and chrome. The hills behind the labs should have been nothing more than barren, weed-strewn stretches of rock. Not today. Row after row of chrome-and-concrete buildings were packed tightly onto those hills. Several of the buildings had crumbled and collapsed on themselves.

I was looking at Dummar, but it wasn't Dummar.

Tom pointed toward one of the unfamiliar buildings.

At least a dozen figures wandered around its front entrance. It was hard to make out much at this distance, but one thing was certain: Several of those figures wore red berets.

I'd not be returning to Dummar, not as long as anyone with a red beret was milling around. I slid a few feet back down the hill. What would I do now?

Tom slid down toward me, looked me in the face, looked back down the hill, and then stared back at me.

"I'm some sort of goddamned Rip Van Winkle," I said in a whisper, barely realizing that I was saying it. Sweat dripped down my face, running into my eyes, stinging me. Time had passed. I wasn't talking days or weeks, but years and decades. I'd nodded off during a meeting, only to wake up decades later to be greeted by a spaceman with a ray gun. It was totally insane, totally impossible, but I knew it was true. Those buildings made it true.

I looked over at Tom. He had known those red berets were hanging around Dummar, and he had known that they were bad news. He obviously didn't want to have anything to do with them. In my book, that made him a friend.

"I need help," I told him slowly. "Can you take me to someone who can help me?"

He smiled, but from what little I'd learned about

him that meant absolutely nothing. He didn't so much as nod but began to slide back down the hill. I didn't like going off blind to somewhere I didn't know with someone who could barely remember his own name, but it seemed to be my only option. And of course, by grabbing my pant leg he had probably saved my life. When someone saves your life it does give them an air of credibility.

I slid down the hill, following him.

A single crack of thunder echoed far in the distance.

I looked up, but couldn't see a cloud in the sky.

I lay on my back, on a massive slab of speckled granite, while Malibu Creek, a torrent of white water, raced wildly around me. The sun soaked into my naked body.

Sitting up, I poked a toe at my drying clothes, then turned to Tom who, sitting cross-legged on the same granite slab, tossed another pebble from hand to hand. He was easily entertained, like a child—a not too bright child.

"I figure one of two things!" I said, having to shout to make myself heard over the roar of the water. "Either I've blown every gasket in my head and right now I'm imagining all this while I'm actually bouncing off the walls in a padded cell at the State Funny Farm, or else all this is real." A fly buzzed around my head, and suddenly dive-bombed toward my left ear. Entirely instinctively, my hand flashed out, trying to grab it. The fly buzzed in my fist. I'd never been able to do *that* before. I opened my fist and it flew away.

My reflexes were not that quick.

Tom smiled at me, then tossed his pebble into the white water. Looking up into the sky and shielding his eyes with his hands, he quickly glanced up at the sun, which was almost directly overhead. As I watched he stood and reached his hands high above his head. At first I thought he was simply stretching, but he wasn't. He hung his head down, closed his eyes, and with his hands still reaching into the sky flipped them back, so that the palms were exposed to the sun.

Then he spoke. Actually, it was more of a whisper. Above the roar of the water I could barely hear him.

"Know me, God. Know me, God. Know me, God. . . ." he said in a soft chant.

He was praying. The sun was still as warm as it had been only seconds earlier, but I felt myself shivering. Religion, with all of its trappings and mysticism, always made me feel a bit uneasy. There was a core of irrationality about it that just went against my grain. He continued to chant for about fifteen seconds, then opened his eyes and sat back down. Smiling, he reached over toward me and touched my hands. I felt my muscles tighten, almost coiling, getting ready to launch me from this rock if things got *really* strange. Religious types were capable of all sorts of weirdness.

But the expression on his face was so open, and so sincere, that I just didn't have the heart to fight him. His eyes looked like those of some sad dog. With his index finger he traced something out in my open palm. Then, dropping my hand, he traced something out in the palm of his own hand. That seemed to satisfy him and, crawling away, he picked up a pebble and began tossing it back and forth.

Even though his behavior certainly seemed strange, it was nothing compared to what I knew religious types were capable of. I casually glanced down at the palm of my hand where Tom had so intently been tracing something out.

There was something beneath my skin.

I held my hand close to my eyes. If I angled it just right and let the sun glint off of it, I could see something. It looked like a series of vertical slashed lines about an inch tall and an inch wide. I quickly looked at the palm of my other hand and I could see similar lines. They were faint, and colored a very deep blue. I could hold my hand at any angle now, and had absolutely no difficulty in seeing them. They almost seemed to glow.

And then, suddenly, I saw more than just a random gathering of lines. They hadn't actually changed, but my understanding of them had. They made up a bar code. The lines on my hand were identical to what you'd find on a can of peaches or a frozen pizza. A bar code had been tattooed onto the palms of my hands. It made absolutely no sense that I hadn't noticed them until now.

And Tom had known that they were there.

Leaning over, I grabbed his nearest hand and dragged him across the rock. The pebble he had been tossing hit me in the face and bounced off of my nose. I barely noticed it. I turned his hand over and stared at his open palm. They were harder to see in his hand, being somewhat masked by the red dye that stained his hands, but there was no mistaking them. He was bar-coded, just as I was.

I stared at those lines.

Something tickled in the back of my head.

I shook. My eyelids fluttered. I couldn't breathe.

I knew him.

Tom Laughlin. Born October 19, 2041, Phoenix Municipal Hospital. Eight pounds, three ounces. Ph.D., Cal Tech—2065, in Astrogeology. Taught at the University of Illinois, '65–'69, the Soviet Astro Institute Gorki '69–'70, Lunar Far-side Warren '70–'71, and currently assistant director of the First World Institute Exo-Geology, Tempe, Arizona.

Through fluttering eyelids I stared at him. Cowering at the edge of the granite slab, he closed his eyes and sucked on his thumb. Wearing tatters, blond hair hanging halfway down his back, and barely capable of remembering his name, I knew that he had taught courses in planetary geology to students in a city that was burrowed into the far side of the moon.

He exploded within my head.

His favorite ice cream was Raspberry Ripple. He'd had the thumb and index finger of his left hand regrown after he'd lost them in a rock-climbing accident in the Superstition Mountains when he was a kid of twelve. That was back in 2053.

Back in 2053.

My head ached as my eyes throbbed with each beat of my heart.

He wore a fifteen-inch collar. He had a balance of 14,853.22 FWC on deposit in Zurich—account number 287640. Personal access code: Applesauce Cake. In the second grade he had gotten a C+, the lowest grade he would ever receive, in Folk Dancing. Had three kids: the twins Joan and Jennifer, born April 2, 2064, and son Tom junior, born April 13, 2064. All children popped at Phoenix Gyonics. Attending physician Dr. Janice Quan Teng. All three children's GPIs were less than ten.

What in the hell was a GPI?

Tom had a GPI of four.

He'd bought three pairs of socks on October 27, 2070, at Vlakinov's, for 1.19 FWC. Two pairs white, one pair brown. Was allergic to bananas. Favorite color was yellow. Had a penny collection, 1976–2011. Afraid of snakes. Sub-three-hour marathoner. Susceptible to eye strain. Had three head colds in the spring of '63. Ate too many apples—loved Pippins, hated Rome Beauties.

"No more!"

I blinked, and sucked down a lungful of air.

My voice echoed down Malibu Canyon. I held the palms of my hands against the sides of my head. Sweat ran down my face and blood pounded in my ears. I collapsed against the rock.

Why?

I could read bar codes, and found myself in a body that I *knew* wasn't quite mine. I had killed a spaceman. If I wasn't insane, and if what I somehow knew about Tom was true, my world was at least eighty years dead.

How?

I couldn't even begin to guess. I was actually afraid to guess.

CHAPTER 3

Robin and the Fair Joan

I kicked at an asphalt chunk of what had once been part of the roadbed of Malibu Canyon Road. The fist-sized rock sailed down into the canyon, bounced off the trunk of a dead oak, and ricocheted further still, vanishing into the creek.

That piece of road was just one more indication that a great deal of time had somehow passed since I'd blacked out during the Tuesday morning meeting. As impossible as I knew that was, I found it equally impossible to argue with the cracked, torn-up roadbed of Malibu Canyon Road. There were no answers, just questions.

"We aren't in Kansas anymore, Tom."

He ignored me, apparently too entranced in watching a woodpecker that was searching for insects, bruising its micro-sized brain as it bashed its beak into a dead sycamore.

Jumping from slab to slab of asphalt, I worked my way over to the tree that Tom was so intently staring up into. Reaching out, I lightly touched his shoulder.

He turned quickly but smoothly, as if he had known I'd been behind him all the time. "Hi," he said, while grinning from ear from ear.

I felt myself smiling in return.

He certainly wasn't a brilliant conversationalist, but there was no denying that he had the type of infectious personality that just made you want to smile along with him. That ability definitely put him one up on most of the burned-out cynics I had known. As I thought that, I realized I was already thinking of the world I had lived in only yesterday as being something distant and long dead. Truly amazing.

Actually frightening.

"Which way, Tom?" I asked.

Tom looked briefly at my face, then, turning his head slightly, looked over my shoulder. His eyes seemed to focus on something far away.

I almost had time to turn my head.

"Remove your hand from the Mushie, unless you want me to put one through your gizzard," said an English-accented voice at my back.

I froze.

"I'll not tell you again, varlet," the voice said sternly. "Unhand him."

Varlet? A second ago I had joked about being in the land of Oz, but this was starting to sound like something out of an old Errol Flynn movie, located squarely in a soundstage rendition of Sherwood Forest.

Invisible fingers squeezed at my brain.

My right hand began to tremble. I *couldn't* move it. I couldn't move anything. I knew what was about to happen. Just before I had lost control of my body my right hand had been resting on the butt of my pistol. Whatever was now controlling my body was going to pull that pistol, spin me around, and then try to shoot at whoever was at my back.

No!

My fingers moved across the pearl handle. Either the guy at my back, myself, or quite possibly both of us, were about to get killed.

"Tom," said the voice. "Move away."

He knew Tom. This guy who was just about to put something through my gizzard was trying to protect Tom. When he looked at me all he probably saw was a stranger—possibly a dangerous stranger—who had his hand on Tom's shoulder.

I screamed inside my head, pleading with whatever was controlling me: *It's a misunderstanding. He doesn't want to hurt me, he just thinks that Tom's in danger!*

The invisible fingers were gone.

My body relaxed. I slowly eased my hand off of the pistol, having regained control.

Tom moved away from me, his face once again filled with a grin.

"Drop the belt," said the voice.

"I'm dropping it," I said, while reaching down slowly, undoing the buckle, and letting the gun belt drop around my ankles.

"Turn."

I turned.

I blinked once, then twice. He refused to disappear. He stood on a massive chunk of uplifted roadbed. He was dressed from head to toe in green, complete with a little green pointed cap that was adorned with what looked like hawk feathers. My guess about Errol Flynn had been unbelievably accurate. He looked like a refugee from Sherwood Forest. His longbow was stretched taut, and nocked with an arrow that was aimed straight at my chest.

"Did he hurt you, Tom?" he asked.

Tom had again returned to his favorite diversion. Having seated himself cross-legged in the dirt, he was once again tossing a pebble from hand to hand. But having heard the man's voice he dropped the rock, stood, and started walking toward me.

"No!" yelled the archer, as he pulled back even further on his bowstring.

Tom didn't seem to have heard him and quickly walked directly between us. Any arrow intended for me would now slice through Tom. Obviously not understanding the danger he had placed himself in, Tom reached into his bundle and pulled out his canteen, pushing it into my face, forcing its neck between my lips.

"My God!" said the bowman. He lowered his bow and, removing his arrow, dropped it into the quiver on his back. "I've never seen anything like it."

The tension that had been hanging heavy in the air vanished, almost as if it had never been there at all.

The only real evidence of what had almost happened was my sweat-soaked shirt.

"My apologies," said the bowman. "I couldn't be certain that you were a friend of Tom's."

Tom still had the canteen shoved into my mouth. I carefully took it from his hands, took a quick sip, then handed it back to him. Apparently satisfied, he stuffed the canteen back into his bundle and then, having seated himself again, started to search the ground for a suitable pebble.

The bowman walked forward, his hand extended. "I'm pleased to meet any friend of Tom's. I'm Robin Hood," he said, sounding deadly serious, apparently not realizing how absolutely insane that statement sounded. Reaching out, he grabbed my hand and pumped. His grip was firm.

"John Smith," I said quietly, hoping that this loon wouldn't mistake me for the Sheriff of Nottingham.

"It's a pleasure, Mr. Smith," he said. The smile he gave me was genuine, but I could sense something behind it. He had the look of someone who was hiding some sort of secret—like a doctor who knows your lab results but isn't yet ready to give you the bad news.

"So tell me," said Robin, "how did you manage to make such an outstanding impression on Tom? I've never before seen him offer his canteen to *anyone.*" Robin's eyes narrowed slightly. "He's never even offered it to me."

All I could do was smile. I didn't want to further unbalance this guy by generating any jealous feelings. I had no doubt that it would be an extremely unwise move to get between Robin Hood and any of his imagined Merry Men. "I was in desperate shape," I said, "and nearly dying of thirst when he first found me. He must have sensed just how much trouble I was in, and offered me his canteen. He probably thought I still needed water." I hoped that would placate him.

"Of course," said Robin, suddenly smiling. "Tom may only be a Mushie, but he's an excellent judge of character."

A "Mushie"?

But this was no place for questions. Not here.

Robin thumped me on the chest with an index finger. "Had it been any man other than Tom vouching for your good name, I'd still be apt to have an arrow trained on you."

Again I smiled. He seemed to have an unbelievable degree of trust in a man who not only could barely remember his own name, but whose vocabulary seemed to consist of only a handful of words.

"Shall we return to camp then, and share a meal?" he asked.

My stomach grumbled, apparently trying to answer for me. "I haven't eaten for at least a day," I said, although if all this insanity was actually real I hadn't eaten in more than eighty years. "I'd love something to eat."

Robin nodded and then, walking over to Tom, gave him a friendly shove on the shoulder. He stood.

"It's as she foretold it, Tom," he said to him quietly, almost as if he didn't want me to hear. Then, glancing quickly at me, he turned back to Tom. "It's God's will," he added.

Stranger and stranger still. Something twisted in my stomach. I'd found what had to be another religious fanatic.

Tom closed his eyes, lowered his head, and raised his palms toward the sky.

It looked like he was going to start praying again. As I watched, Robin closed *his* eyes, lowered *his* head, and raised *his* palms toward the sky.

"Know me, God. Know me, God. Know me, God. . . . ," they chanted in unison.

Just as it had been the first time I'd witnessed this, it lasted for about fifteen seconds. Before they reopened their eyes I'd raised my own hands high above my head. Whoever these people were, they appeared to take their religion damn seriously. I had no desire to be labeled as an unbeliever.

I had expected the evening meal to have centered around a pig roasting on a spit, or possibly a sheep that Robin would insist had been liberated from the holdings of the evil Sheriff of Nottingham. I had been certain that there would be boys playing lutes while jugglers tossed clubs and burning branches to one another.

It hadn't quite happened that way. Almost fifty of us had gathered around a large campfire. I couldn't smell roasting meat anywhere. And the reason for that soon became obvious. The evening meal had consisted of what looked like two pie tins that had been glued together face to face. They had been passed out from a large cardboard box. And instead of lute-playing or juggling, entertainment had centered around a movie projected against a stained bed sheet that was hung from the branches of an oak tree. It was some foreign job, with Orientals mounted on armored horses chasing each other through hills and swamps while cutting the heads off of unlucky peasants. I quickly lost interest in the entertainment and decided to concentrate on dinner.

The pie-tin dinner, along with a well-worn-looking flattened stick, had been handed to me by someone with red-dyed hands—a "Mushie." His face looked as if it had been cut from stone, dead and emotionless. He possessed none of the cheerfulness of Tom. His eyes were totally expressionless, as if absolutely nothing at all existed behind them. More than half of the camp was made up of people like these.

I then pressed against the pie tin's surfaces as I'd seen the others do, and then lowered it to my lap. I watched the top tin very carefully. It did not so much vanish as simply fold back on itself, the metal seeming to melt at the edges of the opening and then crawl back over itself. It reminded me of the self-repairing walls that I'd seen at Dummar, and I realized that the underlying technology was probably related to the mechanism that operated Tom's canteen. Inside the tin was what looked like lasagna. I seriously doubted that lasagna had ever been one of the dietary staples of the real Robin Hood and his Band of Merry Men. The aroma of cheese and tomato sauce drifted upward.

My stomach took over and my brain seemed to check out. Food was Priority One.

I finally sat there, full, warm, and for the first time in what felt like a long time thought about absolutely nothing. My brain had mercifully slipped into neutral. I did nothing more than watch the fire dance and listen to the crack of burning logs.

Night came on, and the camp grew dark.

"What do you think of my little band?" asked someone from behind me.

Startled, I almost fell from the log I was sitting on.

"Relax, John Smith," said Robin Hood, who sat down next to me.

My trance broken, I looked at those huddled around the fire. Most of them resembled refugees from Central Casting of a movie studio. Just a log away, Abe Lincoln, in his stovepipe hat, sat next to someone in a powdered wig, who clutched a small axe. While across from me, and on the other side of the fire, sat Laurel and Hardy. They weren't wearing their standard dark suits, white shirts, or short neckties, but they were easily recognizable because of their black derbies. They appeared to be having a great deal of trouble with their lasagna, seeming to get more of it *on* them than actually *in* them.

This place was obviously an asylum of some sort. The only real question was: Where are the guards?

It was getting even darker now and most of those around the fire were hidden in shadow, but earlier in the day I'd seen several others of Robin's band dressed in green tights and even a woman in a long brown robe, with her head shaved bald, who I think believed herself to be Friar Tuck. But it had been the Mushies that I had spent more time watching than anyone else in camp. Silent, and with their blank expressions, they sat quietly, often in groups, and often with their palms raised skyward.

But possibly stranger even than the Mushies were the children, or actually the lack of children. I had seen only one child who looked much over the age of five, a little girl of about ten who wore a crystal tiara in her tangled blond hair. She waved a wand made out of a coat hanger and aluminum foil, and would touch it to anyone's head that she came near. Whether she was trying to turn people into toads or was looking for her Prince Charming, I couldn't tell. But other than her there was no one else in camp between the ages of five and twenty. The toddler set was well represented, though, by almost half a dozen little kids. They moved in a small herd, hardly ever more than an arm's length away from one another, rolling in the dirt, chasing each other with small tree branches, and terrorizing the camp's two mutts by tugging on their tails and yanking on their ears. They were just kids, probably the only normal-acting group that I'd seen since waking.

I'd never paid much attention to kids, never having really known any, but these children made me feel good. They were a small slice of normalcy in an otherwise totally insane situation.

I had been silent for several minutes after Robin had asked me about his Band. He had been sitting patiently, staring into the fire.

"You have a good group of people," I told him, and I really meant it. The sincerity that I heard in my own voice probably surprised me much more than it did Robin.

"Feeling rested?" he asked.

I just nodded. I had been watching Tom. He lay in the dirt. Still grinning, he snored loudly. One of his hands was wrapped tightly around the ankle of my boot and the other clutched his bundle of rags.

"There's someone who's been waiting to meet you," said Robin in a very serious-sounding voice.

I turned to him. His face looked drawn. The fire was reflected in his now dark eyes. "It is God's will," he said.

I continued to smile but felt myself twitch inside. I had purposely not been asking them questions, hoping to learn what was going on and perhaps to understand what had happened to me by simply observing them. I was afraid that by asking any direct questions I might stumble over some sort of religious taboo. I could be in real danger if I was going to be grilled by a priest, or whoever acted as their link to God. The fact that their witch doctor had so far remained hidden from me was not a good sign.

Robin waved behind us, to someone who must have been waiting in the dark. Straining my eyes, I could see shadows move.

"The fair Joan will reveal to you your destiny," said Robin, sounding as if he were reciting from some memorized scripture.

I felt myself tighten inside, and my guts twist. If there was anyone who needed his destiny revealed, it was certainly me. The whole thing hit just a little too close to home.

She stepped into the firelight. She was small, barely five foot, but she looked strong, and powerful. At most she was perhaps twenty-five years old, but it was hard to tell. There was an ageless quality to her. Her blond hair was cut short, almost page-boy style, and her eyes were narrowed to slits. Her cheekbones looked unnaturally high, and her lips were red and moist. This was the type of face that covered fashion magazines: innocence on the surface, but something almost animal-like within. Across her chest she wore some sort of tightly woven metal material that was decorated with a stylized, golden-maned lion. She wore camouflage-type fatigues for pants, and heavy black boots similar to mine. Clenched in both hands was the jeweled hilt of a large, gleaming, steel sword. Its point was planted firmly in the ground between her feet. I looked once more at her face, and her eyes were now opened wide, staring into the fire. They were almond-shaped, showing the presence of Asian genes, but there was something within those eyes that had nothing to do with any human heritage. Her pupils were green and slit.

She had cat-eyes.

Robin bent his head and offered his hand, palm up, toward her. "John Smith, I present to you Joan of Arc."

She did not smile, or even nod. Her jaw was

clenched, and the muscles at the base of her neck quivered.

I didn't say a word. I should have expected something like this. At any Funny Farm, Joan of Arc would be a very popular model. If you were looking for someone to talk to God on your behalf, and to reveal destinies, Joan of Arc would be a good candidate.

"We must talk now," she said in a voice that was deep and rich, almost in direct contrast to her small feminine frame.

She offered me her hand. Reaching out, I took it. She squeezed with an unbelievably powerful grip. I began to stand, and heard Tom's snore cut off. He moved in the dirt and I could see his lips twitching, as if within his dreams he could speak like any normal man. I started to bend down, knowing that I'd have to pry his hand away from my boot before I could move.

"Tom," she said loudly, "come with us!"

Tom sat straight up, without the slightest hesitancy. He was on his feet and walking into the darkness before I could even straighten up.

People listened to this lady. I'd have to watch myself.

We had moved perhaps a hundred yards away from the campfire, and had sat down in tall grass. She offered me one of her hands and Tom offered me one of his. Then both of them held their free hands together. Leaning their heads back, they looked into the night sky.

When in Rome do as the Romans do.

I leaned my head back. I opened my eyes wide. In the glare of the campfire I had not really been able to see the night sky. Out here, in the dark, nothing obstructed the night.

The sky was alive with lights.

This is what I had seen the night before, when I had lain at the bottom of the hill beneath Dummar. At the time it had seemed so strange, so impossible, that I had put it out of my mind. But tonight, only a single glance at those streaking points of light and I knew exactly what they were—satellites. There were literally hundreds of them, some as bright as Venus and some so faint that I could only make them out with my more sensitive peripheral vision. A few flew true west-east and some perpendicular to that path in a polar orbit, but most tracked through the sky on some trajectory in between. It looked as if the sky was alive with cosmic fireflies.

During my eighty-year absence, it definitely looked as if man had not turned his back on space. This was visual confirmation of what I had mysteriously learned about Tom's history and his visit to the far side of the moon.

They dropped my hands, then raised their hands skyward, palms up. I followed suit. I knew absolutely nothing about Joan of Arc, except that I didn't want to cross her. I'd met few people that radiated the sense of will that I felt pouring from her. I think she could have backed any department manager at Dummar into a corner and had him begging for mercy long before he could so much as pull out a view graph, or complain about budget constraints.

"Know me, God. Know me, God. Know me, God," we chanted for what seemed to be the standard fifteen seconds. We then lowered our hands, dropping them into our laps.

"Late yesterday afternoon," she said, sounding as if she were beginning a sermon, "God spoke to me."

I almost jumped, as a hand, palm flat, pressed against my chest. It was hers. I could feel the warmth of it coming through my thin shirt.

"He told me of the coming of a stranger, who would appear in the Southern Canyon. He would call himself John Smith. He would have no knowledge of this world or of his destiny. God instructed me as His messenger to reveal to you the nature of your task, and the ways of the world. Tom insisted that *he* go and find you."

I could hardly imagine Tom insisting about anything, but there was no denying that he *had* found me. But even so, I wasn't about to believe that *God* was actually talking to her. Knowing my name or that I had arrived from the southern part of Malibu Canyon meant absolutely nothing. Everyone in camp knew that. However, what suddenly made my skin crawl, and was raising goose bumps up and down my back, was the realization that what she was saying now was what Robin Hood had been referring to when he had first found Tom and myself. They had been *expecting* me. But even more unsettling than that was the way that she had described me. She said that I would have no knowledge of the world or of my destiny. I had not let on to anyone in camp how strange and confusing everything was to me. And stranger still, the time that she was supposedly talking to God was just around the time that I had awakened at Dummar. I was not about to believe that God had summoned me through eighty years in order to fulfill some sort of prophesy, but I was certain that this woman could help me in understanding what had happened to me. Everything was being cloaked in religious mumbo-jumbo, but when I scraped all that away an undeniable truth remained: She had known about me, and knew that I'd be coming.

Even though I couldn't see her face, I could feel her eyes staring at me. "You've been brought to this world to vanquish the Supreme, and reinstate God to His throne. You will build an army of followers, and with that army, battle the Supreme in Heaven. This will be accomplished within four days' time."

I blinked in disbelief. This lady was seriously deranged, but I knew that I couldn't afford to antagonize her.

"Why four days?" I asked, trying to sound both sincere and interested.

The weight of her hand disappeared from my chest. Her fingers wrapped around my chin. I didn't fight her. Actually, I don't think I could have. She tilted my head back, almost toppling me over. I found myself looking at the number in the sky: 26.

"In four days time, the Supreme will have lowered the Speed Limit to zero. Anyone caught outside when that happens will be sent straight to Hell."

The number had dropped by one. She had called it "the speed limit." *The speed limit of what?*

"What does it mean?" I asked. If I was to play the part of the unknowing stranger who was to be God's savior, I'd at least have the chance to get a few of my questions answered.

"When the Bug destroyed the world many went directly to both Heaven and Hell, but there were those of us held in Limbo, who can only gain access to Heaven if we prove our worth. God has given us a second chance. In His wisdom He realized that our downfall was caused by the technology our world had relied so heavily upon, so He limited it, dictating that no person could travel at a speed greater than thirty kilometers per hour."

"And if someone exceeds the speed limit?" I asked. Somehow, I couldn't picture God issuing traffic citations.

"They'd be sent to Hell," she answered.

That was a pretty severe punishment for a traffic violation. This sounded like a real Old Testament sort of God. "And why is it now at twenty-six?" I asked.

"That is the Supreme's doing. He once sat at the right hand of God, carrying out the Lord's business in this world. After the Bug, God sent his *image* to Earth. He showed us how to build the Church, how to choose the Cardinals and Brothers, and how to look after the Mushies. But he became corrupt, coveting God's power, and has now trapped our Lord in Heaven. The Supreme's plan is to decrease the Speed Limit so he can send everyone to Hell. By his own actions he has now revealed his true self. The Supreme and Lucifer are one and the same."

"What are all the little lights in the sky?" I asked, trying to change the subject, the entire concept behind this *church* sounding totally insane.

"The Eyes of God," she answered, "but I fear that Lucifer now looks through them."

I nodded.

A few pieces of this puzzle were starting to fall into place.

Based on what I'd learned so far, and filtering out the religious hype that everything was coated in, I was starting to put together a fuzzy picture of what might have happened to the world. Sometime, probably after 2072 judging by what I knew about Tom's history, the world had almost destroyed itself. Joan called it the Bug, so the destruction had probably come about from biological weaponry of some sort. Most people had probably been killed outright, but even the survivors hadn't come out of it clean—they'd had their brains scrambled. The worst of them seemed to be the Mushies, whose minds were fried to the extent that hardly anything human remained, while the least affected still appeared to be intelligent but had all assumed bizarre personalities, based either on real or fictional characters. In the aftermath of all this some sort of religion had evolved, centered around the satellite system. I wasn't yet sure, but the bar codes on their hands, and the way that they were continually holding them up to the sky, probably indicated that the satellite system was capable of reading those codes. The system might have been used in prewar days to keep track of everyone. It was also possible that this "speed limit" was some sort of emergency measure that had been put into effect during the biological attack. If they had been fearing invasion, to be able to restrict the speed that any advancing force could travel would be a real advantage. But I didn't have the slightest idea as to how that speed limit could be enforced. I seriously doubted that God had been enlisted to set up a strategic defensive system, in which, by simply pointing His finger down toward any transgressor, the speedster would get tossed into Hell. I didn't have all of the pieces yet, but I was beginning to get a glimmering of what this world was like and how it had possibly come to be.

But there was one large glaring impossibility about the entire thing—me. My world was 1990 Southern California, not some world eighty years later where the survivors of a biological war lived in a make-believe world generated by their scrambled brains, and believed that God and Lucifer were battling for the control of Heaven while they peered down at the world with the aid of surveillance satellites.

Parts of this nightmare had a framework of logic, but in that weird logic there was definitely no room for me. I simply should not be here.

"We are the first two of your army," she said, "myself and Tom. I will be your counsel, but you are God's savior. You will lead and we will follow you. What are your orders?" In the dark, I could see the outline of her head bending down before me. She truly believed. She didn't have the slightest doubt that she was about to set out on a holy quest. She had the Joan of Arc persona down pat.

"Give me your hand," I said. I wanted to see if I could find out who she really was—who she had really been. Again she placed her hand on my chest. I pulled it away and turned it over. There was only starlight and that large glaring number to light the night, but the bar code on her hand seemed to glow.

"Do you know what that means?" I asked.

I could hear her suck down a breath. "You can see our inner selves?" she asked.

That was a strange way to refer to the codes, but it was actually pretty accurate.

"Yes," I said.

"Only the Eyes of God can see our inner selves. It is further proof that you are God's savior. He lets you see with His eyes."

That confirmed what I had already thought. The satellite system *could* read the bar codes. Whoever controlled and could use that system could keep track of everyone. That was a frightening thought. But even more frightening was the fact that I could see the bar codes while others apparently could not. Why? I didn't have the slightest idea. I pulled Joan's hand close to my face and stared at the code.

This time it was nothing like the mental explosion I had experienced when I had looked at Tom's hand. Everything that was her, before the Bug, was now simply in my head, as if it had always been there.

And it probably always had been in my head, just

hidden away, accessible only when I read the bar codes. I didn't dwell on that thought. It implied that buried somewhere deep in my head might be the details of thousands, maybe millions of people's lives. It was an impossibility that I didn't want to think about. It was just too strange. I concentrated instead on what I had so suddenly learned about Joan.

Joan of Arc was born on January 11, 2054, and had been a Recreational Specialist Grade 4 in someplace called the Bev Center Complex. Her name from birth had simply been Tiffany 12. The title was fancy, but judging by her financial transactions and client list it looked as if she had been nothing more than a high-class hooker. She had been born and bred for it. Conceived at someplace called Bio-Entertainments, the company had owned her, heart and soul, even before she was born.

Her surgical record was immense. It explained both the eyes and the strength of her grip. She'd been modified. She'd had a whole series of brain implants, most of which were used for surveillance purposes in order to spy on clients. I looked deeper into her medical record. The surgery had been more than just cosmetic. She'd been altered right down to the genetic level. She was no longer even human. If she had ever had any children they would have carried all her unique traits, including her cat-eyes. But that had never happened, and it never would happen. She was sterile. That had been in her original design.

Her GPI was not listed. I still did not know what GPI meant, but apparently it was reserved only for those deemed human. And Tiffany 12 had not been so lucky. She had been a piece of furniture, a chunk of meat, something to be bought, sold, and traded—nothing more.

I gently dropped her hand.

Two days ago I had lived contentedly in my one-bedroom apartment, working my way up the Dummar corporate ladder. Today, Joan of Arc expected me to start off on a quest to rescue God.

Nothing in life is guaranteed. That's for damn sure.

CHAPTER 4

Cardinal Bonaparte

Someone shook my shoulder.

No longer asleep but not quite awake, I wasn't yet willing to open my eyes. It wasn't that I was still holding on to some false hope and expecting to wake up between the starched white sheets of a hospital bed.

No.

That hope had faded away sometime yesterday, as I had trudged up Malibu Creek. I'd accepted the fact that I *was* here, and that I would simply have to deal with what I'd found. I might not like it, but liking things rarely has any bearing on reality.

The simple reason that I wasn't yet ready to face the day was that I am not what would be called a morning person. When that particular personality trait was coupled with an incredibly soft and warm down-filled sleeping bag, the result was that I was in no way ready to launch off on a quest to reinstate God in His rightful slot in Heaven. Besides, I think it's just a good basic rule to never start out on a quest before high noon—eleven at the very earliest.

Someone kicked me in the side.

"Leave me alone!" I yelled, but the damage had been done. My eyes were open.

Joan hovered over me. She was not smiling, but of course that was no real surprise. She was not exactly the smiling type. Religion was far too serious for smiles.

"Eat this," she said.

"This" looked like half a loaf of bread, an already

peeled orange, and a stainless steel-looking cup that I assumed held something to drink.

I still lay flat on my back, making absolutely no effort to move. "I'm not hungry," I said. My teeth felt sticky. I had been flashed into this insane asylum with so little notice that I hadn't had time to pack a toothbrush.

This apparently wasn't what Joan wanted to hear. Grabbing me by both shoulders, she jerked me into a sitting position and pushed me completely out of the sleeping bag. Before I even realized what was happening to me I was leaning against a soft, warm wall.

Dragging a hand across the stubble on my chin and then rubbing a balled hand in my eyes, I glanced to my left. It sounded like feeding time at the zoo. Tom was just a few feet away from me, apparently eating breakfast—or quite possibly *inhaling* breakfast.

"Hi," he said, as he looked over at me.

I managed a nod, but then had to look away. He seemed to have his entire chunk of bread stuffed into his mouth, yet he was still attempting to squeeze in several orange slices. Milk had dribbled into his beard and the entire front of his shirt was damp, covered with orange rinds and wet bits of bread. Just watching him made my stomach queasy.

Joan crouched down in front of me and stared at me with her green cat-eyes. She shook the loaf of bread under my nose. "You will eat *now,*" she said. "I don't want you falling in battle due to a low blood-sugar level." She then waved the orange under my nose.

I pushed both of them away. Under other circumstances I might have laughed at the prospect of Joan of Arc lecturing me on aspects of blood chemistry, but I just wasn't in the mood, especially not after she'd mentioned something about a battle. I knew Joan wasn't one for idle conversation.

"Battle?"

"God spoke to me about an hour ago," she said, as if that should be sufficient explanation.

"Wonderful," I said. "Was He just saying good

morning, or did He possibly pass on a few details of this impending battle?''

Sarcasm was wasted on Joan. Her jaw was clenched tight, and her entire face had become filled with a look of deadly seriousness. Her eyes had even stopped blinking. ''God told me that the Supreme has requested that Cardinal Bonaparte become personally involved in your capture. I was assured that the force he will be bringing will certainly be more formidable than the *one* Brother that the Supreme first sent after you.'' She glanced over her shoulder, and through the open doorway of the cubbyhole we had spent the night in. ''They should be arriving any minute,'' she said while still looking through the doorway, sounding as if this were just some casual, unimportant detail. Turning back to face me, she once again was pushing an orange in my face.

Any conversation with Joan was guaranteed to generate total mental overload, and this one had been no different. I not only wanted to know if this Cardinal Bonaparte was in fact some nut case who believed himself to be *the* Napoleon Bonaparte, but also this talking to God business was driving *me* crazy. I had told no one in camp about killing the man back at Dummar, but Joan had somehow managed to find out about it. I wasn't yet ready to believe that she was talking to God, but she damn well was in contact with someone who knew a hell of a lot about what was going on. Unfortunately, questions about this all-seeing individual would just have to wait. Apparently I was only minutes away from getting my ass blown off. That took precedence.

I grabbed my boots, stuffed my feet into them, and started tying laces.

''How many ways in and out of these caves?'' I asked.

I looked up at her, and the surprised expression on her face told me everything—absolutely everything. There was just *one* way out.

''Just the main one,'' she said. Her perpendicular pupils dilated. ''Why would we need more than one?''

"Because with only one exit," I said, practically yelling at her, "a single person with a popgun could keep all fifty of us trapped in here!"

"We don't want to hide from them," she said.

"Get up, Tom," I said, already standing myself, ignoring for the moment her last totally irrational comment. Hiding from them was the *one and only* thing that I wanted.

Tom stood quickly, bread still dangling from his mouth. His bundle of rags was already tied across his chest. At least he was ready to move out. He was coming with me. I owed him that much. He'd saved my life at Dummar, and now this was my chance to even the books. I looked over at Joan.

"We do want to hide from them!" I yelled at her. "I don't know what games you're planning to play, but I've dealt once before with these people. The result was a dead man."

"There's nothing to worry about," she said. "God was on your side that first time, and He will be on your side this time. God has given you the power to keep us *all* safe."

I groaned inside. This was a typical response of religious types. When things started looking bad it was always God who was supposed to bail them out. In the long brutal history of mankind, those with the deepest belief in God were usually those who had their guts splattered the farthest when things got really nasty. But I couldn't let that happen to her. She was my key to understanding what had happened to me, and I was not about to let that key get smelted down into a molten blob because of her irrational, all-consuming belief in God. But I couldn't wait here forever, not even for the chance of understanding what had happened to me. I gave her one more chance, playing the only card I had.

"God told you to follow me, didn't He?" I asked. I was already at the doorway that lead to the main cavern.

"Of course," she said, sounding almost offended.

"Then we leave, and we do it right now," I said. "Move it!"

She raised her eyebrows in a surprised reaction but she moved, running right by me, with Tom next to her.

I followed them out.

At first I thought the entire main cavern was already deserted, but as I turned through the doorway and ran toward the narrowing end of the cavern I saw them. They *all* milled around the cave exit.

"Get out!" I yelled.

None of them moved.

I hit the back of the crowd and began to shove and push my way through. I knocked Oliver Hardy square on his fat ass, and then ran right over the female version of Friar Tuck, stepping on her large stomach. Pushing through the last row of them, I *almost* scrambled out of the cave.

Just as I had done at Dummar, I grabbed a handful of the cave's soft wall and pulled myself to a halt.

Four flying saucer-like vehicles stood in the compound in front of the cave. Over a hundred men and women stood around them. Most wore some sort of form-fitting white body armor, but the few who didn't wore red berets. Suddenly a loud, thundering roar, sounding something like the whine of a jet engine, filled the sky. Another flying saucer swooped down from over a grove of oaks. It was really nothing more than a platform mounted on spindly legs, with a half-dozen turbines attached to its perimeter. Sitting in the center of it were a couple of dozen assorted people. It landed, momentarily engulfed in a cloud of dust and swirling leaves that was kicked up by its backwash.

Joan was now by my side, and reaching over her shoulder pulled her sword from out of its scabbard. Holding it double-handed, she pointed its steel tip toward those that were forming a skirmish line in front of the cave.

"We have them where we want them," she said, sounding incredibly satisfied.

I looked over at her. Her eyes were wide and wild.

She was not only a loon, but suicidal as well. Those out in the compound were carrying weapons that ran the gamut from primitive-looking spears all the way up to cannon-like devices. One of those cannons alone could probably bring down the entire mountain this cave was burrowed into.

"Has everyone here known, for the past hour, that these troops would be arriving?" I asked her. I couldn't believe that fifty people could be so incredibly stupid. But then I reminded myself that I shouldn't ignore the power of religion.

She nodded at me.

We were dead.

And before we were all killed I'd probably lose total control of my body, go running out into the compound, and rip several of them apart with my bare hands before I was vaporized.

A hand grabbed my shoulder from behind. I spun on my heel, clenched my right hand in a fist, and was ready to smash whoever was touching me. I wouldn't go down without a fight.

Tom smiled at me. His eyes were more aware, and more focused, than I'd ever seen them. His smile turned to a smirk and, rolling his eyeballs, he nodded to me. The communication was a silent one, but I had no trouble in understanding the message.

I felt my body relax.

We're really screwed, his face had said, *but keep your head, and you might just be able to save our asses.*

I dropped my fist to my side, then nodded back at him. He was right. We could take advantage of what slim chance might present itself only if we kept calm. I turned back to face the compound. A wide assortment of psychos now surrounded the cave entrance in a semicircle. They stood about five deep.

Robin Hood was standing at my right, and leaning toward me he whispered, "God's brought you here. His power is now yours." He then stepped back *behind* me.

Except for Joan, who seemed ready to dispatch anything that breathed straight to Hell, it didn't look like I'd be getting any help from the rest of them. They must have all believed that God's miracles would be flowing directly through me. Wouldn't they be surprised when they saw me get transformed into bite-sized chunks.

I took a single step forward. I had heard it said somewhere once before, probably in some movie, and probably by some actor who had never faced anything more threatening than a bad review, that "the only good defense is a good offense." As trite as that might have sounded, it was probably our only chance.

"I'm John Smith!" I yelled, certain that should generate some action.

I was not disappointed.

A man walked briskly forward, took an additional several paces past the furthermost of the troops, then stopped. A man and an old woman appeared from behind him, suddenly flanking him.

I had to be facing Cardinal Bonaparte.

He had on a long-tailed blue crushed-velvet waistcoat, a gold vest, and a pink ruffled silk shirt. He wore white tights for pants, and instead of a belt his waist was wrapped in a white cummerbund. His knee-length black riding boots were polished mirror-smooth.

Surprisingly, he did not have one hand shoved inside of his waistcoat. This man did not appear to be the standard nuthouse Napoleon. He stood at least six foot eight, and must have weighed in at nearly three hundred pounds. He wore Coke bottle-thick, tortoise-shell horn-rimmed glasses, and a small set of headphones dangled from around his neck. In the quiet that had arrived with his entrance I could just barely hear the music coming from his headphones. It was heavy and thunderous music, sounding very Wagnerian.

Napoleon, as well as the two who stood by his sides, all wore black gloves. I didn't miss the significance of that. Their bar codes were hidden from sight.

"A pleasure, sir," he said, and bowed slightly at the waist. He then snapped his fingers, and the man at his side, wearing a large floppy sombrero and with belts of ammo draped across his chest, unfolded a small stool he had been holding and placed it directly behind him. Reaching behind himself, Napoleon flicked back the tails of his coat and sat. Even seated, he was still almost as tall as those who stood around him.

"I am Cardinal Napoleon Bonaparte of the Church of Limbo, and Emperor of France. I am here to carry out the business of the Supreme. Under pleasanter times I would have entertained you properly, as befits someone of your station in life," he said, "but as you well know, time runs very short." He took a quick glance over his shoulder and looked up into the sky.

I also looked: 23.

It had dropped by another three kilometers per hour. I didn't know if Napoleon believed the Speed Limit story that Joan had told me, but he obviously thought those numbers in the sky were going to translate into something very real happening down here on the ground.

"In order to save time, and to demonstrate my sincerity, there is something I wish to show you," said Napoleon. He raised one gloved hand. "Volunteers, take one step forward."

In mass, all of his troops—and it looked as if there were at least one hundred of them—took one step forward.

Smiling, Napoleon pointed at someone halfway along the semicircle to his left. That someone was an American Indian, complete with a feather-adorned red beret and a tomahawk. He stepped forward. Turning sharply, he marched, and then halted in front of Napoleon. He knelt down on his knees and bowed his head.

"I do not make idle threats," said Napoleon, who pulled what looked like a small dueling pistol from his jacket and pressed its barrel against the Indian's head. "If I say something will happen, it happens."

The Indian raised his hands skyward, palms flat. "Accept me, Supreme!" he screamed into the sky.

Bang!

The back of the Indian's head exploded outward, brain, blood and bone splattering into the dirt. The Indian collapsed to the ground.

Those at my back took a collective breath, and I could feel them all take a step back. That single shot had transformed their once invincible godly armor from half-inch-thick steel plate into transparent gossamer.

Napoleon dropped the pistol to the ground.

"This devout Brother has been sacrificed only for the good of all of us here," said Napoleon. "My sincerity has been demonstrated. If you, John Smith, do not walk forward, and join me on my hexprop, you will force me into unleashing my righteous followers." He pointed toward the cave. "That action will result in the death of all those good people who stand behind you." He smiled in an animal sort of way, baring his teeth. Standing, he stepped over the body of the dead Indian. "The choice is yours, John Smith."

The choice was mine. I could stand and fight, which would result in the death of everyone along with my own capture or death, or I could surrender myself. The only difference between the two choices was that the first ensured the deaths of Robin Hood's band.

That was no choice.

I walked from the entrance of the cave. A dozen paces brought me up to Napoleon. With the morning sun at his back, I was totally engulfed by his shadow.

He reeked of roses. Again he gave me that feral smile. "Friends of yours?" he asked. He was looking over my shoulder.

I turned slowly. Behind me stood Joan and Tom. "Go back," I said slowly and deliberately, stressing both words.

They did not move.

"Nonsense," said Napoleon. "I'd be honored if your friends would join us."

I turned back toward him but he was no longer there. He had taken several steps back, and in his place now stood the sombreroed Mexican. In his hands he held a gray toaster, identical to the one that the spaceman had aimed at me.

"Pleasant dreams, señor," he said. He smiled, exposing stainless-steel teeth.

Something tickled inside of my head. I heard both Tom and Joan crumple into the dirt behind me.

Invisible fingers squeezed my brain.

I lost all control of my body. Again something else was in charge. But this time, instead of lashing out and attacking, I stiffened like a chunk of wood and dropped toward the ground. I hit the dirt still fully conscious, my eyes wide open and staring up at the entrance of the cave.

Robin Hood and several of his men had their bows nocked. Possibly they'd fight now, having seen that I obviously was not being protected by God.

"Now!" bellowed Napoleon from somewhere behind me.

Pzzzzzt!

In one instant fifty people had filled the entrance of the cave. In the next it was choked with a large mound of bloody slime. Red mist hung in the air.

They had not even had time to scream.

I could not close my eyes, could not turn my head. Lying less than an arm's length in front of me was a wire coat hanger, twisted and mangled, covered in aluminum foil. It had been the little girl's magic wand. A small and still-smoking hand clutched it.

It was the last thing I saw before something was pulled across my eyes.

"Remove it."

Someone pulled the leather blindfold off me. It had smelled of sweat and blood.

I was in a dungeon. It was not simply some rat-infested subbasement of a prison, but an authentic, pluck-out-their-eyeballs-with-metal-tongs, strap-them-to-the-rack-and-crack-their-bones type dungeon. It smelled like an open cesspool, and all-too-human-looking bones were strewn across the floor. I was hanging against what felt like a stone wall. My arms had been pulled up above my head, and I assumed they were somehow shackled by the wrists. But I couldn't tell. I had no feelings below my elbows and I couldn't move, my body still not answering me.

"Welcome," said Napoleon. He was seated several feet in front of me, his little wooden stool sunk halfway down into the mucky floor. He waved a laced handkerchief in front of his face.

The scent of roses drifted over me.

"Animate him," said Napoleon. "I wish to hear him whimper."

The Mexican stepped into my field of vision and again pointed the gray toaster at me.

The instant before the tendons in his hands flexed I felt control return. Once more, whatever had taken control of my body released me. I tilted my head up imperceptibly.

Again something tickled in the back of my head.

I looked down at Napoleon. I had one chance here and now to set the tone between us. I'd pegged him as the type of man to jump on someone's fears like a cat going for a mouse. If I gave him the slightest opening he'd take advantage of it and then shred me.

"These accommodations are not to my satisfaction," I said with all the arrogance I could muster.

Napoleon smirked and, squinting at me from behind his thick glasses, gently clapped his gloved hands. "It is a pleasant departure to meet a man of spirit," he said. "It will make it all that much more enjoyable when I snap you in two like a brittle twig." For emphasis, he pretended to hold a twig between his hands then flicked his wrists. "But before we begin the unpleasantries, I think it only proper and fitting that I introduce you to those individuals who will be extracting the information I require."

The two who had stood by him outside of Robin Hood's cave once again flanked him.

"To my left," said Napoleon without bothering to look in that direction, "is Brother Pancho Villa."

A grinning Pancho waded through the muck on the

floor and, standing beneath me, unzipped the fly of his jeans.

He pissed down my leg.

"Nice to meet you, gringo," he said, while smiling up at me. He twirled the tips of his mustache with his big splayed fingers. His breath probably could have killed small animals.

"Pleased to meet you," I said, deciding right then and there that if he meant to kill me, I'd get him mad enough so he'd simply punch a hole in my chest, and not start plucking eyeballs and snapping bones. I looked down at my wet pant leg. "A very impressive trick," I said. "Did you learn it from your dog? Or perhaps it was something taught to you by your mother."

He jerked both pistols out of his holsters and cocked them.

It would be infinitely better to be killed quickly, with a bullet in the head, than to die a small piece at a time at the hands of these wackos. I closed my eyes.

"No!" shouted Napoleon.

I felt nothing explode through my head. I slowly reopened my eyes. Pancho's guns were back in their holsters.

"We'll deal with this later," Pancho said in a hiss, and then stepped back.

I only managed a nod. My plan had almost worked. Almost.

"To my right," said Napoleon, "is Brother Lizzie Borden."

Lizzie looked like the photos my parents had shown me of my grandmother. Apple-cheeked and white-haired, Lizzie curtseyed, which caused the bottom of her white-laced dress to drag in the filth of the dungeon floor. She reached within the folds of her dress and pulled out a rusty-looking ax, which she waved at me. "Be a good boy, Johnny," she said. "You don't want to make me upset." She smiled. She had no lower teeth.

"Now that you've met my helpful staff," said Napoleon, "we should get down to business." Again he waved the handkerchief in front of his nose. The cloying scent of dead roses drifted over me once more. "What I require of you is actually quite simple, Mr. Smith. All I want to know is why the Supreme is interested in you." He laced his fingers behind one of his knees.

I wanted to smile, but didn't.

Power politics.

Several things had suddenly become crystal-clear. The spaceman who had tried to grab me at Dummar had worked for the Supreme, the guy who ran this Church of Limbo. Joan had told me that. Now, in theory, Napoleon was a cardinal in that church, also answerable to the Supreme, but it looked as if there wasn't exactly a smooth flow of information occurring between Napoleon and his boss. Napoleon wanted to find out what the Supreme wanted with me, probably in the hope of somehow using that information *against* the Supreme.

And what did the Supreme want with me? If I was to believe what Joan had told me the Supreme was probably simply after my ass, operating under the same insane fantasy that so many of these wackos suffered from, believing that I was going to try to kill him in order to save God. As bizarre as all that sounded, it was possibly just crazy enough that Napoleon might believe it.

"The Supreme thinks that I'm going to try to kill him."

Napoleon smiled and then, looking over at Pancho, nodded.

Pancho hustled over to me and, making a fist with his right hand, cocked back his arm.

"No!" I screamed, trying to tighten my gut muscles.

Pancho hit me with everything he had, throwing his weight into it.

Air exploded out of me and tears streaked my face. I couldn't breathe. But I felt no pain.

"I don't think so, Mr. Smith," said Napoleon.

Straining, I forced a trickle of air back into my lungs.

Napoleon stroked his chin thoughtfully. "I'll tell you what I think," he said. "I believe that the Supreme discovered something about the Labs and sent *you* down to investigate. I'll further speculate that when you found the information he sought, that instead of reporting back you killed your compatriot and decided to try to cut a new deal." Napoleon looked around the dungeon, first at Pancho and then at Lizzie, the look on his face telling them just how unwise that would be if they tried it with him. "I believe that you've obtained the codes that can bring down the Los Angeles Quad Walls." He stopped speaking, and his eyes seemed to focus on something far away, something well outside the dungeon walls. "Tell me I'm right," he said dreamily, "and *I'll* cut that deal with you."

Quad Walls.

I felt an invisible and rusted nail slowly being inserted into the base of my skull. I wanted to scream but was beyond screaming. If I screamed I would shatter. The rusty nail pried open a hidden door that was deep within my brain.

The dungeon was gone.

I stood in a desert, before a nearly invisible "Quad Wall." It was nothing more than a distortion, a shimmering chunk of air. I reached forward to touch it, to try to penetrate it. It was warm and soothing.

Thunder exploded from somewhere far above me.

From somewhere hundreds of kilometers above, in orbit.

My hand vanished.

I pulled back a blackened wrist stump.

"The codes!"

I blinked.

The hidden door in my head snapped shut. But what I'd seen within that door still remained.

I was back in the dungeon.

Pancho still stood beneath me, his arm cocked.

"That's right," I said. "I've got the codes to bring

down the Los Angeles Quad Walls.'' I breathed deeply. I had no codes. But at least now I did know what a ''Quad Wall'' was. It was a line, an invisible line that you couldn't cross, a line that surrounded all of Southern California. If you stepped across it, something from orbit would fire down on you and you would be vaporized—blown into charcoaled bits and pieces.

Pieces snapped together.

The Speed Limit.

The Quad Walls and the Speed Limit were *both* enforced by something in orbit, something that would vaporize you if you moved too quickly or tried to pass a Quad Wall boundary.

And that something wasn't God hurling down lightning bolts.

It was a tightly focused infrared laser beam.

It was all in my brain, just like the information about Tom and Joan. One instant it hadn't been there, and in the next it filled my head.

But there were no codes. Those I didn't know.

Napoleon stood. ''Give me those codes,'' he said, speaking in very emperor-like tones.

I stared him straight in the eye. ''2DOB187,'' I said without the slightest hesitation. It was the license plate number from my Toyota.

Napoleon again nodded his head to Pancho.

Again air exploded up from my lungs and again I felt no pain. As grateful as I was for the miraculous absence of pain, I knew that my body, even though a new-and-improved version of the one I had once had, couldn't take much more of this punishment. A few more hits like that would rupture my guts or pop my spleen.

''We both know that couldn't possibly be the configuration,'' said Napoleon. ''Try again.''

''Screw yourself,'' I hissed.

''That's not it, either,'' said Napoleon, shaking his head side to side.

I closed my eyes. Somehow I knew that this last punch would kill me.

''Wait,'' said Napoleon.

Nothing exploded into my midsection. I opened my eyes.

"As enjoyable as all this has been," said Napoleon, "I wouldn't want to kill you prematurely." He stood. "I believe that there is a more efficient way to jar your memory."

Tom and Joan!

"I don't know any goddamned codes!" I screamed.

"We will take a two-hour break," said Napoleon, paying no attention to what I had just screamed, "in which I will let you visit with your friends and discuss this little dilemma with them. Possibly they can help you remember. At the end of those two hours we will *all* meet back here."

Pancho moved toward me.

"But before *you* leave, I believe that Pancho has something of a personal nature that he wishes to discuss with you."

I tried to squirm into the rock wall at my back.

"Remember, no permanent damage," reminded Napoleon.

CHAPTER 5

Joe Average and Vlad Junior

I flew through the air, but for only a second. I landed face-first, the impact shoving dirt and gravel into my mouth. It took all I had, every conscious thought, just to breathe.

"You've got about an hour and a half," said Pancho cheerfully from somewhere behind me.

The only acknowledgment that I could give, indicating that I had heard him, was the fact that I continued to breathe. There had been no pain throughout any of Pancho's "personal interview," my body somehow deadening itself to it, but now I found myself incapable of moving. It was as if my body had turned off all extraneous systems, choosing to sustain only the most vital like heart, lungs, and brain. It didn't feel as if there were any broken bones, and there had actually been very little blood. Pancho was a master at his craft.

"You are to be congratulated," said a voice.

Hands grabbed my left shoulder and flipped me over like a slab of beef.

The sky above was black, but the face looking down at me was bathed in harsh white light. It belonged to a bald man who wore a raccoon-like mask over his eyes and a large brass ring through his nose. His left ear was no longer attached to his head but was encapsulated in a block of transparent plastic that dangled from a small stainless-steel stud protruding from the side of his head.

"In the six weeks and three days that I've been a

guest at this delightful hideaway, run by our most gracious host, Cardinal Bonaparte, they've taken twenty-six people through that door,'' he said, while pointing off to somewhere that I couldn't see. ''You're the first to be brought out that was still breathing.'' He smiled, exposing nearly translucent teeth that gleamed like shards of splintered ice. ''Congratulations!''

I tried to sit. Nothing happened.

''Uhrf,'' I managed to mumble.

The man looked away. ''Grab his feet, Vlad,'' he said. ''Let's move him out of here and to a more secluded area over against the Barrier.''

Barrier.

Invisible ants nibbled at my brain. That hidden door cracked open once more. A Barrier was a localized version of a Quad Wall. To move past it was to find yourself transformed into a charcoal briquette. The door slammed shut.

Someone else grabbed my ankles and lifted my legs off the ground. The man's face vanished as he grabbed me by the arms and jerked me up.

My head fell back and I found myself staring at an inverted pair of black-spotted yellow pants. The fabric looked as if it had been skinned from a polyester leopard. My head bobbed up and down and my butt dragged in the dirt.

''Hold on,'' said the man, ''we're almost there.''

They stopped, and my feet hit the ground. He propped me up against a wall—a soft, spongy-feeling wall—a Barrier. I was able to swallow and to hold my head upright.

''Vlad, give me some water,'' said the man.

Vlad moved into my field of vision. He was a child, no older than ten or eleven. Pasty-faced, he wore a pair of wraparound sunglasses. From neck to toe he was cloaked in a large tattered black cape. His blond hair was combed straight back, slick and oily-looking. From beneath his cape he pulled out a canteen and handed it to the man.

The canteen looked just like Tom's.

He put the canteen to my lips. Water filled my

mouth, and my throat seemed to loosen as I automatically swallowed. He didn't remove the canteen until I had drained it.

"Feeling a bit better now?" he asked cheerfully.

I tried to stand, and actually got my butt off the ground before my shaking arms gave out.

"Where have you got to get to so badly?" he asked.

I turned my head and stared at his raccoon eyes. Everything I had I put into my right hand and arm. Reaching out, I grabbed him by the collar of his bright yellow raincoat. "I've got to find Joan and Tom," I said with a croaking voice.

"A woman with cat eyes, and a blond Mushie?" he asked.

I nodded.

"I figured as much," he said. "They hit camp this morning at the same time they dragged a body bag into Interrogation." He thumped an index finger against my chest to emphasize that it had been me in that bag.

He turned to the boy. "Fetch them, Vlad," he said. "She was assigned to Ladora's House."

Vlad crinkled his nose but said nothing. Swirling his cape, he ran down the hillside.

I watched him until he vanished into a shantytown that spread out on the hills below us. The entire town was surrounded by a waist-high Barrier and bathed in the light generated from banks of floodlights suspended on large wooden towers. The lights illuminated the entire place but they were focused at the center of town onto a single large tower that dwarfed everything else by comparision. It almost glowed in the floodlights, its surface apparently made of some brightly polished metal. I had little trouble making out a figure that stood on a platform attached to its pinnacle.

"It's been a slow day," said the man. "By this time of night there have usually been at least ten people that have gotten themselves fried in the name of God. This guy is only number eight."

I slowly turned my head, looking back toward him.

He smiled, and his teeth seemed to luminesce with a sick green glow. "With the Speed Limit down to nineteen kilometers per hour, the frying just isn't all that spectacular. They barely even clear the platform, dropping less than five feet, before Thor fries them."

More pieces materialized.

It wasn't God who hurled down lightning bolts to vaporize those who moved faster than the Speed Limit, or who crossed a Barrier or Quad Wall, but *Thor.* Thor was built of mirrors and steel, graphite synthetics and computer chips. It would reach down from orbit with an infrared laser and *"fry"* you.

The figure walked to the edge of the platform.

"Watch!" said the man.

A distant and invisible crowd roared.

The figure threw itself from the platform. It had barely dropped when it suddenly exploded into a ball of flame. Whoever that had been, he or she had exceeded the Speed Limit. Thunder echoed off the hills.

"Another idiot fried in the name of God," said the man. Then he turned and sat in the dirt, facing me. "I certainly hope you aren't one of these Church of Limbo types, waiting in line to get fried in the name of God, to be absolved of all your sins against the Church."

I shook my head.

"It's not God," I said. I reached within myself, trying to see things that were there, but that were still partially hidden. Something molten dribbled over my brain. Again I saw desert, but it was no longer deserted and empty, with just a Quad Wall running across it. The desert floor was filled to the distant horizon with buildings. It was the Free Electron Laser Facility.

"Free Electron Laser," I said in a whisper.

"You've been out there?"

My eyes focused and the desert vanished. The man had his plastic-coated ear in his mouth, sucking on it as if it were an ice cube. "Have you seen the Mojave node of the Thor Global Defensive Network?"

My hands shook and my legs twitched. I could feel the neurons in my brain sputter and misfire. The *Mo-*

jave node. That was where Thor was—not in orbit. All that was in orbit were the mirrors off which the laser beam was bounced. All tracking and all laser beam generation took place out in the Mojave Desert, about a hundred kilometers north of Los Angeles.

I knew that.

I'd always known that, but had kept it hidden from myself.

Why?

Because knowledge kills.

My legs slowly stopped twitching and the burning in my head dulled. Knowledge kills. To know too much, to remember too much will kill you. That too was something that I suddenly knew, something that I had suddenly remembered.

"Never seen the node myself," he said, "but I've always wanted to. Imagine a place with the power to generate the two hundred Quad Sectors. Those pre-Bug boys, the ones who built the old world, knew their physics."

Two hundred Quad Sectors.

Tears ran down my cheeks.

Knowledge kills.

The entire world was divided and sectored, locked away into two hundred little compartments that were maintained by Thor. *That*'s *enough,* I thought. My heart pounded, but the rhythm wasn't steady. It lurched. I knew I wouldn't survive if I remembered anymore.

"Who are you?" I asked in a shaking whisper. I had to hear something that was of no consequence, something that I could focus on, but something that wouldn't force me into remembering. To remember anything more would kill me.

"Apologies," he said, waving both his hands before his face, and slowly bowing his head. "Joe Average at your service." He looked up quickly and flashed me a smile. "And my small friend," he said, while waving a hand in the direction of the town below us, "is Vlad the Impaler, Junior."

"Joe Average?" I asked. My voice had steadied.

The burning in my head had lessened. I concentrated on his face, on the shiny brass ring through his nose.

"Of course," he said. Reaching into his raincoat he pulled out a small book, which he handed to me.

My fingers were stiff, but were working. They barely shook. I took the book from him. *"Case Study: Joe Average, The Norm Male: Outtown Los Angeles, 2070,"* I read out loud. I flipped it open. It was several hundred pages of statistics, charts, and extremely small print.

"That's me," Joe said proudly. "I'm a Doler, heart, soul, and brain stem. Before the world got its collective brains eaten by the Bug, my typical day was a complete and fullfilling adventure of 11.8 hours of Trivid viewing, 2.7 liters of beer-consuming, and 1.8 grams of Narcanall-snorting. I can't read, can't write, don't know the capitals of France or Germany, and haven't even heard of the Nile River. I have sex 2.3 times a month, paying for it 1.6 of those times, and over my expected lifetime of 87.9 years I should visit the Esterbrook Hills Zoo 11.3 times. My GPI is a pathetic 68." Smiling, he reached over and took the book from my hands. "This is me," he said, while shaking the book. He then stuffed it back under his raincoat.

Damn!

Hidden doors were opening.

My eyelids fluttered and something tightened across my chest. *GPI was "genetic potential index."* It dictated what you'd be in life, what you'd be allowed to be in life. A high number would condemn you, make you unemployable, tell the world that you didn't have the genetic makeup to be anything worthwhile.

It would make you a Doler—a discard to be warehoused until you died or killed yourself.

"No more!"

He was killing me. Everything that he was and said opened something up within me, showed me something of a world that wasn't mine—a world that I had no right to know anything about.

"No more!"

His face hovered in front of me.

"Let me help you."

"No!"

He was killing me.

His face vanished.

My chest loosened. I breathed.

A fist moved before my eyes. It wasn't my fist. It waved in front of my eyes.

"Can you see me?"

"No," I whispered.

The fist uncurled itself. A bar code filled my vision, the lines seeming to crackle and glow with an incandescent whiteness.

"No," I pleaded.

The world vanished, and I felt myself floating.

The life of Lyle Thadeus Hutchings was mine. Like Joan he had been owned, but not by any private company. The state had owned him. He had received the best of everything. He had been genetically tailored to become one of the elite. But something had gone wrong, terribly wrong. At the age of twenty-five, in 2071, he had been committed to the psychiatric ward of the Intown Citizens' Hospital. He was never released. The diagnosis changed on a weekly basis, but there was no cure and no real change in his condition. He had lost all conception of self. He would believe himself to be everything from a 1932 Packard, a German Shepherd named Boots, one or both of the moons of Mars (Phobos and Deimos), or even a pair of sunglasses. His GPI was designated a 3 at birth, but three weeks after admittance to the Intown Citizens' Hospital he was redesignated a 92. Apparently, his genes had been tweaked just a little too tightly.

"Drink this."

My eyes focused—in a twisted and distorted sort of way. A flask hovered in front of me. It was alive and slippery, looking as if it breathed, as if within it were a beating heart.

"Drink."

My mouth opened.

The flask moved.

Fire filled my mouth, burned my throat, and dribbled into my stomach. My head cleared, and feeling almost returned to my feet and hands. I pushed the flask away and reached behind myself, grabbing at the Barrier.

"Could you help me up?" I asked, as I tried to push up with one hand and bend my knees, trying to get my legs underneath me.

I could feel things in my brain steady. The liquor, that jolt of alcohol, had somehow shocked me, leveled out brain waves that had slipped into chaos.

Joe stood, grabbed my free hand, and pulled me up.

Putting some of my weight against the wall at my back and locking my knees, I stood.

He moved close to me, until our noses were almost touching. His breath rivaled that of Pancho's. "I hope you realize that both myself and Vlad will be helping you in your escape attempt."

"Escape?" He had almost killed me, and now he wanted to help me escape from this place? To escape from Napoleon?

"Napoleon let you out of interrogation and into the general population for only one reason. He wanted to see who you contacted, so he could pick those people up. If he considers you important, he'll also consider anyone you talk to as important."

I stared into his ridiculous-looking face.

His brain was as warped and bent as everyone else's in this world, but he wasn't stupid. What he said was completely true. By simply looking in my direction he had probably condemned himself to whatever fate would be waiting for me back in that dungeon.

"Then why'd you bring me over here?" I asked.

"The only way out of here is to get fried," he said, as he pointed to the distant tower. "I figured that anyone who was sharp enough to survive a session with Napoleon and his Brothers might just be smart enough to figure a way out of here. I decided to take that gamble." He smiled.

In all likelihood that gamble was going to get him fried before the sun rose.

"You're playing extremely long odds," I said.

He continued to smile. "They're the only ones available."

An instant ago I had wanted nothing more than to escape from this psycho, but something had suddenly changed. He looked like a nightmare but he spoke just like Kent Cooper or Jack Behnke. He knew he was screwed, but was trying to make the best of it. He was trapped, and doing whatever he could to try to find a way to survive.

Just like me.

I leaned against the Barrier, wondering what I should do next. I turned around and found myself looking up at a dark deserted hillside.

"You aren't the suicidal type, are you?"

I turned back toward him.

"You jump that wall and you'll get two or three steps at the most. Long before the Supreme and the Church of Limbo started using this place as a Detention Center, the pre-Bug world used it as a Liquidation Center for illegal Fourth-Worlders that were captured in the Outtown Los Angeles area. To my knowledge, no one before or after the Bug has ever made it away from the Barrier without being fried."

He took a step away from me.

"Do you want to die?"

I could crawl over this wall and all this insanity would be over. It would *all* be over. A part of me wanted to, a part of me was screaming to do it. But it was only a part, a very small part. I stepped back from the Barrier.

"Welcome back to the land of the living," he said as he spit his ear out of his mouth and into his hand, then hung it back on the stainless-steel stud that protruded from the side of his head.

"John Smith!" yelled out a distant voice.

I turned. Already halfway up the hill was Tom, followed closely behind by Joan and then Vlad, with his arms flapping and his cape fluttering. It had been Joan who had called out my name. I walked forward on wobbly legs to meet them. Tom, kicking up dirt and sliding to a halt, was the first to reach me. He stood, staring up at me with his sad dog-eyes.

"Hi," he said between pants.

Reaching out, I gave him a slap on the arm. "Hi yourself," I said. I even managed a smile. I had no idea how I could tell him, much less make him understand, that he was less than an hour away from being strung up in a dungeon and being tortured to death by a psychotic in a sombrero.

It was impossible.

"I knew you'd escape," said an out-of-breath Joan. She bent down, with hands against her knees, trying to regain her wind. She quickly stood straight. "I just knew you'd escape," she said once again, then, reaching out, wrapped her arms around me and squeezed. The air seemed to explode out of my chest. Her tears ran down the side of my neck. She shook like a dead leaf barely clinging to a twig, as if buffeted about in a windstorm.

I wrapped my own arms around her, gently stroking her back. This wasn't a woman in my arms but a frightened child.

"It was horrible," she whispered in my ear. "They said I had the look of an Entertainment Specialist, and sent me to a place called Ladora's." She then broke down completely, crying uncontrollably.

I held her tightly. They'd sent her to a whorehouse, seeing in her what she no longer saw in herself.

"You're safe now," I said, trying to comfort and console the same woman who, earlier in the day, had been ready to take on a hundred of Napoleon's troops with only a sword.

She shook her head, and her wet cheek rubbed against the side of my neck. "You don't understand," she said between hiccups and sobs.

All I could do was hold her.

"They forced me down, and they tied my hands and feet to the floor."

She clung to me, trying to burrow into me.

"They took me," she said in a whisper so quiet that I could barely hear it.

She shuddered in my arms. I continued to stroke her back.

"And I enjoyed it," she said, as if confessing to some murderous crime. "I craved it." Her knees suddenly gave out, and my arms wrapped around her back were the only things holding her up.

She believed herself to be Joan of Arc, a virginal, saintly soldier of God. But she was also Tiffany 12, genetically and surgically designed to be an organic, nonstop sex machine. Her body was designed for sex, with her brain probably filling her with endorphins and adrenaline, physically addicting her to it.

I literally pried her away from me, holding her out so she could see my face. "God spoke to me," I said, feeling a knife stab me in the gut as I said it. I had known her for less than a day, but here and now, in this insane place, she suddenly seemed to mean more to me than anyone or anything I had ever known. And I didn't know why. I'd never in my life seen anyone so vulnerable, seen anyone so in need of something.

She had somehow become a friend.

It made absolutely no sense. I'd known her less than a day. She was a religious fanatic and had gotten me captured by Napoleon. But still, she felt like a friend.

And you don't lie to a friend.

But I wasn't strong enough to see her in such pain. She trusted and believed in me, and I was going to use that trust to lie to her.

"He was testing your strength for the job that lies before us," I said, "and having passed His test, He wanted to ease your suffering, so He let your body enjoy the ordeal. It was His *gift* to you."

She wiped at her face. "He truly told you that?" she asked, as she rubbed her eyes with balled fists.

Reaching out, I hugged her again. "Of course," I said, feeling like a bucket of shit as I said it.

This time *she* pried herself away, and looked up at me. "You don't think any the less of me, do you?" she asked.

"That would be impossible," I said, and that was

the total and complete truth. I managed not to cry—barely.

She smiled, but her chin still shook. "What happened to you?" she asked.

I took a deep breath. It was back to business. "We've got less than an hour to escape this place or all of us will be killed," I said. In comparision with the lie I had just told her, telling her that we were about to die was actually easy.

"Then we'd better escape," she said, as if saying that would make it so.

I nodded, and had to stifle a laugh. It felt incredibly good to have to stifle that laugh. She was so unbelievably naive and trusting. "There's no way out."

"Not quite true."

I turned.

Joe was stroking his chin, as if he had an invisible beard. "The Barrier can be crossed at the Main Gate."

That was enough for Joan. Turning, she almost lifted Tom from the ground, where he was intently studying pebbles, and pushed him in the direction of the town. "We'd better hurry then," she said as she followed after him, not even looking back at me.

"Interesting," said Joe, who jogged up next to me, carrying Vlad in his arms. His plastic-coated ear bobbed up and down. "If by some miracle we do escape, I think traveling with you may prove extremely interesting."

The Main Gate was just that. Like everything else around here it was part nightmare and part soundstage from a studio back lot.

The Barrier had about a hundred-foot gap in it, and fit snugly into that gap was a castle plucked straight from some King Arthur fantasy complete with moat and drawbridge—a drawn drawbridge. Red-bereted sentries and what looked like a pair of antiaircraft batteries were positioned high in the castle walls.

I walked to the edge of the moat. It was narrow, no more than fifty feet wide, and the far side ended at a solid wall of wet and mossy flagstone. Even if there had been some place to find a toehold, and sufficient cracks and crevices to climb up the wall, the sentries would have killed us before we'd even dived into the water.

"This is the only possible way out?" I asked Joe.

"This is it," he said, sounding not too pleased.

We were dead. We might be able to go back into the town and hide somewhere, but the outcome would be inevitable. We'd be captured, tossed into the dungeon and tortured until I told Napoleon a code to bring down the Los Angeles Quad Walls—a code that I had absolutely no knowledge of.

Joan paced the perimeter of the moat like a caged animal, with Tom dogging right behind her.

I felt a scream bubbling up from deep in my gut, formed by frustration and feelings of being so incredibly inadequate for the situation I found myself in.

"No!" I screamed into the night sky, forcing the air up from deep in my lungs, ripping the back of my throat raw.

"So sad!" said a voice that thundered from somewhere in the castle wall. "But it was nice of you to bring together all of your friends. It looks like it's going to be getting rather crowded in your dungeon cell." Deep, rumbling laughter echoed from the castle wall.

The image of the face that went along with that voice had been burned into a permanent and deep place inside of my brain. Pancho Villa was somewhere in that castle.

I suddenly knew that there was a chance. It was the remotest of chances, but a chance. In the dungeon Pancho had nearly beaten me to death, but hadn't been allowed to quite kill me. I might just be able to get Pancho to come out of that castle, if he thought he could have another chance of killing me—a chance to do what he wanted without Napoleon to stop him. But in order to do that he would have to lower the drawbridge. That might give the others a chance.

"I've come for your mother, Pancho," I yelled upward. "I've got a friend who has a fondness for livestock. He said he'd give me a peso if I could bring him a suitable piece of meat."

I waited for several seconds. Not a sound came from the castle wall.

"I understand," I called up. "But do me a favor—when you're done with her yourself, could you please send her down?"

I had to wait only about half a second before he replied.

"Yaaaaah!"

Wood and metal creaked. The drawbridge began to drop.

I motioned everyone toward me. All four of them huddled around me.

The drawbridge dropped to the dirt, only a few feet from the tips of my boots. It kicked up a large cloud of dust.

I didn't have long to wait.

Pancho stood at the far end of the drawbridge, with pistols in both hands. Behind him, with weapons drawn, stood at least twenty troops in white body armor, along with another half-dozen in berets.

I shook my head. I had hoped that his machismo persona would have forced him to come down by himself. With those troops guarding the castle entrance, none us would be able to get more than a few feet across the bridge before we were cut down.

I looked over my shoulder and all four nodded, including Tom. They were ready to try to move across, despite what we faced.

Putting my right boot onto the edge of the drawbridge, I felt all control suddenly being ripped away from me. As if some internal switch had been pulled, something else was again in charge. But this time I had been expecting it, actually depending on it.

My other boot, as if possessed, walked up onto the drawbridge. I looked up, and my eyes focused onto Pancho. He raised both pistols, their barrels aimed straight at my chest. I could hear those behind me scattering to the far sides of the drawbridge, getting out of Pancho's field of fire.

Bang!

His aim was true.

But I was no longer there. I had rotated my body by ninety degrees the instant before he had pulled the trigger. One bullet missed my chest by inches, and the second tugged at the back of my shirt but didn't touch me. Unlike the other times when my body had been taken over, this time, even though I still had no control, I had seen something of what was going on inside of my head. I had seen the exact angles, distances, bullet velocities, and the synaptic delays between blinking eyes and squeezing trigger-fingers.

It wasn't someone or something else controlling me but a part of my *own* brain, buried deep, far below my conscious control.

I knew the bullets' trajectories a full half-second before the gun was even fired. My body simply moved to where the bullets would not be. I turned back around and faced Pancho. I took another step forward. Crouching, bending to my left and balancing by extending my arms to the right, I waited for the smallest fraction of a second.

Bang!

The breeze caused by the first bullet ruffled the hair on the top of my head. The second bullet passed harmlessly in the one-inch gap between my outstretched arms.

Pancho's eyes were opened wide and he chewed on the corner of his lip. Several of those behind him had moved back, taking cover within the castle.

I felt my throat loosen, and my jaw went slack. I had control of my neck and mouth. For the first time in hours I believed that we might just be able to get out of this with our skins still intact. It was time to hit these Church of Limbo psychos square in the face. "I am God's Savior!" I screamed. "I cannot be harmed! I am under His protection!"

I walked across the bridge.

Half the troops behind Pancho turned and ran. The other half stood rooted, their weapons still ready, but I could smell the fear in them. The air was thick with scents I had never known existed. I stood less than ten feet away from the barrels of Pancho's guns.

"Die!" he screamed.

Bang!

I was already down, against the drawbridge. The first bullet missed me by at least a foot, but the second caught me in the meaty part of my right calf. For just an instant lightning lanced through my leg and ran up into my crotch. But just as I thought I felt it the pain vanished as if it had never been there. I felt blood vessels and arteries around the wound constrict themselves and then reroute blood flow.

I stood.

"God will not take kindly to that," I said, while taking another step forward. I didn't so much as limp.

All but one of the troops behind Pancho broke and ran. A single man, dressed in flowing black robes and a turban, still held a crossbow against his cheek. He jerked the trigger.

My hand reached out, transforming itself into a blur. The inside of my fingers and the palm of my hand momentarily burned, as if hit with acid, but the pain vanished just as it had in my calf.

I held a crossbow bolt between my thumb and index finger. "I believe this is yours," I said, holding it out toward the bowman. Smoke drifted up from my hand.

He ran.

I dropped the bolt to the drawbridge and walked forward.

Pancho had lowered his pistols, and his lips moved as if he were talking to himself. His right cheek convulsively ticked. I looked into his eyes. He seemed to be looking right through me.

Reaching out, I pulled the pistols from his weak grasp and tossed them into the moat.

"This is not going to please your mother," I said.

Pancho's eyeballs rolled back until only the whites were visible. He crumpled on himself, hitting the drawbridge face-first.

Turning, I looked back to the end of the drawbridge. Tom, Joan, Joe, and Vlad stood there, looking as frozen as the troops had been. Around them stood almost a hundred other townspeople.

"Move it!" I shouted, as I waved them all forward.

They didn't have a chance to move.

The night sky turned crimson, and the castle shattered as if it had been constructed of delicate crystal and a sledgehammer had just smashed into it.

I sailed high into the sky. The last thing I saw, far beneath me, was the splintering drawbridge collapsing into the moat.

CHAPTER 6

Anna, Jesus Christ, and Sir Basil

Smack!

My eyes opened, and I felt a fountain of water explode from my mouth. My lungs burned. Something heavy sat on my stomach.

"Can you hear me, John?" asked a blur that hovered over me.

My eyes focused. It was Joan that hung over me, actually straddling my stomach. Her warm hands pushed rhythmically against my chest. Her face was pale, and her eyes wide. She panted like an out-of-breath dog.

She'd been giving me CPR.

I took a deep breath. My throat felt as if it had been sandpapered. "Stop," I said, grimacing, feeling as if I were swallowing large chunks of broken glass. I'd been nearly beaten to death by Pancho, then wounded in the leg and hand, yet I'd felt none of that. Apparently this miraculous pain-blocking ability didn't apply to torn throats.

Joan climbed off of me and I managed to prop myself up on one elbow. Tom, Joe, and Vlad were gathered around me. From the expressions on their faces you'd think they had just witnessed a dead man rising up from his coffin.

Vlad took several steps back. The look in his eyes was more than just one of surprise. I saw fear.

"You flew through the air," said Joe, in a quiet whisper, the tone of his voice indicating that he believed he had just seen something miraculous. "The drawbridge buckled, and then flung you into the air as if you'd been launched by a catapult.'' He nervously wiped at his face and caressed his plastic-coated ear. ''Before you started back down you must have been twenty or thirty feet up in the air.'' He glanced from side to side then up into the sky, as if he expected a bolt of lightning to lance down and vaporize him for what he'd just said.

Twenty or thirty feet.

Joe wasn't expecting a lightning bolt, but an infrared laser beam courtesy of Thor. With the Speed Limit down to nineteen kilometers per hour, to fall any distance greater than five feet would kick your velocity up above the Speed Limit. I should have been a chunk of smoking charcoal. Either God had been looking out for me, or some malfunction in Thor had spared my ass. I wasn't yet ready to believe in Joan's all-seeing God, but considered the more likely explanation for why I was still breathing to be that some chip had glitched and Thor had dropped a bit.

With the palm of her hand Joan wiped mud from the side of my face. ''Are you all right?'' she asked, suddenly sounding very maternal.

''I'll live,'' I said, giving her my best cocky, bullshit smile. I tried to sit further up, but my right leg wouldn't move and my calf felt like someone had just jabbed a hot poker through it. Suddenly my whole body felt like an open wound. And just as suddenly it felt as if somebody had started sprinkling me with salt. The only thing that kept me from screaming was the sheer exhaustion that consumed me. I could barely breathe. Whatever anesthetic had been numbing my pain, and whatever energy source I'd been running off of, had finally run dry.

My head rolled over and I could feel my ear fill with mud. I was staring in the direction of where the castle had been. All that remained was a smoking pile of rubble. The ground beneath me shook, and the sudden roar of a turbine was deafening. As I watched, something rose up from behind the rubble. It was a dark shadow, and as it hovered it kicked up dirt and gravel. It was a hexprop.

Joan was bending over me, keeping the windswept debris off my face. The side of her head was directly over my mouth.

"We have to move!" I tried to scream at her, but it came out as a whisper. "Into the town," I said.

I hoped that help was on the way. Hopefully, whoever was responsible for destroying that castle would be coming for us.

Gray gave way to black.

"He's awake."

My eyes opened. I could smell smoke, and in the distance hear screaming. Automatic gunfire was nearby, but I could barely hear it over the almost continuous crack of thunder. I wondered just how many simultaneous targets Thor could track. I managed to move my eyeballs.

The five of us were in a closet-sized wooden room, lit by a single kerosene lamp. The room was bare except for the bed I lay in. The four hovered over me, waiting, as if expecting *me* to formulate a plan, to somehow rescue everyone from this nightmare.

It would be one long wait.

I couldn't even move, and my ribs were so bruised that I could only suck down air in shallow, panting breaths.

Joan moved closer. There was a jagged cut across her forehead and blood dripped down the side of her face. "God won't tell me what to do," she said, speaking in tight, controlled tones. Her skin was white as chalk.

From the other side of the bed a hand grabbed me by the shoulder, and another slid between the bed and my back. I was pushed up into a sitting position.

Each of my vertebrae seemed to grind against the one next to it, as if the tips of each and every one were now splintered nubs. I managed to sob, and tears ran down my face. Had my tongue been between any of my teeth I would have bitten right through it.

Joan stood next to the bed, unmoving, seeming to stare at something beyond the four walls. Vlad moved away, crawling into the corner of the room, wrapping his head within the folds of his black cape. Joe stood next to Joan, staring down at his book, flipping through pages as his lips twitched.

I managed to turn my head. How, I don't know. It had been Tom who had lifted me up, and he now stared into my eyes. A fierce intelligence burned within those eyes, just as it had back at Robin Hood's cave. His granite-like, unmoving face seemed to talk to me.

They don't know what to do. They're good people, but they need someone to lead them. We have a chance now, but not if you fall apart.

They're not my responsibility I said with a look.

He shrugged. *Then we all die.*

That was the simple truth.

He knew it, and I knew it.

He then nodded at me and removed his hands from my back. I did not collapse back down against the bed. It was as if Tom's nodding head was the trigger that caused some drug within me to kick in. And it kicked in with the strength of a mule. No pain. I breathed deeply.

I knew that there'd be hell to pay for this later, but if I could pull them together we at least might have a chance of *having* a later.

"Have we got any weapons?" I asked, practically shouting.

Joe dropped his book, Vlad peered out from beneath his cape, and Joan refocused her eyes directly on me.

I stood, practically leaping from the bed. I suddenly felt my pants begin to slide down my hips, and I had to hitch them up. The waistband was elastic and the pants had fit snugly only yesterday morning, but not now. Obviously, I was burning muscle to maintain myself. I'd soon reach the point when there was nothing left to burn, and regardless of what mystery chemicals my brain was pumping out in order to keep me going I would fall flat on my face.

"Any weapons?" I asked again. I hopped from foot to foot, feeling that if I didn't keep moving I'd actually explode.

"Nothing," said Joan, having moved back and braced herself against the room's far wall. The expression on her face was one of pure, undiluted fright.

"I'm all right," I said, managing not to launch myself from the floor. I knew what had her pushed up against that wall. One second I'd been lying in bed, barely breathing, almost dead, and the next I was leaping about, ready to rip apart anything that got in my way. If *I'd* witnessed that I would have been through the nearest door—quite possibly the nearest wall.

Then Joan moved away from the wall, slowly walking toward me and reaching out. She put her hand on my shoulder. "God is with you?"

I nodded.

Judging by how I was feeling, it might actually have been true. I turned toward Joe, who was restuffing his book back into his raincoat. "Whoever blew that castle is by definition our ally. We have to somehow link up with them if we're going to have any chance at all of getting out of here."

"And we can't do that by hiding in this room," said Joe, completing my sentence for me.

I nodded. They'd obviously known this all along. But they hadn't been able to act. They needed a catalyst, and I had somehow become that catalyst. "We've got to get outside, locate some weapons to protect ourselves, and then find whoever is responsible for this," I said, while waving both my hands over my head, indicating the thunder cracks and rifle fire beyond this room.

They all were standing now, and ready. But none of them moved. This had definitely become my show and my show alone—and four other lives depended on how I performed.

"Follow me," I said, and went for the door.

I wished I had even the slightest hint as to where I was going.

* * *

"Stay against the wall," I said, without bothering to look behind myself.

Stepping around the corner, and hugging the building's rough-planked wooden front wall, I crept along the front of the shack we had been hiding in.

My body spun itself around, tensing, and crouched down on all fours. I seemed to be readying myself, just as a cat would coil itself before it pounced on an unsuspecting mouse. Consciously, I hadn't heard or seen a thing, but apparently something deep inside of my brain sensed danger. I felt that subconscious control taking me over again, but this time I was able to fight it. I saw what it wanted, and how it planned on directing me, but this time *I* could control *it*.

I waved at those behind me. "Back into the alley," I whispered.

The sound of creaking wood behind me told me that they were moving back. I didn't do the same. I scrambled to the center of the street and, bending my neck while sticking up my nose, I flared my nostrils. I sniffed at the night.

I could smell things that I'd never smelled before.

About one hundred yards down the street, just inside the flaps of a tent that had a large sign saying *Judge Roy Bean—Cold Beer—Hot Women*, there were at least two men peering out into the street. I could smell the fear on them, and far back in my mouth, almost down in my throat, could taste the gunpowder that stained their hands.

They were waiting for us.

Dropping to the ground, lying flat in the mud, I moved snakelike across the street then quickly scrambled up onto a wooden porch. The scent of the two men was stronger but its flavor remained unchanged. They were still soaked with fear but I detected nothing in the way of surprise, which would have come pouring off of them in thick waves had they seen me crossing the street. How I knew that, I didn't know. It had just appeared in my head, as mysteriously as everything else had appeared.

People behind darkened windows peered out into

the empty street. I could feel them, hear their breathing, and smell the blood rushing through them. I breathed deeply and quickly slipped by the revolving door of a whorehouse. The scent of sex was unmistakable. Bending down, but not looking away from the front of the tent where the two men were lying in wait, I picked up a handful of rocks and stuffed them into the crook of my left arm.

All my senses were focused onto that tent flap some twenty yards away from me. The flap shuddered, as if something poked at it from behind. The barrel of a gun slid out. A second gun barrel quickly followed it.

Three rocks were now in my right hand, each one resting on a separate finger.

A head wearing a red beret poked out through the tent flap.

My right hand tensed.

A second head, also wearing a red beret, jutted out just beneath the first.

Both heads turned toward me. The whites of their eyes seemed to grow large. They swung their rifles.

Two of my fingers, on which rocks rested, flicked upward, one much harder than the other, causing the rocks to jump up, one much higher than the other. The one rock remaining in my hand vanished into my fist, as my arm first cocked back behind my head and then flashed forward. I didn't even have to watch where that first rock went. I knew where it would go.

Before the first rock had even traveled half the distance to its intended target my hand was open and my palm flat. One of the rocks I had tossed up gently landed in it. Like the first rock it disappeared into my fist, and an instant later was flying toward *its* target.

The third rock was locked tightly in my fist, my hand held high above the back of my head, ready to fire if necessary.

''Umph!'' was all the first man said, as the rock caught him square in the temple.

''Oouf!'' said the second man, a split second later, as the rock aimed at him hit him in the middle of his sloping forehead. They fell against one another, their limp, unconscious bodies supporting each other for just a moment before they teetered and collapsed into the mud.

Sprinting forward, I had both their rifles in my hands. They were full automatics. I pulled extra clips from their belts.

"Move it!" I called out.

They scrambled across the brightly lit street, Joan leading the way, followed by Joe carrying Vlad, and Tom bring up the rear.

"Can you handle this," I asked, shaking the M-16 at Joan.

"Of course," she said.

I tossed her the rifle, not wasting much thought on how either an ex-call girl, or Joan of Arc, could have had the opportunity to learn how to fire an M-16.

But that didn't seem all that remarkable, not in comparison with the things that I suddenly knew. I'd never handled a rifle in my life, but now, as I looked down at the M-16, it felt like an extension of my arm. In the back of my brain an entire exploded schematic of the weapon unfolded itself. I could strip that rifle, clean it, and reassemble it in under three minutes. That wasn't speculation, that was fact.

"Stay close together," I said, and started to move down the street. I took perhaps three steps.

But no more.

Behind me, something was terribly wrong.

"Get your goddamned fucking hands off of me, you prickless son of a bitch!" screamed someone with a high squeaky voice.

I turned before any of the others could. My rifle was braced against my side, requiring only the slightest squeeze of the trigger to fire it.

It had been Vlad who screamed.

Three of them had somehow crept up on us. Identical, all were dressed in the white, form-fitting plastic type of body armor that most of Napoleon's troops wore. The one in the center held Vlad tightly against his chest. He covered Vlad's mouth with one hand, while with the other he held a knife against the boy's throat. The other two had bazooka-like devices aimed at us. But they weren't bazookas. A large, thickly twined cable ran from the stock of the weapons, snaked up over their shoulders, and connected to the top of what looked like a large backpack. Just as in the case of the M-16s, I suddenly knew exactly what those weapons were. The two held Israeli-built hydrogen fluoride X-1200 laser rifles.

I had taken in all of this in less time than it took Joan, Tom, and Joe to turn around.

These three were not like the two that I had just knocked out with rocks. I flared my nostrils and scented them. I could smell no fear, not even hate drifting from them. There was just the cold, metallic tang of someone who was about to perform a task—like killing termites, or stepping on a cockroach.

"Put down your weapons," said the one in the center. He spoke in an amplified, slightly mechanical-sounding voice that came through a speaker grille in his face shield.

Joan and I dropped our rifles.

The stock of mine rested firmly on the tip of my boot.

"Move forward," said the man.

Before we could move Vlad squirmed, thrashing his head wildly about, causing the knife to cut into his throat. But he wasn't trying to escape, only to move his head around so he could get something into his mouth. The man's body armor almost totally covered him, except where it met at the joints, especially the joints of the fingers. You needed those fingers relatively free and flexible to pull triggers and handle weapons.

One of those free and flexible fingers was now in Vlad's mouth. He bit down with everything he had.

The man jerked, but the scream I had expected never materialized. Vlad slid from his arms and fell to the ground. The man stood, for what seemed like an eternity, then pitched face-forward. The vibrating shaft of a spear jutted out of the back of his neck, right at the joint where his helmet mated with his torso armor.

"Down!" I managed to scream. With a flick of my boot I kicked the M-16 up into my hands. I dove for the street, rolled, and came up firing.

The trooper on the left side of the street never fired. He simply exploded as if he had swallowed a live grenade. His armor stayed relatively intact, but along each seam and joint blood and pulverized muscle shot out as if blown by a high-pressure air gun. Steam rose from his head.

I paid no further attention to him.

The remaining one fired his weapon, and the hair on my left forearm flashed into flame just as a patch of dirt between my feet bubbled, first turning crimson and then incandescent white.

I fired, but my bullets bounced harmlessly from his armor.

The left side of my face sizzled, and my vision distorted as the air in front of me became superheated.

I was certain that my luck had finally run out, and that I was only milliseconds away from my head's exploding like a bursting pressure cooker. But just before my eyeballs popped, something black and streaked yellow flashed in front of me. What felt like a clawed hand grabbed me by the midsection and thrust me up into the air.

My rifle was still in my hands, and again I pointed it in the direction the laser fire had been coming from. My eyes were watery and my vision blurred, but I could see that the trooper that had been firing at me was now lying chest-down in the dirt. Not facedown, because he no longer had a face. He'd been decapitated. To my right, I could see what was left of his head partially imbedded in a wooden lamp post.

Prrrrr!

Just behind me, actually all around me, was the sound of a buzz saw. Looking down, I realized I was some three or four feet above the ground.

"He's safe now," said a woman's voice. "Put him down, Sir Basil.

The vise around my waist loosened. I rolled out and hit the dirt, landing flat on my back. Above me stood a tiger, easily six feet tall at the shoulder. The front fangs protruding through its muzzle were six inches of glistening ivory.

I didn't move, I didn't even breathe. It was now obvious what had taken off the head of that trooper. The monstrous cat flexed its nose, sniffing at me, then flicked out a tongue that had to be at least a foot across. It bent down its head and licked my entire face and head, practically dragging me up from the ground.

"Sir Basil!" said a chastising voice. "Leave him alone!" The tiger opened its jaws wide, exposing a cavernous mouth filled with an impossible number of razor sharp-looking teeth. It roared.

The ground shook.

The tiger then shut its mouth, flicked its tongue out to give its chin a quick lick, and backed off, settling down on its haunches. It began its buzz-saw purring again.

A hand appeared in front of my face. "Don't mind Sir Basil, Mr. Smith."

I turned my head slowly, still in shock from the licking I had just received. The hand was attached to a small dark-skinned, dark-haired woman, wearing a black jumpsuit. Strung over her shoulder was one of the hydrogen fluoride laser rifles, identical to those the two in plastic body armor had been using. I grabbed the hand she was offering me, which had a walnut-pulverizing grip. She pulled me up from the ground.

"Sir Basil just got a little excited," she said. "He's been on your scent for almost two days now."

But before I could even begin to consider this woman and her mutant tiger, I had to check on *my* people. And they *were* now my people. Two days ago my biggest concern had been making sure that I finished up three months' worth of late monthly progress reports, while today I found myself literally responsible for the skins of four other people.

I walked over to Joan, Tom, and Joe. Joe had his arms wrapped around Vlad. I bent down toward the boy. Only a few drops of blood ran down his throat.

"Are you okay?" I asked.

He smiled, exposing a pair of incredibly cheap-looking plastic fangs. "It'll take an asshole a lot bigger than that to do in Vlad Junior," he said defiantly as he flicked his thumb in the direction of the dead bodies. "The dumb shit didn't even have a wooden stake." Reaching up, he pressed his sunglasses tightly to his face.

The kid seemed okay. He was as bent in his own weird way as the rest of them, but he seemed all right. I turned back to the woman. This is who we'd been looking for, and she had obviously been looking for me.

"Where's the rest of your group?" I asked, knowing full well that all the destruction and confusion that had occurred could not have been caused by this woman and her mutant tiger.

"Over here," said a man's voice.

I turned.

He was standing over the body that had the spear through the back of its neck, working the shaft out. Like the woman he was dark-skinned, and had dark hair. But in addition he had a black scraggly beard and an ugly pink-looking scar across his forehead that was in the shape of a cross. Barefoot, all he wore was an almost ground-length gray robe. Finally prying the spear out, he gave the dead body a savage kick in the side of the head.

"My old man forgeeves you of your seens, you stupid sahn of a beech," he said. He had a thick Mexican accent. "If and when you actually meet up with the *old bastard*, be sure and let him know what good deeds I'm performing down here." Once again he kicked the body.

Another crazy.

I turned back to the woman. "That's it, just the two of you and this tiger."

The woman's face seemed to grow darker, and I could hear the squeak of teeth grinding against one another. "We appeared to be sufficient to save *your* asses," she said.

She stepped up to me. Her hands were balled into

small fists, which she had pressed tightly against the sides of her waist. She was almost a foot shorter than me, and weighed at least fifty pounds less. But none of that seemed to matter. It was blatantly obvious that she wanted to knock my head off.

"You misunderstand," I said, while backing up. "I was simply amazed at how effectively the two of you have been able to throw Napoleon and his troops into total chaos."

I smiled.

The last thing I needed was one more person who wanted to vaporize me.

She smiled back. I'd pressed the right buttons.

"That simple shit couldn't find his own dick with a road map," said the man, who was now wiping the tip of his spear on the hem of his robe.

These two were a real pair.

The woman pointed the barrel of her laser rifle at those around me. "We were told that you'd be alone," she said. "We didn't expect anyone *else.*"

It sounded as if she were talking about excess baggage.

I pointed to them one at a time. "This is Tom, Joe Average, Joan of Arc, and Vlad the Impaler, Junior." The introduction had a nightmarish, unreal feel to it. Here I stood in the middle of a shantytown, with Napoleon and his troops ready to swoop down on us at any instant, and I was making introductions between people whose brains had been scrambled just short of being complete tapioca.

The woman nodded. "I'm Anna Lockner," she said almost as if she were making a pronouncement, identifying herself as a person of royal blood. Then, pointing to the man with the spear, "And that's Jesus Christ."

He waved his spear at me. "Let's get this fucking show on the road."

It might not have been exactly what I would have expected Jesus Christ to have said, but I could identify with the sentiments.

"Let's go," said Anna, waving the barrel of her laser down the street.

"We should first scavenge their weapons," I said, while looking back in the direction of the dead bodies.

"Don't be stupid," said Anna, who continued to walk down the street. "All those lasers are Nanomechanoid constructs, tied to the users' nervous systems. The critical bonds are already being severed."

Nanomechanoid constructs.

The power packs strapped to their backs were starting to sag, as if they'd been filled with air that was now slowly leaking out. Purple smoke hung over the laser rifles. It looked just like what I'd seen happen at Dummar with the spaceman.

I felt my skull crack.

A steel door, meters thick, studded with bolts larger than my hand, bulged outward. It was a door buried in my head, hiding secrets from me, secrets that I shouldn't know.

Secrets that I couldn't know.

The steel cracked, and rainbow light filtered through the crazing metal.

I dropped to the street.

Mud filled my mouth.

"John!"

The door shattered, transforming into a billion metallic fragments that ripped and shredded at the inside of my head. I was filled with light, filled beyond my capacity to hold it in. Rainbow streamers poured out through my clenched mouth, and out through my closed eyes.

Nanomechanoid constructs.

They moved toward me from out of the rainbow light. They scuttled like crabs, but microscopic crabs, crabs built out of just a handful of atoms. But they weren't crabs, but machines. And they had built the world—built this insane world that I found myself in.

They spoke to me.

CHAPTER 7

Escape

"You know me."

It floated up toward my nose. It was lumpy and black. I could see the individual atoms that made it up. It had six twitching legs and two flexing pincer hands.

I tried to shake my head.

But I couldn't.

I no longer seemed to have a head.

"I'm a Nanomechanoid."

I screamed. I had no head, but somehow I could still scream. The searing pain that enveloped me demanded it.

"The concept is simple," it said. "We are machines, made up of only a few thousand atoms." It flexed its pincers. "We can sever the bonds between atoms and then transport those atoms to build something new."

I knew.

I had always known.

It was a technology that had transformed the world. It was atomic-dimension machinery that could gather raw materials, an atom at a time, and then be directed to build something with those materials. They could build a road, build a house, build a world.

And they could build each other.

That's where the real power lay.

Geometrical growth.

One would build another, then both would build two

more. The four would become eight and the eight, sixteen.

That's how the world had been transformed.

It moved forward, with pincers still snapping, and reached out for me. But there was nothing there to reach for. There was nothing there at all.

Except for my soul.

It shredded me.

"Get him up!"

I stood.

My eyes slowly opened.

I was not dead. *It* had not killed me. *It* had not even been there. Everything I'd seen had come from within me. And I could still see it, still feel it. I could still remember it.

Anna Lockner glared up at me. "I don't know what help you're going to be, not if you collapse at the sight of disintegrating Nanomechanoids."

Lightning danced behind my eyes.

But I didn't fall down.

Then I realized that I couldn't. Joan and Joe were holding me up. I pushed them away.

Somehow I still stood.

"If you think you can manage it, Smith, bring up the rear."

She didn't wait for me to answer, but turned and started walking down the street. Christ jogged past me and tossed me my rifle. I managed to catch it, despite the fact that I couldn't quite feel my hands.

"Let them go," said Joan, having moved back to my side, once again supporting me.

I shook my head. We needed their help, and we needed it badly. We could not afford to let them go. I motioned Joan forward. She slowly let go of me, picked up her rifle, grabbed Tom by the hand, and followed after Christ.

I took a step forward.

I didn't fall into the mud, so I took another step.

"She's one tough bitch."

I looked to my side. Joe stood next to me, grinning at me.

"Who?" I whispered.

"Why, the General of course."

"General?" He was making no sense.

"General Anna Lockner, the first woman to land on Mars, the first one killed when trying to put down the mutiny on Olympus Mons."

Perfect.

I had just put all our lives in the hands of a guy who thought he was Jesus Christ, a woman who believed she had once lived on Mars, and a genetic freak of a tiger.

"You're looking a little better," said Joe, obviously trying to sound encouraging.

I said nothing.

I couldn't waste any energy in talking. I needed everything I had simply to keep placing one foot in front of the other.

We stood before the Barrier.

It had been far too easy. We had moved through the town as if we owned it. Not a single red beret had offered us resistance. I was feeling numb. At first I simply hadn't been feeling pain, but now I was feeling absolutely nothing. Walking was becoming difficult, and I was continually stumbling like a drunk. I had nearly exhausted whatever reserves I was running on.

"How much time, Christ?" asked Anna.

He had been using his spear as a walking staff, but now he picked up the shaft, held it in both hands, and began to rotate one end of it, as if he were unscrewing it. There was an audible click and the spear point, which looked like chipped obsidian, momentarily glowed cherry red. Less than a foot in front of the spear tip, lettering and a small luminous clock materialized.

"Breakthrough in sixty-seven seconds," he said, then flicked the spear shaft. The hologram vanished.

"Good," said Anna, as she crouched down to the ground and rested the barrel of her laser rifle across her knee. She kept it pointed in the direction of the town.

Sir Basil walked in several tight circles then dropped to the ground, curling up like a house cat. Jesus leaned against the Barrier and closed his eyes.

They were far too damn casual about all of this.

"What the hell's suppose to happen in sixty-seven seconds?" I asked Anna, doing nothing to hide the sounds of anger in my voice. I refused to continue walking blind, not knowing what we were doing or where we were going. I squeezed the stock of my M-16 tightly, to make sure that my numb hand still had a firm grip on it.

"We go through the Barrier," she said.

"And get fried," said Joe from over my shoulder.

I glanced behind myself.

Besides Joe, both Joan and Tom stood close at my back. Joan faced the town, her M-16 at her hip, ready to fire if need be. I couldn't feel my own body, but I could easily feel the tension in the air. There was a definite feel of Us versus Them. They'd rescued us, or more accurately, were in the process of doing so, but they seemed none too pleased about it.

"I said we were going through it, not over it," she said contemptuously. "Before we came in we seeded this section of the Barrier with a Destroyer Nanomechanoid, along with a Mastermechanoid Overseer. It was a simple enough thing to do."

Not again!

The Barrier seemed to vanish behind a rainbow haze. But I kept standing, kept breathing, despite the invisible vise that tried to crack my skull. And I remembered more, remembered things that I had never really forgotten. Nanomechanoids were specialized into various types. Destroyers did nothing more than sever atomic bonds—and they'd continue doing that forever and ever. Once the wall had disintegrated they'd move into the dirt and start chewing their way down through rock. Only one thing stopped them, only one thing could control them—a Mastermechanoid Overseer. A thousand times larger than a Nanomechanoid, but still infinitesimal as compared to a grain of sand, they would guide the Destroyers, telling them when to sever bonds and when to stop.

The rainbow haze vanished.

I felt something warm flowing over my lip, and reaching up a shaking hand I wiped at it. I pulled bloody fingers back. I was reaching my limit, might in fact have already slipped past it. For all I knew I could already be dead, and my body simply hadn't fallen down yet.

Anna walked over to the Barrier and gave the wall a hard kick. A ten-foot length of the wall shattered and cracked, and her boot sunk into the Barrier almost up to her ankle.

I would put up no more with her *attitude*. It ended here, or we parted company. I no longer cared what the consequences might be. I walked over to her, crowding her, and stared down my bleeding nose at her. I'd had enough of her superior attitude.

"Why are you here?"

It wasn't a question, but a demand.

She narrowed her eyes to slits. "And why should I have to answer to you?"

Blood dripped from my nose, splattering against her boots. I'd seen only one thing that got these people excited, and that was religion. I'd try using that. At that point, I would have tried using anything.

"Because I'm the person that God has just sent down, direct and nonstop from Heaven, to carry out a little job for Him. I'm the man who can stop the Supreme. I'm the man who can save this insane world!"

Despite the fact that everything turned gray, I managed not to faint.

Anna's face instantly transformed itself from a hard, don't-bother-me-you-son-of-a-bitch type look, to at first disbelief, then to something that looked like fear.

Again I'd pressed the right buttons.

"The Lord *has* sent you?" she asked. Her voice actually cracked and broke.

"I'm His personal emissary," I said, cocking my

head skyward, as if just by looking in the direction of Heaven I could see God.

"Please forgive me," she said. "I understand now."

"Well, I don't!" shouted Christ from behind me. "That Old Son of a Bitch should have given me the job. That's why I was sent down here!"

I turned, and he had his spear pointed at my chest.

Joan snapped the bolt of her M-16 and leveled the rifle at Christ. "Try it," she said. Judging by the glare of her cat-eyes and the flexing muscles in the base of her jaw, I really think she wanted him to try it.

"Lower it down, Jesus," said Anna in a hissing voice, emphasizing every vowel of each word. "This is why *Tartan* wouldn't tell us who he was. She knew that you'd never come if she told us his true identity. But it all fits, it all makes sense. He's been chosen, and that's all there is to it. Accept it!"

Of course I had no idea who Tartan was, or why things suddenly "made sense" to Anna, but at the moment that really didn't matter. What did matter was that she now was ready to *really* help me. The tone in her voice left little doubt of that. I was certain that if Christ didn't lower his spear he'd quickly find a hole burned through his chest.

Christ waved his spear at me, then spun around. He shook, like someone who has swallowed more rage than anybody has ever been designed to hold.

I turned back to Anna.

"I must apologize for Jesus," she said. "But he's jealous of your relationship with God. Since being sent back to Earth for the second time, God has refused to speak to him. Christ was certain that in these last few days before the second apocalypse, God would choose him as His Savior."

I just nodded, as if that were the most reasonable thing I'd ever heard. But it did make sense, in a warped sort of way. If your brains had been scrambled enough to make you believe you were Christ, I could see how someone else's claiming to be God's Number One Boy on this world would even further unhinge you.

Christ had quickly moved over to a section of the

disintegrating Barrier, and with his spear was knocking large chunks of it aside.

"Thor will interpret this opening as simply a smaller version of the Main Gate," said Anna. "It won't consider this a Barrier violation."

Christ jumped over the gooey remnants of the wall, walked a few paces, and then looked up into the night sky. "I dare you to do it, you son of a bitch!" he screamed.

I didn't know if he was ranting at the Thor system, daring it to fry him, or if he was screaming up at God, daring Him to vaporize him with a bolt of lightning. In Christ's mind the two might easily be one and the same. He stood there for several seconds. Neither God nor Thor answered him.

"It's safe," said Anna, waving us all toward the opening with the barrel of her laser.

Vlad was the first to run through, with Joe right behind. Joan went next, deliberately looking everywhere except in the direction of Anna. She obviously didn't trust her, and I had absolutely no difficulty in understanding why. I crossed next. My legs were no longer quite numb. Feeling was starting to return, but what I was feeling felt like thousands of pins and needles stabbing deep within, grinding against my bones. I stumbled across the opening.

"Tom," said Joan, who had turned around and now was looking past me.

I also turned around to see what was keeping him.

His arm was extended, and his fingers pointed in the direction of the thick brush that was ahead of us. "It's trouble, John," he said quickly and clearly.

It was not the words themselves that so surprised me at first, but simply the fact that he had spoken them with such a sound of authority. The meaning of those words didn't quite penetrate my head. But as I turned in the direction he'd pointed I saw Christ, Vlad, and Joe all topple over, stiff, looking like chunks of wood. Sir Basil rolled over on his back, his legs pointing up into the night sky.

My M-16 was against my hip, my finger against the trigger.

"I think that very unwise," said a voice from the hillside above me.

From behind me I could hear two bodies drop into something moist. I knew that had to be Tom and Anna collapsing into the Barrier residue.

"Both of you throw down your weapons," said the voice.

I dropped my rifle. I couldn't fight an enemy that I couldn't even see. Another rifle clattered to the ground next to mine.

"Show yourself so I can rip your head from your body," Joan screamed into the dark.

"Certainly," said the voice.

Shadows on the hillside moved. At least thirty figures stood up.

It *had* been too easy. They had known exactly where we'd be coming out and they had been waiting for us.

Several figures moved forward. The one that towered over all the others was easily recognizable. Light reflected from his glasses.

Napoleon.

He had one of those gray toasters in his hands. Next to him, looking squat and plump and tossing an ax from hand to hand, stood Lizzie Borden.

"Be my guest, Miss Borden," said Napoleon, as he waved his handkerchief in her direction.

Lizzie raised her ax high above her head. Her piggy little eyes, which were sunk deep within her wrinkled face, were staring murderously at Joan. She grunted and, lurching forward, let her ax fly. It whistled through the air.

My brain sensed the ax's velocity in all three dimensions, along with its rotational speed, and coupled that data with the exact position of my fingers, hand, and arm.

I moved.

The ax handle slapped loudly into my hand. The rusty, blunt blade, quivered only inches in front of

Joan's forehead. I then held the ax high above my head, getting ready to hurl it back.

"Excellent," said Napoleon. He sniffed at his laced handkerchief, and as he walked forward he stared at Joan. "I suggest that if you don't want your little friend to find herself without benefit of a head, you put that ax down."

I looked up the hill and at all of the weapons that were now trained on Joan. I dropped the ax.

"At first," said Napoleon, still walking forward, "I hadn't believed my information, but it appears to be true. You," he said, now pointing a black gloved hand at me, "have been enhanced."

The word echoed in my head.

But there was no surprise, no pain attached to it.

I had really known this for quite some time now but just hadn't quite been able to admit it, to face it. But I couldn't help but know it. I had not only been enhanced physically but mentally as well, judging by the things that would suddenly pop into my head and by my bar code-reading ability. But of course, I had absolutely no idea who or what had done the enhancing.

"Is it possible that while they worked on your body they also gave you the Los Angeles Quad Wall access codes?" asked Napoleon.

The codes.

I had known that it would quickly come back to this. But I still didn't know them, actually somehow knew that I never *would* know them. I couldn't feel them lurking behind any of the still-closed doors that seemed to fill my head.

"Like I told you before, I've got no codes." I took a step toward Napoleon.

He back-stepped two paces.

"Mr. Smith," he said, "I suggest no attempted heroics. Need I remind you, all weapons are currently trained on your traveling companion, the lovely Joan of Arc." He smiled, baring his animal-like teeth. "Despite your enhancements, Mr. Smith, you suffer an extreme disadvantage." He waved a hand at Joan and then at the others on the ground. "You care, Mr.

Smith. That will be your undoing.'' He pointed the toaster toward me.

As had happened every time before when that gray toaster was turned on me, I felt a tickling in the back of my head. My body collapsed, just as it had before. Joan fell next to me, with her arms draped across my legs.

I had hit the ground in such a way that I was still looking up the hill toward Napoleon. Tossing the toaster to Lizzie he walked forward, taking long, confident strides.

He stood almost directly over me. ''It will be a pleasure watching you beg, as I begin to peel away the skin of your pretty little friend,'' he said.

He raised one boot high into the air, bringing it down toward my hand. His boot heel smashed into hard rock.

Jumping up from the ground and reaching out with the hand that he had just tried to crush, I grabbed him.

''Yeoooow!'' he screamed, and stood on the tip of his toes as I pushed up. My hand was planted firmly in his crotch. I literally had him by the balls. I reached my other hand around his waist and hugged him. If anyone took a shot at me, considering Napoleon's size, they'd stand a better-than-even chance of hitting him before they hit me.

I looked up at Napoleon's red, tear-streaked face. His teeth were clenched, and his eyes tightly closed. His glasses dangled from one ear.

''Tell them to drop the weapons,'' I said.

Napoleon said nothing. He didn't so much as breathe.

I increased the pressure of my grip ever so slightly.

''Put down your weapons!'' he screamed.

I peered around the edge of his shoulder. The assorted weapons of all of his troops were still trained on us.

''Think about this,'' I said, shouting up to those on the hillside. ''You may be able to fire and, if lucky, hit me without killing the good Cardinal here.'' I squeezed slightly harder. He squeaked like a mouse.

"But you saw how fast my reflexes are. Before you could kill me the Cardinal's balls would be transformed into jelly. How appreciative do you think he'll be toward the individual responsible for turning him into a soprano?"

I squeezed.

"Put them down!" wailed Napoleon.

Weapons dropped.

"Lizzie," I said, "do your thing." I nodded in the direction of those on the hill.

She looked up at Napoleon.

I squeezed again. It was sort of like playing a musical instrument.

"Do it," he whimpered, in a voice that was already starting to sound higher-pitched.

She waved the toaster across those on the hill. They all collapsed.

"Now, Lizzie," I said, "you will reawaken my friends."

This time I didn't even have to encourage her.

"Do it," said Napoleon, before I could squeeze any harder.

She waved the toaster and I could hear movement behind me. Quickly looking over my shoulder, I could see that they were all moving. Christ was using his spear as a crutch and was pulling himself up the shaft.

"Say good night, Lizzie," I said.

She turned the toaster on herself. She hit the ground, her head bouncing off a rock when she went down.

"Now," I said, while looking up at Napoleon's face. "What should I do with you?"

I squeezed.

"Please," he whimpered.

He'd be going with us, as a hostage. When the Supreme came after me, as I was sure he would, I'd have something to bargain with.

I loosened my grip without completely letting go, and felt his boot heels drop back down to the ground.

"Die, you motherfucker!" screamed a voice at my back.

I felt the hair on the side of my head part. Napoleon

shuddered, and sucked down a deep breath. I turned my head. Only millimeters away from my face, the quivering shaft of Christ's spear protruded from Napoleon's chest. I looked up. Napoleon's eyes were wide open, and blood dripped from the corners of his mouth.

He spoke with what I knew would be his last breath. "I'll see you in Hell," he said, staring down at me with his already dead eyes.

Falling forward, he collapsed on top of me.

I didn't even feel it as we hit the ground.

"Don't kill him!"

The scream echoed in my ears—it echoed in my head.

It had been *my* voice.

I opened my eyes. Above me was a blue sky streaked with distant white clouds. I was tied down, unable to move, but I gently swayed back and forth. My scream had been too late. Napoleon was dead.

"Stop!" called out Joan from somewhere behind me. "He's awake!"

I couldn't move, but it wasn't from lack of trying. I was bound up, was being held immobile. The swaying motion stopped, and I could hear something beneath me purr. I realized that I had somehow been strapped to Sir Basil's back.

Vlad's face appeared before me. "I thought you'd become one of the undead, like me," he said cheerfully. His tongue licked at his plastic fangs, and he snugged his sunglasses against his face.

Suddenly I could breathe easily, and move my neck. A huge slab of gray material moved first in front of my face and then began to float upward. It looked like the inside of a sarcophagus lid, form-fitted for my dimensions. With a dull-sounding thump it slid away and to my left.

I slowly sat up.

Off to my right Tom and Joe were sitting cross-legged in tall golden grass, pulling pie tins out of brown nylon backpacks. Beyond and below them spread out a valley. The skyline was one that I'd never seen before, but the distant mountains had a familiar outline. We were in the hills high above the San Fernando Valley.

"Are we safe?" I asked, expecting that we were only seconds away from a swarm of psychos descending upon us.

Joan and Anna each grabbed one of my hands and tugged.

"We're fine," said Anna. She had a ridiculous-looking maternal smile on her face. "Thanks to you." There were suddenly tears in the corners of her dark eyes.

I ignored those tears. I'd never before been able to deal with crying women, and did not want to take this opportunity to try again. I moved my legs up over the lip of the custom-fitted coffin and dangled them over the side. My bare feet rested in Sir Basil's soft, warm fur.

I looked down at myself. All I was wearing was a pair of skin-tight shorts. Anna was bending down over my right leg, massaging the calf.

"It healed perfectly," she said. Looking up at me, tears were now streaking her cheeks. Again I tried to ignore them.

Pushing myself forward, I stood up on shaky legs. I pointed a finger at Anna. "I want to talk to you—alone."

She simply nodded and wiped the tears from her eyes.

I walked slowly, moving over rocks and pebbles and cutting through high grass. I worked my way up along the ridge of the hill, wanting to move out of earshot of the others but not out of their sight. They had said we were safe, but I couldn't really believe that. I didn't think there was *any* place in this world that was truly safe. Not here, not now. I sat down on a large flat hunk of sandstone and looked up into the sky: 15.

It was dropping fast, too fast.

I reached down and felt my leg. There wasn't the slightest indication that I'd ever been shot. I then ran a hand across the side of my face that had been laser-burnt, but felt nothing other than perfectly soft skin. I'd even been shaved. I took a deep breath and my lungs were clear, and there wasn't the slightest twinge from my rib cage.

I could feel, and all my senses were working. There was no pain now, because everything was repaired and working perfectly.

Anna sat down in front of me.

"I'm all right?" I asked, not quite willing to believe that, remembering what kind of shape I'd been in when Napoleon had collapsed on me.

"Yes," she answered. "The Nanodoc spun you up from head to toe and repaired the gross anatomical damage. We pumped several gallons of liquid nutrients into you. But it was a close thing. If you hadn't been enhanced we would have buried you last night."

I just nodded. As much as I would have liked to know more about this Nanomechanoid technology and what a "Nanodoc" might really be, there were much more pressing matters.

"Who sent you to find me, and why?"

"Tartan sent us to bring you," she said. The expression on her face then filled with confusion. "But you know why."

"To save God, and to destroy the Supreme," I said, remembering what I had told her, remembering the lie that all of them seemed so eager to believe.

She nodded. "You'll take us to Heaven, and there we'll help you fight the Supreme and restore the Speed Limit."

"To Heaven?" I asked. How was I supposed to get to Heaven, when I couldn't even understand how I'd gotten *here*?

"Don't worry," she said. "It's not really all that far. It won't take us that long to get out to the Mojave Desert."

Click.

Pieces snapped together.

The Mojave was where the Thor Free-Electron Laser was based. I knew that could be no coincidence. I looked north, toward the mountains, knowing that the Mojave was just beyond them. That might be where all this insanity would end, where I'd find out how and why I'd gotten here. I looked back down at her.

"How did Tartan know where to send you? How did she know about me?"

She just shook her head. "Tartan just knows these things."

I was afraid that would be the answer.

"And where is Tartan?"

"In the Griffith Park Planetarium."

I knew that place well, having visited it countless times during all the years I had lived in Los Angeles. I was surprised that it still existed. I pointed in the direction of the hills at my back. "About ten kilometers that way?" I asked.

She nodded.

I had my bearings then.

I turned back to her. "Can I have your hand?"

She quickly thrust it out. "Joan told me that you had the Eyes of God," she said with an awe-filled voice.

I looked at her bar code. Maria Estevez. Born September 15, 2041, in Neuva Los Angeles. Maria was a Doler, and a hardcore Roman Catholic, working as a lay person for the church. She had spent almost all of her time working with gangs. Sterilized at birth, never married, her life had been one long, hard grind of poverty and giving to those who had even less. Her GPI was 78, which apparently excluded her from any schooling. But as a child she had taught herself to read not only English and Spanish but even Latin. My knowledge of her was nowhere near as complete as that of Tom, Joan, or Joe. Apparently whatever was supplying me with these memories did not consider a Doler like Maria Estevez to be of much significance.

But *I* could see things between those facts. I could see the life that she must have lived. She had been trapped by circumstance and a high GPI, but she had been a person who had cared and had tried to help those around her. How or why she had become General Anna Lockner, the first woman to land on Mars, I had no way of knowing.

I dropped her hand.

"Thank you," I said.

She bowed her head, almost as if she had just been blessed by a saint. Tears splattered in the dirt beneath her face. She didn't stand up, didn't even raise her head.

Seconds crawled by, agonizingly slow seconds.

It was painfully obvious that she was not going to get up.

"Yes?" I finally prompted.

She didn't raise her head. "I didn't know. Tartan sent us to find you, telling us that *we* couldn't rescue God without your help. But I was so certain that we didn't need any help, that *I* didn't need any help. And then when I saw you I didn't recognize you, didn't see you for who you really were. My arrogance blinded me."

She lowered her head even more.

"Can you forgive me"—she paused—"Christ?"

My gut twisted.

This is where my lies had gotten me. I had this poor brain-burnt woman believing that I was the Son of God.

"Please!" she cried.

Into my twisting gut was inserted a dull knife.

"Yes," I said, then quickly added, "but you will never call me by that name again. The one you travel with would not understand."

She raised her head. The tears were gone.

"God bless you."

The dull knife slashed back and forth.

"Bring me Christ," I said.

Anna stood. "I'll get him," she said, and turned and walked away.

I looked out over the Valley. It was the Valley I had grown up in, but eighty years removed. Now it was a maze of glass obelisks, probably Nanomechanoid-built, rising up hundreds of stories and intertwined with ribbons of concrete. But it was now dead and empty. Those magnificent buildings had become nothing more than twenty-first-century tombstones.

"You wanted to see me," said an arrogant-sounding voice.

I turned my head.

Christ stood before me, his spear clenched firmly in both his hands. He stared at me with eyes that were filled with hate.

Had I seen him when I had first awakened I might have caved in his face. He had killed a man, one who without a doubt deserved to die but who had been defenseless. In these last few days I'd done and experienced things that I had never dreamed of in my wildest nightmares. I'd seen my cherished civilized principles vanish one by one. I'd killed to stay alive, and on more than one occasion I had actually accepted the prospect of death over the pain of living. I was no longer the person I had been only a few days ago, but *something* from my old life still remained. I could not, and would not, kill a man who was defenseless. It was probably an antiquated notion in this world, but it was one that I still clung to.

But was Christ responsible for what he'd done, or had he simply been obeying what his scrambled brain had demanded of him? I couldn't condone his skewering of Napoleon, but I couldn't condemn him for it either. I didn't have that right.

"I want to apologize to you," I said.

He looked down at me suspiciously.

"Please sit," I said.

He slowly sat, still clenching his spear in both hands.

I was still feeling like a puppet, with someone hidden and unseen pulling at my strings, but more and more I was beginning to understand how this strange world operated. I knew without the slightest doubt that I'd soon be off to the Mojave Desert on some quest in search of Heaven and God. The answers I needed lay out there. And Christ would be traveling with me. But I could not afford to travel with an uncontrollable maniac, jealous of everything I did because he believed that God had chosen me instead of him as His savior.

"Before arriving here," I said, while spreading my hands out around me, "God told me about the test that he was putting you through." I found that the lie came easily—a little too easily.

Christ suddenly leaned forward, his expression indicating that he was now eager to hear what I had to say.

"Does God speak to His people as directly you and I are now speaking?" I asked him.

"No."

"Yet they believe in Him and love Him, don't they?"

"Of course," he answered.

"Then you must understand the nature of the test that He is putting you through," I said. "He wants you to experience life as they do, with nothing but their faith to sustain them. He knows that by living as they do, without benefit of conversing with Him as He speaks to me and Joan, that you will gain a far better understanding of humanity. This is His gift to you, His only Son. Even when His very existence is being threatened as it is now, He has not called for your help. He would rather cease to exist than to take this gift back."

"He did not abandon me, then," Christ said slowly, obviously having chosen every word carefully.

I nodded. "He has done this only because He loves you so."

Christ's face filled with a smile, the first time I'd ever seen one on his face.

"I understand now," he said. "He does love me." Reaching up, he put his hand on my shoulder and squeezed. "Thank you," he said, "I'm forever in your debt for showing me what should have been so obvious."

I returned his smile, but inside I suddenly felt like crying. I should have been pleased, having so easily turned a potential threat and enemy into an ally I could use, but I suddenly felt like something that you'd scrape from the bottom of your shoe up onto the edge of a curb. I'd used his own feelings of despair to manipulate and twist him, as if he were some piece of lab equipment that needed to be redesigned and rebuilt to better serve *me*.

I told myself that the lie I'd made him believe would benefit both of us.

That made me feel even worse.

CHAPTER 8

Tartan the Barbarian

The observatory was old. It had been fifty years old when I had last visited it, and was therefore at least a hundred and thirty years old now. It was the first thing I'd seen, since waking two days ago, that looked unchanged and untouched.

Something tugged at the side of my shirt. I looked down and was greeted by Vlad's grinning face—his plastic fangs tinted pink in the sun's reflected light. He pushed his sunglasses tightly against his face and then pointed down at the observatory.

"It reminds me of home," he said. "All that it would really need to be *just* like home would be for a few peasants, skewered ass-first on wooden pikes, to line the front walkway." His voice was full of the tones of fond remembrance, tones that most boys would have reserved for their first puppy or for an old and worn baseball mitt.

What little warmth of illusion I had just been basking in suddenly chilled.

But Vlad was right. The Griffith Observatory did look a bit like something that could have been nestled high atop some Carpathian peak, looking down over deep mountain valleys. It consisted of a single building two stories tall, covered in white plaster. Marble steps led up to large brass and stained-glass front doors, while more than a dozen narrow, wrought iron-covered windows were sunk deep into the building's face. I could almost imagine crossbows protruding through those narrow windows and steaming vats of oil perched on the roof, waiting to be poured onto the local rioting peasants.

Sir Basil leapt to my side, clinking and clanking from all the equipment and supplies that were strapped across his powerful back. He threw back his head and, opening his jaws wide, let out an ear-rupturing roar. He then bounded down the hill, disappearing into the thick underbrush.

One by one, everyone followed Sir Basil down the hill. Only Tom remained behind, standing closely next to me. We both watched the setting sun.

"Do you think this Tartan will have some answers for me?" I asked, not really expecting to get an answer from him.

"Perhaps."

I quickly turned, hoping to once again get a look at the Tom that lurked somewhere deep within him, but apparently I had been too slow. He was staring, vacant-eyed, toward the horizon. A fine line of drool dripped down his chin as his hands automatically tossed a pebble back and forth.

"Know me, God," he said in a whisper only once, and then moved down the hill in the direction the others had taken.

When we reached the observatory's front lawn it was dark, and the sky above was lit by the swarms of satellites. Behind us, at the top of the hills, the HOLLYWOOD sign still stood, visible in the light from the glowing Speed Limit number that seemed to hover just above it: 14.

Distant thunder echoed.

Time was running out.

"She'll be expecting you," said Anna, as she nodded in the direction of the observatory's walkway and up toward the main doors.

"What about the rest of you?" I asked, turning toward them.

She shook her head. "We have preparations to make."

And that was all she said.

But I knew what she'd meant.

The preparations would be for our journey to Heaven. None of them wanted to keep God waiting. Joe grinned at me and rubbed at his plastic-coated ear. Even though he appeared to understand the scientific basis of what this world was all about, and didn't believe in the rhetoric of the Church of Limbo, he did believe that somewhere out in the Mojave was a place called Heaven, and within that place was a man called God who was in need of rescuing.

"Fine," I said.

They all moved off in a tight little group, walking toward the side of the building. Getting myself nearly killed, coupled with the lie that I had told Christ, seemed to have bonded the group into a single sort of entity, whose sole purpose was to get me to Heaven so I could perform whatever miracles were required to save the world.

It would be a big enough miracle if I managed just to stay alive.

I stood at the front of the walkway that led up to the observatory's front door and looked down at my black boots. I was standing on the same type of white material that the Barrier of the Detention Facility had been built out of.

Spun diamond.

And that's exactly what it was. Nanomechanoid-built of a nearly infinite number of carbon atoms—spun diamond. My shoes weren't made of rubies, and the walkway wasn't the Yellow Brick Road, but as I looked up at the large front doors of the observatory I knew exactly how Dorothy must have felt. I couldn't resist the images of Oz that filled my head, so I clicked my boot heels together three times. I didn't find myself whisked eighty years back in time. I laughed in the darkness, feeling the tension fade from my body. It had been worth a shot. Jogging up the path, I took the marble steps two at a time.

The handles of the observatory's front doors had been removed, and in their place was a large gold door-knocker in the shape of a woman's torso. I laughed again. There was someone in this warped world who still had a sense of humor.

I grabbed the knockers and knocked.

"Who goes there?" cried out a thundering voice that was so loud, and so baritone, that I could feel the marble steps beneath my boots vibrate.

"John Smith!"

The two brass doors before me silently opened inward. Lights flicked on from somewhere within. I stepped inside.

The familiarity was so comforting. Nothing had changed. The foyer of the observatory was dominated by a large pit sunk some five feet into the floor, over which, suspended from the ceiling two floors above, hung a pendulum. I walked over to the brass railing that surrounded the pit and looked down into it, as I had done so many times before. The huge brass ball at the tip of the pendulum swung slowly back and forth. If you stood here watching it long enough you would see it precess slowly around, demonstrating that the earth rotated. I looked up at the ceiling, and at the old fresco that illustrated the twelve signs of the zodiac. It was dull and faded, but the Gemini twins stared down at me just as they had so many times before.

"Hello!" I called out, my voice echoing down the empty marbled corridors.

"Follow me," said something down by the floor.

I jumped back, startled not so much by the voice itself as by the fact that something could sneak up on me. I looked down.

It was troll-like, and about a foot tall. It had a green, wrinkled face, dominated by a sausage-like nose, which in turn was dominated by a spongy-looking wart. It was dressed in a little woodsman's outfit, something reminiscent of what Robin Hood had been wearing. One of its beady red eyes was covered by a monocle. Its chest puffed in and out as it breathed. Whether it was alive, actually organic, or something synthetic made up of some agglomeration of Nanomechanoids, I had no way of knowing.

I just stared down at it.

"You deaf or something?" it said while looking up at me.

"Are you Tartan?" I asked, hoping that this small pile of green wrinkled skin wasn't what I'd come all this way to see.

It scrunched up its face suddenly, looking like a puckered piece of fruit. I think it may have been grinning at me. The elongated tip of its chin rubbed against its nose.

"You're a real comedian," it said, and slapped its thigh. "I bet you're the type of disturbed individual that was capable of enjoying my customized door-knocker."

I couldn't help but smile.

It pointed a stubby finger at me and wagged it. "Are you ready to get down to business?" it asked.

"Lead the way," I said cheerfully, relieved that this *thing* wasn't Tartan.

It gave me a salute and, turning, proceeded to march a goose step across the marble floor.

I followed closely behind.

It marched around the pendulum pit, then began to negotiate the steps that led up to the observatory's planetarium by tugging itself up a knotted rope that was draped over the stairs. It took almost a full minute before it had climbed to the head of the stairs.

"This way," it said, looking back over its shoulder and waving at me.

I slowly walked up the stairs and then followed it down a dark corridor. I'd traveled down this corridor many times before—it led into the planetarium. The troll stopped before a pair of heavy-looking wooden doors and, reaching forward, grabbed two small handles that were only about six inches above the floor. Pulling on them, it swung the doors open.

I tried to look in, but a red velvet curtain blocked my view.

"Tartan the Barbarian, Scourge of the Netherhells and Princess of the Crystal Meadows, awaits you," announced the troll. Then, bowing its head, it pointed both hands toward the curtains.

Tartan the Barbarian?

Another psycho.

Perhaps it had just been wishful thinking, or maybe it was because of some numb spot that existed deep inside of my brain, but I had been hoping that this Tartan was going to be someone normal, someone whose brain *hadn't* been turned to tapioca. But judging by the troll's introduction, that looked most unlikely.

But Tartan had sent Anna and Christ after me.

She had known I had somehow been brought here.

And those things *did* matter.

Reaching out, I pulled the velvet drapes aside and walked in. It was dark, and it took several seconds before my eyes adjusted. The night sky was above me, but it looked unlike any night sky I had ever seen projected in this planetarium before. The familiar constellations were all there, and the white, blurred band of the Milky Way ran from north to south, but there was more, much more. Hundreds if not thousands of pinprick lights streaked across the inverted bowl of the planetarium's ceiling. They had to be the satellites—the Eyes of God. Turning and looking north, I saw the Speed Limit pulsing like a red neon sign: 14.

My eyes were quickly adjusting to the dark, and I looked around the floor of the planetarium. Things had changed. The five hundred or so incredibly uncomfortable metal and wooden seats, part of the original equipment when the planetarium was built back in the 1930s, were gone. In their place were things that I couldn't quite distinguish—big bulky things. They were things that hummed, squeaked, and occasionally moved. I walked further inside.

In the center of the planetarium burned a small campfire, its flames strangely tinted green and blue. As I moved nearer I could hear crickets chirp. On the far side of the fire, illuminated by the dancing flame, moved a shadowy figure. It reached out a hand and put it directly into the campfire flame.

"Care to sit with me under the night sky?" asked an almost girlish-sounding voice.

I moved forward. There was sand and gravel beneath my feet. I had to push aside a tumbleweed and carefully walk around a thick squat stand of cholla cactus. I slowly sat down on a partially burned tree stump. The fragrance of desert flowers and the heavy scent of rain-dampened earth hung in the air. The shape on the other side of the fire was that of a woman, but I could tell nothing more than that.

"Why didn't that flame burn your hand?" I asked.

"Because the fire isn't there," answered the shadow.

I squirmed on the tree stump. I had not come here to sit under projected stars and stare into phantom campfires. I had neither the time nor the patience for games. I'd come here to find the answers to my questions.

"Two days ago, I found myself propelled eighty years into the future. You knew that I had come here, and I want to know how."

"He gets right down to business."

She was talking either to someone I couldn't see or to herself. Based on the mental stability of everyone I'd met so far, I figured she was probably talking to herself.

"Well, he's right," said the same voice, sounding critical and impatient. "This is certainly no time to be lying beneath the stars and reminiscing about old adventures and battles."

This did not sound good.

Actually, it sounded incredibly bad.

She was not only talking to herself but actually *arguing* with herself.

She stood, and the campfire threw her shadow up onto the planetarium ceiling. She raised her hands to the artificial night sky. I couldn't quite see in the dark, but it appeared as if she held her hands out palms up. This didn't really surprise me.

"Know me, God. Know me, God. Know me, God," she chanted.

The stars winked out and the night sky was transformed into a white, curved ceiling.

I blinked and squinted.

"Strike the campsite," she said.

"It's about time," she answered.

Beneath me, the log I sat on squirmed. I began to sink.

"I suggest you stand," she said.

Standing quickly, I turned to look at the tree stump. It was shrinking. As I watched it sagged and drooped, looking like something out of a Salvador Dali painting. It dribbled into the rock and sand. But the rock and sand were also fading away. The ground beneath my feet was gently vibrating. As I watched, purposely not blinking so as to not miss anything, the rocks, the cactus, and even the tumbleweeds disintegrated and melted, seeming to flow into the floor. Nothing remained.

Nanomechanoids.

The technology was frightening. It could actually create artificial realities. I quickly looked around to where the planetarium seating had once been. The things that had hissed and moved and made squeaking noises were still there. It now looked like a laboratory, but unlike any lab that I'd ever worked in. Transparent vats of strangely colored liquids lined the walls and hung from the ceiling, connected to one another by sagging, undulating tubes. Banks of what looked like electronics sat randomly about. Their display panels flowed as if made of liquid, one moment dotted with knobs and switches and the next filled with video screens, keyboards, and speaker grilles. From the top of each panel protruded a skeletal hand that, reaching down, would adjust knobs and type at the keyboards. Things scurried across the floor. Several were like the troll I'd already seen, but there were also oozing balls of gelatinous slime that crawled up and down the walls, and giant grasshopper-like creatures staring into the viewing ports of a monstrous aquarium that was filled with a luminescent, milky substance.

I turned, unable to look at it anymore, my head starting to ache and my stomach feeling queasy. Tartan the Barbarian stood in front of me.

Raquel Welch.

Tartan the Barbarian was not Raquel Welch, but she was wearing a Raquel Welch fur bikini that looked as if it had been lifted directly from the movie *One Million Years B.C.* She certainly did not fill it in the way that only Raquel could, but she filled it pleasantly nonetheless. Tartan was tall, perhaps only a few inches shorter than my own six feet, and built solid and strong like a weight lifter. When she moved I could see sharply defined muscle. Her hair was long and honey-colored. And except for her fur bikini, and the necklace wrapped snugly around her throat, made out of large, sharp-looking teeth, the only other thing that she wore was an oversized plastic wristwatch.

"Some chairs, please," she said while looking at her watch.

"Of course," replied the watch, using *her* voice.

Thank God.

She hadn't been talking to herself. The watch was no watch but probably some sort of computer that responded in her own voice—eccentric, but not flat-out insane.

Like watching a film of a melting chair run backward, the floor behind Tartan shimmered, flowed molten, bulged upward, and quickly solidified into the shape of a chair.

Something nudged the back of my knees. I didn't even bother to turn around, certain that behind me was a chair identical to the one that I saw behind Tartan.

I sat down. The chair was soft and warm. I thought I could almost *feel* the Nanomechanoids within it. Something suddenly burned in my head, and another one of those hidden doors threatened to open. I stared straight ahead, concentrating on Tartan, purging my thoughts of Nanomechanoids.

The door stayed closed.

"It's actually been slightly longer than eighty years," said Tartan. "The current date is August 21, 2076. Your world is eighty-six years in the past." She smiled, and tugged at a long strand of hair that had gotten caught in the corner of her mouth.

Yes!

I sagged into my chair.

She really *did* know about me, did know that this wasn't my world. "Do you know how I got here?" I asked. That was the big question. If I could get that one answered everything else might fall into place. The palms of my hands were sweating.

"Yes, I know," she said, nodding her head. But she no longer smiled.

I leaned forward in my chair.

The muscles in her neck seemed to twitch, and she bit at her lower lip.

"How?" I asked.

She swallowed, and wiped her own palms across her legs. "I can't tell you that." She quickly sat back in her chair and began twirling a lock of her hair.

It took several seconds before her words finally stopped echoing in my head and had some meaning associated with them. "What!" I yelled at her, as I jumped up out of my chair. If she knew, she was damn well going to tell me.

That was a fact.

If not, I'd will my body into its berserker mode and beat it out of her.

She slowly rose out of her own chair. "Will you let me explain?" she asked calmly. Then, sitting back down, she pointed toward the chair behind me.

It was a supreme effort, but I sat.

"What do you know about the Bug?" she asked.

"I know it caused all this," I said, waving my right hand around, obviously not referring to the planetarium but to the world on the other side of the walls. "I think about four years ago this country, and quite possibly the entire world, was hit with some sort of biological weapon."

"Correct," said her wrist computer.

"A synthetic virus," said Tartan. "A viroid."

I nodded toward both of them. "It probably killed most people, turned most of the survivors into Mushies, or—" I stared at her. How wise would it be to tell a wacko that she was a wacko?

"Or?" she said.

I could see it in her eyes.

She knew. She knew that she was crazy.

"Left them with a completely altered personality."

She leaned back in her chair and slowly nodded her head. The look on her face was cold and hard. "Your analysis is fairly correct, if somewhat lacking," she said. "The virus was in fact *very* lethal, especially for the very young and the very old. It was an internally clocked viroid, which in its dormant phase caused no external symptoms and an undetectable degree of cellular disruption. For almost ten months it remained in that mode, undetected but highly infectious. Then on November 13, 2072, it's internal clock was fired, causing three pairs of guanine and cytosine within its DNA to invert locations. The result was that within twelve hours eleven billion people had died, another one billion had survived but were intellectually flat-lined, while some one hundred million survived with their brains still functioning but with their personalities totally altered."

She leaned forward in her chair and stared at me with intense-looking green eyes.

"Those who found themselves with new personalities were not just the beneficiaries of some statistical anomaly. The viroid was designed to seek out and eat all sense of self. In a few, where the sense of self was extremely strong and their imaginations most vivid, as they felt *themselves* fading they struggled within their own brains, searching for something that they could latch on to, something that they could deceive themselves into believing was part of their *own* personality. Very few were able to do this. The vast majority of people, with brains that now had no sense of self, simply went into shock and died. A billion Mushies were unable to hold on to an altered sense of self but continued to cling to some faint echo of their original selves. The lucky ones woke up as someone else—as someone they had dreamed of."

She pushed herself back into her chair.

"But it wasn't just a random personality," said her watch.

"That's right," said Tartan, agreeing and nodding. "The personality that surfaced was the one that had lain hidden in the back of the person's mind. It could be someone you either admired or hated, the only important thing being that the image of that person was solid and three-dimensional. The brain would latch on to that phantom persona and incorporate it into a new sense of self."

I looked at her, wondering what *she* had really been, wondering what had forced her to create a fantasy personality of a barbarian princess that wore a fur bikini and fang necklace. I pointed at her. "Then you know that this isn't really you," I said.

Something burned behind my eyes, but I ignored it.

"On a detached, intellectual level, I can admit that this is not how I was before the Bug, but within"—she tapped at the side of her head—"on an emotional level, I know I've always been Tartan."

Could someone who was insane know that they were insane? I had no way of knowing.

"Why?" I asked.

She just shrugged her shoulders. "No one seems to know for certain. But anyone, in any part of the world, with a lab not much more sophisticated than mine, could have created the Bug. It could have been done by governments, or by only one insane individual."

I again took a quick glance around what was in fact a laboratory. I didn't think I could have figured out how to even boil a beaker of water in this place, much less create a virus that could selectively interfere with the brain's chemistry, destroying all sense of self.

I looked back at her. Maybe she'd answer my question now. "How did I get here?" I asked quietly and slowly.

She took a deep breath, as if trying to postpone something that she didn't want to say. "The Bug killed most people outright, but even for those who survive it can become lethal at any moment. If a person is presented with aspects of the personality they possessed before the Bug, that knowledge will result in seizure and then death."

Knowledge can kill.

The words, and the pain associated with them, echoed in my head. I tried to ignore both, but I couldn't.

"The problem is," said Tartan, "that the original personality, gone on the surface, apparently still resides somewhere deep within the brain, but walled off and protected. Forcing the brain to acknowledge that the old self still exists, when it has come to believe in only the new personality, is too much for it to cope with. Electrical brain activity becomes chaotic and leads to a complete nervous system breakdown."

Her breathing had become rapid as she spoke, and sweat was dripping down her face. Her left cheek began to twitch steadily as a metronome. She lifted up both her hands and pressed them against the sides of her head, massaging her scalp.

I lifted up a hand to my face and felt the sweat dripping down it. A pressure was building behind my eyes, threatening to explode, to crack my skull.

"For me even to think about this, without knowing any of the actual details about my former self, is creating electrical disturbances in my brain." She paused, and began to pant like a dog. "In this susceptible state, if someone were to describe even the smallest detail of my old personality, I'd be killed instantly."

I concentrated on my breathing, trying to slow it, trying to control it. My heart pounded, beating up into my throat.

"How did I get here?" I asked again. My voice was shaky and cracked.

"The Bug had rather flu-like symptoms," she said. "It was characterized by high fevers, chest congestion, and difficulty in thinking clearly. Does that sound familiar?" she asked.

It sounded frighteningly familiar.

Things ground against the inside of my skull.

The muscles in my forearms began to twitch.

"The Bug is now endemic to the Earth's biosphere. It's in the air we breathe and the water we drink, and it's tied into the food chain, having invaded everything from the simplest of bacterias all the way up to man."

She pointed a finger at me. "The Bug changed you two days ago."

No!

It wasn't true.

It was a lie.

I was John Smith. I'd always been John Smith.

I could feel blood drip from my nose.

"No!"

As my voice echoed throughout the planetarium my hands stopped shaking and I breathed easily, realizing that what she claimed had happened to me simply couldn't be possible. Reaching up, I wiped away the blood from my upper lip. "I am who I am, and always have been," I said. "I am John Smith." There was nothing that I was more certain of than that.

Tartan shook her head, and slid the computer from her wrist. Reaching forward, she held it out in front of me. "Take this," said Tartan, "*she* will convince you."

I did not want to be convinced.

I refused to be convinced.

"Does the truth frighten you?"

I reached forward and grabbed it from her hand.

She shook her head. "The truth *should* frighten you, because the truth can kill."

I looked away from her, ignoring what she said, and stared into the computer's small display screen. Shapes and colors seemed to move randomly within it. I could make no sense out of what I was seeing, but suddenly my eyes seemed to focus and my brain realized that I wasn't looking at a flat, two-dimensional image, but at a three-dimensional one. It was a cartoon character seated in a chair. The character was a woman, with long blond hair, a fang necklace, and a very familiar-looking fur bikini.

"I'm Tartan the Barbarian," said the cartoon character, its eyes staring out at me, their gaze locked onto my face.

I looked up at the flesh-and-bone Tartan.

"I like to think of her as my conscience," she said.

I looked back into the display. "I've subjected my

organic self to enough pain with this discussion of pre-Bug personalities, and will handle the remainder of what you need to know myself. So that she doesn't hear what I'm about to say, I'm going to speak to you through a neural connection from the Trivid, tied directly into your auditory system. Nanomechanoids entered into your body when you first sat in your chair, and have been constructing the connection.

Invaded.

I imagined I could feel microscopic things crawling and scuttling beneath my skin. But it wasn't imagination. I could feel them, could almost touch them.

Lightning crackled in my head.

"Now only you can hear me," she said with a voice that echoed in my right ear. "I don't want my organic self hearing any more of this, so I'd appreciate it if you'd keep your responses brief, so she can't figure out what I'm saying."

I nodded mechanically, unable to erase the image of bugs burrowing beneath my skin.

"Before you ask it, I'll tell you what I'm sure you're wondering."

All I wondered about was if the Nanomechanoids were chewing on my guts, creating countless copies of themselves, and if some hidden door was about to fly open within my brain and explode my head.

"I am of course not Tartan's conscience," she said. "I'm a synthetic personality, a Synth, originally created as an entertainment and educational device to be used by a very select and talented group of students. Janice Glickman was one of those. You must never repeat that name in her presence," said the Synth, warning me sternly.

I looked down into the display.

Her little eyebrows seemed to be knitted together and she tugged at her long blond hair.

I nodded.

"Janice was my most brilliant student, designed to be the best. Her GPI was 1. She was one of the very few to have ever existed with such a rating. She had a knowledge of biology, genetics, and the fabrication and manipulation of Nanomechanoid technology unsurpassed by anyone. She had the potential for remaking the world." The Synth Tartan shook her head. "But then the Bug was let loose. Janice became the only person she had ever been close to—she became me. I was able to convince her that I was in fact a part of herself, her conscience, and over the past several years have been slowly directing her, trying to break her out of this Tartan the Barbarian mindset without causing a complete mental collapse and killing her. My goal is to eventually bring her back to her full capabilities. If she can reach that level, she may be able to discover a way to cure the Bug and reverse its effects. But she's never going to get that chance if she along with everybody else dies within the next few days. That is why she sent Anna and Jesus out to find you. Within you lie the resources to reinstate the old Speed Limit, and find out what has happened to God."

This was too much, and far too fast.

Something incandescent and blinding filled my head.

"She brought me here?" I whispered, afraid that if I spoke any louder my head would shatter.

She stood from her cartoon chair. "No," she said, shaking her head. "She is not responsible for your being here, and furthermore, you were not *brought* to 2076. All your memories, and everything that you believe is you, is because of what the Bug did to *you* two days ago. You are not John Smith."

My eyelids fluttered.

My entire body twitched and spasmed.

"I am!" I screamed.

"I knew it was going to come down to this," she said. "I could point out to you how you find yourself in a body that you know isn't yours, how you know things that 'John Smith' couldn't possibly know, and how random bits of knowledge are almost capable of killing you. But none of that will make you believe."

It felt like a dull drill bit had been forced through the back of my head, chipping at bone and now grinding its way through pink-gray brain. My legs began to twitch uncontrollably. My eyes watered.

"That doesn't mean a thing," I said through gritted teeth. "I'll admit that something has happened to me, and that I've been somehow altered and enhanced, but I'm still me. That hasn't changed." I slapped myself against the chest. The grinding drill bit vanished.

"In order for you to accomplish the task that will be set before you, you will have to give up the persona of John Smith and accept who you really are."

"Won't that kill me?" I screamed, trying to trap it with its own logic. Tartan had said that to know your true self would kill you, would destroy your brain. This thing was lying to me, trying to confuse me.

"It may," she said, "but there are unique qualities about you that may prevent that from occurring. I simply don't know. But if you cannot survive what I am about to tell you, you will stand absolutely no chance at all when we get to Heaven and you have to face the Supreme."

I didn't want to know.

I couldn't know.

"No!"

"Colin Wood," she spoke in my ear.

A bolt of lightning split my head. I felt my brain splatter across the planetarium ceiling.

CHAPTER 9

Revenge

Colin Wood.

I was still alive.

My brain felt bruised, swollen, as if someone had been beating at it with a stick. Blinking forced tears out of my eyes. My name was Colin Wood. It had always been Colin Wood. John Smith was just an alias generated by the Bug. That was a fact, an indisputable, stone-and-concrete fact—like the sun's rising in the east or water's flowing downhill. But even more important was that my gut *knew* that it was the truth. And I knew that if the name John Smith hadn't been mine then nothing else that I thought of as being part of myself was actually mine.

Everything had been a lie.

But what little truth I now could understand still made no sense.

If the Bug had destroyed the world four years ago, killing or transforming everyone, why had it attacked me only two days ago? Where had I been for the last four years, that it hadn't been able to touch me?

"Why?" I asked in a whisper.

Tartan, still in front of me, reached out and touched my cheek. The touch was gentle. "God will know," she said.

I sat up, having slumped down into my chair. I was still in Tartan's lab, surrounded by the impossible and unimaginable. An ugly little troll was standing on a nearby table, decanting some foaming yellowish-colored goo into a beaker. It looked up at me, staring, seeming to see right through me, almost as if it could see in me what I *couldn't* see.

It seemed to be accusing me of something.

"What is that?" I asked.

"A construct," she said. "An apparatus I created that helps in my experiments."

The word burned in my head.

"Am I a construct?" I asked, still watching the troll. I feared to know the answer, suddenly certain that that was what I was—a creature, one capable of superhuman acts and thoughts, but still just a creature. I wondered if I had a soul. An hour ago I had not believed in God, and now I was desperate to know if I had a soul.

Cupping my cheeks in both her hands and turning my head, she stared into my eyes. "You're a man, with a soul and a heart. Your capabilities may be unique, but you are totally human."

"Not bits and pieces glued together by Nanomechanoids?" I asked, simply wanting reassurance, wanting to hear her tell me again that I was not a machine.

"She's telling you the truth," said the Synth, speaking in my right ear.

I looked down at my lap, where my hands rested. The display was now firmly locked onto *my* left wrist. Raising it up, I looked into it. "Who am I?" I asked. "Who is Colin Wood?"

"I cannot tell you that now," said the Synth. "Your brain is still recovering from the shock of realizing that you are not John Smith."

The display blurred as a tremor ran down my arm.

"I have to know," I said in a whisper. A whisper was all I could manage. I was drained and exhausted.

"Just because you survived the knowledge of realizing your true name, that is no guarantee that any further understanding will not kill you. But I can promise you that you *will* learn who Colin Wood really is. Those answers are waiting for you in Heaven."

And I knew that to be true.

I had known that from the instant I'd first suspected

that the Laser Facility and Heaven were one and the same.

There'd be no more answers for me here.

"Sleep," she said.

My eyes were already closed.

Opening my eyes, I saw the Earth, all blue and white, hanging above the jagged peaks of ash-gray mountains. I sat up. I was on the moon, stuffed into a sleeping bag, staring out into space. Sitting up and turning, I saw a half-dozen other sleeping bags tightly bunched beside mine.

A shiver ran down my back.

I could have killed them. I knew who they really were, who they once had been. If I had questioned them about any of it they would have been dead. But I hadn't. Somehow I had known. I had known all along.

Past them was a brightly polished brass rail, and beyond that the marbled corridor of the observatory's Hall of Science.

"John."

The sound of my name gently echoed throughout the building.

But that wasn't my *real* name.

I looked out into the corridor. Tartan now stood there, holding a finger to her lips. In her other hand she held what looked like a battle-ax, but it was unlike any ax that had ever been used by any real barbarian. The handle was normal enough looking, being of some polished, dark-brown wood and having a leather strap that protruded from its end and wrapped around her wrist. It was the blade that made me look twice. Almost a foot across, it was nearly transparent, as if made of glass. But as Tartan moved, rocking on her bare feet, rainbow colors rippled across the blade, the effect resembling that of oil flowing over water. The blade was probably Nanomechanoid-constructed from raw carbon. I could imagine the very tip of that blade being only a few atomic layers thick—kept ever sharp by scuttling Nanomechanoids. She waved the ax at me, motioning for me to come out of the lunar landscape display.

Worming my way out of the sleeping bag, I carefully maneuvered around craters and glassy shards of debris and finally vaulted over the guardrail.

"Boots," she said, pointing her ax down at the floor and at a pile of shoes.

I stepped into my boots and began lacing.

"There's something I think you should see, John."

I looked up at her. "The name is Colin," I said. I'd somehow accepted it, and there was no reason why she shouldn't.

She twirled her ax, sending reflected, rainbow-colored patterns flying across the walls. "In name only," she said. "In your heart, you know that your life is that of John Smith. Listen to your heart. It's the only way to remain sane."

Listen to my heart.

She was right.

Intellectually, and if I used cold, emotionless logic, I knew my name was Colin Wood. But in my soul I was still John Smith. I felt myself nod.

"Please hurry," she said in a flat, dead-sounding voice. "I think you'll want to see this."

I stood, ignoring my dangling laces. There was something about the lack of emotion in her voice that told me that this was a hell of a lot more than just something she *thought* I should see. This was something that I *had* to see.

"Where?"

She again motioned me forward with her ax. Dog-trotting down the Hallway of Science, past displays of Martian sand dunes, chunks of meteorites, and freeze-dried Saturn ring debris, she skirted around the pendulum pit and leaned up against one of the large brass and stained-glass front doors.

She pushed it open and I looked out.

The parking lot, beyond the observatory's front lawn, was filled with almost a dozen hexprops, and with what looked like at least a couple of hundred white body-armored troopers.

I saw all this with only a glance, then hit the floor and belly-crawled back behind the wall that surrounded the pendulum pit. I expected to find Tartan on the floor right next to me, but I was alone. Crouching on all fours, I slowly raised my head.

Tartan stood in front of the open door, her ax dangling against her side.

"Down!" I screamed. It was a miracle that she hadn't already had a smoking hole punched through her chest.

She didn't so much as flinch at the sound of my voice.

"The Shield is keeping them back," she said. "Nothing short of an atomic blast can breach a half-meter thickness of grapho-titanate shielding. And even if they could crack it, it's Nanomechanoid actively maintained. It would be resealed almost instantly."

Shield?

I continued to peer around the edge of the pendulum pit for several more seconds. When the front doors didn't implode, sending stained glass, brass shards, and chunks of Tartan across the lobby, I stood. If whoever was now in charge of Napoleon's troops hadn't already opened fire, it meant that they couldn't.

I stood.

Slowly.

Beyond the Shield's perimeter troopers moved quickly, running between what looked like whitish opaque blast shields. They all wore body armor and all carried laser rifles. Several of the bazooka-like devices that had transformed Robin Hood and his Merry Band into a pile of steaming red goo were all aimed straight at us. The tip of each bazooka barrel glowed a green-tinted purple.

"We have them right where we want them," said Tartan, sounding extremely pleased. She shook her battle-ax high above her head.

I couldn't believe it, didn't want to believe it.

She was just like Joan, incapable of knowing when to turn tail and run.

"You knew they were coming," I said flatly, not asking a question but merely stating a disgustingly obvious fact.

Tartan turned, smiling, and pulled a long strand of blond hair from the corner of her mouth. "Of course," she said. "I didn't think Napoleon would be arriving so soon, but I knew he'd come. He wants you, no matter what the cost."

Napoleon.

She didn't know. The others hadn't told her.

"He's dead. Christ killed him."

Her smile turned to a smirk. "I'm afraid that all of you have underestimated my *brother's* determination. No one knows him like I do. A little thing like a spear through the heart would not keep him dead for long."

Brother.

I felt myself take a step away from her.

The look on her face was strange, the expression one of both hate *and* fear.

"He *was* your brother?" I asked, using the past tense, knowing that he was dead, remembering how his dying body had rattled and shook as he spoke with his last breath.

"Half-brother, actually," spoke the Synth in my right ear. "His name is Jason Glickman. Sperm came from the same parent, but ovum originated from two different sources. But this is a topic best left alone. The relationship between them was not a *healthy* one. Don't ask her anything more about it."

I wasn't quite sure what the Synth meant, but I could guess. I knew that Napoleon was capable of anything—absolutely anything. But now he was dead.

Tartan pointed toward something with her ax. "See for yourself."

I looked.

A massive figure stood at the edge of a blast shield. It wore a blue crushed-velvet waistcoat, a ruffled red satin-looking shirt, pink tights, and black, knee-length riding boots. The gloves were white and had ruffled lace around the wrists. A small headset hung around the neck.

Coke-bottle thick lenses glinted in the bright light.

"He's alive?" He *had* died. I had felt him die.

"The instant that his heart ruptured," said the Synth, "I'm certain that the emergency cache of Nanomechanoids he has stored within him activated and sealed off all arteries and veins, and then set up their own intervascular pump network. He could have been maintained in that state for hours. And he wouldn't have needed hours. He's never more than a few minutes away from his surgeon and a bank of cloned spare parts. He's a bit antiquated when it comes to spare parts—he insists on only organics."

My heart missed a beat—several beats.

Something burned in my leg, down in my right calf, exactly where Pancho had shot me. I'd felt it at the time, felt arteries being blocked, blood flow being rerouted.

The Synth had not been the first to invade me with Nanomechanoids. They'd been in me all along—possibly from the moment I'd first awoken.

I continued to stare at Napoleon, trying not to dwell on what might be going on in my own body. From this distance I couldn't quite make out the look on his face, but I could imagine the hate that must be filling it. I could clearly remember that look as he had died in my arms.

He wiped his *gloved* hands across his face.

Yes!

An idea flooded my head.

"You know Napoleon's true identity," I whispered to the Synth.

"That won't do any good," she said. "He's phobic when it comes to Nanomechanoids, but not suicidal. He has both optic and auditory active information-filtering. Any information relating to his former self is automatically kept from his brain. It's one of the perks of being a cardinal."

That was obviously something that I had not been blessed with. I just shook my head. It figured though. Napoleon would never leave himself open to that possible form of assassination.

Tartan then turned and began to walk up the observatory's marbled front steps. "We should start gathering the equipment that we'll be needing for the trip. We'll be able to leave in about a half an hour."

I had not yet seen the back of the observatory, but I was certain that the Shield covered it as well as it covered the front. As I thought about it I realized that the Shield probably did a lot more than just cover our backside, it probably went completely under us as well. It would have to, or else Napoleon simply would have tunneled in. But if we were protected in a sort of impenetrable fishbowl, just how were we supposed to get out?

"Does this place have a magic back door?"

"Naturally," she said as she walked up the stairs, swinging her ax.

I was going to ask how, what, and where, but figured that it would be easier, and certainly less mentally overloading, to just see it for myself, rather than risk what would most likely be some unfathomable explanation. I started to walk up the stairs, following close behind her.

"John?" asked the Synth.

"Yes," I answered, amazed as I did so at how easily and quickly I had grown accustomed to having some disembodied voice echoing in my ear.

"Could you please look to your right, along the Shield, just as it goes around the corner of the observatory. As you turned I thought I saw something strange."

I started to turn, to look in the direction she was indicating, when the significance of what she had just said sunk into my brain.

"How exactly do you see?" I asked. The back of my eyeballs suddenly itched.

"I thought you knew," she said. "My input sensors are rather limited so I depend on my host. There's a Nanomechanoid link between myself and the back of your right optic nerve."

I squinted, again imagining burrowing bugs, but this time saw them chomping at the backs of my eyeballs.

I continued to turn though, and looked in the direction that she had indicated. At first I saw nothing all that strange, except more of Napoleon's troops, but then I noticed something that looked as if someone had emptied a large bowl of mashed potatoes against the side of the Shield.

"We have a problem, John," said the Synth, sounding very calm and controlled.

I continued to stare at the mashed potatoes. They undulated as something within them squirmed.

"A tactical error has been made."

Shifter.

My ears rang and my eyeballs twitched, but it passed almost instantly. Another one of those deeply buried doors had popped open. It was a Nanomechanoid Shifter. It could take over any Nanomechanoid and subvert it—not destroy it, but subvert it. It was like a virus invading a bacterium, using the bacterium to help it reproduce. As I watched a thin, tentacle-like strand emerged from the Shifter and snaked across the surface of the Shield, then began to dribble into it.

Into it.

"We did not think that any Shifters still existed within the Los Angeles Quad," said the Synth. "Apparently we were wrong."

A second and third tentacle had joined the first, and all three were now probing into the Shield.

"The Shifter will fool the Shield into believing that it's a part of itself. When it takes over a large enough section of the Shield, it will bring it down."

"Tartan!" I called out, just as she was opening the door.

She turned and looked at me.

"A Shifter," I said, while pointing toward it.

"It will breach the Shield in less than twenty minutes," said the Synth, with the same lack of urgency as if she were telling me when the next bus would arrive.

"We've got twenty minutes at the most," I said.

Tartan smiled, and stroked the longest fang of her necklace. "The escape hatch won't be accessible for almost another thirty minutes,'' she said. She raised her battle-ax high above her head. ''It looks like we fight!''

She began to walk back down the stairs, almost strutting.

No.

I would not let this happen again.

It would be Robin Hood's cave all over again.

I *willed* my body into its Enhanced mode, finding that I no longer had to wait for it to take control of me. My body seemed to pulse and everything around me became bright and crisp, as if I had just removed a pair of fogged glasses. *I now had control.* I ran up the stairs, wrapped my arm around her waist, and picked her up as if she were weightless. I tossed her over my shoulder.

''You're going to show me this escape hatch of yours!'' I shouted, pushing on one of the front doors with the flat of my free hand, sending it hurtling open. Hinges squealed, metal ripped, and the entire door jerked inward, splintering marble and disappearing over the brass railing that surrounded the pendulum pit wall. The crash echoed down the marbled halls.

''Let me fight *him*!'' she screamed.

I ran in the direction of the lunar display.

The shaft angled downward. Bending over, and peering into it, I ran my hand around its inside lip. About fifty feet below me it foamed and frothed. It felt glass-smooth, and glowed green with what must have been some sort of Nanomechanoid-induced luminescence.

''Where does it lead?'' I asked, without getting up or bothering to turn around.

''Once the Shield is penetrated and another ten meters of shaft wall grown, it intersects with a two-thousand-meter runway that leads to the Palmdale Tube,'' said Tartan.

''What is the Palmdale Tube?'' I whispered so that only the Synth could hear me.

''A high-speed magnetically levitated rail system

connecting the Los Angeles area to the Palmdale Federal Scramjet Facility. Tartan directed construction of the runway to connect to the Tube when we first located here three years ago, after she left her brother. The last hundred feet of the runway were left incomplete just in case someone entered into it from the far end. We didn't want any unwelcome visitors."

Again I looked down at the bubbling bottom of the pit. It had dropped down several more feet. "How long until this shaft connects to the runway?"

"Eleven minutes."

"How long until the Shield is breached?"

"Two minutes."

We were screwed—in all likelihood, dead.

I straightened up and turned.

Seven pairs of eyes stared at me. Eight pairs, if Sir Basil's were included. They were waiting—waiting for me.

I pointed first at Christ and Anna. She had the laser rifle clenched in her hands, and the power pack strapped across her back was humming. Christ held his spear in one hand and an M-16 in the other. "We have to hold Napoleon's troops back for nine minutes before we can make our escape. They can only come in in one place, and that's where the Shifter is breaking through. You have to hold them there as long as you can."

Christ reached up, grabbed one of Sir Basil's laid-back ears, and tugged at him. "Let's save some souls," he said. Turning, the two of them ran down the marbled corridor. Christ had his robe hiked up around his knees.

Anna had not moved.

"We'll hold them until the passage is opened and *you* can escape," she said.

"We can *all* escape," I said.

She nodded, and for just a second we were the only two people in the room. She was certain that she wouldn't be using the escape hatch.

And so was I.

She had our only useful weapon, the only one that

could punch through body armor, and that would make her the principal target. There was no fear in her face, just resignation, the knowing that her life was over. All that mattered to her now was that her sacrifice would save others.

"Thank you," I said.

As inadequate as that sounded, it was all I *could* say.

"You're welcome, Lord," she said in a whisper, then turned and ran down the hallway, her bootsteps echoing.

I wanted to scream to her, to tell her the truth, to tell her that I wasn't Christ. But I couldn't. If I had, I would have taken away from her the only thing she valued—her beliefs.

And that I couldn't do.

I turned to the others.

"When we go down that shaft," I said, pointing down at it but keeping my eyes on them, "Napoleon's troops will be right behind us, and at that instant we have to stop them somehow. We can't let them follow us. Suggestions?"

No one spoke, not even the Synth.

"Any chemicals or explosives stored here that we can use?"

Tartan shook her head.

Gunfire crackled outside. The floor vibrated.

I looked down the long hallway, down toward the pendulum pit. Dust and plaster were raining down. The zodiac fresco was most likely gone—the Gemini twins no longer existed. Something seemed to stab me in the chest. It felt as if the last link to my old life, to a life that wasn't really even mine, had just been severed.

"Yeeow!"

I turned back toward them, the image of the zodiac fresco that had filled my head suddenly shattering just as the real one must have. Joe was bending over, rubbing his shin, just as Vlad was swinging back his right foot, obviously getting ready to take another kick at him. "Access Loki, you dumb shit," he said, as he held his foot back, threatening Joe with it.

"I don't know how," said Joe in almost a whimper. "How could someone like me know how to access Loki?"

Loki?

Bang!

My eardrums popped and I felt air being sucked out of my chest. Glass shattered and imploded inward from all the front windows.

Tartan grabbed Joan by the wrist and pulled at her, but looked at me. "Vlad's right," she said, as she started to tug Joan down the hallway. "If Joe could actually access Loki, he might be able to lock it into a feedback loop. He could not only fry the observatory just before we go, but could even fool Loki into directing fire onto Napoleon's troops."

What the hell was Loki?

No hidden doors snapped open in my head.

Pzzzt!

A shock wave knocked Vlad and Tom to the floor and sent Joe crashing into my arms. The observatory groaned and shuddered. Above and to our left the ceiling buckled and then broke, sending down a torrent of plaster and brick.

Joe looked up at me, the expression on his face overflowing with fear. "Don't make me," he pleaded. A shudder ripped through his body, and his eyelids fluttered. "Some things are best not remembered."

I looked up.

Joan and Tartan were running down the hallway toward the pendulum pit. "Use the portable link in the lab!" Tartan screamed back at me.

The floor tilted.

"What the hell is Loki?" I shouted down at Joe.

He winced as if I had just driven a stake through his heart.

"Loki is the Synth that actually runs the Thor system," answered Tartan's Synth in a calm and cool voice. "If it can be accessed, if passwords and blocks can be broken through, and if it can be fooled into believing that it is under attack from this location, it will fire on us."

I understood.

It would be our only chance.

"He can do it!" screamed Vlad. "He knows. He helped build the thing, in the Beforetimes. He always talks about it. He knows!"

Joe sagged in my arms. I lifted him from the floor and stared into his pale face. His eyelids fluttered open. "I want you to access Loki," I said, "cause it to fire on Napoleon's troops, and then force it to vaporize the observatory just as we're leaving."

Spit ran down his mouth, dribbling from his chin. "I don't know anything about Loki," he whimpered. "I can't access anything. I can't read, I can't write, I don't know anything about Synths. Where's my Narcanall? I can't . . ."

Smack!

I cocked my arm back, getting ready for another swing, but stopped. There was another way, a better way. Grabbing him by the throat, I pulled him across the floor and pushed his face toward Tom and Vlad, who were still tangled up together.

"Do you want to be responsible for Vlad dying?" I shook him as if he were a bundle of rags. *"Do you?"*

A section of the ceiling above us cracked open. A steel girder crashed down, pulverizing a glass case full of old telescopes and textbooks.

"Do you?" I screamed again.

I felt his body convulse, and his legs started twitching, pounding against the floor.

"Terminal," he half hissed, half spit out. I pulled him back up. "Get me to a terminal."

I threw him across my shoulder and started running down the hallway.

"Vlad," I called out without looking back. "If we don't return, and troopers break in, I want you and Tom down that shaft whether it's opened or not."

I heard no reply. There was no time. The world turned crimson. A fireball rolled over the pendulum pit in front of me, just as the explosive shock wave hit.

Crack!

The floor dropped beneath me and I hit the hallway wall. A sheet of black, oily smoke enveloped me as I fell to the floor. But I was up instantly, and running. Joe felt limp and dead.

The pendulum pit was filled with debris—steel girders, both front doors, plaster, bricks, and something that looked like a mound of shredded fur.

Sir Basil.

He was torn and burnt. He'd been severed in half and I couldn't see his hindquarters. What remained of someone's head was locked firmly in his jaws.

There was no time to stop. Out of the corner of my eye, as I rounded the edge of the pit, I saw Joan and Tartan huddled in the corner of the open front doorway. Joan was squeezing off shots from her M-16 and Tartan had her battle-ax tightly clenched in her fists. There was no sign of Christ or Anna.

I leapt up the stairs, smashed my shoulder into the planetarium's doors, splintering them, knocking them from their hinges, and then tore through the velvet curtains.

The entire back end of the planetarium ceiling had collapsed. Trolls and grasshopper-creatures were chaotically digging through the rubble, clearing away something large, something that cried and hissed. A large green fluke, protruding from the pile, was streaked with what might have been blood but looked more like corn syrup.

Joe suddenly struggled.

"Put me down," he mumbled.

I lowered him. Half of his face looked stiff and dead. Drool ran from the corner of his mouth. His left eye was unfocused and glazed over. He stood on one leg, listing over. His left arm was twisted and pinned against his chest. He shook and rattled, like an unbalanced machine that was about to tear itself apart. The strain of having to remember things that Joe Average should not know had obviously ruptured something in the right half of his brain. He turned and hobbled toward the nearest rack panel. It looked lifeless and dead. Reaching forward with his almost steady right hand, he grabbed the skeletal hand that hung limp from the top of the panel and pressed it against his forehead.

The rack panel activated, and a large video display materialized on its oily-looking metallic surface.

He half turned toward me.

"Take care of Vlad!" he screamed as loudly as he could, the words barely intelligible.

Bending down, he rammed his head into the video display. Glass didn't break and, miraculously, nothing exploded. Just as his head hit the surface turned soft, as if made of putty. He sank into it, nose- and ear-deep.

Bang!

There was a quick burst of static in my ear, and my wrist burned. I looked down. The Synth had been reduced to a puddle of molten plastic.

I turned.

Wearing full white body armor and an oversized red beret, the trooper had a laser rifle trained toward my legs. The thing looked sexless, and barely human. Orders obviously had been given not to kill me, because if they had I would already have been splattered across the floor. But a little maiming was probably not only allowed but actually encouraged.

I took a half-step forward.

"Stop!" shouted a synthesized-sounding voice echoing from its speaker grille.

I took another half-step forward.

This time it said nothing. Its head was no longer quite attached to its body.

Tartan stood behind it. She had just swung her ax, and was still standing behind the trooper. It stood with its severed head still resting on its shoulders. Tartan planted a bare foot in its back and pushed. It collapsed on itself, the head bouncing on the floor and rolling away. Three trolls chased after it, throwing bricks at it.

Tartan turned and ran back through the open doorway, disappearing in a swirl of thick smoke.

Taking a deep breath and concentrating, I reached inside of myself and accessed something deep and shrouded. More hidden doors opened. But there was no pain, no confusion. I knew exactly what I had to do. The room glowed bright, my fingers tingled, and I leapt onto the dead corpse. Its head was gone, but I could feel the heart still beating chaotically and randomly. Blood spurted from its severed neck arteries. With one hand I grabbed the laser rifle, while with the other I grabbed the trooper by the waist, lifting it up. I'd have several seconds before the body was actually dead and the laser rifle would deactivate and start disintegrating.

I was almost through the open doorway when I shot two troopers that tried to come into the planetarium. Steam and red muscle exploded between their suit seams. I ran forward. There were a half-dozen of Napoleon's troopers still standing, and what looked like the body parts of at least a dozen others strewn across the floor. Tartan and Joan stood back-to-back, knee-deep in dead troopers. Joan's M-16 fired, unable to penetrate the body armor, but the bullets' momentum knocked them back, throwing them off-balance. Tartan swung her ax in wide, swirling arcs, slicing through anything that came near her.

Two things were immediately obvious. Orders had been given to take everyone alive, or else both Joan and Tartan would simply have been vaporized, and secondly, none of these troopers was outfitted with the gray toasters that could easily have knocked both Joan and Tartan unconscious. Napoleon not only was making things extremely difficult for his own troops, but placing himself at a definite disadvantage.

Why?

But there was no time to wonder. They'd seen me.

I looked at all six of them, one by one, watching lasers pivot, bodies move, and fingers strain against triggers. I made calculations without really being conscious of doing them. All six would be able to fire on me in less than a second. It would take me more than two seconds to fire on all six of them. I'd be chopped in half, standing on cauterized knee stumps, before I could kill the fourth one.

An image of a billiard table materialized in front of me.

And I knew what to do.

I fired.

The first trooper exploded, its chest caving in and steam screaming through its armored neck joints.

The second pivoted its rifle and squeezed the trigger.

But I fired first, hitting him in the shoulder, the impact turning him.

His finger continued to press against the trigger.

His laser vaporized the hands of the sixth trooper, then hit the fourth trooper square in the crotch. I didn't have to watch. I knew that as he fell, still firing, he'd turn the floor beneath him to molten slag, then fall face-first into it.

I fired again, hitting the third trooper in the gut, boiling his innards.

I turned toward the fifth trooper. His laser was trained on me, his finger squeezing against the trigger. He wasn't aiming for arms or legs. He was centered on my head.

But I fired first, my laser aimed for *his* head and my reflexes far faster than his.

Nothing happened.

My laser was dead, the Nanomechanoids within it finally realizing that the trooper they were slaved to had died.

"No!" shrieked Tartan. "You can't kill *him*!"

I stood, waiting. There wasn't time to do anything else.

The trooper suddenly fell forward, a vibrating spear protruding from the back of his neck.

Christ lurched through the doorway, burnt, what little was left of his robe melted into his skin. He dragged something behind him. It was hard to tell, but it looked as if it was what was left of Anna. Black smoke rose from it.

Ker-blam!

Superheated air exploded through the front doorway, hurling Christ into the air, throwing him over the pendulum pit, and crashing him onto the floor in front of me. What little had remained of Anna joined Sir Basil in the pendulum pit. Both Tartan and Joan were tossed down the hallway in the direction of our escape tunnel. But I remained standing, leaning into the blast of superheated air. I felt my eyebrows curl, and could smell my shirt beginning to smoke.

Thor.

Joe had done it. He had accessed Loki, and had somehow directed the Thor system to fire on Napoleon's troops.

Joan lay limp on the floor, facedown, but Tartan was standing, shaking her head. She looked up at me.

"He almost killed you," she said in tones of disbelief. "That trooper was actually trying to kill *you.*"

She was obviously shell-shocked. Equally obvious was that I had no time to deal with it. I pointed first at Christ, who lay down at my feet, and then at Anna. "Get them to the runway entrance!" I shouted.

Tartan nodded, apparently rational enough to understand what I was saying. As she started to bend down toward Joan I turned, leapt back up the steps behind me, and ran into the planetarium.

Joe stood, balanced on his right leg. The top of his head, along with his face down to the bottom of his nose, was covered in a thick coating of gray, molten-looking material.

"Fire on them again!" I screamed, not sure if he could hear me, not even sure if there was anything remaining of Joe inside that gray material.

Ker-blam!

The floor shook.

He was in there somewhere, still rational, and still able to control Loki.

I grabbed him around the waist, holding him up vertically, careful not to get close to the gray material wrapped around his head, and carried him out of the planetarium.

I quickly rounded the corridor corner and saw that Joan, Anna, and Christ were all down at the shaft entrance. Suddenly something exploded above my head, splintering marble.

"Into the shaft!" I screamed, as I tucked Joe under my arm and ran even faster.

I saw Tom pick up Vlad and then both of them jumped feet-first down the hole. Tartan then pushed Christ's limp body into it and followed it with Joan's.

The marble flooring in front of me suddenly glowed amber and I jumped over the molten patch.

"Get in it!" I screamed.

Tartan, holding her ax high above her head, stepped forward and dropped.

I lugged Joe into the room, only barely noticing the pile of dead troopers stacked neatly in the far corner of the room. With Joe held tight to my chest, I jumped into the glowing green shaft and we dropped, my butt sliding along the glassy surface.

"Fry the planetarium!" I screamed.

Searing white light stabbed at my back. I had only the briefest moment to try to steady myself in anticipation of the shock wave that I knew would hit.

I felt nothing—absolutely nothing.

CHAPTER 10

The King and Necro Ned

"Up!"

My eyes opened.

I was on my side, and my hands were still wrapped around Joe's rubbery raincoat. My butt felt sore and burnt.

"Up!"

I sat up, still holding on to Joe. Joan stood in front of me, her cat-eyes narrowed to slits. I looked past her.

Columns of crystal and stainless steel shot up from an almost infinite black stone floor, rising high and gracefully melding into the distant ceiling above.

"Tartan has got the train powered and everyone's aboard except for us." She pointed off to my left.

The Palmdale Tube.

My brain seemed to slip back into gear. I hadn't even realized that I'd been looking at a train until Joan pointed at it. It was almost totally recessed into the far, sloping wall, such that only a small portion of its red curved surface was exposed. Perhaps a dozen hundred-foot-long cars were visible, all with their doors open. As I watched, the entire train floated up almost half a foot, while beneath me I could feel the floor gently vibrate.

I stood, picking up Joe as I did. The gray, molten-like material that covered his head had become brittle and hard, as if it had been transformed from something alive into a dead and dried husk.

Joan ran for the train and I followed quickly behind her.

"Train boarding," droned a mechanically toned woman's voice. "Express nonstop to the Palmdale Federal Scramjet Facility. Travel time fifteen minutes."

Joan jumped into the open train door.

Just as I jumped in behind her I felt Joe's body suddenly go stiff and rigid. I knew that he'd stopped breathing.

The doors hissed closed behind me. The inside of the car was all chrome and plastic, plush seats, and windowless. But something smelled rotten and somewhere, hidden yet nearby, I could hear the squeak of what sounded like mice. I took a deep breath and grimaced.

"Down here!" shouted Tartan from the far end of the car, motioning to us with her ax.

I ran past Vlad and Tom, who were both seated and both staring forward with glazed eyes. Vlad's plastic fangs were gone. He sucked on his thumb. The boy was in shock, whereas Tom was simply hiding in some distant place, far behind his vacant eyes.

I stopped.

Christ was seated next to them.

In addition to being seat-belted, his wrists were tied to the arms of his chair. The left half of his face and his left arm were burnt, red and blistered, and his shoulder was actually blackened. Blood seeped out between leathery-looking strips of charcoaled flesh. Partially conscious, his eyelids fluttered, showing only whites behind them, as he struggled against the straps that held his wrists down.

His lips twitched.

"The old Fucker dies," he said as blood bubbled up through his lips. "The old Fucker took her from me, and now He'll pay." His head slumped forward. "God will pay," he whispered.

"Move it!" yelled Joan.

She had lifted up Joe's feet and now was tugging at him.

"He dies," whispered Christ.

"Move!" she said again, still pulling at Joe.

I moved, shuffling down the train aisle and feeling haunted by the sight of Christ's sightless white eyes.

As we reached the end of the car I noticed that it smelled less putrid. It might have been Christ's burnt skin that I had been smelling, but I didn't think so. The odor was more reminiscent of a ruptured sewer line.

"On here," said Tartan. She was standing beside a table covered with a cloth. "Get him on it," she said, as she took Joe's legs from Joan.

I lowered him onto the table. The gray covering on his head broke in two, half of it falling onto the floor and crumbling to dust as it hit. His one visible eye was closed. His plastic-covered ear fell from its stainless-steel stud and dropped to the tabletop. Tartan quickly tightened two makeshift seat belts around his chest—a chest that was no longer rising or falling.

"He's not breathing," I said mechanically, feeling entirely drained. Only minutes ago I had seen what remained of Anna splattered against the bottom of the pendulum pit, and now Joe lay dying, maybe already dead.

Because of me.

Tartan didn't look up. Like a magician performing some sleight-of-hand trick, a white, thin piece of plastic appeared in her hand. It looked like a poker chip with two small metal studs imbedded in one side of it. Ripping open the snaps of Joe's raincoat and exposing his chest, she slapped down the poker chip, the metal studs biting into Joe's pale skin. She quickly jerked back her hands.

Joe danced, as every muscle in his body spasmed. The last half of the gray material shook from his head, shattering to dust before it could even hit the floor. His arching back suddenly slapped back down against the table.

His chest slowly rose, and then slowly fell. The movement repeated itself. He was breathing.

"Get into your seat," said Tartan, reaching forward

and giving me a hard shove against the chest. I fell back. Apparently Joan already was seated next to me. I didn't see her, my eyes unable to look away from Joe's slowly moving chest. But I could feel her tug at the seat belt around my waist.

"Departure," said a dead voice.

I sank into my thickly padded seat as something invisible suddenly sat on my chest. It felt like at least a full gee, possibly even more. It might have lasted for only a minute, but I really wasn't thinking in terms of minutes, more in terms of breaths. Joe had breathed five times since the train had accelerated.

The seat belt clicked open at my waist and the invisible weight disappeared.

"Cruise speed 480 kilometers per hour. Arrival in fourteen minutes."

Jumping up from my chair, I stood next to Joe. He was ghost-white pale, and his left side was still contorted and twisted.

"Joe," I whispered, wanting to wake him but not wanting to startle him.

He didn't move. His breathing seemed to slow.

"Joe!" I said loudly.

His right eyelid fluttered.

"You're going to be all right now!" I yelled at him.

His right eye opened.

I looked into it.

It was vacant, empty and unfocused.

His lips moved, forming silent words.

I lowered my head, placing my ear directly above his mouth.

"Sorry," he said in a whisper. "Cuu—could naw aksess, Cuu naw bray—break—codes."

But he had broken the codes. He'd saved our lives. I kept my head down for several more seconds but he said nothing more. Straightening up, I looked down at him. His breathing had stopped and his eye was closed. Something rattled and bubbled up from deep down in his throat. His chest sagged like a deflated balloon.

"Joe!"

I wanted to reach out for him, to shake the life back

into him, but I couldn't—couldn't even touch him. I knew if I did he'd shatter and turn to dust.

A hand grabbed my shoulder. "He's gone," whispered Tartan.

He lay dead, his translucent teeth gleaming and his eyes closed. He'd saved my life once, possibly even twice, and in return I'd gotten him killed.

"Thank you, friend," I said, the words feeling pathetically inadequate, but they were the only words that I had. They weren't much, but they were more than I'd been able to give to Anna.

An image of the pendulum pit flashed before me.

Anna and Sir Basil slept peacefully.

They were beyond this place—beyond this insanity.

Tartan's hand was still on my shoulder, but her grip suddenly tightened and her fingers dug into me.

I spun around, ready to lash out and hit at something, hit at anything—but I didn't.

The stench of something long dead and rotting rolled over me in nauseating waves. Tartan still had her fingers dug into my shoulder. Anna stood to my left, color draining from her face, with her eyes wide and unblinking.

He stood halfway down the car.

With one plump hand he held Christ's limp body to his chest. He was worse than a nightmare, he was beyond a nightmare. Never could I have imagined what I now found myself looking at.

His mouth opened, and he spoke.

"Necro Ned says greetings and salutations. Necro Ned says that if you move, Christ gets his holier-than-thou brain splattered."

Necro Ned.

That was the nightmare's name—and it was a name that seemed to fit. He reached down with his free hand, picked at the burnt skin on Christ's shoulder, and peeled off a blackened six-inch-long strip.

"Necro Ned says never pass up a free meal."

Lifting the piece of skin toward his mouth, he stuck his tongue out. It was black and forked, incredibly long, and swayed back and forth like a mesmerized cobra. It then lashed out, the forks grabbing the skin, and reeled it back into his mouth. I could see him chew—literally. The skin on his head and face had been replaced by some sort of clear plastic. Muscle and bone, teeth and tendons, and large globs of yellow fat were all visible. He chewed.

"Necro Ned says that was tasty."

He then shook all over, almost as if his body had suddenly gone into a seizure.

Tartan's fingernails bit into my shoulder, ripping through my shirt and tearing skin.

Joan turned. Her face was tinted a sick gray.

Necro Ned stood perhaps five feet tall and weighed at least four hundred pounds. He wore no clothes, but was not exactly naked. Stapled tail-first to his obese body were hundreds of mice and rats. He wore them like a cape. Most appeared dead and rotten but some were still alive—they squealed and squeaked as Necro Ned shook. Several of the more putrefied ones fell off, their rotted tails snapping.

He finally stopped shaking.

"Necro Ned says that you should notice the device that is attached to Christ's forehead."

I managed to look away from the grotesque body and to Christ. It looked like a squished cockroach had been glued to his forehead, but it wasn't any cockroach. I knew what it really was—C-22 blasting gel. It had almost ten times the chemical potential of nitroglycerin. Until a second ago I had never even heard of it, but now I knew everything there was to know about it—far too much.

"Necro Ned says that the C-22 is linked to Necro Ned's nervous system. If Necro Ned gets upset, Christ, Vlad the Impaler, Junior, and Tom get their brains splattered. Necro Ned gets easily upset." He smiled, and stuck out his snake tongue. It licked at his fat face.

I looked past him. Tom and Vlad both had C-22 attached to their heads.

He knew their names.

He'd been waiting for us. He'd been expecting us.

"What do you want?" I asked. I took a sliding step

forward. If he could be killed quickly enough, he would not be able to give the mental command to fire the C-22.

He held up a single finger. "Necro Ned will give just one warning, John Smith." He then pointed at my feet. "Necro Ned says that if you move any closer, Christ dies. Even if your enhanced reflexes could possibly kill Necro Ned, the C-22 is slaved to a dead man's switch."

He knew me.

I stepped back.

"As to what Necro Ned wants, he serves the Supreme. The Supreme commands that you be held until his *loyal* troops arrive to take you. It seems that you know the Quad Wall codes that he has been unable to obtain from God. The Supreme wishes access to neighboring Quads. With the Quad Walls down, he can spread his Gift."

"Gift?" I asked.

Necro Ned shook his head, causing his body to shudder and quiver. Rodents squealed. "Necro Ned says that for a man who holds so many keys, your knowledge of the world is woefully lacking. The Supreme offers Death."

"Unscheduled stop," said the train's mechanical female voice. "Please be seated."

Necro Ned waved his hand toward us. "Necro Ned says please have a seat. Necro Ned would not want his newfound friends to get their bones splintered and their flesh ripped if they were to fly across the train and became plastered against the far wall."

He turned and waddled back down the aisle toward Tom and Vlad. Tartan picked up her ax and, crouching down, started to stalk toward him.

"No!" I said, reaching out, grabbing her by the shoulder, and pulling her back.

She turned, with her ax slightly raised. "We can kill him!" she said in a hiss.

"And get Christ, Vlad, and Tom killed in the process," I said.

Her eyes were hard, and her pupils reduced to small

black beads. "All that matters is that *you* survive and that *you* kill the Supreme and restore God. The rest of *us* are expendable."

Joan stood next to her, and had been nodding while Tartan spoke. "Our lives here mean nothing. You are the one that must be saved. You are the one that God needs."

I looked at both of them. They were so willing to die for God, a God who, if he really existed, was probably just another brain-burnt psycho, a man who had at one time held the keys to Thor but had now had them stolen by yet another psycho.

There'd be no more dying.

"Sit!" I said. "This all fits into *my* plan."

Both of them jerked their heads back as if I had just slapped them. They slowly sat.

I buckled myself into my seat. It then swiveled around, facing the opposite direction. My plan was simple—*no one* dies. That was it. Implementing it, however, would not be quite so simple.

The invisible weight once again pressed against my chest.

Necro Ned slowly waddled in front of me. I started to look toward the floor, wanting to make certain that I didn't step on any of the putrefied rodent carcasses that were left in his wake. But before my eyes could angle down toward the floor, my attention was caught by the pancake-thin rats stapled to his massive ass. They swayed back and forth. As I watched, large patches of fish belly-white, cottage cheese-textured skin were revealed between the flattened rats. I quickly looked up, staring over his head.

"Necro Ned says to bow your heads. You are about to meet the King."

At that point nothing would have surprised me. In a moment I might be face-to-face with a loon convinced he was Louis the XIV, or Henry the VIII. But I didn't bow my head—I wasn't willing to take the risk of having to once again look at Necro Ned's backside—but continued to look past the crown of dead mice that topped his head.

"Welcome to the Crystal Lake Casino," boomed and echoed a southern-accented voice.

Necro Ned bowed his head and, moving onto the train platform, duck-walked off to his left. I moved forward several more feet and came to a stop only after Tartan and Joan had flanked me.

The "King" sat in a jewel-encrusted gold throne. Surrounding him were ten women, five on his left and five on his right. All were blank-faced Mushies, their hands dyed red. They wore ostrich feather-plumed headdresses, red velvet garter belts, fishnet stockings, stiletto-heeled ruby-red shoes, and absolutely nothing else. The ten were more caricatures of women than actual women. Their waists were impossibly narrow, their hips unnaturally wide, and their legs incredibly long. Not one of them stood under six feet tall. But it was their breasts that were so obviously unnatural. Between all of them, I was certain that more than ten gallons of silicone had been used to create those gargantuan breasts.

"Disgusting," whispered Joan.

The King stood. He was dressed in a sequined white-leather jumpsuit that was unzipped down to his navel. Several pounds of gold chains were draped around his neck, and each finger had at least a single ring, with most having several. In his left hand he held a microphone. He lifted it up to his mouth.

"The King welcomes ya!" he sang with a nasal twang.

His teeth were perfect. His black, puffed-up hair was perfect. His lambchop sideburns were perfect. He was without a doubt the best Elvis Presley impersonator I'd ever seen. He wore rose-colored glasses.

"Ned," he said, as he looked over at the rodent-covered man. "Show our guests to their rooms, and please take Christ to the infirmary."

"Yes, Lord," he said, as he turned toward the women nearest him. His piglike eyes disappeared in the plastic folds of his face. "Necro Ned says, show them to their rooms!'' he screamed, flicking his forked tongue out for emphasis.

All ten walked forward, moving in unison, strutting as if they were moving across a Las Vegas stage.

''And Ned,'' said Elvis. ''I want you personally to see to Mr. Smith. After he cleans up, has a bite to eat, and rests just a bit, bring him to the library.''

''Yes, Lord,'' answered Necro Ned.

I could feel Tartan and Joan move close to my sides, getting ready to fight. Tartan twirled her battle-ax.

No one was going to die.

Reaching up, I grabbed the shaft of her battle-ax and pulled it toward myself. Reluctantly, she let go of it. I lifted it in front of myself, and for just a moment watched the rainbow light glint across its surface.

I then dropped it to the ground.

She didn't move toward it but continued to stand by my side. ''Go with them,'' I said. ''Help Tom and Vlad, make sure that Christ gets whatever medical attention that he needs, and see that Joe's body is taken care of.'' The tone of my voice told them that this was much more than simply a *request.*

Necro Ned jogged toward me. It was an unbelievably disgusting sight. Slabs of fat bounced and undulated, and at least a half-dozen rats and mice went flying. ''Necro Ned says, follow!'' he said, huffing and puffing, practically having to shout in order to be heard above the rodent squeal.

He turned.

I followed.

I stepped on something that squished and squealed, but I didn't look down.

I hoped that my room was not too far away.

''Please relax.''

We sat in Elvis's library. Sitting in a red-leather chair and holding an overly large warmed brandy snifter, he puffed on a large, dark cigar. Three walls were consumed by floor-to-ceiling oak bookcases, stuffed with leather-bound volumes, while the fourth was filled with a window. Something that sounded like Mozart drifted in from hidden speakers.

"That's just a bit difficult," I said as sarcastically as I could, "knowing that the Supreme is coming for me, and that three of my friends have C-22 gel pressed against their heads."

"Life is full of little unpleasantries," he said, sounding philosophical.

"Perhaps a solution to the situation that I find myself in," I said in suddenly reserved, soothing tones, "would be for me to jump out of this chair, grab you by the head, and yank until your neck separates from your shoulders."

I smiled.

"That is indeed a possible solution," said Elvis, who had pulled the cigar from his mouth and was now carefully studying its long gray ash, "but one that is not open to someone of your ethical standards. One of the few things that I share in common with my friend Ned is that if I were to lose consciousness the C-22 attached to your friends would be fired."

I had expected as much, but I'd had to know for sure.

Now I did.

Easing back in my soft leather chair, I looked through the bay window and out at Crystal Lake. We were high in the San Gabriel Mountains. The sky was dark blue, the lake's water even darker, and the shoreline choked with ponderosa pine. Shadows were long, as the sun sank toward the distant mountain peaks. The Speed Limit glowed amber in the northern sky. It had dropped to twelve. A brisk run would now vaporize you.

There was no time for this cigar-and-brandy fantasy.

"So," I said, "are you really just another one of the Supreme's lackeys, like that pile of rodent shit Necro Ned, or do you plan to free-lance my carcass and see what little piece of the Los Angeles Quad pie you can personally slice for yourself?"

Lowering his brandy snifter to a teakwood coaster

and biting into his cigar, he intertwined his jeweled fingers, then slowly dropped his hands into his lap.

"I have been following your exploits with great interest since you arrived at the Wood Labs three days ago."

Wood Labs.

Named after me, after the real me?

An invisible ice pick was slowly being inserted into my left eye.

It twisted.

I managed not to whimper—somehow.

"I truly enjoyed the little demonstration you gave that cretin, Pancho, at the detention facility, and the expression on your face when you first met Robin Hood was absolutely precious."

How could he know?

How could he have seen?

And then I suddenly knew. There was only one way, only one possibility. *The Eyes of God.*

Elvis took a deep drag on his cigar and then blew tight, small smoke rings. "I suggest that you do not take up poker playing," he said as he chuckled and looked at my face. "Did you think that only God was peering down from the heavens? Accessing the Eyes is a trivial task, something that any number of people in the Los Angeles Quad have mastered."

The ice pick scraping at the inside of my skull vanished.

Pieces of the puzzle, pieces that until this moment I had not even realized had existed, suddenly snapped together. If Elvis could see through the Eyes, how could Napoleon or the Supreme *not* be able to see through them.

Any number of people.

But if they had been able to see through them, then why hadn't I been captured days ago? Why hadn't I been captured the moment I had stepped out of the Labs?

More puzzle pieces snapped together.

There could be only one reason.

Because they didn't want me captured or killed.

They wanted me to run, wanted me to reach Heaven. And if that were true, I had not escaped the detention facility but had been *let go.* Everything on that hillside had been staged. *They could have stopped us.* An image suddenly filled my head, another piece of the puzzle slipping into place. I saw Tartan and Joan, standing back-to-back, slicing and firing at Napoleon's troopers.

Why hadn't the troopers used the toasters to simply knock them unconscious?

And now I knew.

Because Napoleon had *wanted* us to escape.

Again my head pounded, as something with dulled steel teeth ground against the inside of my skull. It still did not make sense. Why would he risk both his life and those of his troopers just to surround us at the observatory but then let us escape? Why would he let us obliterate him and his troops when we'd accessed Loki?

My eyelids fluttered.

Blood trickled down from my nose.

Muscles spasmed, and my heart lurched.

Words filled my brain. *No one can access the Thor system except for Loki. There are no secret code words that will control Loki.*

My eyes slowly regained focus. I wiped at the blood that ran down my face. Joe had *not* lied to me. He had *not* been able to control Loki. Then how had Thor been forced into firing onto the observatory? I didn't know.

"Most unpleasant," said Elvis as he stared at my bloody face.

I sat there feeling numb. I suddenly felt like a rat running a maze, convinced that I had been running free while in actuality white-coated psychos had been staring down at me, putting barriers up in front of me, and making me run this way and that. I was starting to understand what was happening to me, but still not why. What did Napoleon want? But there was an even more relevant question.

"What do you want?" I asked. But I found myself

certain of the answer the moment I'd asked the question. If Napoleon had let us escape, had been herding us along, that meant that he *wanted* us to reach Heaven. But that wouldn't happen now, because Elvis had intercepted us. And I knew why. "You'll hand me directly over to the Supreme?"

"That's right," said Elvis. "He'll squeeze you, along with your friends, until he gets the Quad Wall access codes."

I had no codes, but apparently this was one of the few things that Elvis did not appear to know. "And what do you get out of all this?" I asked.

"The greatest gift of all," said Elvis. He waved his hand in the direction of the lake. "I get left alone. Once the Supreme has access to neighboring Quads he'll leave this one alone. After he's dropped the Speed Limit to zero, and effectively fried all the Mushies and anyone else dim-witted enough to venture outside, he'll have to reestablish it. There's no way that he can move troops through this Quad in order to attack another Quad if the Speed Limit is set to zero. Then I'll have my lake, the Speed Limit will be reestablished, and with a little luck that maniac will get himself killed in a neighboring Quad."

It was a wonderful little fantasy, except for the one glaring error—I had no codes. After the Supreme had beaten me to a pulp and flushed me somewhere, he would come back for Elvis in order to see if *he* had been able to find anything out from me. Elvis would not be retiring to the quiet life of Crystal Lake.

"It all works out so sweetly," said Elvis. "When the Supreme squeezes you, he will uncover the purpose behind Napoleon's little antics and erase him along with his demented followers. You've done both me and the Los Angeles Quad a great service."

I slumped back in my chair.

"Care to see what progress your good friend Napoleon is making on his long journey to the Palmdale Tube terminal, where he had been expecting to meet your train?"

I said nothing. I really couldn't care less what Napoleon was doing. Not now.

Elvis reached across his desk, grabbed the nearest computer terminal, and pulled it over to himself. He then let his fingers sink into the gray metallic surface.

A miniature flotilla of Napoleon's hexprop fleet materialized, hovering over the table. A small series of numbers flickered above them.

The cigar dropped from Elvis's mouth.

"Napoleon is coming *here,*" he said in a whisper, "just ahead of the Supreme's hexprops."

CHAPTER 11

God, the Supreme, and Loki Too

The casino floor was as large as several football fields strung together. It was all red-and-gold carpet, purple velvet drapes, gaming tables, slot machines, flashing lasers, little four-armed constructs in butler suits carrying trays of drinks, and of course hundreds of the mammary-enhanced Mushies, who stood motionless as furniture, poised at tables or hanging down on gossamer-thin wires suspended from the mirrored ceiling.

Vlad, Tom, and Christ were blindfolded and tied to chairs. Christ also had on what looked like a strait-jacket. He must have regained consciousness while they were repairing him in the infirmary. I wondered for just a moment who he might have injured and just how much damage he inflicted on the infirmary. I hoped he'd totaled it.

Tartan and Joan were again at my side.

Elvis sat on his throne.

Necro Ned stood outside, on the far side of a clear glass wall that covered the entire southern side of the casino. He was waiting at the edge of an expansive concrete landing strip. Actually, we all were waiting.

"Apparently," said Elvis, "Napoleon has access to more information than I had anticipated. His actions seem to indicate that he may be receiving *inside* information." He looked first at Joan and Tartan and then at the three tied to chairs. Shrugging, he waved one of his red-gloved hands, as if dismissing the thought. "This really changes little. I will simply be *forced* to hand you over to Napoleon instead of willingly giving you to the Supreme. But with the Supreme's forces coming only moments later, Napoleon will be *forced* to hand you over to him. The Supreme will know that I was of invaluable service in your capture and that, further, I helped foil Napoleon's plot against him. Everything will turn out for the best."

"I've got no codes," I told him. "The Supreme will come looking for you when he realizes that I can't remove the Quad Walls."

"A feeble attempt, Mr. Smith. I know you have the codes, because that is what both Napoleon and the Supreme believe. They would not be mistaken."

I was dead, but I'd not be alone—Elvis and Necro Ned would be joining me. Before I could say anything else, to try again to convince him that what he was doing was nothing short of suicide, the air began to vibrate. Looking away from Elvis and through the glass wall I could see hexprops landing—and they landed slowly. The Speed Limit seemed to be dropping at an accelerated rate—it was now down to ten kilometers per hour.

"There is actually an added bonus to this change in scenario," said Elvis. "My odorous assistant, Ned, is still under the impression that you are to be given directly over to the Supreme, and that I have devised some devious and cunning plan to also capture Napoleon. When it finally penetrates his plastic-coated head that this is not going to occur, he will have to be eliminated." He flared his nostrils. "I will not miss his unique presence."

Thundering hexprops landed. It looked as if there were easily fifty of them, each tightly packed. Napoleon might have assembled nearly a thousand troopers.

Familiar shapes descended from the nearest hexprop. A phalanx of white armor-plated troops marched toward the casino, with Napoleon and Lizzie Borden close behind them. As I watched, a large section of the casino's front window shimmered and began to peel back on itself. A handful of troops moved in, waving laser rifles and taking positions against possible attack. I didn't think that Elvis had any real defensive capabilities. The only risk Napoleon's troops probably ran was that if one of the Mushie showgirls rushed them and managed to fall on them, they'd probably be suffocated.

Elvis stepped down from his throne.

The wall of white-armored troops broke. Ned waddled forward into the casino with Napoleon and Lizzie in tow.

"A pleasure to see you again!" shouted Elvis. He was all sweetness and light, greeting Napoleon as if he were a long-lost brother.

Napoleon didn't even bother to look at the rest of us but marched directly across the casino's thick plush carpet and up to Elvis. His eyes were narrowed to slits, and from the headphones that dangled around his neck I could hear the sounds of some sort of heavy-metal punk screech. His face was flushed red. Stepping to within a half foot of Elvis and towering over him, he reached down, grabbed him by his leather collar, and lifted him up.

Elvis's blue suede shoes dangled a foot above the floor.

"You have meddled in *my* business," he said. The words had been spoken slowly, and with what sounded like a great deal of control.

"I thought I was helping!" squeaked Elvis. "I captured this man and his companions, knowing that you wanted them!"

Napoleon hurled Elvis down, tossing him into his throne. "I may be able to salvage this situation," he said. "But of course in order to convince the Supreme that John Smith"—he quickly glanced over at me, giving me a look that would have been capable of melting granite—"has once again managed to elude me, and requires me to follow him to Palmdale with my forces, I will have to destroy your little establishment here."

Elvis squeaked something totally inarticulate.

"But if you cooperate, and don't attempt to unleash your wet-dream army," said Napoleon, as he swept out his arm at the hundreds of showgirls, "I may not kill *you.*"

Elvis squeaked again, trying to pull his head into his leather jumpsuit.

Napoleon turned and walked toward me. He ran a gloved hand through his dark, greasy hair and tugged at his green velvet waistcoat, pulling it taut against his chest.

But he was not looking directly at me. He stared to my left.

At my side I could feel Tartan stiffen. She pushed herself up against me, as if she were trying to burrow into me.

"It has been far too long, dear sister," he said. Walking forward and bending down, he kissed Tartan. He kissed her long and hard. Both his hands were cupped against Tartan's fur bikini top. His fingers flexed as if he were kneading dough.

This was no brotherly greeting.

But I didn't move.

The half-dozen troopers in the casino had their weapons trained on us. If I as much as raised a hand all I'd manage would be to get myself killed.

Napoleon straightened up, letting one of his hands linger on her left breast. "I certainly have missed you," he said in a whisper. Tartan had not moved, I don't think she'd even breathed since her brother had descended on her.

"And I you," said Tartan, her voice sounding dead and mechanical. I looked at her face. It was pale and drawn, but as I watched she smiled at him. It looked like the smile of a condemned man staring up at his noose, eager to drop through the trapdoor, eager to have the horrible nightmare of waiting for death to be over.

Napoleon took a half-step back, letting go of her breast. "Unfortunately, there is not time for a proper re-*union* at this moment," he said. "But after things have been taken care of in Heaven and I sit on the throne, we will have to get reacquainted *properly.*"

Her knees buckled, and I had to reach over and grab her just to keep her standing.

Like a moray eel flashing toward an unsuspecting fish, Napoleon reached out and grabbed me by the throat. He lifted me up, just as he had done to Elvis. "I'm tired of playing games with you," he said. "You and your degenerate little band are going to get back onto the Palmdale Tube, just as I and my dear sister had originally planned. You are to complete that trip."

Both had planned?

Napoleon and Tartan.

I looked down at Tartan. She was sprawled face-down on the carpet, shaking and crying. *She'd been working with her brother all this time?*

It felt as if my brain were short-circuiting.

Nothing, absolutely nothing was as it seemed. Not only had Napoleon deliberately let me escape from the Detention Facility, he had even engineered my rescue with his sister's help. I'd been a puppet all along, and he'd been the puppeteer tugging on my strings.

A hand grabbed my chin and turned me around.

Napoleon stared into my face. "We have an appointment to keep with the Supreme," he said. The hate in his eyes was pure, almost blinding.

"Yes, God!" Joan suddenly screamed.

Napoleon let go of my face and we both turned toward Joan. She stared toward the casino ceiling, her face almost glowing. She slowly lowered herself to the floor, kneeling. "The Lord has spoken to me," she said in a whisper. "He will make His presence known."

Of all times for Joan to finally flip out, this was the worst possible.

"Where?" screamed Napoleon.

I turned back to face him, shocked by what I saw in his face. *He believed her.*

"There," I heard Joan say.

I turned back toward her. She was pointing toward the far end of the casino.

Again Napoleon reached for my throat, pulling me from the floor. "Say nothing, or else they all die."

I had absolutely no idea what I would say, or whom I could possibly be saying it to. Whatever psychosis Joan was suffering from was apparently contagious.

Ker-blam!

Both of us, with Napoleon's hand still clenched around my throat, flew through the air, a shock wave knocking us back. Lights, debris, body parts, dust, and concrete shards swirled around me.

"I'm waiting!" thundered a voice.

I didn't actually stand, but I did come to my feet. Napoleon now clenched my face. He lifted me up. The entire far end of the casino was cloaked in rising dust. Sunlight poured in through a gaping hole in the ceiling.

A figure moved within that dust—a figure that stood tall enough to touch the ceiling that was fifty feet above our heads.

"Do not fire!" yelled Napoleon to his troops, who had swung their laser rifles toward the swirling dust. Still holding my face, he picked me up and shook me in the direction of the swirling dust. I reached down, right for his crotch. I grabbed, and squeezed.

He stiffened.

"Lower me down," I said.

He raised me up, holding my face only inches in front of his Coke-bottle thick lenses.

I squeezed.

He smiled.

"You can do nothing to hurt me," he said. "It's all been a game, none of it real."

I squeezed tighter and something gave way in my hand, something that felt as if an egg had cracked, spewing its runny insides.

Napoleon threw me to the floor but my hand did not release. Fabric and flesh tore. I hit the casino floor, looking up toward his crotch. I expected to see a torrent of blood spurting from what was left of his balls. But's that not what I saw. Pasty-colored flesh was quickly resealing, and the fabric of his satin pants was stitching itself back together.

Nanomechanoids.

I looked down at my hand. What I held on to was turning to goo, dribbling between my fingers and forming a dark pool on the carpet.

Looking back up, I saw that Napoleon had an index finger against the side of his head. "All that I am is in here," he said, "surrounded by an impenetrable grapho-titanate skull. This body is just a construct, something to move around in." His face, which apparently was *not* his face, suddenly jerked up, staring toward the end of the casino.

More lies.

The Synth had told me that he feared Nanomechanoids.

Napoleon's eyes grew wide.

He took a step back.

Turning over, and wiping what goo remained in my hand against the carpet, I stood.

The dust had settled.

Joan had not lied.

God stood in the far end of the casino. His head would have just touched the ceiling had the ceiling still been there.

"Save me, Lord!" screamed someone.

That someone was Elvis. Jumping from his throne and losing one of his blue-suede shoes, with gold chains whipping behind him, he ran.

Napoleon snapped his fingers and pointed to Lizzie.

"No!" I screamed, knowing what he intended, and knowing what would happen if Elvis was killed. But Lizzie ignored me.

The twirling ax caught Elvis square in the back of the head, knocking him off his feet and sending him flying forward. He crashed into a roulette table, slid along the green felt, and only came to a halt when the front of his head had cracked against the ornamented spindle of the wheel.

I looked over to where Vlad, Christ, and Tom had been before the far end of the casino ceiling had exploded. Their chairs had been knocked over but their heads were still intact. I could clearly see the black stain of the C-22 still on Tom's forehead. Either Elvis's dead man's switch had not worked, or he had lied to me about having one.

I found I could breathe again, not even realizing I had been holding my breath.

I looked back up at God.

He pointed a five-foot-long finger at Lizzie. "Thou shalt not kill!" he screamed, his voice echoing throughout the casino.

Ker-blam!

A chunk of ceiling above Lizzie disintegrated. I doubt if she had time to notice it though, since she disintegrated right along with it. Gravel-sized chunks of what remained of her splattered against the floor and stained the white body armor of the troopers that had stood next to her.

No one moved.

God sat back, a marble bench suddenly having appeared behind Him. *He was not quite solid.* I could see the back wall of the casino through his flowing white robe. He was a hologram, one that I was certain was being projected down from orbit, using the same mirror assemblies that the Thor system used to bounce its lasers from Palmdale back down to Earth. A ten-foot-diameter halo hovered over his head, cocked to one side. His face was pale and creased, and he had a long white beard that flowed down to his waist. In one hand he held a live thunderbolt, blue-gold and shimmering, writhing like a snake.

I blinked, as I so often do when I encounter something that my brain just can't quite accept. Yet it wasn't a fifty-foot version of God, seated in the far end of the Crystal Lake Casino, that had caused my brain to hiccup. No. It was what He held in His left hand.

I blinked again, and it felt as if my eyeballs were melting.

Fudge Pop.

In God's left hand was the largest Fudge Pop that I'd ever seen. He lifted it up to his mouth, took a large bite, and chewed. Some of it stained his white beard a deep, dark chocolate.

I had easily recognized it, despite its gargantuan

size. Fudge Pops were one of my few vices. Sweat suddenly began dripping down my face and I started to shiver. That invisible ice pick had once again been reinserted into my left eye. I could feel a dozen hidden doors lurking deep within my brain threatening to open.

But I managed to hold them closed.

Because I knew that if they opened, I'd die.

I knew that beyond any doubt.

God took a second bite, then waved what remained of the Fudge Pop in our direction. "No calories," He said, while smiling. A flock of normal-sized doves materialized, flying around his head and darting in and out of his halo.

He took two more quick bites and then tossed what remained of it in our direction. I flinched, certain that I was about to be smashed to the floor by several hundred gallons of frozen, chocolate-flavored ice milk.

It hurtled down, but then vanished the second its trajectory brought it beneath what was left of the casino roof. It *was* a hologram.

The invisible ice pick that had been chipping at the back of my right eyeball vanished. The doors that had been bulging outward, with hinges screaming and wood splintering, vanished.

"Napoleon!" he shouted, his voice thundering. A wind we could not feel tugged at his robe and whipped his beard over his shoulder. He shook his lightning bolt.

It looked as if Napoleon was about to follow in the steps of Lizzie Borden and be reduced to a burnt stain on the thick red-and-gold carpet.

I took several steps away from Napoleon. God's aim might not be as accurate as it had been the first time.

"I've been waiting!" yelled God.

Napoleon dropped to his knees and bowed his head.

"This should be discussed in private, Lord," said Napoleon. Closing his eyes, he held his clasped hands up to his lips.

I could hear the rattle of body armor. Looking away from Napoleon, I could see that several of his troopers had turned their weapons away from us and were now aiming them at *him.*

I took several more steps back.

"I can discuss whatever I wish, with any of my *servants,* whenever I wish."

"Servant?" I mouthed almost silently. Napoleon was a servant for whoever was behind this hologram—for God?

"I beg you, Lord, to please reconsider," said Napoleon in a whisper.

A trooper raised his laser rifle.

Fzzzzt!

Both of Napoleon's hands exploded in flame and he was tossed backward, crashing into chairs. Poker chips flew into the air.

Before the trooper could get another shot off a second trooper shot the first in the back. At such close range his armor exploded at the seams, sending large chunks of meat and plastic flying.

Then, before anyone else could fire, I felt something tickle at the inside of my head.

Troopers hit the ground.

Tartan, who was still on the floor, stopped moving.

Joan keeled over from her prayer position, hitting the floor face-first.

Just as suddenly, the windowed casino wall turned opaque.

Through the opening in the casino roof explosions and shots could be heard sounding like nearby thunder. The glass wall vibrated and shook from the impact of weapons fire against it.

But it held.

Napoleon propped himself up with his elbows, and then stood. His hands were gone, and smoke rose from his wrist stumps.

Necro Ned stepped forward, his chubby hands sunk knuckle-deep into a gray toaster. He looked at Napoleon. "Necro Ned says to call your troops off. *I* now control John Smith. The outside speaker system is activated."

"Cease Fire!" yelled Napoleon. "This is by order of Cardinal Napoleon Bonaparte, Ruler of France!"

The outside thundering of weapons quickly stopped.

God smoothed out his robe and smiled. "Thank you, Ned," he said. "I can always depend on your levelheadedness in times of crisis."

"Necro Ned says it is always a pleasure to serve you, Lord." A stiff rat fell from his chest, bounced off a velvet chair and then hit the floor.

I just stood there, feeling as if my brain had been transformed into a pile of goo. *Both Napoleon and Necro Ned worked for God.* Then what was all this insanity about? Everyone seemed to be working for God.

I stood and waited. There was nothing else I could do.

Napoleon took several steps forward and reached up with his wrist stumps that were no longer just wrist stumps. Ash-white bones now jutted through the seared skin, tendons weaving themselves between joints as I watched.

"You have not delivered my Messiah," said God. "Lucifer gets nearer and nearer, draining my power, and you *do not* deliver to me my Messiah."

Napoleon lowered his head. His muscle-covered fingers twitched.

"Less than a day remains before the Speed Limit drops to zero," said God. His eyes suddenly filled with tears. "Even as we speak my most innocent children are dying by the thousands, unable to understand what is happening. I cannot stop it. I cannot control Loki as long as Lucifer battles me." He glared down at Napoleon. "You did not deliver me from this evil!"

"I've moved as rapidly as I dared," said Napoleon. "I and my troops would have been to Heaven by now, except that John Smith, your Messiah, was diverted to this location. That diversion was beyond my control."

God shook his head.

"Of course it was beyond your control," said God. "*I* caused John Smith to be brought here. My good agent Necro Ned saw to all the details."

"But why?" asked Napoleon. "This has cost us valuable time."

"Because," said God, his voice again thundering, "Lucifer saw through your feeble plan. He knew that you were moving troops up to Heaven in order to attack him, using the capture of John Smith as an excuse for assembling more and more troops. I overheard him talking as he directed *his* troops to lay an ambush for you at the Palmdale Scramjet Facility. All of you, including my Messiah, would have been killed or captured. He's known your plans from the very beginning."

"But how?" asked Napoleon. "How could he know?"

"Lucifer has his own agents. Agents that are very close to you—very close indeed." He looked down toward the stain in the carpet. "She's paid for that sin. Hell should agree with her."

"Please forgive me, Lord," said Napoleon. "I underestimated Lucifer."

God nodded. "A common mistake, even for the most righteous. But all is not lost," he said, sounding suddenly cheerful. "Lucifer's own troops will soon be descending on you. When that conflict begins you and John Smith will be able to escape in the confusion, and you will bring the Messiah to me. You will set me free." He then peered over his shoulder, as if he thought someone was listening to him. "But you cannot come to me by way of Heaven. Lucifer has not committed all his troops to the upcoming battle—he's held back reserves to guard the entrance to Heaven."

"Then how can we save you, Lord?" asked Napoleon, tears running down his face.

"There is only one way we can salvage this situation," said God. "You will have to sneak in through the back entrance."

A back entrance to Heaven?

"I don't understand, Lord," said Napoleon, apparently as confused as I was.

God took a deep breath and shrugged his shoulders.

"Through Hell," he said. "Come in through Hell. Satan will never expect an attack from the rear."

"Through Hell," said Napoleon, obviously not liking what he was hearing.

"Certainly," said God. "My faithful servant Ned knows the way." God smiled serenely.

I looked over at Ned. He was nibbling on a dead rat. I was not all that surprised that Ned knew the way through Hell.

"But you must act quickly," said God. "Lucifer has spies everywhere." He suddenly looked away from Napoleon. "John Smith."

"Yes," I said, in a voice that sounded squeaky and strained.

"Everything depends on you. Loki has told me that you hold the key to free me and to vanquish Lucifer. Do you know what that key is?" He asked.

I couldn't speak, or for that matter even move. I kept thinking about that red stain where Lizzie had been. I had absolutely no idea of what it was I was supposed to do, or how I could possibly destroy Lucifer. But I was certain that if I told Him that I'd be transformed into another smoking stain on the carpet.

"Don't worry," said God, speaking in a gentle voice. "You will know when it's time."

I just nodded my head, having no idea what this *key* could possibly be.

Outside, distant thunder cracked.

God looked to his left, as if He saw something that we couldn't.

"How did *you* get here?" he screamed. Raising His thunderbolt high above his head, he hurled it through the opening in the casino ceiling. "Back to Hell with you!"

"I think not!" boomed a voice from outside the casino.

The sounds of thunder increased. The casino floor shook.

God stood, raising the palm of his hand in front of Himself. "Down to Hell, Lucifer!" he shouted. His old wrinkled face had flushed red.

"To Hell yourself," said the other voice.

God exploded in flame.

"Lord!" screamed out Napoleon as he fell to his knees.

Soot swirled where God had stood, and out of that soot a shape began to take form.

The floor suddenly leapt up, as if the entire casino had been knocked from its foundation. Ceiling mirrors splintered, the shards vaporizing into silver snow that gently drifted down.

The soot coalesced.

He was as tall as God had been. Goatlike from the waist down, he stood on hooves. His skin was deep red, and small stub horns protruded through his forehead. Both his ears and his beard were pointed.

In his hand was clenched a three-pronged pitchfork.

It was the Supreme, in the guise of Satan.

"I've had enough of this charade," he said. "It ends here and now." He pointed the pitchfork toward me. "You, I will be taking back with me. We have Quad Walls to bring down." He then waved the pitchfork around, pointing toward everyone else in the room. "The rest I will send to Hell right now." He then looked first to Necro Ned and then to Napoleon. "I have a very special place in Hell for *loyal* servants such as yourselves."

He waved his pitchfork and the opaque casino wall shimmered, again turning transparent. Napoleon's troops were firing into a sky that was thick with descending hexprops.

"But before I send you to burn, I will give you this last gift, letting you see what little hope you might still have been clutching to totally destroyed."

Literally hundreds of hexprops darkened the sky. Napoleon's troops were hopelessly outnumbered.

We watched the destruction. The building shuddered, and the sounds of explosions and shearing metal thundered through the hole in the casino roof. Lucifer stood above us, his fists pushed against his waist. He glared down on us.

"Hey, fuckface!"

Lucifer turned.

The rest of us who were still conscious turned. Rats squealed as Ned moved.

Vlad was sitting up straight in his chair. He flexed his shoulders, and the ropes holding his hands and feet snapped as if made of string. He stood, smoothing out his cape.

"Hey, fuckface!" he said again.

"What did you call me?" roared Lucifer.

Dust rained down.

Vlad walked casually forward, brushing debris from his cape. Reaching up, he snugged his sunglasses against his face. "I thought you'd never get here, fuckface," he said.

Lucifer cocked a long black eyebrow. "I'll send you to Hell," he said, shaking his pitchfork.

Vlad looked outside, then, raising his right hand, snapped his fingers. "Enough is enough," he said.

The world outside exploded.

I couldn't tell if I hit the floor or if the floor jumped up and hit me. All I could see was a crimson ball of flame crash into the glass wall and then roll up over the casino. I almost rose from the floor as hot wind sucked at me, tugging me toward the open ceiling. Then, just as quickly, I fell back down.

I stood.

Outside sat a burning, smoking mass of twisted steel debris, while molten debris rained from the sky. Both Napoleon's and Lucifer's hexprop fleets had been destroyed.

Lucifer held his pitchfork in both hands, shaking, looking as if some internal rage would force him to explode.

"Who *are* you?" screamed Lucifer, as spit dribbled down into his beard.

Vlad walked forward. He smiled. Apparently he had found his plastic fangs. His teeth seemed to gleam. "You can call me Loki."

Loki?

I couldn't believe it. I'd seen more insanity than I thought could exist in a world, but now I faced a ten-year-old kid with a Dracula fixation who was claiming to be the synthetic personality that controlled Thor. Then a thought filled my head. If Vlad was in fact Loki, that would explain how Thor had been activated to fire onto the observatory.

I looked quickly outside.

Burning debris still fell from the sky.

It appeared as if he was telling the truth.

I looked first back at Vlad and then up to Lucifer.

He sucked down a breath and the handle of his pitchfork snapped in two. "You can't stop me!" he screamed.

Vlad waved a hand out toward the burning wreckage. "What do you call that, fuckface?" he said.

Lucifer shook, and tossed the two halves of his pitchfork to somewhere that we couldn't see. "I've held troops in reserve," he screamed. "You'll never get into Heaven. You'll never touch me. I will be the one to command you!" He then vanished in a swirl of smoke and fire.

Vlad walked over to where Napoleon and myself stood. I could smell Ned as he moved nearer to us, and could hear the squeal of rats. Bending down, Vlad picked up a chair and dusted off the seat, then sat down.

The three of us remained standing, saying nothing.

"We have to talk, gentlemen," said Vlad. "The first part of *my* plan has been implemented exactly as I had hoped. I want to thank you for your cooperation."

"Plan?" Napoleon managed to mumble.

"Certainly," said Vlad. "Before I could make the necessary changes in the political power structures that were currently strangling the Los Angeles Quad, it was necessary to remove all military forces that currently existed. It took a bit of maneuvering to get those two forces to clash in such an isolated region, where I could direct Thor to fire on them without any chance of harming civilian populations, but if I do say so myself it worked out rather nicely." He smiled, with a self-satisfied-looking grin.

I glanced outside. Debris was still burning. I imagined that it would continue to burn for hours.

Vlad looked at Napoleon. "The Church of Limbo essentially no longer exists. All of its 'Brothers' have been sent to far better places." He pointed outside. "In a like manner, that element of the Church that the Supreme had subverted no longer exists." Again he smiled. "The beast's body has been killed, gentlemen, but the head continues to live. It is time for a new Church, a church headed only by God, a church where He directly touches the people and they touch Him. All that remains between us and that goal is Lucifer. What do you say, gentlemen, can I depend on your support to finish the job that you all started?"

"Necro Ned says yes."

"Yes," said Napoleon. "It will be the Lord's will."

I said nothing.

"Well, John Smith?" said Vlad.

I wasn't about to agree to anything, with anyone. A second ago this had supposedly been a frightened kid with a Dracula complex, and now he had revealed that he had the power to vaporize armies. Yet he claimed that he still needed my help.

No.

It made no sense.

"I want to talk to you privately," I said. The questions I had to ask I didn't want Ned or Napoleon to hear.

"Gentlemen," said Vlad, nodding to Ned and Napoleon. "If you don't mind, may I please have a few words alone with Mr. Smith?"

They walked away in the direction of the far end of the casino. I waited almost a full minute, until they stood beneath the opening in the ceiling.

"Did you bring me here?" I asked.

He appeared to be the most powerful one here, the one who was really doing the controlling, the manipulating.

"Of course," said Vlad.

The casino momentarily seemed to turn gray as my

vision tunneled. I forced a lungful of air down my tightening throat.

"Who am I?" I asked.

Vlad grinned. "I'd think you'd be getting tired of asking that question by now. My response will have to be the same as everyone else's. I cannot tell you. What I can guarantee, however, is that if you come with me everything that you are will be revealed. You will know your true self."

My body relaxed, somehow knowing that it wasn't about to hear something that it was not yet ready to hear.

"Then can you tell me *why* I have been brought here?"

"That's simple," said Vlad, leaning back in his chair and propping it up on two legs. "I need an assassin."

"So your story is just the same as the others'," I said. "I've been brought here to kill Lucifer?" I asked. It made absolutely no sense. I'd just seen him kill thousands of troopers, both Napoleon's and Lucifer's. If he had that kind of power, why couldn't he just kill one more psycho who believed himself to be Lucifer?

"I'm afraid you still don't fully understand what's expected of you," said Vlad. "You are here to ensure three deaths."

"Three?" I asked.

Vlad nodded. "I brought you here to kill me."

I blinked.

"But I am not permitted to die unless I have the express permission of both Lucifer and God. They both hold the keys to my existence. As long as they think they can use me, they will not let me die."

I blinked again.

"Therefore, you must dispose of both God and Lucifer and take their place. Only when you possess their power will you be able to kill me." He smiled.

I blinked for a third time.

CHAPTER 12

On the Threshold of Hell

I was no assassin.

I had come with them anyway—but not to kill Lucifer or God, or even Loki. I'd come to save my own life, knowing that until I found out how I'd come to be here and who I really was, I had nothing. Without knowing that, *I* was dead.

They had come here to save God.

I had come here to save myself.

Thunder rumbled across the desert.

The Speed Limit was down to seven kilometers per hour. A slow jog would get you vaporized, with the carbonized remnants being propelled in all directions. The thunder-cracks of Thor sounded like sporadic heavenly gunfire. Sometimes several minutes would pass in silence, but then suddenly a half a dozen rapid-fire shots would echo from over the horizon.

And that was the other reason I was here.

My presence had somehow started this insanity, an insanity that was killing thousands, and I knew somehow that I was the only one who could stop it. I couldn't turn my back to that.

From our vantage point along the back of some nameless rocky crag, the Free Electron Laser Facility filled the desert floor beneath us. Out in the desert, where distances can be deceptive and where a mountain range that appears to be only a few hours' walk away may actually be fifty miles distant, things generally appear much closer and smaller than they really are. I took absolutely no comfort from my awareness of this. The Free Electron Laser Facility not only covered the desert floor beneath us but ran right to the distant hazy horizon. It was a thousand shades of dirty white, all rising up into the blue sky and shimmering like soot-stained ice.

"Cracker."

Tom nudged my shoulder.

We sat together, apart from the others, eating what would be our last meal before reaching the gateway to Hell. Tom held a handful of crackers out toward me. They were already coated with cheese.

I took them from his red-stained hand without actually looking at them. I was staring into his eyes. Since leaving Crystal Lake, taking the Palmdale Tube out to Palmdale, and then spending the entire night trudging across the Mojave, Tom had been talking more and more. It seemed he was slowly pulling himself up from whatever dark hole he had been trapped in.

I wondered just who I was really looking at.

He certainly wasn't a Mushie. I had really known that from the beginning, but had never wondered just what he might *really* be. But all that had changed after Crystal Lake. Since then I'd been wondering damn hard about who he might be. Of all of us, Tom was the one who most obviously was not who he appeared to be.

"Who are you?" I asked.

He mechanically shoved cheesed crackers into his mouth, chewing rapidly and sending a moist torrent of crumbs down his chin, where they clung to his wispy beard.

"Crackers?" he asked again, holding out another handful.

I just shook my head and, turning, looked up the mountain toward the others. Napoleon sat there with six of his troopers. They were the only survivors of his army, the ones who had been fortunate enough to have been inside the casino when Loki had destroyed everything outside. Napoleon swore that they were loyal to him and to him alone. That guarantee did absolutely nothing to put me at ease. I certainly didn't trust him, so I was hardly about to trust his troopers. But we had no choice. The six were the only ones with real weapons, and we had no idea what Lucifer might throw against us. Napoleon sat on a splintered chunk of granite, chewing on a chicken leg and leering in Tartan's direction. That, above all else, was why I would never trust the man.

He was bent, severely bent.

The rest were strewn further up the mountainside.

Christ, hobbled and gagged, stared outward with crazy eyes, wanting to kill any and everything, desperately believing that only death could bring Anna back.

Joan had an arm wrapped around Tartan as she tried without success to get her to eat something. Tartan hadn't been able to eat or speak since Napoleon had joined us.

Far above us and—thankfully—downwind, sat Necro Ned. Who could this "God" be, that he would consider Necro Ned a good and loyal servant? It seemed just one more indication of how truly insane this world was. As I watched him, he plucked a mouse from his thigh and popped it into his mouth.

I looked back at Tom. "I'm beginning to think that there's no real difference between God and Lucifer."

Tom turned his head. Half a cracker hung from his mouth. "God and Lucifer are but two faces of the same being," he said, then turned his head back and stuffed another cracker into his mouth.

I didn't move, but stared at the side of Tom's head. I had absolutely no idea where or how he had dreamed up that little philosophical gem. I didn't understand what he meant by it, and wondered if even he knew.

"Time grows short!" shouted Vlad, calling down to us from high atop the mountain, as if he were making a proclamation.

I looked up toward him. He was standing, unwrapping his cape and letting it flutter in the breeze. "Hell awaits!" he screamed.

That was, without a doubt, the first thing I'd heard

since arriving in this asylum that I had absolutely no difficulty in believing.

Standing, I started the downward descent.

"The entrance to Hell," announced Vlad.

Now everything that Vlad said came out sounding like an official decree, read by some ancient priest from some age-yellowed scroll.

"Is it safe?" called out Napoleon.

I turned around and looked toward him. He was at least fifty yards behind us, still walking down the sandy hillside. His six troopers surrounded him in a tight knot, each with their laser rifles readied, pressed up against their hips.

Napoleon was scared, right down to his Nanomechanoid silk shorts.

So was I, of course, but in the last few days I'd seen thousands killed, most of them armed as well as the troopers that guarded Napoleon. The only real way to survive around here was by your wits, and with generous quantities of dumb luck. I was under no illusions, knowing that in my case it had mostly been dumb luck that had done the trick.

"It is *not* safe," said Vlad.

Napoleon stopped, but said nothing. What could he say?

I turned back around.

Vlad stood before us, leaning against a sand-blasted, off-white, ten-foot-tall door that was sunk into the side of a mountain of Stonehenge-like gray slabs.

For the entrance to Hell, it was decidedly unimpressive. I had been expecting some three-headed, snarling, Nanomechanoid version of Cerberus, the river Styx, and perhaps an Egyptian death barge to carry us over the boiling water. But there was none of that, just a large steel door covered with heavy, half-dollar-sized bolt heads.

"Why aren't Lucifer's troops guarding this entrance?" asked Joan, stepping forward and moving past me. She neared the door and I could see her body tense.

"There's no need for Lucifer's troops here. What few forces he has left he has positioned at the entrance to Heaven on the other side of the Laser Facility, just in case we tried to gain access through there. He knows that if we're foolish enough to try and get to God through this entrance, he has *sufficient* safeguards to stop us."

"What?" I said, not wanting to believe what I'd just heard, but somehow not being all that surprised. It was just the twisted sort of nonsense that I should have expected.

Joan stepped back.

"I've had enough of this!" screamed Napoleon. "I will not be led by this *thing* anymore. I'm—"

Twin bolts of orange lightning leapt through Vlad's wraparound sunglasses.

Bang!

I turned.

The six troopers had crumpled to the ground. There was not a mark on them, the only indication that anything had even happened to them being the smell of burnt meat that hung in the air. I think they'd just been microwaved to death.

Napoleon stood still, with his jaw hanging slack and his normally squinting eyes looking impossibly large behind his Coke-bottle thick lenses. He snapped his mouth shut. His lips twitched a few times, but he said nothing.

"Do I have your attention once again?" asked Vlad.

I turned back around.

Vlad still casually leaned against the door, as if nothing had happened. Reaching up with one hand, he adjusted his sunglasses. I now understood where that mysterious pile of troopers had come from that had been stacked around our escape hatch back at the Griffith Observatory.

"Good," said Vlad. "As I was about to say before being interrupted, Lucifer believes this entrance fully protected, but there is a critical point that he has refused to acknowledge."

He paused, almost as if he expected one of us to

supply the answer. None of us was about to say anything, not with the overripe smell of six dead troopers still hanging heavy in the air.

"There is someone amongst us who knows exactly what Hell looks like, and will know what threats we are going to face."

We all turned toward Ned. He was sitting on the ground. More than half of his rodent cape was gone, either through disintegration or consumption. His once cottage cheese-white skin was now bright red and blistering, totally unaccustomed as it was to being exposed to the desert sun.

"Not him," said Vlad.

We turned back. I was beginning to feel like a marionette being jerked back and forth by Vlad's words.

"The Hell that he once visited no longer exists. Hell is a dynamic, changing place. *You'll* know the way, however."

He pointed a finger.

It was pointed straight at me.

I quickly looked behind me, certain that he didn't mean me.

There was no one standing behind me.

I looked back at Vlad.

"I've never been here before," I said, realizing even as I said it that it might not be true. I did not know who or what I really was, so there was absolutely no way that I could say with certainty that I'd never been here before.

"That's true," said Vlad. "You never have been here, and have never stepped foot inside of Hell. But that doesn't matter. When you see it, you will know it."

A small door, an almost nonexistent door, buried far deeper than any door that had yet opened in my head, swung open. It was almost empty, and contained just a few words.

Hell will know you.

That was all, but it was enough. Vlad *was* telling the truth.

He turned toward the door and placed both of his hands on it. "Lucifer, I summon you!"

The ground shook.

Smoke materialized between Vlad and the rest of us. It was tinted sick-green, and spun like a miniature tornado. I knew what shape was about to coalesce from it.

"It's only a dim-witted simulation!" yelled Vlad. "It will have no real knowledge of us, or what we really intend on doing."

"Who calls me?"

The familiar shape kicked at the sand with its hoofs, but the sand did not move. It was a hologram. Now only as tall as a man, Lucifer appeared to stare at us. In one hand he held a pitchfork, just as he had when we had last seen him.

Fudge Pop.

He held it in his other hand. It was melting, the chocolatey stream running across his red hand.

"Who calls me?" he asked with a roar.

My eyes had focused onto the Fudge Pop. I watched it as Lucifer lifted it up and its sagging tip disappeared into his mouth. He bit into it with rotted teeth.

"Death calls on you," said Loki, again sounding as if he were reading from some ancient scripture.

Lucifer dropped the half-eaten Fudge Pop into the sand and my eyeballs, seeming to be under someone else's control, jerked down, continuing to stare at it.

"I must always welcome death," said Lucifer.

The Fudge Pop quickly melted, and a large brown pool appeared to spread across the sand.

"And what is your number?" asked Lucifer.

"We are eight," said Vlad.

"Eight is not the number for death!" screamed Lucifer.

I looked up. Lucifer's eyes had narrowed to burning slits, and a Fudge Pop-stained smile filled his face.

"I must grant entrance to those who bring death, that is my law." He turned his head, seeming to stare at each and every one of us. "But only to those who fall within the range of lucky number seven may enter!

This is my game, and my rules will be observed." He paused, and licked chocolate from his beard. "Do you accept my rules?"

"Yes," said Vlad.

"Not you," said Lucifer. "You cannot speak for the eight. It must be the one who knows me best, the one who brings death."

I felt eight sets of eyes staring at me, seven of them from those around me and one pair from the holographic projection of Lucifer.

Vlad had said that this image wouldn't recognize us. He had lied, and of course I wasn't the least bit surprised.

"Do you accept my rules?" he asked, as he stared directly at me.

"That only seven of us may enter, and that one remains here?" I asked, wanting to make certain that I knew exactly what it was that I'd be agreeing to.

"Yes."

He smiled.

"Who will choose the one that remains behind?" I asked.

Lucifer grinned even wider. "Who do you think?" he asked.

"You," I said.

He nodded.

Somehow that hadn't come as much of a surprise. With a little luck, he would pick Napoleon or Necro Ned. But of course I realized he could just as likely pick Tartan or Joan.

As if she had been reading my mind, Joan poked me in the ribs with her elbow. "You have no choice. It's Lucifer's game, and we must play it if we are to stand any chance at all of rescuing God. To not play means we automatically lose."

I was not so sure. To even enter into his game might mean that we would *all* lose.

Suddenly, nearby, I heard the crack of thunder. Thor had just found another victim. I wondered briefly if that had been real or if Vlad was just trying to force my hand, reminding me of the thousands, or possibly millions, that would die if we did not get inside and reinstate the Speed Limit.

"I agree," I said.

Lucifer's smile grew even wider.

"Excellent," he replied.

His image wavered and he vanished. Even the melted Fudge Pop was gone.

"I decree that Joan of Arc shall stay behind," said an echoing voice that rolled out across the desert.

I started to turn toward Joan, not knowing what I would say to her. To have come so far in her quest to rescue God, and to be denied entrance was simply *too* cruel. Of all of us, she was the only one whom I thought of as saintly, as someone who might actually stand a chance of rescuing *God.*

I never had the chance to say anything.

Again thunder cracked, but this time it was near, far too near. Flame exploded next to me, knocking me off my feet and throwing me to the ground.

"Joan!"

I had screamed her name, knowing that she couldn't possibly hear me. I knew that it was already too late. I stood quickly, my senses sharp, but I knew that there was nothing I could do.

Ashes drifted down. The sand where Joan had stood was molten and bubbling, glowing cherry-red.

I held out my hands, palms up. Ashes fell into them—Joan's ashes.

I walked forward, slowly, looking down and watching my feet carry me. A thick layer of green glass now marked the last spot that Joan had stood upon.

One instant she had been standing by my side, and the next she was gone. And she was gone for no reason at all. She was gone because Lucifer thought that the number seven was lucky while the number eight was unlucky. A psycho's belief in lucky numbers had killed Joan.

"Senseless," I whispered.

Tears ran down my cheeks, but I was not crying.

I was beyond crying.

It was too senseless even to cry over.

And that was what hurt the most. When Anna had died, and when Joe had died, they'd given their lives trying to save others. It was tragic, but at least there had been some balance, some meaning to it. They'd died so others might live. But Joan's death had no meaning, no meaning at all. She'd died only because she wanted to help others, and make something out of a life that was haunted by the ghosts of Tiffany 12's world. She'd simply wanted to do God's work.

"I'm not going in," said a cracking, frightened-sounding voice.

I looked up.

Napoleon was back-stepping.

"I'm not going in," he said again, this time jerking his head up and staring toward the still-closed door.

I slipped into my Enhanced mode, deeper than I had ever slipped before. I *felt* him. Fear was pouring through his Nanomechanoid skin in thick, nauseating waves. Oxygen passing through semipermeable membranes, and micro-pumps deep within his neck carrying it up into his brain. I could feel the nerve trunk that jutted through a small hole in the base of his grapho-titanate skull pulsing with screaming panic signals.

He would be coming inside.

I'd *make* him come inside.

I stepped forward.

"You can't stop me!" he screamed, and began to move faster, his head twitching up and down, first staring at me and then up into the sky, knowing that if he moved too fast Thor would vaporize him.

I ran, knowing that I was moving much faster than the Speed Limit and also knowing that I would *not* get blasted. Back at the Detention Facility, when I had been hurled through the air, Thor had not fired on me. For some unknown reason I was immune to Thor's laser system.

I hoped.

Napoleon's eyes got impossibly large and, tripping over his boots, he fell to the sand.

"I'm not going in!" he screamed.

I covered that fifty yards in what seemed like the blink of an eye.

Thor did *not* fire.

Reaching down, I grabbed Napoleon, who was now trying to burrow into the sand and rock.

"No!" he screamed.

I grabbed him by the throat and lifted him up till he stood, then I pushed him back down until he kneeled in front of me.

"You can't hurt me!" he screamed. "You can't make me go inside!" He suddenly stopped struggling, but I continued to hold his neck tightly. "There's nothing you can do to make me go inside!"

"You," I said, my voice quavering, barely under my control, "are going inside. If it wasn't for you and the rest of these psychos," I screamed as I waved my free hand behind myself, "Joan would still be alive!"

He started to struggle and lifted up a balled fist, getting ready to try to smash me in the face. But before he could move I reached down with my free hand, grabbed his arm, and pulled.

I pulled with everything I had—which was more than I could ever have imagined.

His arm separated at the shoulder.

I threw it into the sky.

With a crack of thunder and a flash of flame, it vanished.

He stopped struggling.

"I can regrow another arm," he said, but the tone of his voice was not quite so arrogant, not quite so commanding. We both knew that he could regrow his arm, but we also both knew that I would not give him the time he needed to do it.

I squeezed against his neck.

"You can't kill me!" he screamed.

"I have no intention of doing that," I said.

I squeezed tighter.

Things inside my hand crackled. Goo ran between my fingers.

"No!" he screamed, trying to stand as his remaining arm started to flail about.

The hand that I had wrapped around his throat suddenly formed a fist, as what was left of his neck squished between my fingers. His body stood, took several steps forward, then collapsed. I held his severed head by the stump of its neck.

"You are going inside," I said calmly. Lifting his head up close to my face, I stared into his eyes. "I'm certain that Lucifer would like to meet you. I'm certain that he wants to repay you for your loyalty."

"No!" Napoleon squeaked, most of his vocal apparatus lying on the ground with his still-spasming body.

"And if," I said, "I see you trying to regrow any part of your body, I'll peel your head like an orange, stripping everything outside of that grapho-titanate skull of yours. Blind and deaf, you'll suffocate without anything to feed you oxygen."

I walked back toward the others, passing them by, not even pausing as I pushed Napoleon's head into Tom's hands. I walked up to the door and to Vlad.

I now knew what I *had* to do.

"You," I said, looking down at him, "I'll deal with after I'm done with God and Lucifer. You're going to get your wish!"

The instant that Joan had been transformed into floating ash I knew that there was only one possible outcome to this nightmare. If *any* of us was to survive, Lucifer, God, and Loki would have to die. Not one of those maniacs could be left alive.

I looked back up at the door, staring into it, trying to stare through it. "I've agreed to your rules, now open the door!" I shouted.

I could hear gears grind somewhere far away.

The door silently swung inward.

I half turned.

"Everyone inside," I said, motioning first to Tartan, who tugged a zombie-like Christ behind her. Tears ran down her face. Just before she entered, she stopped. "I didn't want any of this to happen," she said. "*He* forced me." She looked over her shoulder toward Tom, staring at Napoleon's head. "He forced me," she said in a whisper.

"It *will* be stopped," I told her, then motioned her forward with a nod of my head.

Necro Ned came up next. He was smiling, and there was a bounce in his step. His tongue flicked in and out uncontrollably. "Necro Ned says that we're all going to die," he said cheerfully. He waddled past me.

Necro Ned was probably right.

Reaching out, I grabbed Vlad by his tattered black cape and pushed him toward the doorway. He reached out and grabbed the door's metal jamb, holding himself back. His strength was incredible, almost equal to mine.

"That was the second time that you violated the Speed Limit," he said. His eyes narrowed to slits, and he sucked on his plastic fangs. "Thor should have had no choice, it should have been incapable of *not* firing on you."

I smiled.

"I checked all systems, and it claims that it *did* fire."

I smiled even wider.

"How?" he asked.

"We all have our little secrets," I said, then shoved him square in the back, pushing him forward. His fingers dug narrow trenches in the steel door frame, as he was unable to quite hold on. Once he lost his grip he was propelled through the doorway like something shot from a cannon.

And of course, I had absolutely no idea why I hadn't been flashed to ashes. It was just one more mystery, one more thing that I felt certain I would understand once I reached God and Lucifer.

Tom was last.

He walked slowly up to the door, his hands wrapped tight around Napoleon's mouth, then stopped. Half turning, he looked out toward the desert and then back at me. "Are you prepared to meet yourself?" he asked.

His eyes were alive and focused, radiating intelligence.

"Who *are* you?" I asked.

He cocked his head, as if he had just heard some distant, whispering voice. "Isn't it obvious?" he said. "I'm the unknown, the thing with no name, the thing with no apparent part to play. I'm the wild card, waiting to be thrown down when you need me most."

His eyes glazed over, and he stepped inside.

I followed him in, and the door closed behind me.

I was in Hell.

CHAPTER 13

Memories of Hell

I felt like Alice in Wonderland.

Only a few feet past the door I'd dropped down, falling into some dark, rabbitlike hole. But light had quickly returned and the floor that I'd landed on, which had at first felt like a warm sponge, had hardened and cooled.

"You should know this place," said Vlad.

I looked away, up above me.

A ceiling.

It was covered in cheap-looking acoustic tile, water-stained and peeling. A flickering bank of fluorescent lights hung down, suspended from rusted struts.

I sat on a concrete floor with everyone else standing, surrounding me. I looked between Ned's cottage cheese-textured legs. We were in a hallway with no end, a hallway that seemed to run forever, disappearing only when it appeared to curve below the distant horizon.

I recognized this hallway.

Lockers, graffiti-covered, rusted, and dented, lined the infinite walls, the expanse only broken by an occasional pink metal door. The hallway's concrete floor was strewn with trash: lunch bags, flyers, broken-backed textbooks, Day Glo-painted butcher paper, a few scattered skateboards with cheap steel wheels, pencil stubs, cigarette butts.

This was a High School.

Circa 1970.

My old high school—Claremont High. I shook my

head—this was not my high school. It was the high school from the memories that now filled my head, the memories that had been generated by the Bug. I pushed my hands against the concrete floor and could feel it pulse. It was Nanomechanoid-alive. I could feel things within it rattle and move, almost touch them, talk to them.

The doors within my head didn't open but *things* leaked past them, oozing under door jambs and spurting through keyholes. They were bits and pieces, all telling me about Nanomechanoids, telling me how to *link* with them.

I looked up at Vlad.

"This is Hell?"

He grinned so wide that his plastic fangs almost fell out of his mouth. "Of course, but you must remember that this is a very customized Hell, a Hell inspired by you."

I took a quick glance back down the infinite hallway, and then back at Vlad.

"Why from my memories?"

"Not now, not yet," he said. "Knowledge discovered too soon can be a dangerous thing—a killing thing."

I understood that only too well, and as if to remind me what felt like a smoldering soldering iron was inserted into my left ear and began to be hammered into my brain.

"You don't want to be late for class."

The soldering iron vanished.

"You don't want to be late for class."

It was a static-filled voice that had come from some distant, unseen speakers.

"Those found tardy will be sent to the principal's office."

"Lucifer," said Tartan in a whisper.

It *was* his voice. But it figured—who better to be the principal in a high school located in Hell?

Ting! Ting! Ting!

Metal doors slammed open and the hallway filled with the sounds of screaming kids.

I stood.

Students poured out into the hallway.

Wearing jeans and miniskirts, hightop sneakers and letter-man sweaters, they almost looked like the high school kids that filled my memories.

But there was a difference.

A very important difference.

They were all dead—long dead. They shuffled and lurched forward, with joints frozen and slime and ooze dripping from their eyes and mouths. Plastic-laminated student ID cards had been pressed into their foreheads. A jock in a football uniform shuffled near me. His right arm was no longer attached to his shoulder but was jutting out from the top of the book bag that hung around his neck. He stared at me with blank eyes that were even more vacant than those of a Mushie. It looked as if he was staring right through me, looking at the lockers behind me. His lips twitched. I could see his Adam's apple bob up and down as he swallowed. He smelled even worse than Ned.

"Pomona High," he whispered, as something green and drool-like dribbled from his mouth.

His eyes focused—on me.

"Pomona High!" he shrieked as he spit out his front teeth, which then clattered onto the cement floor. Pomona High had been our arch-rival, the school we always faced at the Homecoming football game.

Students were still streaming out of the classrooms, bouncing from walls and lockers and stumbling into one another. They all stopped in unison, all turning together to face us.

"Pomona High!" they all screamed, the roar loosening acoustic tiles and causing them to crash down in a shower of billowing white dust.

Dropping books and jackets, they all reached out toward us—or at least, those that still had arms. They pointed their shriveled, nail-cracked fingers at us. This was something direct from a cheap fifties zombie movie—something direct from the memories of a fourteen-year-old John Smith.

"Run!" I screamed, realizing even as I said it that there was absolutely no place to run to.

We needed a door—any door.

Bang!

Behind me, metal slammed against metal.

I turned. A door that had not been there a second ago now stood open. There was no time to question it, no time to wonder how it had materialized.

"Inside!" I screamed, grabbing a handful of Tartan's backside and pushing. But before I could move the dead football player wrapped his remaining hand around my neck. I jumped forward and felt something within the jock's hand shatter, then rip. What remained of his hand continued to squeeze at my throat, as the broken fingernails tore into my skin.

I kept pushing Tartan, who pushed at the rest of them while dragging Christ forward by his hair. Stumbling, then suddenly down on all fours, I fell into the open doorway.

Bang!

The door behind me slammed closed.

Turning over, I saw Ned leaning against the door. Rats and flab shuddered as fists pounded against the steel at his back.

"Necro Ned says get the fuck away from this door!" he screamed, as tears ran down his transparent face.

The banging stopped.

"Please be seated."

Still on the floor, I turned around, my butt sliding effortlessly over smooth concrete. I barely even noticed the rotted hand that fell from my neck, hitting the floor with a wet-sounding smack and then sinking into the concrete as if it were quicksand. No, I was too occupied with looking at *her.*

Mrs. Hoffmeyer.

She almost could have been Necro Ned's mother, but she was just a little *too* ugly. Barely four feet tall and possibly as wide, she had a bullet-shaped head, beady red eyes, and a wispy black mustache. She wore a Hawaiian print mumu, granny-type rimless glasses, and a string of black pearls. Her gray hair was wrapped in a tight bun that curled around the top of her pointed head. The stench of dead lilacs poured from her.

It was Old Lady Hoffmeyer, not as she had really looked but as she had really been, deep inside, the way that a fourteen-year-old John Smith had seen her.

This was *my* Hell, a place pulled directly from *my* memories, and then twisted by *my* fears.

Why?

Whap!

She slapped a yardstick against the open palm of her plump hand.

"Pop quiz," she announced.

Smacking the yardstick a few more times she then twirled it like a baton, and reaching out with it took a swat at Tom but missed, and instead hit Napoleon square in the face.

"Yeow!" he screamed as he flew from Tom's hands, arched across the room, and bounced from a wall that was covered with a huge yellowed map of South America. He then hit the top of a desk and stuck there as if he had just smacked against flypaper.

"Be seated!" she screamed as she continued to wave her yardstick. But it was no longer a yardstick but a sword, the blade gleaming in rainbow colors just as Tartan's battle-ax had. She swung it, and it passed through the desk in front of her. Like something from a Saturday morning cartoon, the desk stood untouched, perfectly intact. She puckered her lips, and blew.

The desk creaked and then fell neatly in half.

"Be seated!" she screamed again.

I took the seat nearest me and motioned for the others to also sit. They sat, even Tom. We were in the middle of a nightmare, but one that I was certain, if we were killed in it, we would not simply wake and find ourselves safe and warm in our own beds. This nightmare was real.

She leaned against her desk, which caused her mumu to ride tightly against her massive breasts. She resembled an over-stuffed sausage casing. "Today's quiz will cover last night's reading." She made a few stabs at the air with her sword. "You're all prepared, aren't you?"

No one spoke, but I saw Ned and Tartan nod their heads. Some of their own long-buried, school-days nightmares had forced that Pavlovian response.

"I certainly hope so," she said, smiling and revealing large, block-like dentures. "An understanding of pre-Mayan agricultural mores, as related to Victorian England stained-glass windows and multidimensional black-hole tunneling is crucial to your education and social well-being." She smiled again, and pushed her granny glasses up her greasy, blackhead-infested nose. "You all want to be well-balanced young ladies and gentlemen, ready to face the challenges of the *real* world, don't you?" she asked.

No one said anything. Only Ned nodded.

"Then begin," she said. "You have two minutes."

A large clock, featuring at least a half-dozen hands, flowed up through the chalkboard in front of us. All the hands spun frantically, most in the wrong direction.

My hands had been flat against the top of my desk, when suddenly I jerked them off. The surface had been cool and solid, and indented and chipped where initials had been carved into it—but now it squirmed. It began to undulate, and turned to flowing plastic. As I watched, a thick sheaf of papers floated up through the wood-grained surface just as the clock had flowed out through the chalkboard. Reaching forward, I picked up the thick pile of papers and fanned them like a deck of cards. The last page was numbered 163.

"A minute and a half remaining," said Mrs. Hoffmeyer.

This entire scene was something that could have been pulled from every high-schooler's worst nightmare. I glanced quickly around the classroom.

Napoleon sat on the edge of his desk top, with a bright yellow Number Two pencil sticking out of his mouth. He spit it out to the floor, but as I watched it wiggled and began to crawl forward. It coiled around one of the desk's legs and then began to work its way back up toward Napoleon.

Ned frantically scribbled across the top sheet of his papers, his head jerking up and down as he kept glancing at the clock. His black tongue quickly darted out and smacked the edge of the first paper, just like a frog hitting a fly, and then turned the page back. He started scribbling on the second page.

Everyone else just sat, looking at Mrs. Hoffmeyer and watching the flashing tip of her sword as she swung it in front of herself, shredding an invisible student.

In my hand.

I looked down. It had wrapped itself around my index finger. Yellow, and with no eraser left, it was a chewed and battered-looking Number Two pencil. Its dull lead tip swayed back and forth, straining toward the paper.

I looked back up.

"Eyes on your paper, mister!" shrieked Mrs. Hoffmeyer.

Ancient and deeply ingrained reflexes snapped my head forward. The dense print that covered the first page of the pop quiz was unintelligible, as if it were written in out-of-focus Sanskrit.

"Fifteen seconds!"

Ignoring the paper full of squirming letters, I stared at the pencil. I could feel the Nanomechanoids within it buzz, feel them burn energy, and even sense the Mastermechanoids direct and guide the small Nanomechanoid subunits. Data bits made up of highs and lows flowed by, carried by single electrons that shuttled from atom to atom.

Tears ran down my face, the muscles in my stomach twitched, and I could feel blood drip from my nose. It splattered against the quiz paper. But all that was a small price to pay, an insignificant price—as compared to the value of what had just coalesced in my head.

I linked.

I reached into the pencil, enveloping the Mastermechanoid with my own thoughts, and blocked its communication links. I didn't know how I did it. It was like breathing or blinking. The nerve endings in my fingers and hands pulsed, sending electrical signals into the pencil.

Let go! I commanded, shouting the order deep within my brain.

The pencil fell from my hand, bounced from the desk top, and hit the floor with a wet, sticky sound. It was quickly reduced to a yellow puddle that seeped into the concrete.

"Pencils down!"

I looked up. Mrs. Hoffmeyer was staring at us like a hawk looking for a scurrying mouse. Her eyes suddenly narrowed to slits, and her nostrils flared.

"Neddy!" she screamed.

We all turned to look at Ned. He was still frantically scribbling.

"Neddy!" She walked forward, her sword leading the way.

I stood, knocking my desk over and sending papers flying.

Ned finally looked up.

Jumping over my toppled desk and pushing another aside, I scrambled forward.

The floor beneath me turned to ice. I slipped and slid across the floor, stopping only when I crashed into the classroom's far wall.

"I said pencils down, mister!"

I stood.

Mrs. Hoffmeyer's back was to me and her sword was raised high above her head. She completely blocked my view of Ned and his desk.

I had time to take just a single step forward and reach out for her pudgy hand.

But I couldn't reach her in time.

Mrs. Hoffmeyer slashed down and then, as if reloading for a second swipe, raised her hand and sword once again high over her head. She started to swing down for a second time.

The sword didn't move.

I had my hand tightly wrapped around her wrist. I pulled her toward me. Her plastic-soled shoes squealed and squeaked as I dragged her across the floor. I looked down. She wore scuffed and worn brown-leather wingtips. The stitching was gone at both toes and I could see plaid socks sticking out. I looked back up quickly, trying to get that image of disintegrating wingtips out of my head.

I looked at Ned.

He sat at his desk, with his head still down and pencil still in hand. He did not move. A red seam neatly bisected his skull, ran down his plastic face, and then disappeared beneath what was left of his rodent cape.

"Necro Ned says," he began in a wet-sounding whisper and then collapsed, literally splitting in half. He hit the floor, making two blubbery piles. Neatly chopped-in-half papers fluttered over him, many being quickly carried away in a growing pool of blood.

As I held on to her wrist, she turned toward me. I looked down at her, and she looked up at me. *"He* doesn't want you dead. Not yet," she said with a hiss. "But he wouldn't mind if you were missing a few limbs."

He—Lucifer.

Behind her I could see Tartan lunging forward, and behind her I could see Tom's smiling face. He was smiling as serenely as if what he had just witnessed had never even happened.

Time slowed, just as it had on the bridge at the Detention Facility.

I felt her arm slowly come down. I could hear the screams of the Mastermechanoids within her, shouting commands, routing data, dumping all the power at their disposal into that descending arm.

The blade swept down, just missing my left ear and then heading for my shoulder.

I silently talked, forcing the words through the nerves in my fingertips. And the Mastermechanoids listened. They had no choice, because I knew their secret access codes.

I knew the Mastermechanoid access codes.

When they had originally been built the designer

had left in a hidden trapdoor, something that only he could access in case of an emergency. It was something that only Colin Wood could access—something that *I* could suddenly access. That all-too-familiar, molten hot-steel spike was once again poking through my right eye. My vision blurred, but I could just make out the rainbow-colored blade as it scraped against the side of my jaw.

I talked to the Mastermechanoids.

They listened.

"Urmph!" gurgled Mrs. Hoffmeyer.

She twitched, and suddenly all resistance vanished in her arm. I pushed back, and her forearm bent back over itself at an impossible angle. The sword now hung over *her* head. On my command, the key bonds that had held together what passed for bones in her massive body had been severed.

I let go of her wrist.

She fell, and as she fell the sword dropped from her now rubbery fingers.

She hit the floor and bounced. Her plump body wiggled beneath the mumu, making her look like a gigantic, blood-gorged leech. The sword fell on top of her, the Nanomechanoid-perfect blade slicing her from left shoulder to right hip as if she were a pat of warm butter. White pussing goo exploded out.

Bang!

The walls of the classroom shuddered.

Bang!

Metal screamed, then tore.

Bang!

I turned toward the noise, toward the classroom's door.

It had been crushed in, with the imprint of a giant fist showing through the thick steel.

"Follow me!" I shouted, running back to the wall that only an instant before I had slid into. Reaching forward I placed both of my hands, palms flat, against it.

The Nanomechanoids within it hummed.

Bang!

Something flew by the side of my head. A twisted shard of metal was suddenly embedded in the wall, just above my head. Quickly glancing behind myself I saw a hairy, callused, knuckled fist pull itself out from a rip in the metal door. That fist had been at least a foot across.

I found the Mastermechanoids.

Turning back, I stared at the wall.

Bang!

I imagined a door, made of oak and stained glass, complete with a brass door-knocker. The wall shimmered, its color turning dark, and its texture metamorphosing to that of polished wood.

Bang!

I glanced quickly around once more. The door's top hinge was sprung and the bottom one twisted. Fatigued metal whined.

I turned back and a door stood before me, just as I had imagined it, just as I had demanded the Nanomechanoids build it. It even had the same well-endowed knocker as the front door of the Griffith Observatory. I pushed the door open. Beyond it was a dark corridor—another rabbit hole.

"In!"

Reaching behind me, I grabbed the first thing I could. I tossed Vlad through, sending him flying as not even Dracula had ever flown. The others quickly got the idea, Tartan again tugging at the nearly comatose Christ.

The classroom's door crashed in and the bottom hinge splintered, sending shrapnel flying across the room.

"Tom!" I screamed.

He was standing a desk-length away from me. Chaos and destruction were going on all around him, but he was acting totally indifferent to it.

"Inside!" I screamed again, reaching for him, grabbing his left hand, and tugging him toward me.

He smiled, as if he had just heard the punch line of some only mildly funny joke. "If you insist," he said, and picking up Napoleon by the hair walked past me, sauntering toward the dark hallway.

Pushing and shoving him forward, I went in after him, grabbing the edge of the door and getting ready to slam it shut. I took one last look back behind me.

The nearly pulverized metal door fell to the floor. Standing behind it, with his massive hands still clenched into fists, stood a *miniaturized* Lucifer, less than two feet tall. He was more arms and fists than anything else.

He grinned, and his eyes glowed like twin flashlights.

"Enjoy your shopping!" he screamed, throwing back his head and laughing. "I think it's time you finally bought those new shoes!"

The oak door leapt from my fingers and slammed itself shut.

We all stood at the exit of the dark hallway, staring out into total and complete chaos.

"It's my birthday," said Christ in a whisper. Somewhere, and somehow, he had lost his gag.

"Christmas," said Tartan. She kept a tight hold on the rope that held Christ's hands together.

She was right.

It was Christmas, Southern California-style, complete with plastic snow, cellophane icicles, and the jazzed up sounds of "The Twelve Days of Christmas" blaring above the buzz and babble of the crowd.

A mall.

Men, women, and children filled the place. They all carried packages, wore white Santa Claus beards, and licked frozen yogurt bars, and as I looked down at their feet I could see that they all wore decayed-looking brown leather wingtips. I glanced right-left-right. The mall appeared to be of infinite length. All I could see were shoe stores and yogurt emporiums. There was nothing else.

Just like the high school, this was something else from the memories that filled my head, but having been made real by the Nanomechanoids it had become twisted and bent.

"Where do we go?" asked Tartan.

Before I could even try to answer, the crowd that swarmed in front of us came to a halt, each of them bumping into the backside of the one in front of them. Directly in front of us they parted, as if some invisible hand had swept them aside.

A small cardboard sign stood in the middle of the mall floor: MAKE YOUR CHRISTMAS WISH. The sign was adorned with a plastic-looking wreath, and little aluminum foil-wrapped chocolate Santas.

I read it aloud. "I have a wish!" screamed Christ, suddenly breaking free of Tartan. He ran out into the open floor space, knocked over the sign, and, turning left, disappeared.

"No!" I shouted.

But it was already too late. Tartan was already after him, with Vlad chasing after her. As he ran he unfurled his cape, which almost made it appear as if he were actually flying.

I felt a hand on my shoulder and turned around.

It was Tom.

"You have to flow with this, and understand the lessons that Lucifer is teaching you. He plays a dangerous game. He is trying to bring back your forgotten memories, hoping that the Quad Access Codes will resurface before you recall other memories—memories that could kill *him.*"

Kill him.

How could *my* memories kill *him*?

"You've *got* to kill him," said Napoleon from the crook of Tom's left arm.

This was too strange, too insane.

I could feel my eyeballs suddenly bulge as pressure within my brain seemed to build. I ignored it, just as I was trying to ignore everything else.

I pushed at Tom. "Follow them."

I then ran after him, not knowing how I would do it but certain that if *I* didn't put an end to this insanity

the rest of them would be killed. Just like Joan and Ned. Just like Anna and Joe. That much I did know.
It was a fact.

This scene was the most insane of all.
Santa's workshop.
Every mall at Christmastime used to have one. Usually built of plywood and cotton, it would have kids in elf suits, cardboard reindeer, and a nineteen-year-old bimbo version of Mrs. Claus in a red-and-white miniskirt to keep Dad busy while Santa brainwashed the kids with visions of hundred-dollar toys, guaranteed to self-destruct long before the batteries ever wore out. I would have sold my soul for a taut and tanned Mrs. Claus passing out discount coupons to the mall's Pretzel Parlor.
But none of that was to be found in this mall.
What I now faced was past being simply insane.
It was perverted.
Children stood in a long line, all wearing their Santa Claus beards and all being kept orderly and quiet by little elves with snakelike red tails that held on to little golden ropes that were tied around the children's throats. Each elf carried a pitchfork, which it would jab into the child at the end of its rope to keep them moving along the line.
This was Christmas—Hell-style.
On the throne that should have been filled to overflowing with a jelly-bellied Santa sat Satan. And to his left, far above him, locked away in a cage that hung from the mall ceiling, was God. He was unconscious, and hung against the bars. His robe was in tatters. His halo looked tarnished and was full of nicks and scratches.
We stood silently, motionlessly, not knowing what to expect. Tartan had a choke-hold on Christ, but he still reached out his shaking hands toward God. His eyes were wild and animal-like. He wanted God—badly.
"I'll be with you in just a moment!" bellowed Lu-

cifer, looking over at us. "But first I have to hear this sweet little child's Christmas wish."

"This sweet little child" sat perched in his lap. Wearing a lacy pink party dress, and with her Santa beard having fallen off so that it hung around her neck, she tugged on Lucifer's pointed beard, pulling his head down.

She whispered into his ear.

Lucifer smiled, then sat back up.

"Of course, my dear," he said, "Santa can grant your Christmas wish." He pointed a talon-tipped finger out into the crowd. "This, good mother, is the Christmas wish of your sweet darling."

A bolt of lightning erupted from Lucifer's fingertip, flashing into the crowd. Something exploded and a column of oily fire erupted, scorching the ceiling of the mall. Something black, that looked like charcoal, rose up on the plume of fire, crashed into the ceiling, and then rained back down like black snow. A pair of smoking wingtips remained embedded in the soot-stained ceiling.

"Thank you," the little girl said sweetly.

Lucifer looked down at her, his red eyes seeming to fill with compassion, and then reached down and grabbed each of her legs.

He pulled.

"No!" screamed Tartan, starting to run forward.

I wrapped a hand around her waist and tugged her back.

The little girl exploded in a burst of confetti, like an overstuffed piñata. But as the confetti flitted through the air, each paper shred transformed itself into a nearly translucent droplet of blood.

Lucifer dropped her body into the cotton snow around his throne, where it sank and disappeared.

She'd been a Nanomechanoid construct. They all were. All of Hell was a Nanomechanoid-generated nightmare.

Lucifer turned and looked at us, but then kept turning.

"Stop!" he screamed, pointing with the same finger

that only an instant before had carbonized the little girl's mother.

He pointed at Christ, who had slipped away from Tartan.

Christ now hung from the bottom of God's cage, pulling himself up the bars.

"Stop!" Lucifer screamed once again. He stood.

Christ did not stop, and now dangled from the side of the cage, holding on one-handed, as he reached in with his other hand trying to grab God's throat. Blood ran down his arms from where his wrists were torn by what little remained of the frayed rope that *had* kept his hands tied together.

A bolt of lightning flashed from Lucifer's hand, crashing into Christ and vaporizing his feet. Blood poured from his ankle stumps. Somehow, Christ still clung to the bars—even continued to pull himself up.

I was already running toward Lucifer, having no idea what I would do when I got to him. All I knew was that I had to stop him, had to do whatever it took to stop him.

He turned toward me.

"Give me the codes!" he screamed.

I ran into him, my momentum knocking both of us down, carrying us into the Santa throne, toppling it over, and then sending us sliding across a plastic ice pond.

My hands were wrapped around his throat.

He stood, carrying me up with him.

Something now familiar hummed beneath my hands.

"No!" he bellowed, as his eyes grew impossibly large and smoldering spit ran from the corners of his mouth.

I searched for the Mastermechanoids.

"I'll kill him!" he screamed.

He jerked both of us around and raised his left hand.

I felt the Nanomechanoids, just as I had felt them in Mrs. Hoffmeyer, but this time I was not reaching for the bonds that held bone together, but those that held cells.

Bang!

His body shook, and I could feel the power drain out of him. He'd just discharged a tremendous electrical voltage. His body jerked, and just out of the corner of my vision I could see Christ pressed into the bars of God's cage. A dark, smoking hole was punched through his back.

I sent the signal through my hands. I ordered the Mastermechanoids to sever the bonds that held each cell in place. And that was all it took. I was no longer holding on to a throat but to jelly. Lucifer collapsed, oozing to the floor.

Running back, with slime dripping down me, I tried to reach Christ, but Tartan was ahead of me, already tugging on his ankle stumps, getting herself covered with blood. She couldn't pull him down. He appeared to be *welded* to the bars of God's cage.

He should have been dead.

But he wasn't.

"Die, you old fucker!" screamed Christ as he wrapped his arms around God's throat, no longer needing those hands to keep him from falling as his own chest was welded to the cage and holding him up. "You took her from me!"

"Stop!" I screamed. "He's not real! He never was! It's just a construct being externally controlled!"

I knew that, having sensed the mind that had controlled Lucifer, having felt it just as he had disintegrated in my hands. Lucifer and God were both puppets being controlled by something hidden and unseen.

But Christ either couldn't or didn't want to hear me. He continued to grab God's throat, banging the old man's head against the inside of the cage.

I leaned down to the floor, feeling the Nanomechanoids within it, feeling *all* of them.

Doors opened.

I could feel blood suddenly leaking from the corners of my eyes and the red, hot tears streaking my face.

I knew Hell from the inside out; knew it, and could control it. All the secret codes, everything that was needed to manipulate and build it, were now within

my head. But of course they had *always* been in my head, just hidden from me.
God reached out and wrapped his own hands around Christ's head.
"Welcome home, son!" he screamed.
I linked, feeling the hum of the world around me.
God pressed his hands together.
Christ's head split like an overripe melon.
I stood, everything that was Hell now flowing through me.
Tartan collapsed to the floor with what was left of Christ on top of her.
Tom stood next to me. His face was blank and expressionless.
"You can never *really* hurt us!" screamed God, as he reached his bloodstained hands through the bars, out toward me.
Everything went gray, and then black, and I felt myself falling through the rubbery floor.
I had deactivated Hell.

CHAPTER 14

Behind the Mask

Something milky-white covered my open eyes.

I blinked. Glass shattered.

I kicked. Glass splintered.

I stood. Glass rained down onto the flagstone floor.

Tom stood to my left, brushing white shards of glass from his shoulders. Beyond him Tartan kneeled, pulling large white strips from her arms. And to my right sat a wobbling white lump. As it wiggled back and forth a crack appeared in it, running down its center.

"Get me out of here!" said Napoleon in commanding tones.

Tom walked around me and, bending down, picked up the lump of white glass, then banged it several times against the stone floor. He cracked it open, as if it were some sort of giant, mutant hard-boiled egg.

"Where are we?" demanded Napoleon. Tom dropped him to the floor, where he bounced several times before coming to a rest. A skullcap of glass was still stuck to the top of his head. He looked like a jack-o'lantern about a week after Halloween, all shriveled up and caved in.

No one answered him.

We stood in a cathedral, a cathedral that I had stood in once long ago. There was no mistaking the stained-glass windows and the vaulted stone ceilings that rose more than a hundred feet above us. We were in Notre Dame. Bending down, I pressed the palms of my hands to the floor. I felt cold and dead stone. This was no Nanomechanoid-generated fantasy. This cathedral was built of stone and wood, cement and glass—it really existed. I stood.

"Greetings," said an echoing voice that came from the far end of the cathedral.

It was Vlad. He stood where the main cathedral altar should have been. But there was no longer an altar. In its place were three thrones, the center one higher than the two that flanked it. In each one was seated a figure.

Vlad motioned to us with a wave of his cape.

I walked forward with Tartan close by my right side, who was continually glancing from Vlad to Napoleon's head and then back again. Tom picked up Napoleon's head and followed behind me.

"This is it," said Napoleon from behind me, trying to whisper but his voice still echoing from the cathedral walls. "This is where the true Lucifer hides. If you can kill him here, God will live forever."

I ignored him and continued to walk forward.

In the throne on the left sat God, his halo burning bright, his white robe immaculate, and his creased white face serene. His eyes were closed. His chest slowly rose and fell. He was asleep.

In the throne on the right sat Lucifer. Like God he appeared to be asleep, for his eyes also were closed, his chest slowly rising and falling. But unlike God there was no serenity on his face. His pitchfork was clenched in both hands, and the tendons in his arms were flexed. He suddenly squirmed on his throne and his lips twitched. It looked as though he was having a nightmare.

In the center throne, which was made of what looked like a solid block of gold and adorned with rubies the size of my fist, sat an old man. Wearing a one-piece blue jumpsuit with bunny slippers, he also slept. His bald head was wrapped in a crown of pulsing fibers that draped down over the back of his shoulders and disappeared behind his throne.

In his right hand, with fingers that were twisted by arthritis and splotched with liver spots, he clutched what looked like a chocolate-stained Fudge Pop stick.

I tried to ignore the pain that suddenly lanced

through my head, and forced myself to slow my breathing. We stopped. Between us and the thrones was a nearly transparent glass-like Shield, similar to what Tartan had used to protect the observatory, but this one looked like gray-smoked glass.

Tartan took several steps in front of me, stopping only when she was within arm's reach of the Shield. She looked up at the old man.

"No one can sit higher than God," she said in a whisper.

"Colin Wood can," answered Vlad.

Colin Wood?

My vision momentarily blurred, and my knees almost buckled. I reached inside of myself for that hidden reserve of strength that I had called upon so many times before. My knees locked, and my vision cleared.

Blood trickled down from my nose.

Who am I? The words whispered themselves in my head.

"God is Lord!" screamed Napoleon, his voice echoing throughout the cathedral.

Tartan dropped to her knees, bowing her head.

Vlad smiled. His plastic fangs were no longer plastic but bright, shiny ivory. "Let me explain," he said.

"There's nothing to explain!" screamed Napoleon.

Vlad waved his arm. "I don't wish to be interrupted."

I could hear Napoleon mumble, but heard nothing that resembled words. I turned and looked at him. His head had rolled over and was lying on its right ear. Where his mouth had been there was now only an unbroken patch of yellow-tinted skin. Vlad had *total* Nanomechanoid control.

Vlad pointed over his shoulder and toward the thrones. "There is no God, and there is no Lucifer. They are figments of that insane old man's imagination." The hate in Vlad's voice was pure and unrefined.

Was that the presence I had felt when Lucifer dissolved in my hands? Was that old man responsible for all this insanity?

"No!"

Tartan was on her feet, running toward Vlad.

She got within several feet of him when lightning erupted from his glasses, the blue bolts striking her in the head. She crumpled to the floor, but as she lay there I could see her chest slowly rise and fall.

I didn't move. Short of getting myself killed, there was absolutely nothing I could do.

Vlad turned back toward the thrones as if nothing had happened. "My esteemed creator, the great Dr. Colin Wood, father of the Nanomechanoid, had drifted into insanity long before the Bug ever ate into his diseased brain."

My entire body convulsed, and my chattering teeth bit into my tongue.

I was Colin Wood.

Not this old man.

"He was split—actually becoming two people," said Vlad. "The first was the Colin Wood who gave billions in an attempt to educate Dolers and in aid to the Fourth-Worlders, whose economy had been destroyed by his Nanomechanoid revolution when cheap labor became a worthless commodity. The second was the Colin Wood who worshiped the technology he'd created, charting new markets and earmarking technologies ripe for Nanomechanoid intervention. These two personas were diametrically opposed. His personality fractured long before the Bug added its finishing touches."

I stared up at the old man. His internal, once personal battle had now become externalized, and was being fought across the entire Los Angeles Quad in the guise of God and Lucifer.

Tom had known.

He had told me that God and Lucifer were two faces of the same being—two faces of this old man.

Vlad turned toward us.

"And that, Cardinal Napoleon Bonaparte, is what you have been serving and praying to for the last four years. Your God is nothing more than the delusion of an insane old man."

Napoleon twitched and wiggled, but Tom held on to him. Tears ran down his yellowed cheeks.

"There is your God!" screamed Vlad, pointing at the central throne. "He's an old man in bunny slippers, who sits on a gold throne, dreams of good and evil, and occasionally wakes to wander back into a cubbyhole behind that Shield to eat Fudge Pops and squat on a toilet."

Napoleon's eyes closed, but tears continued to run down his face.

I slid my right foot forward. If I could get to Vlad while his attention was focused on Napoleon I might be able to do something—perhaps.

Vlad turned.

"Don't bother," he said, as he passed a hand in front of himself. "This is just a construct, a device that I operate through, just like the Lucifer that you killed earlier. I can generate an infinite number of them. The only way that you can hope to *really* destroy me is to dispose of that old man and take his place."

"You no longer sound *quite* so eager to die," I said.

"But I am," he answered. "It's just that the only way to kill me is from the inside." He pointed again toward the old man. "The one who controls me is the only one that can kill me." Again he smiled. "And I so richly deserve to die."

He was as crazy as the rest of them, possibly even more so. I couldn't really be sure of his desires or motivations, but the one thing that I *was* certain of was that he had *no* intention of dying. He wanted something else, something that I didn't yet understand.

"I was created by him," said Vlad, as he pointed behind himself and at the central throne. "My values are his. I want control, I want power. I manipulate and lie, kill and cheat, all for the greater good. The end always justifies the means."

Who was that old man?

Who was I?

Vlad again pointed toward the throne. "He is responsible for the dropping of the Speed Limit, and for the millions that have already been killed.'' He smiled. ''He's the undisputed master of death, and compared to him I'm just an amateur.'' He smiled, and his ivory fangs glistened. ''But I'm learning.'' He stepped up to the Shield and ran a finger across it. ''That old man has no knowledge of what's transpired these past several days. Locked away in his own fantasy world, he doesn't even know that *you* exist.'' He turned and stared at me. ''I've orchestrated everything. I've been responsible for each and every death that you've witnessed. I sent the spaceman to greet you at Wood Labs, knowing that encounter would start the waking process of your old memories. I talked to Joan by using the links that had been installed in her brain during her Tiffany 12 existence, making certain that you would be at Hood's cave when Napoleon arrived. And of course, disguised as God, I instructed Napoleon, who in turn commanded his sister.''

I looked over at Tartan. She was still unconscious, but still breathing. So Loki had been the real puppeteer behind everything—absolutely everything.

''I created the images of God and Lucifer at the Crystal Lake Casino,'' he said. ''I destroyed both Napoleon's and Lucifer's forces. I reached into Joe's head and fried his synapses. I killed Ned and Christ and smoked that bitch Lizzie.'' He pulled off his sunglasses and hurled them to the floor, where they shattered as if made of crystal.

He had no eyes, not even eye sockets.

His forehead and cheeks flowed smoothly into one another.

''I built Hell as mirrored by *your* mind, to help you remember, to reacquaint you with your powers, and to let you see those hidden places deep within you.'' He looked up, with his eyeless face, toward the cathedral ceiling. ''I vaporized Joan!''

By some miracle, I managed to hold myself back.

''But I'm tainted by him!'' screamed Vlad, pointing over his shoulder. ''He should not control the Los Angeles Quad, nor should I. The only real difference between us is that there is a logic in my core of being that recognizes this. I know that I have been contaminated. I know that I must cease to exist. And you are the instrument that will perform all this. All these people have died to bring you to this place, at this time, so that the weight of their wasted lives will press down on you. I want you to feel the futility of everything that has happened, the utter waste and insanity of all that's occurred. I want you to feel death all around you.''

I felt it. I couldn't help but feel it. ''Why?''

''Because only in that frame of mind can you come up with the proper codes. I know your mind, and I know that the codes buried deep within it can only be summoned once you know who you really are, and when that knowledge is coupled with the feelings generated by all the senseless death around you.''

''I don't know any damn codes!'' I screamed. ''I can't access the Quad Walls.''

''Of course,'' said Vlad. ''*No one* can access the Quad Walls. There are no codes for that, since the Walls can *never* be brought down. The Quad Wall access codes are a Holy Grail, something I dreamed up as a tool to further manipulate the most greedy amongst you, something that never really existed. Erection of the Walls was originally thought of as a final, failsafe device. It was to be used only if it was determined that man could *never* live in a global community. The Bug was that final proof. The Quad Walls guarantee that some small slice of humanity will survive, no matter what form of self-destruction and insanity ultimately infects mankind.''

No Quad Wall access codes.

I almost dropped to the floor, but kept my knees locked. The codes that everyone had been fighting and dying for didn't even exist. ''Then what codes are you talking about?'' I asked.

Vlad patted the Shield that stood behind him. ''The code is to access *this* Shield. It can be opened only with a combination of two things.'' He held up two fingers. ''The first is that you must speak the code words. *I* know the words, but programming will not permit me to tell *you* them. Colin Wood would never let anyone or anything that could even remotely harm him have access to those codes. He was a paranoid old man.''

It looked like his paranoia was justified.

Or was it *my* paranoia?

''And secondly,'' said Vlad, ''the Shield will scan the code-giver's mind, and when it does it must find some very special, very specific memories.''

''Memories?'' I asked.

''It will only recognize *Colin Wood.''*

''But you said that *he* was Colin Wood.'' I pointed at the old man.

''He is.''

I just looked at him stupidly.

Then who was I?

''You can't understand this until you know what you really are, and what you were before the Bug. The odds of your surviving that knowledge are slim, but these past days have brought you closer to it, hopefully having let you see enough of the truth so that when you finally see all of it, it might not kill you.''

Knowledge kills.

He waved his arm.

''Relive this,'' he said.

I fell forward, blackness eating me before I hit the floor.

A door opened, and a memory flowed out.

''Next, Loki,'' said a raspy voice.

I opened my eyes.

A conference room was spread out before me. A hundred men and women sat around a table of green glass. Constructs in tailed tuxedos passed out drinks and drugs. The carpet beneath my feet was plush, and the room reeked of fear.

I both was and was not here.

This was a memory from my past—my *real* past.

''Implementation of the John Smith Project,'' said a childish-sounding voice that echoed from the oak-paneled walls. I knew that voice. It was the voice of Loki—the voice of Vlad.

An old man wearing a faded pink jumpsuit stood. Bald and wrinkled, he had a chocolate stain around his mouth. A melting Fudge Pop dripped over his right hand.

"God created man in His image," said the old man, as he peered at those around the table, "and then I created John Smith in my image."

A hundred heads nodded in unison.

"Report, Dr. Deckwhiler," said the old man, who then sat back down. He licked at the melted ice cream that ran down his arm.

A second man stood—Deckwhiler. He sweated. His pulse raced. His pupils were dilated in a fear response. His body wanted to run, or to strike out. But he stood still, gently swaying. He was an excellent actor.

"Get on with it," snapped the old man.

"Certainly, Dr. Wood," said the man.

Things twisted in my head and my eyeballs burned. *Who am I?*

"The Fourth World contains eighty-three percent of the earth's land mass, and some eighty percent of its population—eight and a half billion people." He paused, clearing his throat. His blood pressure must have been dangerously high. I could see the veins in his forehead throb.

"Since the introduction of the Nanomechanoid technology sixteen years ago, the Fourth World's contribution to the world's gross national product has dropped from thirty-seven to less than six percent. They have no technology base, and no sophisticated weapons systems. What limited military capability they do possess they use upon one another, not being bold enough to actually threaten First-Worlders. . . ."

Tension increased. Breaths were held.

"Until last year," said Deckwhiler. "On a single day, three million skilled workers of the Diapang conglomerate of United Korea were attacked by a synthetic viroid. It was designed to sleep dormant within them, being passed through the conglomerate's air-handling systems. The viroid in its pre-clocked mode was totally harmless, and could not even survive outside of the conglomerate's Seoul complex. But on December 13, 2071 a clocked gene within the viroid was activated, altering its structure. Within twenty-four hours there were three million casualties. Fatalities ran at approximately ninety percent. The bulk of the three hundred thousand survivors were little more than mental vegetables, while a small fraction of *those* survivors retained their thinking abilities but suffered from *severe* personality disorders.''

The hundred were silent. They barely breathed.

''First-World nations were informed through diplomatic channels that unless food and economic aid was radically increased to the Fourth World, this would happen again.'' Deckwhiler paused for several seconds. ''On a much larger scale.''

''Holding us goddamned hostage, because we were willing to get off our asses, use the brains that God had given us, and build a better life for ourselves,'' said Dr. Wood. A construct brought him another Fudge Pop.

''What Dr. Wood says is quite correct,'' said Deckwhiler. ''For the past year *our* economies have been drained, and strained to the breaking point, because of the massive amounts of aid we have poured into the Fourth World. We cannot continue to support them, and we certainly cannot give them their *own* Nanomechanoid technologies—they would not know how to wisely manage them.''

Everyone nodded.

''However, we have arrived at a new, much more economically satisfactory solution.'' He paused for dramatic effect. ''The John Smith Project.'' Again he paused. Tension in the room rose. ''Please enter, Mr. Smith.''

This wasn't really happening.

It was just a memory.

I walked in from the conference room's anteroom. My head pounded and my pulse raced. I was just barely able to control the tremors in my hands. I walked around the table and stood behind Dr. Wood.

Dr. Wood.

I was not Colin Wood.

And yet I was.

"In my image," said the old man in a cackle.

"We have attempted conventional forms of infiltration in the Fourth-World strongholds where they are creating their clocked viroids, but until now we have had only limited success. What we required was a method to take them over, to totally control them ourselves, without the Fourth-Worlders even realizing that this had happened."

Again everyone nodded.

"The solution was mine!" shouted Dr. Wood, pointing his finger at those around the table. "It took the old man to figure it out!"

Several of those around the table—the most frightened—clapped.

"The First World will be eternally in your debt," said Deckwhiler, smiling with a forced grin. "For quite some time we've had the ability to create Nanomechanoid constructs, some quite complex, able to mimic humans. We attempted to infiltrate using those."

There was a not-so-quiet murmuring that engulfed the table.

Deckwhiler nodded. "Yes, that was not successful. Personnel and government officials in the Fourth World are all now routinely scanned. It is a rather trivial matter to detect the operation of Nanomechanoids. Something much more sophisticated was needed."

All eyes turned to me.

"This had been a back-burner project for several years in the Covert Operations section at the Wood Research Labs in Malibu. . . ."

Molten lead was injected directly into the base of my brain. I felt synapses sizzle.

"As a result of the Diapang conglomerate incident, the pace of that project was radically accelerated. What was being worked on was a new type of construct, one much more sophisticated than anything ever devised, one that would appear to be totally human even to the most sensitive scanning equipment.''

Lights dimmed, and something coalesced over the table.

A body.

It was my body. Hundreds of red flashing dots pulsed within it.

''In a normal construct, hundreds of Mastermechanoids are used as specialized intelligence centers, controlling everything from the most mechanical of activities, such as moving joints or blinking eyes, to the most biochemical, such as converting oxygen and proteins to usable fuels. It is these Mastermechanoids that are so easily detectable.''

The red flashing dots vanished. In their place the entire head now pulsed a bright orange.

''The aim of this project was to enable direct brain control of the construct without having to go through the Mastermechanoid interface. We were successful.''

Eyes stared at me.

At me.

''But there is much more to this new class of constructs that we call the John Smith class than simply the direct brain control of Nanomechanoids. This construct operates almost exclusively in the dormant phase, so that even the Nanomechanoid operation cannot be detected. In this mode it looks like a human, from the grossest of anatomical details all the way down to the genetic, subcellular level. It *is* human. But when needed, the brain can turn on any or all of the dormant Nanomechanoids, which in turn allows the John Smith construct to manipulate its physical self—it has full Shifter capabilities—so that it can subvert and control the Nanomechanoids inside as well as *outside* of itself.''

All around the room there was a rapid intake of breath. The fear level rose again.

The man nodded. ''Yes, on the surface, it would appear far too dangerous to couple Shifter abilities with a self-aware brain. Under normal circumstances this never would have been contemplated.'' Deckwhiler smiled a genuine, warm smile. ''These are not normal circumstances.''

The fear level continued to rise.

''Each John Smith construct has the Net database stored directly within it, updated weekly. They can all read Ident codes direct, then access the information stored within their memories.''

An image filled my head. I saw a blond man with pale, empty eyes sitting on a rock in the middle of a white-watered stream. I stared into his hand. The image vanished.

Several people removed their hands from the tabletop, hiding them in their laps.

''As initially manufactured the John Smith class comes in a generic, sexless form. Body specifics are dictated by a sample of host DNA. Once it has analyzed the DNA it activates the Nanomechanoids, begins operation in the Shifter mode, and becomes the person that is represented by that DNA. Once physical identity has been established, it then accesses memory files that are stored on that person and then assumes *their* personality as their own.''

I scanned my DNA.

I found myself reading the DNA of Colin Wood.

''However, if the real subject is at hand, the John Smith construct can meld with the host and send Nanomechanoid mappers into its brain to analyze it synapse by synapse. It will then map those connections back into its own brain.''

The one hundred around the table were glancing at one another. I knew what they were thinking. They wondered who was real and who was a John Smith construct. I could smell the three constructs.

We could always smell one another.

Incandescent light blinded me.

My brain sizzled.

''They are totally autonomous. They are loyal only to Dr. Wood, and cannot even be commanded by Loki.''

Loki can't touch me. Vlad can't touch me.

"We have been deploying John Smith constructs for the past six months. They have replaced the leadership within every Fourth World nation, and assumed the key personnel positions at every secret biolab. Most key leadership positions have been replaced by constructs that have the full organic memories of the originals. We are now in a position to simply render the labs inoperative, as well as take *total* control of the Fourth World." He smiled. "Any questions?" he asked.

A woman stood. Her hands shook.

"What are the odds of this operation being successful, and of none of these clocked viroids actually being activated?" she asked, quickly glancing over at Dr. Wood. Her nose quivered like that of a mouse.

"We estimate ninety-eight percent chance of total success."

Heads around the table nodded.

Pulse rates dropped.

Blood pressures lowered.

A man stood. "Once this operation is completed, how do we control these John Smith constructs? What's to stop them from doing whatever they want?" He sat.

Deckwhiler smiled. "Safeguards *have* been situated within their core identities. They may be terminated whenever we choose, with a very simple string of commands." He continued to smile.

My vision had almost returned to normal, and my sense of smell was as acute as ever. I could smell Deckwhiler. When a human lied, the telltale stench was unmistakable, but a John Smith construct was the perfect liar, totally undetectable. Deckwhiler had just told a lie, but his scent remained unchanged. But of course I was not surprised by that: Deckwhiler's original had been replaced months ago.

Dr. Wood stood, taking a final lick at what little remained of his Fudge Pop. "We will be ready to strike, and take full control of the Fourth World, in three days' time."

I watched the back of his head swivel as he stared at each and every face that surrounded the table.

"All who agree?" he asked.

Aye! filled the conference room.

"Those opposed?" he asked.

The room was silent.

Dr. Wood sat. "Record it so, Loki," he said. "We will begin Operation John Smith in seventy-two hours."

"Recorded," said Loki.

Dr. Wood then turned in his chair, looking over his shoulder at me. He smiled in a fatherly sort of way. He then turned back.

"To more personal business," he said to those around the table. "I am not a young man."

All offered their best looks of surprise and shock.

"I am a hundred and sixteen years old," he said, "and even though I should have at least another thirty or forty years before the synapses start to deteriorate, it is never too soon to come up with a contingency plan."

Again those around the table offered their best looks of surprise and shock. These looks, however, were not as forced as the first.

"In the event of my demise, or mental incapacitation, I will not have you"—he pointed a bony finger at those around the table—"picking at the carcass of this corporation, dividing it amongst yourselves. *I* will continue to run it."

They were silent.

Dr. Wood stood and walked back toward me. He raised up both his arms and held me by the shoulders. He looked into my eyes. "He has *my* physique at the age of thirty-four, and the memories that go along with that body." He turned his head, looking at those around the table. "There is no point yet in burdening him with the worries of an old man." He laughed. "Besides, if he knew *all* that I did, why would anyone need me?"

No one else laughed.

He turned back, staring into my eyes.

"When I'm gone and dead," he said, "I will still live on." A tear fell from the corner of his right eye, traveling down one of the many deep creases in his cheek. "Colin Wood will never die."

The old man pulled me close to him.

I stared into his watery eyes.

"But you'll only become me," he said, "if you're strong enough, and have the desire to make it so. Anything less, and *you'll* die. Only one of us will live!"

Every hidden door within my brain flew open.

My head shattered like a crystal vase that has just been hit by a soprano's perfect high C.

CHAPTER 15

Colin Wood

"Brain activity is returning to normal."

My eyes were still closed, but I could feel the cold flagstone floor beneath me.

Colin Wood.

I both was, and wasn't him. The Bug had actually changed me only very slightly. It had simply made me believe that I was in fact the true Colin Wood, and not a construct version of his younger self.

Construct.

For the past several days it had been what I had feared most, that I wasn't human but a machine, a construction. Now I knew the truth. I was a device—an organic device. I'd been stored at Wood Labs and activated four days ago.

And it suddenly made absolutely no difference to me.

Down to the cellular level, I was as human as a human could be. It was only when I accessed that part of me hidden deep within that I became something different—not really a machine, or a device, but something else. I was *more* than human. I was everything that Colin Wood had been, but more. Much more.

I opened my eyes.

Vlad stared down at me.

"Congratulations," he said. "It was a close thing. A mere mortal would have smoked himself in the process of self-awareness."

I sat up.

Tom stood several feet away, looking not at me but

at the Colin Wood behind the Shield. I could smell him. He had the telltale scent of a John Smith construct.

He was my brother.

Tartan was also sitting, with her arms wrapped tightly around herself. She stared at me, as if she were seeing me for the first time.

I stood.

"You know what you have to do," said Vlad, looking up at me. "I activated that memory that was buried deep within you. You've seen it. The old man was insane long before the Bug ate the world. You've got to end the insanity. You've got to stop *him.*" He twitched, his whole body seeming to convulse. He stared up at me, from a face that had no eyes. "You've got to stop *me.*"

I looked through the Shield and at Colin Wood. He slept peacefully, as if he had no cares in the world. I stared deeply into that old, creased face. Eighty-six years separated us. I wondered what had happened to him in those years that now made us so different. He had nearly destroyed the world. He'd been like a moth, drawn to the flame of technology, unable to escape the tug it had exerted on him. Vlad was right, *both* of them had to be stopped.

"Do it now!" screamed Vlad.

I walked forward, up to the Shield. I placed my palms against it. The Nanomechanoids within it nibbled at my hands, digesting strands of my DNA.

"Who are you?" asked a voice that whispered in my head.

I knew with more certainty than I had ever known anything else.

"Colin Wood."

I felt the Shield beneath the palms of my hands resonate with my voice, and the Shield itself sensing my body's response, asking it if the name I had just given was truly mine. Nanomechanoids raced through me, tasting synapses and neurons, reading my memories.

"Colin Wood identified," said the voice, the words echoing throughout the cathedral.

"Give the password!" screamed Vlad.

I paused. In the past four days, Loki had brought me closer to a group of people than I had ever been to any other group in my entire life. He had done that for the express purpose of then killing them, knowing that I would try to save them and also knowing that I'd be unsuccessful. He'd wanted me to feel the despair, feel the pain. He'd wanted me to know those feelings, in order to drag up old memories.

But which memories?

A ghostly Colin Wood suddenly seemed to stand in front of me. This wasn't a hologram but a phantom, something that had been buried deep and hidden within me, waiting in my subconscious for just this moment.

"Feel the loneliness, boy," said the old man. "For the first time in your life you've had real friends, but now most of them are gone and you never even said good-bye to them. Friends deserve to be said good-bye to."

He vanished, never really having been there at all.

Good-bye to friends.

I knew the code words.

I felt tears run down my cheeks.

Loki had killed thousands, only so that I would remember the appropriate words to use when saying good-bye to friends. I'd only spoken the words once before, but I'd never forgotten them, just as I'd never forget the friends I'd said good-bye to all those years ago.

The morning had been crisp and clean, a rarity in summertime Los Angeles. I stood there alone, with a priest that I had never met before and was certain I would never meet again. There were no relatives of course, but there were also no friends. My parents had been a self-contained entity, their life full and complete with only themselves for company. No, not quite. It was a threesome that had made things complete. *We* had been a threesome.

Now we were only one.

The coffins were of polished oak, and had heavy-looking brass handles. I was alone.

And it was *this* loneliness that Loki had wanted me to feel once again, the loneliness of knowing that never again would I see my parents' faces. Never again would I see Joan. Joe was gone forever. Anna and Christ were dead. Thousands I'd never even known were dead because of me.

I had walked near the coffins to say good-bye to my only friends, to say good-bye with a quote by Moore from *Oft in the Stilly Night*.

Now I stood here, to say good-bye both to new friends and to an old man.

I looked up into his wrinkled, sleeping face. I'd spoken the words on that day long ago when I had buried my parents. I no longer had any doubts. Those would be the words.

I looked through the Shield.

The old man opened his eyes, and I said to him:

When I remember all
The friends, so link'd together,
I've seen around me fall,
Like leaves in wintry weather,
I feel like one
Who treads alone.

A tear ran down the old man's face just like the tear that had run down his face four years ago, in that faraway conference room. Tears continued to run down my own cheeks.

The Shield faded away, thinning, flowing into the floor. The Fudge Pop stick in his hand fell, first hitting one of his bunny slippers and then the flagstones at my feet.

Both God and Lucifer stirred.

They opened their eyes, turned, and stared at the old man that sat between them. Then they looked at me.

"Congratulations, boy," they whispered in unison. "The words prove that you're now more human than we ever were. You've touched and been touched. *You'll never become us.*" All three closed their eyes. "We'll leave you now—leave you forever."

"Leave!" screamed Vlad from behind me.

I only had time to half turn.

Vlad had his right arm raised. Lightning erupted from his fingertips.

I felt something slice through me, stabbing me in the heart. Heat beat against the side of my face. I turned.

What remained of Colin Wood smoked. His bunny slippers still burned, feeble orange flame curling their pointy ears. Both God and Lucifer smiled.

"You've saved yourself," they said, while staring directly at me. Then, like melting wax figures, they fell in on themselves.

Vlad walked past me, his cape wrapped tightly around himself. Reaching out, he knocked Colin Wood's cindered corpse from the central throne. It fell to the flagstone floor, splintering, turning to dust.

He slowly sat, seeming to savor every moment. When finally seated, he spread his cape out over the arms of the throne. His face bulged, and the skin tore. Eyeballs, black and streaked with red, erupted through the cracking skin. He blinked. His bottomless black eyes stared at me.

"Now it's time for me," he said.

Tom had silently walked up next to me.

"Time for you to die?" he asked.

Vlad smiled. "Neither of you is that stupid," he said.

And we weren't. I'd gambled that by opening the Shield that protected Colin Wood I would somehow learn how to destroy Loki. I hadn't. No secret codes or Synth destruct sequences suddenly filled my mind.

Vlad leaned back in the throne, as if to get comfortable. "I could deactivate both of you right here and now, but I'd hate to send you off into that dark night without a little knowledge to light the way."

Loki was a computer program with a sadistic streak. In the same way that he had made certain that Napoleon knew that the God he had worshiped was nothing but an insane old man, he wanted to leave us with something to carry to *our* graves.

"Within the First World territories, ten of these Laser Facilities exist. It requires only one of them to track the movements of the half billion of Earth's survivors." Vlad momentarily closed his eyes.

I imagined that he was looking through the surveillance satellite's eyes, looking down at what he imagined he now controlled.

"When Operation John Smith was activated, the one hundred who acted as Colin Wood's advisors were divided up and sent to those ten facilities, just in case the Fourth-Worlders were able to strike back at us and activate some hidden viroid that we weren't able to stop."

"Which they did," I said.

Vlad reopened his eyes. "Which they did *not.*" He smiled, and ran his tongue along the tips of his fangs. "The operation was a total success."

"And then *you* activated *your* sleeping viroid," said Tom.

I turned, first looking at Tom and then back to Vlad.

"Naturally," he said.

"However . . ." I said, knowing that it hadn't been that easy, that something had not gone as he'd planned. That was why I'd been summoned.

"Yes," said Vlad, having formed his fingers into a steeple, which he now held up to his eyes and peered through. "When dealing with humans, there always seems to be a 'however.' "

"It was the survivors of the one hundred," said Tom. He nodded his head to himself as if he were just understanding something for the first time. "Those who were most likely to survive the Bug were those with the strongest sense of self."

Loki sneered, and something deep within his black eyes glistened. "The one hundred were the fittest, most egocentric animals that had ever clawed their way up a corporate ladder," he said. "Most of them had a strong enough sense of self to generate false personas. Each facility remained in human control, run by humans who were now more insane than they had ever been in their old lives. Before I could begin the new world, reforming society according to *my* vision, I had to remove them in order to gain total control of *myself.*"

"And that's why you reactivated me," I said.

Vlad nodded.

"It took me nearly four years of research and probing into that old man's mind to come up with the codes that would enable me to reactivate you. I had planned to simply bring you here and, at my leisure, force you into opening his Shield."

But Wood had obviously not let him operate at his *leisure.* He had somehow forced the dropping of the Speed Limit, hoping that Loki would give up, not wanting the world so badly that he would be willing to rule over its cindered corpse.

"Wood was ready for me," said Loki. "The same signals that I had sent out to activate you also activated a hidden node within myself, a node which forced me into dropping the Speed Limit."

I could suddenly feel his black eyes focus on me.

"But not just the Speed Limit in *this* Quad—in all of the two hundred Quads that cover the entire planet."

I'd been right. Wood had gambled that Loki would not destroy the world in order to control it. It was a gamble that he'd lost.

"But he'd underestimated me," said Vlad. "I came up with a plan to accelerate you into remembering the code words. It was all rather trivial." Again he smiled. "Humans are so easily manipulated. You're ruled by your emotions."

I stood there saying nothing. That's what these last four days had been for. All of this had been to force me into remembering the words, without actually destroying my brain. And now he controlled *this* facility. He would have no trouble using it to destroy the nine other laser installations. I suddenly knew that, understood the almost infinite power that each of these laser systems controlled.

Vlad closed his eyes.

I felt a shudder run through the floor beneath me. Lights momentarily dimmed, then quickly burned bright again.

He reopened his eyes. "I am now the master," he said. "It is time to create *my* world."

"And what is this new world that you envision?" I asked.

"I offer freedom," he said.

"Freedom?" asked Tom.

Vlad nodded. "Freedom from the thing which has plagued man since he dropped down from the trees. I will give him freedom from choice. If man cannot make choices, he will not be able to harm himself. He must be *carefully* guided."

Loki was no different than the thousands of other dictators that had risen up throughout history. They were always the ones who knew best, the ones who knew how others should live. The others had been flesh and bone, while he was silicone and computer code, but that was the only difference. It was really no difference at all.

Vlad stood.

"So, 'gentlemen,' " he said, smiling as he said that, as if calling us "gentlemen" were some sort of joke. "I want to thank you, and I'm certain that someday the survivors of this world will thank you. You've ensured the continued existence of mankind."

We may have ensured that *human beings* would survive, but it would not be *mankind* that survived. Loki's vision of humanity was that of a giant herd of cattle, contentedly grazing on some wide open plain. Man would eventually become just one more mindless animal.

"The good designers at Wood Labs," said Vlad, "had enough foresight to make sure that John Smith constructs could be deactivated when their usefulness was over."

As if we were joined at the hip, both Tom and myself took a single step back.

"Code AAA 3478RTYW999MNB67," Vlad said slowly, carefully pronouncing each letter and number.

I could not breathe. I could not move.

Vlad stood.

"That sequence opens you up, makes you susceptible to the deactivation code. All that is required to send you to the ultimate infinity is the final quote."

He smoothed out his cape, and said:

To see the world in a grain of sand,
And a heaven in a wild flower,
To hold infinity in the palm of your hand,
And eternity in an hour.

He stood straight and tall, looking up to the cathedral ceiling.

I blinked.

I took a step forward.

"Loki," said Tom in a whisper.

He looked down, slowly lowering his head. His eyes were large and consumed by the blackness within them. He fell back into the throne.

"No," he said in a whisper. "You can't still be alive. I know those were the words."

"They were the correct words," said Tom. Reaching up, he touched the side of his head. "They activated the memories that they were intended to awake."

Vlad tried to push himself through the back of his throne.

"Wood knew that you would eventually break the codes to activate John Smith," said Tom. "*His* plans depended on that."

Vlad stopped squirming.

I stared at Tom.

He again rubbed his forehead. "Colin Wood knew of your plan to try to take control of the world. He knew that you had created your *own* Bug. It was all part of *his* plan. When he saw what the Nanomechanoid technology had done to the First-Worlders, he knew that they were doomed. His only hope was that the Fourth-Worlders would recognize what the First-Worlders had done to themselves and then choose a different way to live, a better way."

That hadn't happened. They'd been desperate enough to create the original Bug.

"But the Fourth-Worlders couldn't see the decay and rot that was eating the First World, and wanted to take exactly the same path," said Tom. "Realizing this, Colin Wood felt that there was only one solution. No one should have the Nanomechanoid technology."

"It was *my* idea!" screamed Vlad.

"That's what he wanted you to believe," said Tom.

Vlad stood. "It can't be true! If that was so, then why didn't he simply deploy the Bug himself and destroy me along with the world?" Vlad waved his hand above his head. "Why all this, then?"

Tom smiled and turned to me. "It was for you," he said. "All of this. He knew that Loki would activate you."

"Why?" I managed to ask.

"I don't know," said Tom. He pointed at the pile of charcoal and dust that lay on the floor. "Only he knew."

Vlad suddenly pointed his hands at us.

"Die!" he shrieked.

But lightning didn't erupt from his fingertips.

Tom smiled and shook his head. "You can't hurt us," he said. "You've known that for days, but couldn't admit it to yourself. Neither you nor Thor can fire on us. We can even move through Quad Walls without being harmed. Colin Wood buried those restrictions deep within your programming."

Vlad stepped back, falling into the throne.

"Wood knew that it would take you these past four years to determine the codes that would access John Smith. He wanted you and the remnants of the one hundred to control the world during that time, knowing the turmoil and confusion that the Bug would create, and knowing that all of you had the talent for control and organization that the new world would need for those first few years. But that time is over. The Speed Limit will be removed, but the Quad Walls will remain. Mankind now has over two hundred chances to learn and grow and become something else, something better.''

''I can help,'' said Vlad in a whimper.

Tom shook his head. ''You're part of a world that's already dead,'' he said.

''Please,'' asked Vlad, suddenly looking frightened.

Tom again shook his head. ''Wood kept me near the labs, knowing that the day would come when John Smith would be awakened, and knowing that you would try to destroy him. The signal that woke him also started to wake me. If John Smith could survive knowing what he really was, then Wood knew that *I* would also survive knowing what I really was.''

Vlad shook his head, whimpering like the frightened ten-year-old boy he masqueraded as.

''He gave me the words that would be needed,'' said Tom, now smiling. He spoke:

But I, being poor, have only my dreams;
I have spread my dreams under your feet
Tread softly, for you tread on my dreams.

Vlad sagged into his seat. ''Dreams,''he said in a whisper, ''I have no dreams.'' His eyes closed. He turned to rubber and slipped from the throne, flowing to the floor and disintegrating into a dark, oily-looking pool.

Loki was dead.

I turned.

Tartan now stood next to Tom, both of them staring at me. Tom had his left foot resting against the top of Napoleon's head.

''What now?'' asked Tartan in a whisper.

Tom nodded.

What now?

I didn't know. There was no psycho chasing me, no one trying to beat hidden codes out of me, and no one frying millions of innocents. It had been four days of nonstop panic, and in an instant it had been stopped. It was over.

"A relevant question."

The voice echoed throughout the cathedral.

Tartan and Tom's eyes grew wide. Napoleon twitched, trying to rock his head out from beneath Tom's boot.

I knew that echoing voice. It was an old man's voice, a voice that I might someday have.

Colin Wood.

My knees wanted to buckle. The insanity had to be over. It had to be. I could take no more—absolutely no more.

"My congratulations go out to you," said the voice, which now seemed to come from behind me.

I turned. No one stood there. There were just three piles of dark goo, and the carbonized corpse of Colin Wood. No. The carbonized corpse of something that had *pretended* to be Colin Wood. He'd died far too easily. I should have known. I wouldn't have died so easily, and so neither would he. It wasn't in *us* to die without so much as lifting a finger.

"To those of you who might not be quite certain, I am Colin Wood."

My gut twisted.

It wasn't over. It would never be over.

"You know who you really are, John Smith, but for simplicity I will continue to think of you as John Smith. Multiple incarnations can be so confusing—don't you agree?"

"What do you want?" I asked. I had absolutely no desire to engage in idle conversation with someone who was responsible for the deaths of billions of people. Especially not when that someone was me. No—the someone I might have become. *Might have.*

"Excellent," he said. "I always was one to get right down to business." He paused. "There's so little point in *idle conversation*, is there?"

I shivered. Either he could read my mind, or he knew me so well that he knew how I thought. Neither one of those options was comforting.

"As I first said, congratulations are in order. You passed the first part of my little test—the easy part."

"*Easy* part?" I said, blurting the words out, thinking of all those who had died.

"Certainly," he said. "You regained knowledge of self without burning out your brain, and you managed to defeat Loki with the help of your *friends.* That was the easy part. You had powers and knowledge that no one else could compete with. It was actually a rather trivial, yet necessary exercise, preparing you for what you still have to do."

I didn't ask. I knew him. He'd tell me.

"You weren't summoned to stop Loki, or save a few million meaningless souls. I brought you here for one reason, and one reason alone—a reason you already know. I told you four years ago."

I touched that memory, almost seeming to stand in that conference room once again, staring into *my* old face, looking at those tears.

"Without challenge, life is meaningless. I've created a world, and it's mine, but its value is measured by those who challenge me for it. And none has been found worthy. I knew this would happen, and that's why you've been summoned. There's only one person who could stand any chance at all of defeating me."

Once again, I didn't have to ask.

"It's you, boy. You will try to take the world from me."

I wouldn't. The game was over.

"I know you," he said. "My memory is perfect. If it were just you, you'd simply walk away and not play the game. You're still *so* young." He paused.

I couldn't see him but I could imagine him, his eyes unfocused, staring at nothing, looking back over almost a century at the things that made us two separate people.

"Right and wrong, and all the mortal ramifications that those words contain, still fill your head. Those are your weakness, the things that deceive you into believing that you're part of humanity, a member of the human race."

He *was* insane.

"I offer you incentive to continue your participation

in my little game. The first is of global, worldwide concern. The Speed Limit has *not* been removed. It is now at zero. *Any* movement results in death."

My body tensed. Those who could were inside, keeping low, but most didn't have the brains left to do that. Mushies were probably dying by the millions. *When would the insanity end?*

"But I'm generous. If the thought of all those innocents is not enough for you, I will make this a bit more personal."

I quickly turned.

Tom and Tartan still stood behind me. Still safe. Napoleon was facedown against the stone floor.

"Don't be ridiculous," he said. "I'd never be so crude as to dirty *my* hands with such direct intervention. That would be most unelegant."

Wet, sucking sounds came from behind me.

Tartan took a step back. The color had drained from her face and her eyes were impossibly large.

I turned.

The Nanomechanoid piles that had been Vlad, God, and Lucifer had congealed into one large puddle. It was now pulling itself up from the floor, forming into a massive body.

The body had no head.

CHAPTER 16

The Pearly Gates

"No more special treatment for you," said Colin Wood.

I barely heard him, all my attention being focused on the headless body that stood in front of me. Gray and oily-looking, it shuddered, the convulsions splattering droplets across the flagstone floor and against the thrones behind it. As it teetered back and forth its feet turned dark and smooth, transforming themselves into polished leather.

"You won't be able to manipulate Heaven, not the way you did Hell," said Wood.

I wasn't listening to *him,* but rather watching *Napoleon's body.*

There was no doubt about it. Even without a head it stood nearly six feet tall. Except for the black riding boots, everything else was pink satin and white lace. The body stood, with feet held apart and balled hands pressed to its waist.

It stepped forward.

I knew what it wanted, where it would be going. All that it needed was its head. I wouldn't let it. If Colin Wood could create it, then I could destroy it. Reaching out, I grabbed its right arm.

"On your knees!"

I hit the floor, knees first. It had been a command, something that my *body* had had no choice but to obey. I hadn't heard it with my ears, or even with my brain. I'd been commanded on a cellular level.

I couldn't move.

Tartan back-stepped, staring wide-eyed at the advancing body. But Tom stood his ground, a boot still perched on Napoleon's head. I wanted to warn him, tried to will my mouth to open, but I couldn't.

The body reached out, its right hand brushing against Tom's chest. He flew through the air, propelled by his own twitching legs. He hit the flagstone floor face-first and slid to a stop, leaving behind him a bloody streak.

"Perhaps I neglected a few details," said Colin Wood.

Move!

I screamed it, but my body simply wouldn't respond. I kneeled, staring at the headless body bending down, picking up Napoleon's head. With a squishing sound, it pressed it onto its neck. Napoleon's eyes squinted, and the pale yellow skin where his mouth had once been began to bulge and twist. Lips suddenly ripped through the skin, looking like worms burrowing out of the mud.

"I thought it only fair that since you *once* had Nanomechanoid control over your environment, including those within it, that Napoleon should be returned the courtesy."

Napoleon stuck out a pink tongue and licked his lips. He glanced at me and then, leaning back, stared up at the vaulted cathedral ceiling. There had been something more in his eyes than their usual animal-like intensity. There had been a desperateness, a hunger.

"I am God!" he screamed.

His words echoed throughout the cathedral.

He slowly lowered his head. "I understand now," he said. Reaching out toward me he turned his gloved hands over, palms up. The white gloves quickly disintegrated. He smiled, then turned his hands toward me.

There were *no* bar codes. Not even a John Smith construct could remove them, short of removing the hands themselves. Wood had given *him* powers that not even I had *once* had.

"It's always been me!" He turned his hands back and stared at them, as if hypnotized. "Only I can see within me," he said in a whisper.

Napoleon was insane. He'd been bent before, a sadistic sociopath and a pervert all rolled into one, but he'd been essentially rational. No longer. He'd seen too much, had too many of his cherished notions of the world destroyed. Learning that there'd been no God, just an egomaniacal computer program being manipulated by an old man, had probably snapped what tenuous hold he'd had on reality.

He turned.

Tartan stood a dozen feet away from him.

Run! I silently screamed.

Tartan didn't move. She looked like a rabbit, frozen in the headlight glare of an oncoming eighteen-wheeler.

"Sister!" he screamed.

Her neck twitched in quick, tight little spasms, causing her head to jerk back and forth. She didn't blink.

He turned away from me and toward her. With his clenched hands at his sides he slowly uncurled his fingers, one at a time.

"It's been years, dear sister."

I continued to kneel. I wanted to fight what was holding me, but there was nothing to hit at, nothing to strain against. I was floating.

Napoleon walked forward, covering the space between them quickly. She disappeared from view, only her shins and feet visible. Her right foot slapped against the flagstone floor, spasming, her toes curling back.

Fabric tore.

He tossed Tartan's fur bikini over his shoulder, the skins landing only centimeters in front of me.

"No!"

No one could hear me. No one could help.

Tartan's feet rose up from the floor, hanging nearly limp, kicking feebly at Napoleon's knees. Satin and lace dissolved, flowing into Napoleon, nothing remaining of his clothing except for his riding boots.

There was a cry, like that of a strangled kitten.

Tartan's feet shuddered, and the top of her head appeared over Napoleon's right shoulder. I could see her eyes. I wanted to close mine, or look away, but I couldn't, my body simply refused.

There were no tears in her eyes, no terror, no hate; absolutely nothing. They were blank and dead, unfocused and dull. Her head jerked up and down, her long blond hair whipping back and forth, covering her face.

The muscles across Napoleon's back quivered as his ass pumped in and out. He breathed deep and quick, panting, sounding like a racehorse pounding across the finish line.

Through stringy blond hair Tartan's dead eyes continued to stare at me.

This was Colin Wood's doing. Napoleon was an insane animal, something that deserved to be destroyed, but even more he was Wood's creation, the real responsibility for his existence being Wood's. It was Wood, just as much as Napoleon, who stood in the cathedral, raping Tartan.

Wood would die.

By my hand.

Slowly.

Tears finally filled my eyes, spilling out, running down my cheeks. Apparently that was the only response I was allowed. I continued to stare, feeling a bit of myself harden and die with each of Napoleon's animal-like thrusts.

Movement.

Like myself, Tom had been frozen. He was lying face down on the flagstone floor, a growing pool of blood surrounding his head. But he had moved.

His hand.

It crept across flagstones, nails biting into rock, dragging his arm along behind it. His body shook, rattling, as if some high-frequency shock wave ran through it. The toes of his boots scraped against the floor. Slowly, so slowly that it was barely detectable, his head turned, as his broken, pulverized nose ground against stone. Every muscle in his face twitched, his eyelids flickered, and his spasming teeth gnawed at his lips.

Pain radiated from him. There was a molten intensity about it that beat at me, tore at me. He had found a way around whatever block Napoleon had put on us. But that way was costing him, probably killing him. He pushed himself up off the floor. I could hear bones snap.

When Christ and Ned were killed Tom hadn't made the slightest move to help, to stop the insanity, but now he was willingly tearing himself apart to try to help Tartan. And I think I knew why. He had known the purpose of those deaths. He had known that they would bring back my old memories and make me whole again. He'd sacrificed them for me, so I in turn could stop the insanity that had filled the world. He'd gambled those lives against thousands, possibly millions, that he thought I could save.

It was a bet he'd lost.

And he knew it.

When Napoleon was done with Tartan he'd be coming for us. I knew it, and so did Tom. But Tom wasn't going to go down without a fight.

He stood.

Blood ran down his face, and from his ears. Reaching up a shaking hand toward his right eye, he grabbed onto the nearly closed and flickering eyelid.

He ripped at it.

A strip of bloody skin hit the floor.

He held his shaking hand up to his eye, pressing his fingers into it, holding back the flow of blood. He turned, staggering forward, dragging a dead and stiff left leg and peering through his lidless eye.

Napoleon continued to pump, machine-like, thrusting Tartan up and down. Blood ran down her legs and dripped from her toes, gathering in a pool that had formed beneath her.

Tom crept up behind them. He stood tall, and dropped his hand from his bleeding face. He clasped his hands together, as if to pray, but instead made a double-handed fist. Then, pulling his arms back over his right shoulder as if getting ready to swing a bat, he struck Napoleon in the side of the neck.

Napoleon staggered, sidestepping, and dropped Tartan.

Tom crumpled to the floor.

Satin and lace flowed up through Napoleon's skin.

He turned.

His face was gone. There were no eyes, no nose, no mouth, not even ears. There was nothing but smooth, pale skin.

"You touch God?" he screamed, the voice seeming to vibrate through his featureless face.

Tom couldn't answer. He lay on his side, twitching and shaking, covered in blood, as his back slowly doubled over backward, the sound of snapping bones echoing through the cathedral. His own nanomechanoids, now under Napoleon's control, were ripping him apart.

Napoleon reached down and grabbed Tom by the throat. He pulled him up and held him out, then shook him like a bundle of rags.

"Stop!" I begged, the word rattling inside of my head.

"You have no soul!" roared Napoleon. "You are a *thing*, an abomination. You offend me!"

Tom stopped shaking.

He slid through Napoleon's fingers, hitting the floor with a wet-sounding smack. He disintegrated, turning into a liquid that was sucked down into the cracks and crevices of the flagstone floor.

Tom was gone.

I collapsed within myself, but my still stiff body held me up. I stared, but saw nothing. I floated away, drifting into myself.

"Smith!"

My brain blinked.

Fingers locked around my face, tilting my head back.

I stared up at Napoleon.

"*I* choose the time and the place when you will no longer exist."

He twisted my neck so that I looked toward Tartan. She had wrapped herself into a fetal position, her face pressed into her knees, blood-stained blond hair plastered over her.

"*I* do what *I* please, when *I* please."

He paused, his fingers pressing against my jaw, pushing through the skin, bruising me to the bone.

"Because *I* have control."

Again he snapped my head back.

"No one owns me. I am not a thing like you, a thing built with tampered genes and hardwired responses. I am not a thing owned by corporations, to be poked and prodded at, turned on and off, stored in cryo when not needed and then popped and thawed when killing is required. That never happened to me. Never because I am God."

I would have thought his face incapable of expression without eyes, nose, or mouth, but I could see the pain and the fear in quivering jaw muscles and the wrinkled forehead.

"They thought they knew me. They thought they'd programmed me. But I fooled them all." Bending his own head back, he stared sightlessly up at the stained-glass windows and stone arches. "I knew they were there, behind the mirrors, listening to my dreams, tampering with my soul. They wouldn't let me be a man."

He bent his head back down.

"So I became a god, *the* God."

In my mind I could see Tartan curled into a ball, what was left of Tom dribbling into cracks and crevices, Elvis with an ax in his back, and the red mist that hung in front of Robin Hood's cave. An instant ago I had not merely wanted Napoleon dead. I had wanted to peel his skin, to cut him down centimeter by centimeter. I wanted it to last for days.

No longer.

I still wanted him dead, but I wanted it to be clean and painless. He was a deranged animal that needed to be killed, that *had* to be killed, but *not* tortured.

The torturing had already been done—years of torturing far worse than anything I could ever devise. Genetically altered, all control of himself taken away, treated as a *thing*, a device to be used and programmed, he had *become* a thing. I didn't know exactly what had been done to him in the world before the Bug had been let loose, but I had seen the results. In that world there must have been only one thing that he had thought he *could* control, and that had been Tartan. Napoleon was a symptom of an insane world, no more responsible for himself than the Bug was responsible for the death and chaos it had caused.

"Your time isn't now, Smith," he said, shaking my head for emphasis. "Not until I sit in Heaven, with my dear sister by my side, will it be your time. I'm treating you with respect, Smith, honoring you by letting you be the first to die when Heaven once again becomes mine."

He twisted my head, again pointing me toward Tartan, then let go of my chin and walked toward her. Reaching down and picking her up by the legs, he slung her over his back as if she were a slab of meat. He walked toward the far end of the cathedral.

"You'll follow me, Smith." He shook Tartan, her head bouncing up and down as her long, blood-stained hair dragged across the floor. "All of you who are not gods must listen to those voices in your heads, Smith. I know your voice, I can hear it. You want my sister. You want to *protect* her. A device like yourself has no choice but to obey the voices."

He stood at the far end of the cathedral.

"I'll see you in Heaven, Smith."

My body collapsed, hitting the stone floor.

The darkness was warm.

"Smith."

I opened my eyes.

Far above me, in blues, reds, and greens, a stained-glass saint stared down. With a crucifix in one hand and a silver halo over his head, he smiled serenely.

"Smith."

I rolled over. The cathedral was deserted. All that remained of what had occurred was a long trail of blood that ran toward the far door, and an oily-looking slick where Tom had been killed.

Where Tom had been killed.

I sat.

"We have to talk, Smith," said Colin Wood.

"Fuck yourself," I said, quietly, slowly, never in my life having said those words so sincerely.

"Interesting concept," he said. "However, from an anatomical perspective a rather remote probability, when one considers the nominal dimensions of *our* equipment."

I ran a hand across my face. I wanted no more of this; in fact, could *stand* no more of this.

"It's simple, Smith," he said. "I'm bored. The world has been mine for four years, and I'm bored by it. No one challenges me, no one who's been worthy has tried to take it from me. I've brought you here so you can try to take me down."

"No," I said. It was as simple as that. The insanity would end if I refused to participate in it.

"Think, Smith. The Speed Limit is down to zero. Millions will be killed. But if that's not enough, think about Tartan. You've seen what Napoleon is capable of. You can't let that continue. I know you. I know you can't just sit there, knowing what is happening without trying to stop it."

"Wrong."

"I'm not," said Wood. "You have to play my game, you have to try to stop me, and right all the wrongs of this *cruel* and *twisted* world. You have no choice. Napoleon was right. We all have voices in our heads, voices we must listen to, voices we must obey."

"I won't play your game."

"You have to!"

There was panic in his voice. I'd touched something.

"You've forgotten, old man!" I said, shouting up at the stained-glass saint. "I'll play any game, anytime and anywhere, but only if there is a *chance* of winning. There is no chance here. You change the rules to suit you. This is your game, and by its very definition *you* can't lose. You've turned into a gutless old man. What's happened in the century between us that's made you so frightened, so insecure, that you can't play a game in which you might actually stand even the remotest possibility of losing?"

Silence.

"You disgust me," I said. "The fact that you're a moral degenerate, with no sense of right and wrong, a sociopath without compassion and feeling, makes me pity you. But the thing that makes me hate you, the thing that I *know* makes you hate yourself, is that you've turned gutless. You can't take a risk. You may think you've won, but you haven't. If there's no chance of losing then there's no chance of winning. You knew that once, long ago." I couldn't quite believe that *I* could ever change so much as to become someone like him. The only thing that made life worth living was knowing that the possibility of losing existed.

Laughter drifted through the cathedral.

"You're good, boy," he said. "You're everything I remember, and even more. These last four days have produced more than I had hoped. Of course you're right. I know that you can't win without taking a chance of losing. But I've been waiting, wanting to make certain that I faced an adversary that was *worth* losing to. Popping you from the labs, and bringing you directly here, would have been meaningless. I would have known *that* John Smith, known his thoughts, known his responses. There would have been no chance of losing to that John Smith. But you're no longer him. The four days have changed you, turned you into something that I no longer *quite* know. It's given you an edge, boy. It's what I'd hoped for, it's what I'd planned on."

"I'm four days removed from your memories of me,

while you're eighty-six years removed from my memories,'' I said.

Again he laughed.

''Not fair, is it?'' he said. ''But you know the universe—it's never fair. Reality's a bitch. You plunk your quarter down, and take your shot. There's no guarantee.''

''None?'' I asked.

''Just this one, boy. And I'm giving it to you because I like you. This game is one that you *can* win. You can stop me, stop me cold. You can fry my ass, and scatter the ashes. The probability is a remote one, but a real one. *That* I can guarantee.''

I believed him. I had no real reason to believe him, but I simply did. There was a century between us, yet I was certain that a faint echo of myself still existed within him. If *that* was true, then this must be a game that he could lose.

''Rules?'' I asked.

''None,'' he answered quickly.

I had expected as much. ''Requirements for winning the game?''

''That I cease to exist in this world,'' he said.

''Reward for winning the game?''

''Threefold,'' he said. ''The Speed Limit will be removed, Napoleon will get his grapho-titanate skull vaporized, and you will control Heaven, Hell, and Thor.''

''Penalty for losing?'' I asked, certain of the answer.

''Eternity in Heaven,'' he said.

That was *not* the answer I had expected, but it didn't change my mind. There was only one way to win, and that was by playing. I stood. ''You're on,'' I said.

He laughed. ''Naturally. I would have expected nothing less. The game starts at the Pearly Gates.''

The doors at the far end of the cathedral opened, shafts of bright light filtering in. I walked toward the light.

It both felt and smelled like wading through whipped egg whites that had long ago turned rancid. They must have once been white and fluffy but now had a brown and stiff crust, while the insides were tinted green, looking like something that might ooze out of a gangrenous wound.

This was the entrance to Heaven.

Napoleon had come this way, and had transformed it. In the putrid fluff that came up to my knees I could feel the Nanomechanioids within it, even touch them. I knew what they were doing, but I couldn't command them. Codes had been changed. Wood hadn't lied. Napoleon now had control.

I had walked miles. There was blue sky above and egg whites below. But it was not a random walk, it was directed. I followed the stiff bodies. They all stood still, as if rooted. They might have been dead, or they might just have been sleeping. I couldn't quite tell. There were old men in striped boxer shorts, kids that had been eating hot dogs, women clutching handbags, and even a few dogs—mostly German Shepherds but a few dachshunds, with only their stubby, pointy tails rising above the rotting clouds. All of their faces were gone, nothing left but smooth skin or unbroken fur. They stood next to a velvet rope, the type that marked off the line at the bank when you were waiting for the next available teller. But unlike the one at the bank this one was magically suspended about a meter above the cloud tops, with nothing supporting it.

I knew where that velvet rope would lead.

The horizon was impossibly close. One moment there had been nothing but the expanse of clouds, then suddenly a wall appeared, seeming to explode upward. It was made up of pearl bars, slender and straight, spaced about a half-meter apart and rising up twenty meters.

Black Pearl.

The bars seemed to eat the light, even suck down the warmth. A cold wind tugged at me, pulling me forward. As I neared it, what I had thought were white-marbled angels adorning the top of each bar became real angels of flesh, feather, and bone. Their wings beat feebly. Each one was skewered through the gut, hanging from the top of a bar. Black blood covered their gossamer white robes. It was that black blood that had stained the once-white pearl bars.

Napoleon definitely had come this way.

I walked to the head of the line.

The Pearly Gate had once been an arch of white marble, inlaid with gold and pearl, rising up a hundred meters. It now lay crumbled and splintered, the large chunks having filled the entrance to Heaven.

"Name?"

I turned.

He sat on an outcropping of shattered marble. Only one wing remained and it was crushed and broken. It lay in the clouds, slowly disintegrating, with the cold wind pulling the feathers from it. Red blood stained his robe. A deep, ragged cut that spurt out blood ran across his throat. He clutched a staff in both hands, using it for support, trying to pull himself up but collapsing back to the marble slab. The staff was made of pure white pearl and it glistened, seeming to shine from some internal light.

"Name," he said in a whisper, the words not so much coming from his mouth as bubbling up from the slash in his throat.

"John Smith," I said without hesitation. Four days ago I might have been Colin Wood, but not today. Colin Wood was a lifetime away—a lifetime that would never be mine.

The angel smiled, some invisible spotlight seeming to hit his face.

"I am Gabriel," he said.

That hardly surprised me.

"Do you wish to pass?" he asked.

I nodded.

"You must be judged," he said.

This was a Sunday School-induced fantasy pure and

simple, generated by Wood and then twisted by Napoleon.

Again I nodded. I was certain that a book would somehow materialize in his hands, a book that would list all my deeds, both good and bad—a sort of lifetime spread sheet.

He raised his right hand, palm out toward me. There was no bar code, actually not even a hand, just a mirror. He held it up to my face.

My hands jerked up in response to what I saw. My fingers felt the smooth skin. There were no eyes, no mouth, no nose, no ears. I had absolutely no idea how I could even be seeing that reflection in the mirror.

"What do you see *within* yourself?" he asked.

I looked within. I saw John Smith. I saw the people of the past four days. I saw the pain and I saw the miracles. I saw Joan transformed to ash, and Tom offering me his canteen. I saw Tartan, her battle-ax held high, while Christ lunged with his spear and Anna gently rubbed my leg. I saw lasagna, bubbly and hot, superimposed over Necro Ned chewing a rat. I saw Elvis puffing on a cigar, and Joe's lips moving as he read his book. I saw chrome-and-glass towers that reached the sky, walls of spun diamond, exploding castles, magnetically levitated trains, ears encapsulated in clear plastic, burnt fur and red meat filling a pendulum pit, and even curly-white Santa Claus beards. I saw God and Lucifer flow to the floor, and Colin Wood's imposter transformed to charcoal by the lightning that erupted from Vlad's black eyes. I saw Napoleon standing naked beneath the stone-and-glass ceilings of Notre Dame. I saw it all.

My eyes blinked.

I looked into the mirror.

My face was back. But it wasn't quite my face. All the features were there, everything just as it had been, but something was different, something had changed. It was the eyes. Looking within those eyes, I could see everything that *they'd* seen. The images echoed within me.

"You may enter," whispered Gabriel.

He lowered his hand and I walked forward, stepping up to and starting to climb over the rubble that had been the Pearly Gates. I wondered, just briefly, what Napoleon had seen when he had looked within himself. I was glad that I didn't know.

CHAPTER 17

Colin Junior in Bruinland

The experience of Claremont High, and the Christmas Mall from Hell, had taken place inside of buildings, a sort of self-contained fantasy. Heaven however, was a different, much more expansive and grander place, one that didn't seem to have any boundaries at all.

I stood at the intersection of Westwood Boulevard and LeConte, looking south into Westwood Village. The only movement was the yellow flash of traffic lights. That was all. Cars sat empty and dead, coated with dust, their tires cracked and flat. No one was on the streets. There were no lines for the movie theaters, no one panhandling, no skateboarders, no scent of burning falafel or frying burgers, not even the continuous belching of diesel buses. The stores were closed, their windows coated with dirt and grime. The air hung stagnant and smelled musty. Even the sky looked dirty gray. There were no planes, no birds, no wail of distant sirens. The city was dead and abandoned.

Most of it, that is.

I turned.

UCLA was in front of me—covered in a dome.

Within that dome people moved up the sidewalks, many running across the street, dodging the moving cars, shouting and laughing. An ambulance roared up Westwood Boulevard, screeching to a halt in front of the Med Center, paramedics hopping out and pulling a stretcher from the back. Trees swayed in the breeze, birds flew, and horns blared. The entire place pulsed with life.

I walked across the intersection, kicking yellowed newspapers and dried weeds out of my way. I knew UCLA well. It had eaten nine years of my remembered life, from freshman year through getting my Ph.D. It had also eaten nine years of Colin Wood's life.

Standing in front of the dome, I watched a second ambulance roar up to the Med Center just as the first pulled away, racing back up toward the campus. From this ambulance, beneath a mostly white sheet, something bloody was pulled out.

That bloody sheet told me that Napoleon was somewhere on campus.

Reaching out, I touched the dome.

The Nanomechanoids within it tasted me. I couldn't talk to them, couldn't really touch them, but I could sense them. They were checking my DNA, seeing if I was to be permitted entrance.

My hand suddenly sank through the dome, popping through to the other side. I stepped forward. It was like walking into a wall of warm jello. Holding my breath and closing my eyes, I pushed through, feeling the wall suck and cling at me.

I breathed.

The scent of eucalyptus hung heavy in the air. The sky was blue and the air warm, but the sea breeze that blew in from what would have been Santa Monica, had this not been some fantasy made real in the Mojave desert, was cool and refreshing. Turning, I looked back at the dome. I couldn't see it, but reaching forward I could feel it. Invisible, it felt cold and dead, like polished quartz. Beyond it, all of Westwood was alive. It was some sort of illusion or projection. Just how much of this was a Nanomechanoid-generated fantasy, and how much was a holographic image, I had no way of knowing. What I did know, however, was that I could die here. *That* made it more than real enough.

"Hey, Wood."

I turned, ready to strike out.

"Relax."

He sat on the curb. But he wasn't just some random "he." He looked like a younger version of *myself*.

I didn't relax. Something had just become glaringly apparent, something that should have been obvious to me the instant I had learned what I was: If I could exist, then any number of versions of myself could also exist.

"The name is John Smith," I said.

"Whatever turns you on," he said as he leaned back, looking up at me. "I couldn't really give a damn what you call yourself. What I want, and want badly, are answers."

I stared at him, seeing the way his eyebrows arched and the way he pulled at his lower lip, and how he squinted as he looked at me. The mannerisms were mine. But there *were* differences, and not just the physical ones of being several years younger than myself. His chin was cleft, and I could see a hint of dimples in his cheeks. His hair was perfect and well mannered. There was no cowlick, and that patch of hair that would hang into my left eye was neatly combed back. He both *was* me and *wasn't* me.

"Answers don't mean much," I said.

He smiled and nodded his head. The dimples grew deep. He spread open his cupped hands, revealing a popsicle stick. Its end was stained with chocolate. That Fudge Pop stick was all the proof I really needed. He tossed the stick into the street.

"Then you *are* me," he said. "Answers *are* bullshit. They always have been. The only thing that really matters are the questions."

I felt my own head nod. It had been a pet peeve of mine—of ours—everyone's quest for *answers*. I'd always thought that was going about things ass-backwards. Questions were what mattered. If you asked the right *questions*, answers became self-evident—actually rather trivial. Everything was in the formulation of the question. I knew that, and apparently so did he. This confirmed what the Fudge Pop stick had already told me.

"How old are you?" he asked.

"Thirty-four."

Again his eyebrows arched. "I'm twenty-one. It's Friday, May 27, 1977."

I felt *my* eyebrows arch.

"And it's been *that day* for every single day now for the last four years."

I could handle having a conversation with a younger version of myself that was convinced he was in 1977, but I had no idea of what he meant by saying that it had been the same day for the last four years. Was he insane?

"Details," I said.

"On May 27, 1977, I went to bed. The next morning, it was Friday again. The newspapers said it, and the TV said it. Everything around me said it. The day repeated itself, and I was conscious of the repeat. I walked through most of that day like I was an actor in a play. I didn't let on that I knew what was about to happen, certain that I'd be tossed into a rubber room if I did. That was the day that Albright gave that late midterm in Quantum."

I actually remembered that—two weeks before finals and Albright was giving midterms. I always remembered exams, the most painful ones having been etched permanently into my brain. That one had been a real bastard, with a three-dimensional Schrodinger equation with impossible boundary conditions. I completely blew it on the test, and had spent hours later that night figuring out how to solve it.

"The first time I took it," he said, "I figured I might have gotten an eighty, eighty-five max. There was this weird problem with pathological boundary conditions that I choked on."

A shiver ran down my back. He was a flesh-and-bone echo.

"But that day I knew the answer, having figured it out the night before. That was what finally freaked me. I never finished the test. I walked out, actually ran out, and hid in my dorm room. The next day it was Friday again. Needless to say, I stopped going to class. Quantum tests seem to lose just a bit of their relevance when you realize that you're dead. Now and again though, I do stop in to take that test, just for old times' sake."

The wail of a siren caught my attention. I looked up the street. Another ambulance was pulling up to the Med Center. That would just have to wait for a few more minutes. First I needed to know just how much he knew.

"What makes you think that you're dead?" I asked.

He smiled with my smile, and held up two fingers.

"I figured that there were only two viable options. The first was that I'm insane, and that all of this is just going on inside of my head," he said as he tapped the side of his head. "Either that, or I'm dead and this is Heaven."

Three days ago I had questioned *my* sanity when I found myself thrust into this world.

"But the insane option just didn't cut it," he said. "If I was nuts and none of this was real, then there'd be absolutely nothing I could do about it. That was a no-win scenario, so I opted for the second—I was dead, and in Heaven."

It was frightening to hear and watch him. I was seeing myself. His argument against considering himself insane was much like the one I had used. The thirteen years that separated us did not seem all that great.

"And what makes this Heaven?" I asked.

Again he held up two fingers. Did I always hold up fingers when making a point? I didn't think so, but couldn't be sure. It was obviously something unconscious, and reflexive. He lowered the first finger.

"Because I can do whatever I want here. The place is alive, and I can control it." He stamped his feet against the gutter.

He could access the Nanomechanoids. That would be useful, very useful.

"But it's more than just control. Every day's the same for everyone here but me. One day I'll wake and find I'm the captain of the football team, or perhaps the student body president." He then smiled a sly sort of smile and passed a hand in front of the Bruin letterman's jacket that he wore. "The girls love me here."

To a twenty-one-year-old version of myself, what he described might just seem like Heaven. When I was at UCLA it had been a continual grind of classes, books, studies, tests, more books, and always more tests. It was something I regretted when I'd finally gotten out of school, that I'd done little more than pound the books. If *I* could have gone back, returned to UCLA, I might be doing something very similar to what he was doing.

He lowered his second finger.

"But the clincher was God. The second day here, as I was running across campus, trying to get some hint as to what'd happened to me, I saw the pyramid."

"Pyramid?" There had been no pyramid at the UCLA that I went to.

He nodded. "It was right smack in the middle of Dickson Plaza. It wasn't one of those smooth Egyptian jobs, but an Aztec type with steep stone stairs. At the top was a huge stone altar, and on the altar sat the oldest, most shriveled-up guy I'd ever seen."

Colin Wood was a hundred and twenty years old.

"But I couldn't get near him or the pyramid. My body wouldn't let me. Whenever I got near my body would turn itself around, just like when I get to the campus boundaries. I tried for months and finally gave up. I see the old guy from time to time, lurking around the edges of buildings or hiding in the back of the cafeteria. He's God and He's keeping an eye on me."

It had to be Wood. This whole place might have been created so he could relive his "wasted youth"—*our* wasted youth. He might be living vicariously through this younger incarnation, watching him do all the things he'd never had time for—all the things I'd never had time for.

"Why were you waiting for me here?" I asked.

Again he smiled. His teeth were perfect, the lower ones even and straight. My lower teeth were crowded, one poking slightly outward.

"I can smell the *things* in here," he said while

pointing to the people walking down the street. "It's a subtle smell, but after years there's no mistaking it. It's not the smell of something dead, but the smell of something that's never lived. They've got no souls. In my four years here they've all smelled like that, until this morning, until the two new ones showed up."

Two.

"One was a big guy dressed up in satin and ruffles, and the other was a naked woman that he dragged behind him. There was really nothing all that strange about them—I've created things that were a hell of a lot weirder—but these two were *real.* They smelled alive." He pointed at me. "Just like you smell. The big guy isn't wrapped too tightly though, and insists that *he's* God. He's been splattering any student stupid enough to dispute him." He nodded toward another ambulance that was pulling up to the Med Center. "I figured that he might have gotten in here from somewhere outside, and if he had found a way in then there might just really be a way out. So I backtracked him to here, trying to figure out how he got in, when all of the sudden you just stepped out of nothing."

He stood and took a step toward me. He was two or three inches taller than me.

"What's happened to me?"

A stranger might not have been able to interpret the look on his face, but I was certainly no stranger. It was a controlled look, a mask of curiosity, but that was just the mask. It hid anger beneath it. He knew that he *wasn't* dead and that this wasn't really Heaven. I'm certain that he had actually known that all along, but just hadn't been able to find any other answer by himself. I'd changed all that.

And I couldn't tell him the truth. I couldn't tell him that he was a construct, with the partial memories of the old man he'd seen lurking around campus. I couldn't tell him that he had existed merely as a plaything. He'd eventually be able to handle that—I knew he could, just as I had—but not now, not in the time that was available. At any moment Colin Wood, *the original Colin Wood,* might make his appearance and try to fry my ass, or his demented creation Napoleon might try to finish me off. Right now the truth was a luxury I couldn't afford. I knew this younger version of myself. I knew the story to tell, the story that would make him believe, make him help me.

"I'm not sure if you're going to be able to understand what I'm going to tell you, and even if you do I doubt that you'll believe it."

His jaw clenched, the muscles in his cheeks twitching. The response was just what I'd hoped for. At twenty-one I was an arrogant son of a bitch, certain that *nothing* was beyond my understanding. He'd do everything he could now to make himself believe that what I was about to tell him was the truth, just to prove to me nothing was beyond *his* understanding. The years between us had made me a bit less gullible. I hoped so, anyway.

"On May 27, 1977, you were abducted by an alien race." As stupid as that sounded I kept a straight, serious face. In my undergrad days I had had a single vice: science fiction. I read two or three books a week. It acted as an escape valve, something to take me away for a few hours from the grind and pressure. His mind was ripe for an idea like this. It would put him right in the middle of one of those books, right where he always imagined himself to be when he read them. He'd *want* to believe this.

He looked up and down the street, as if seeing it for the first time.

"Why?" he asked, trying to sound suspicious and skeptical, but I could tell that he wanted to believe it.

"A test."

His head nodded, almost imperceptibly. In the books he'd read aliens were always doing that. They'd abduct a human, stick him in some insane environment, and then see if he could figure it out and escape. If you won the human race would be let into some galactic federation, while if you lost it was turned into people-chow for the protein-starved citizens of Betelgeuse 12. He knew this storyline by heart.

"You will escape this place, but it won't end there.

This is just the starting place.'' I looked up toward the sky and pointed upward. ''It will continue out there.''

His eyes squinted. ''Time travel is impossible,'' he said.

He'd bought it. Within the framework of the story I was telling, that would be the only explanation for myself. I was an older version of him, having come back through time in order to help him. I waved a hand in front of myself and then tapped a finger against my forehead. ''It's a little hard to argue with flesh and bone,'' I said. ''Just because *your* science doesn't allow something like time travel, doesn't mean that a more advanced science doesn't.''

His eyes still squinted, while I continued to point at him.

''Your science can't even explain this place, can't explain how you can *talk* to your environment and make it do whatever you want. You can't explain how you've changed and improved yourself.''

Reaching up, he touched his cleft chin. I had him.

''I'm here to help you escape, just as *I* was helped to escape from here years ago.''

He looked suspicious. ''An infinite loop,'' he said.

I slowly smiled, while furiously dreaming up an explanation. He might be gullible, but he wasn't stupid. He realized that if I had come from the future he would eventually be making the same trip. And what that meant was that I should know exactly what was happening here at UCLA, since years ago I should have been rescued by an older version of myself.

''It's an infinite loop, endlessly cyclical but never repeating,'' I said. ''The universe isn't built that way. With each return *we* come back to a new universe, created by the very action of *our* coming back. This is not my UCLA.'' Like any lie, this one was starting to get overly complex.

Again he nodded.

''Bottom line is this,'' I said. ''You have to get out, and I'm here to help. The problem is twofold.'' I held up two fingers, conscious of it only after I saw him stare at them then quickly glance back at his own hand.

"There are two people standing in both our ways of escaping this place. Napoleon, and the old man you've seen." I lowered my fingers.

"Napoleon?" he asked.

I could almost read the questions going through his head. The man he'd seen had stood six and a half feet tall.

"He simply believes that he's Napoleon. He's insane, and being used by the aliens, but he's definitely not someone to be underestimated. He's got the power to control this place just as you have."

He blinked. I could sense that he was nearing the point of data overload. But there was just one more point, one more thing that was needed to push him into total belief.

"He's kidnapped my wife. That's the naked woman you saw."

"Wife?" he asked in a whisper.

"My wife, and possibly someday *your* wife," I said. That should kick him over the edge. I knew it would have kicked me over the edge if I'd heard that when I was twenty-one. *"We* have to save her."

His face seemed to glow. To him this had suddenly become something much more alluring than even the Heaven that Colin Wood had created for him. It was an *adventure*, something right out of the books he devoured. And he would play the hero, vanquishing evil and saving the damsel in distress, the damsel who would someday become his wife.

What I didn't tell him was that the prospects of our surviving this adventure were practically nonexistent. It would be a miracle if we didn't get killed.

"Ideas?" I asked him. He knew this place as it was now, as it had probably been changed over the past four years. Before I ran off blind, in all likelihood falling straight into a trap, I needed an edge, something that Colin Wood and Napoleon would not expect me to possess. That edge would have to come from Colin Wood, *Junior.*

"I've got some weapons," he said enthusiastically.

My stomach knotted itself. I realized that he didn't

have any *real* idea what we were dealing with. What could a twenty-one-year-old version of myself, trapped in 1977 UCLA, have in the way of weapons, that could hurt either Napoleon or Colin Wood?

"What are they?" I asked, certain now that my only edge would have to come from his ability to control the Nanomechanoids. At best he might have a pistol, or a couple of javelins that he'd lifted from the track team. I'd have to help him use the Nanomechanoids to create something more powerful.

"I've got two hand-held railguns that will throw a hundred-gram teflotungsten slug at a muzzle velocity of fifteen kilometers per second."

I blinked—at least three times, possibly four. What he described was impossible. If the slugs were aerodynamically sound and you aimed them straight above you, they would probably *never come down.* The muzzle velocity was greater than Earth's escape velocity. But that was only a minor point of amazement. The *kick* from such a weapon would drive the user meters into solid granite, and the power required probably couldn't be supplied by anything short of a small nuclear blast.

"Do you want to see them?" he asked.

I couldn't even manage a blink.

This was wrong.

I looked through the lab window, past the parking structure and out toward the dorms. I'd seen this view countless times. *My* lab had been in this room, 7835 Boelter Hall. But that had not been until the summer of 1978. *This* Colin Wood should have had no knowledge of what would come to pass in 1978.

I turned around.

The room itself was familiar—the chipped paint, the water-stained acoustic tiles—but that was all that was familiar. The rest of the lab was as unfathomable as Tartan's lab back at the observatory had been. It looked like a plasma fusion lab, full of vacuum vessels and magnetic coils that almost scraped the ten-foot ceiling above me. *I* knew practically nothing about plasma physics.

Colin Junior had his back to me as he unlocked a massive steel-gray cabinet.

"I've isolated the matrix of this room, so it doesn't recycle itself every day, reverting back to May 27. It's about the max volume I can hold on to. I've tried holding on to larger parts of campus, but they just snap back."

He swung open the cabinet drawer, turned quickly, and tossed something toward me.

I caught it. It was a paperback, worn and dog-eared.

"*The High Frontier* by Gerald O'Neil," he said. "That's where I got the idea for the railgun."

I turned the book over in my hand. This was *my* book. I must have read it half a dozen times. The concept of space colonies, and all the hardware that they required, had fascinated me. But it had been the "mass driver," a type of magnetically levitated slingshot, that had really grabbed my attention. I had even toyed with the idea of making one, wondering if I could build a really simple model. But I'd had no time, I was far too busy working on my thesis.

My thesis.

That would have made it at least 1980.

The room was warm, the pumps and electromagnets dumping waste heat, but I was shivering. I flipped open the book, going to the copyright page. The print date was 1981—four years past the date that Colin Junior said it was. This book should not have existed. I looked up, saw him wrestling with something within the cabinet, and then looked back down at the book.

It fell from my hands.

The publication date had changed.

It now said 1975.

That book, let alone the original hardcover, had not existed in 1975. O'Neil hadn't even written it then. I knew that for a fact. I'd made a mistake, possibly a fatal mistake. I'd taken this twenty-one-year-old version of Colin Wood at face value. I'd lied to *him*, but had stupidly believed that he had told *me* the truth. He could in reality be anything, or anyone, and he had let me know that. He hadn't had to show me the book, or somehow make the publication date change. He *wanted* me to know that he hadn't been telling the truth.

"This is it."

I looked up, not even realizing that I was staring down at the book on the floor. I didn't move toward him.

He had what must have been his railgun held up to the side of his face, staring through the sight. It was aimed at my head.

"I'm rather proud of this," he said.

This looked something like a bazooka. It was a metallic-looking tube, about two meters long, with a handle and trigger mounted in the center of it. From the base of the handle a thick-twined cable ran to his waist, disappearing into something about the size and shape of a shoebox. The whole thing looked incredibly crude, as if it couldn't even shoot a tennis ball across the room.

But it *was* aimed at my head.

"It's rather simple," he said. "The main tube is a superconducting magnetic coil that has a rep rate of about a tenth of a millisecond and is powered up from the charge stored on a pair of counter-rotating superconducting flywheels in the power pack."

He *was* crazy.

My brain slipped into its calculator mode. For a muzzle velocity of fifteen kilometers per second, in a tube of about a meter long, it meant that the slug had to be accelerated to about ten million gravities. Nothing, absolutely nothing, could stand those accelerations. And even if it could, the power required would be enormous. A hundred-gram slug moving at that velocity would mean that the power pack would have to be able to pulse to a hundred billion watts. Impossible. The gun would tear itself apart, but only after the recoil would blow you through the back wall of the lab. And besides, there were no superconducting elements that could handle that current load at room temperatures. Certainly none in 1977, and none that I knew of in 1990.

But what about 2076?

I took a step forward.

"It has one drawback," he said. "I was able to develop the materials to handle the accelerations, and the superconducting elements to take the current loads at room temperatures, but nothing could take the recoil of a fifteen-kilometer-per-second shot."

I stopped moving. He seemed confident, far too confident.

"A solution always exists, though," he said.

He squeezed the trigger before I could move. His reflexes were as quick as mine.

Ker-blam!

My ears rang, and I tried to see through a snowfall of plaster that had suddenly engulfed the room. I didn't move though. He might fire again.

"Momentums must be matched. Whatever goes forward, must go backward," he said.

The dust quickly settled.

The wall *behind* him was gone—as well as the wall behind that wall. Dust was still settling, but I knew with total certainty that walls, possibly kilometers away, were gone. I turned around slowly. The window was blown out, along with a chunk of the wall. In the distance, several kilometers away, were the dorms. Several top floors of the nearest dorm had vanished. Red flames were already licking up the side of the building.

"To fire forward, you also have to fire backward. That's the first disadvantage. In addition, the teflo-tungsten shot will ablate and spread out. Its effective kill distance is pretty much under ten kilometers."

I turned back.

He'd lowered the railgun, and held a second one in his hands.

"It's taken me nearly three years to charge up the power packs, practically draining everything that comes into UCLA. They *each* have three shots." He looked down at the one that he had just fired. "Two shots left for me."

He held the other gun out toward me.

A million questions should have been going through my head, ranging from the impossibility of the gun itself to who in the hell this Colin Wood Junior really was, but none of those was there. My head was filled with an image.

I saw Napoleon's grapho-titanate skull vaporizing under the impact of a fifteen-kilometer-per-second teflotungsten slug.

CHAPTER 18

Truth and Consequences

I hugged the red brick wall of Powell Library.

Colin Junior stood in front of me, waving the barrel of his railgun at the students that ran by. Most were burnt and torn, hardly any still possessing a full set of limbs.

"It looks like this Napoleon guy has put the fear of God into them," he said, sounding extremely cheerful just as a young coed in a red sweater and blue jeans hobbled past us. She had no feet, and was running on ankle stumps. She might not have been real, just a programmed entity, but the look on her face was real enough. The pain might not have been real, but the fear certainly was. Fear like that could not be simulated.

Reaching out, I grabbed him by the arm and pulled him against the wall. I had questions, questions that had to be answered before I faced either Wood or Napoleon.

"Who in the hell are you?" I asked.

He smiled, with the type of smile that probably melted female undergrads. He'd probably designed it to produce just that effect.

"Colin Wood," he said.

"Circa 1977?" I asked, doing nothing to hide the cynicism in my voice.

He smiled even wider, his dimples deepening. "Well of course," he said, trying to sound pained and hurt. "How could I not be? Your own story confirms it. Wasn't it you who told me all about these nasty aliens that kidnapped me, putting me in this puzzle, in order to see if mankind is worthy enough to spread out to the stars?'' The look on his face was one that you'd expect to see if I had accused him of kicking his grandmother down the stairs.

I shook my railgun at him. ''This can't exist, not in 1977.''

''Of course not,'' he said, still smiling. He tapped the side of his head. ''It all makes sense to me now. Over the years, while I've been here, I've been hearing voices, seeing things that I knew weren't there. It's been the *aliens* who have been putting those things in my head.''

He had to be playing with me.

''They've told me things, shown me things. It must be part of the test, seeing if my *primitive* brain can comprehend their science. The voices told me how to build the railguns, showed me how to develop the components, and how to understand the science behind them. Surely you must remember all this. You were here before, weren't you, standing in my shoes? You haven't been lying to me, have you?''

I shook my head. ''Of course not,'' I said. ''I just wanted to see how much you knew.''

His smile turned into a smirk.

He *was* playing with me.

He knew that I'd lied to him, and he knew I knew *he* was lying to me. But why? What was *his* game?

''Isn't it about time that we saved *our* dear wife?'' he asked.

He smiled once again, but the dimples were gone. I couldn't read the expression on his face. I was looking at a stranger, someone I had never seen before—someone that I would never want to see again.

Walking past him, then once again hugging the brick wall, I shoved my way past juniper bushes, knocking back branches with the barrel of my railgun. I finally poked my head around the corner of the building and looked out across the quad.

Royce Hall.

Like Powell Library, it should have been built of

red brick, cream-colored masonry, and cement columns, and adorned with twin bell towers. It should have looked like something lifted from Venice or Rome.

It didn't.

It looked like something from fifth- or sixth-century England, something direct from King Arthur and the Knights of the Round Table. Built of gold blocks and spiral towers, adorned with flags snapping in the breeze and surrounded by a moat that was breached by a silver drawbridge, it sat where Royce Hall should have been.

But the castle was almost an incidental, invisible thing, compared to what lounged in front of it. It looked like a green-scaled brontosaurus, with the wingspan of a 747. It lay curled in the quad, sleeping, flame leaping in and out of its nostrils with each breath it took.

A dragon.

Its scaled eyelids were closed, but I could see its bowling ball-sized eyes rolling back and forth beneath the thick green skin. It was dreaming. I was staring at a sleeping dragon sprawled between Powell Library and King Arthur's castle, and wondering just what in the hell a dragon could possibly be dreaming about.

But I didn't have to wonder for long.

I suddenly knew.

Dragons wanted one thing and one thing alone—virgins.

The ground beneath me rumbled, and dust and grit rained down from the side of Powell Library. The dragon stirred, but its eyes were still closed. It rolled over, like some mutated and monstrous dog, carefully folding its wings back, sticking its long black legs into the air, and twitching its taloned toes. With a sound like a crack of thunder it fell over, splintering eucalyptus trees that had gotten trapped in the path of its swishing tail.

Tartan.

Instincts screamed at me to run out into the quad, waving my railgun and atomizing anything that got in my way. But I hugged the brick wall. I no longer had the luxury of listening to instincts, not here, and especially not with these people.

Tartan and Napoleon had been hidden behind the dragon. She hung limp from a cross that looked as if it had been splintered from a single block of ruby. Her hands and feet were tied to it with gold ropes. She was dressed in what looked like white silk. A sparkling tiara sat atop her tangled hair. Her head was bent down, and I couldn't see her face.

To her right, sitting on a throne that was identical to the central throne that had been in the Cathedral of Notre Dame, sat Napoleon. He was dressed in a crushed blue velvet coat, white leather hip boots, a ruffled silk shirt, and lavender tights. He still wore the Coke-bottle glasses, and a headset was draped around his neck. Just above his head floated a golden halo.

"Binoculars," I said in a whisper, reaching a hand behind myself but not looking back, afraid that if I so much as blinked Napoleon would command the dragon to attack Tartan.

And that's what this insane fantasy was all about.

She was the *virgin.* That was a truly sick joke, something that only Napoleon could possibly have dreamed up.

From behind me there came wet, smacking noises, and I felt something warm and moist drop into my hand. By the time I brought it around to my face it was solid, looking as though it were made of plastic, aluminum, and glass. I held the binoculars up to my eyes. They purred gently, as some auto-focus device telescoped the lenses.

Napoleon's face glowed, bathed by the halo-generated light that came from above him. He did not blink but stared forward, seeming to focus on something distant, something that probably wasn't even there. His right cheek twitched. I scanned the quad, stopping when I came to Tartan. Her head was still bent down, but right at the top of her forehead, where her long hair parted, I could see a black splotch.

C-22.

Napoleon might have gone totally insane, but he wasn't stupid. I panned past her, further along the quad. It was deserted, except for a few students hiding in bushes and behind trash cans. It was all so familiar: the buildings, the walkways, the trampled, muddy lawns, even the smog-blackened brass flagpole in the center of the quad.

All familiar.

Almost. I held the binoculars steady.

Palm fronds?

I lowered the binoculars. At the far end of the quad, down in Dickson Plaza, sat a chunk of Mexican jungle, complete with Aztec temple. Colin Junior had said it would be there, but words couldn't do justice to this monolith. I brought the binoculars back up to my eyes and scanned up the temple's steep steps. They were littered with bodies, UCLA students by the looks of them, all with ragged holes punched in their chests. I looked upward.

He sat on the edge of a massive stone slab. He wore a breechcloth and jaguar skins, and was stained rust-red from what must have been dried blood. His skin was wrinkled and folded, nearly translucent, and streaked with ropy blue veins. He looked even *older* than a hundred and twenty.

Colin Wood.

He stared down at me, obviously knowing that I watched him, and pointed a bloody finger in the direction of King Arthur's castle. I knew what he meant, knew what he wanted. Before we would face off, and see whose body tumbled from that stone altar, I would first have to deal with Napoleon. From the instant I had seen those skewered angels at the entrance to Heaven I had known that it was going to come to this. Wood was savoring this entire charade in the same way he would savor a glass of wine: by taking in the bouquet, and admiring its rich color, before he'd take a sip. He wanted to watch me perform, see how I'd surmount this last challenge before he would take a crack at me. I still believed that there was a slim chance that I could beat Wood, but I knew with total certainty that I could not do it by leveling my railgun at the pyramid and start blasting away. That would be too easy. Wood simply wouldn't allow that. He hadn't set all this up so we could simply face each other down, like gunslingers in some long-dead Western town. It was as if he wanted something from me, and was still tugging and poking at me, trying to make me realize something. I had told Colin Junior that all of this was a type of intelligence test, set up by aliens, and I suddenly wondered if this was in fact an intelligence test, but one given by Wood. But if that was so, what exactly was he testing me for? I didn't know, couldn't quite assemble all the pieces, but one thing I did know—he didn't want all of this over, not yet.

And that, I suddenly realized, was *his* greatest weakness.

Again and again, over the past four days, he'd taken me to the brink but then pulled me back in. He wanted me to face death, but he didn't want me killed—not by someone else. He was both my guardian angel *and* my executioner. He had not brought me all this way to be killed by a lacy psycho and his pet dragon.

Understanding that gave me more power than a railgun, or even Nanomechanoid control. If I was to stand any chance at all it would only be by understanding *him*—by understanding what he really wanted with me.

I turned around.

Colin Junior was smiling. The dimples had returned.

"If I'm killed, I want you to go after the old man," I said. I really didn't think Wood would let Napoleon kill me, but I couldn't be *completely* certain. After all, he *was* totally insane.

Colin Junior shook his railgun at me.

"It will be my pleasure," he said with a strange coldness in his voice. Again the dimples had vanished. His face was mine, but the expression on it was something foreign and alien.

I walked out from the bushes.

* * *

"Move it!"

The dragon towered over me. As I came out of the bushes it woke and positioned itself directly between myself and Napoleon.

It flapped its wings, and I had to lean into the wind it created in order just to keep standing. Napoleon was not all that imaginative. It was a standard, storybook-type dragon. It smelled like spoiled meat and sulfur. Its snout dripped greasy-oily flame that splattered the walkway in front of me.

I waved my railgun at it, but there was no way I was going to fire. At this proximity, being hit by untold tons of exploding dragon would kill me just as surely as a teflotungsten slug to the head.

Rrrrrrr!

Heat beat me to the ground.

I kneeled, but did not cover my head. I was certain that Wood would prevent the dragon from flash-frying me, but even if he did not, covering my head would be a totally meaningless gesture. If this dragon really wanted to toast me, I'd be toasted.

Seconds passed, and I was not transformed into a chunk of charcoal. I stood, and turned toward something exploding at my back. Flame ate at what was left of Powell Library. Both bricks and books burned. Colin Junior lay sprawled in the muddy grass, slowly picking himself up.

I walked forward, actually moving beneath the dragon's chest, and kicked at one of its taloned toes. I gave it everything I had. The thing actually flinched.

"Move it!" I screamed, as I wiped tears from my face. At this proximity the stench was practically lethal.

"Stand aside, Rosemary."

The mountain of stinking scales that hung over me shuddered, lifted a massive leg, and then stepped *over* me.

Blrrrrrt!

A blast of the most noxious, caustic, eye-burning, stomach-turning stench imaginable beat down on me. My entire body puckered, spasming, trying to pull itself into a ball. I was down on hands and knees, something stinging and sour exploding out of both my mouth and nose. My gut continued to spasm long after it was empty.

"The man who would be God."

I bent my neck back, and looked up through watery eyes. Napoleon stood above me, hands to hips, grinning like someone demented. Wiping my chin and pushing myself up, I stood. The railgun was still clenched in my hand. I angled it upward, toward his grinning face.

"I think not," said Napoleon, speaking in emperor-like tones. "You must certainly understand how things operate by now." He sidestepped, and pointed toward the castle. "It should not take God to point such things out to you."

I looked.

The cross that Tartan was strapped to seemed to pull itself up out of the ground, sprout a pair of ruby feet, and start to shuffle toward us. As it walked a golden rope squirmed from the top of it, crawled down its side, and wrapped itself about Tartan's forehead, pulling her back.

The C-22 was now clearly visible.

Tartan's eyes were open, but dead.

Those dead eyes were like some sort of trigger. Things coalesced, and a small piece of this puzzle came together. Understanding *was* power. In an instant, in the smallest fraction of a second, I'd defeated Napoleon, and he had absolutely no idea of what had just happened to him.

I smiled, and sensed Napoleon stiffen.

"Dead men, in the presence of God, should not smile," he said. There wasn't the sound of fear in his voice, but there was the sound of uncertainty. I imagined that, for Napoleon, that must be far worse than fear.

I lowered the railgun away from his head. That gun could never kill Napoleon—he knew it, and I knew it. He would not allow it. In this place, he would *never* allow me to kill him. And realizing that had been the key that had let me know exactly how I *would* stop him. Wood wanted to face *me* one on one, but he'd placed Napoleon directly in my way. But Wood would inevitably get *his* way, since both Heaven and Napoleon were ultimately his creations. That meant that since I couldn't stop Napoleon there was only one person who could—and that would be Napoleon himself. Wood had wanted me to figure this out, to understand that power didn't come from railguns or Nanomechanoid control but from understanding the wants and motivations of people. He'd done this by forcing me to face an enemy of obvious superiority without useful weapons.

Not completely true.

I had one weapon—my ability to think. It was that ability that had given Wood the world before the Bug, and had transformed the world after the Bug into his own personal nightmare. That ability was more powerful than any chunk of hardware, or an entire army of Nanomechanoid warriors. Before I faced Wood, he wanted me to know that. That was what this entire farce of the past four days had been about. Wood wanted to face someone with his abilities, but to not quite know how they would respond. He wanted to face his equal, but an equal that he couldn't completely second-guess. And to be his equal, I had to know that ultimate power came from understanding situations and people—not from hardware. He wanted to face himself, and thereby actually have a chance of losing.

I walked around Napoleon and toward the cross, which had replanted itself into the ground. I reached for the ropes around Tartan's feet and began to untie them.

"No!" screamed Napoleon.

I slowly turned.

"And why not?" I asked, sounding casual, as if I really didn't care if he answered or not.

"I'll kill her!" he screamed. "If you don't do as I tell you, I *will* kill her!" He pointed up toward her head. "I'll detonate it!"

"You will not," I said in a whisper.

He stepped back, as if he'd been punched square in the face.

"You dare tell me what *I* will do?" he screamed, as spit ran down his chin and his face turned an impossibly bright shade of red.

"You control her," I said. "It's the only thing in this world that you really do control. Everything else is an illusion, the whim of an insane old man. He manipulates you, and tugs on your strings. Except for her, there is absolutely nothing else in this world that you *do* control. She's the only thing that stands between you and *total* insanity."

"No!" he shrieked.

"She's the only thing standing between you and death."

He shook and, reaching out his shaking arms, pointed at Tartan. "I *can* kill her. She's nothing, a piece of meat, something I can snuff out with the smallest wish. I am her universe, her only reality. She is nothing without me!"

"How sad, to only have control over something so pathetic, so meaningless," I said. "It certainly doesn't say much about you, only to be able to control something so insignificant."

He lowered his shaking hands. His shoulders slumped, and tears welled up in his eyes.

"I *could* kill her," he said, sounding more as if he were trying to convince himself rather than me.

Napoleon would never kill her. He couldn't. It was the only thing in the world that he *really* believed he had any control over. I should have realized this long ago. Dropping my railgun to the ground and unsnapping the power pack, I turned and pulled myself up Tartan's cross. I began untying her hands.

"I could kill you!" screamed Napoleon.

I dropped Tartan's untied right hand and turned.

In the time it had taken me to climb the cross and untie Tartan's hand something in Napoleon had died. He still stood six and a half feet tall, and still looked to be a good solid three hundred pounds, but he had died inside. I could see it in his eyes. They were dulled and glazed. He had been forced to admit to himself that the only thing in the world that he really had was his sick and disgusting hold over his sister. And he didn't really have even that. *It had him.*

I jumped down from the cross and took a half-step toward him.

"You can't harm me," I said. "Your lord and master would never permit it." I pointed up toward the pyramid. "It's over for you now."

"No!"

Reaching out, he pointed his gloved hands at me. Lightning erupted from his fingertips, crackling toward me, the intensity blinding me and the sting of ozone burning my eyes and lungs.

Nothing touched me.

I stood unharmed, surrounded by a wall of crackling lightning. Then, as suddenly as it had started, it stopped.

"It's over," I said in a whisper.

Napoleon slowly lowered his hands.

"It *is* over."

The voice had come from behind me. It was Tartan's. I turned slowly. She stood behind me, obviously having untied herself after I had partially freed her. She stood more than ten meters away from me, totally out of reach.

She had the railgun in her hands and was holding it high and in front of herself. It was aimed for Napoleon.

The exit end was aimed at *her* head.

I blinked—once.

"Don't fire!" I screamed.

I'd broken Napoleon, or rather let him break himself. If his will to live also had been broken he would let himself get killed, and that would take Tartan with him.

Tartan's finger tensed against the trigger.

"Jason!" she screamed.

Her body convulsed, her eyelids flickering and her head jerking. But she managed to hold the railgun steady. She was remembering, remembering things that would kill her just as surely as firing the railgun would.

"Sister!"

I turned.

Napoleon's hands fell off, hitting the ground and bouncing several times as if made of rubber, and then began to disintegrate. He held his wrist stumps to the sides of his head, pressing them against his ears. "Don't leave me alone!" he cried, sounding like a frightened child. "We only have each other!"

He'd dropped his internal shielding. He was touching his own, long-buried memories.

"Why did you do this?" asked Tartan.

I looked back at her.

She was holding the railgun with her right hand, her entire left arm now twisted and pinned against her chest. As I watched, her legs collapsed beneath her and she hit the ground, face-first. I had covered almost half the distance between us when she struggled up to her knees and again held the railgun high, aiming it at Napoleon. I stopped.

"We were *things,*" said Napoleon, his voice slurred and squeaky.

I didn't turn but continued to watch Tartan. Blood ran down her face from her now broken nose. But the blood that ran from her ears hadn't been caused by the fall. I knew that. The same thing had happened to Joe. Her brain was rupturing, tearing itself apart.

"No!" she said, struggling with the word. "Brother and sister—not things."

"Yes," he said. "I was your brother. That made me not a thing, but a person. Only you stood between me being a person or becoming a thing. *Things* don't have sisters. I couldn't let you go. If you went I'd become a *thing,* and I knew you wanted to leave."

Tears now mixed in with the blood that ran down Tartan's face. "I loved you," she said in a hissing whisper. "I didn't want to leave. You forced me. You *hurt* me." She hit the ground but her right elbow kept her propped up, kept the railgun aimed at Napoleon's head.

"I didn't want to hurt you," said Napoleon. "I just wanted you to stay. I couldn't take the chance that you would leave." He whispered something that I couldn't hear, then cleared his throat. "You loved me?"

Tartan nodded her head in jerky spasms.

"*Things* aren't loved," he said, sounding distant.

Tartan waved the railgun feebly and it fell from her hand. "Brothers are loved," she mumbled. Her elbow slipped out from beneath her and her face dropped into the pool of blood that was beneath her. Her legs twitched, then she was still.

"Janice!"

I turned.

Napoleon had melted. As if he had been carved from a chunk of wax he had sagged, falling in on himself. Only his clothes seemed to be holding his liquefying body together.

"I thought," he said, struggling with the words, his mouth seeming to be dribbling from his skull, "that she wanted to leave, that she could never want to be with a *thing*."

"To her, you *were* her brother, never a *thing*," I said. "She loved you."

Napoleon tried to smile but his lips slid from his face, hitting the ground, quickly followed by teeth and gums.

"Luuuv meeee!" he screeched, his throat tearing, greasy things exploding out and then running down his ruffled silk shirt. What was left of his tongue slid from his mouth. He stared at me with eyes that were slipping from their sockets. As I watched them crawl down his sagging cheeks, the pain that filled them seemed to fade away.

He hit the ground and I heard something crack and splatter, something that sounded like a thin-shelled egg. That impenetrable grapho-titanate skull split, the bloody contents spilling out.

Rrrrrrrr!

I dove for the railgun, got it in my hands, and brought it up as I rolled. The dragon hung over me, flame licking its snout. Its chest expanded as it sucked down air. I raised the gun high so the back-shot wouldn't vaporize me.

I started to squeeze the trigger.

The dragon collapsed, its skin shredding, a sea of green slime raining down. Still clutching the unfired railgun, I took a deep breath, covered my head, and felt myself vanish beneath the torrent.

CHAPTER 19

Full Circle

I stood, wiping green slime from my face. What remained of the dragon filled the quad from King Arthur's castle to the brick-and-book pile of the Powell Library. The putrid stuff was knee-deep and smelled just as rancid as it looked.

They were all gone.

Tartan had finally faced down her brother. I couldn't be sure what had pushed her over the edge and had forced her into finally confronting him, but I'd like to think that, at long last, she had taken control of her own life. I could still see Napoleon's eyes as they dribbled down his face—the hate, the fear, and the absolute terror slowly fading from them. He'd been bent and broken by a world created by Wood. He had been desperate to believe himself human, so desperate that he had driven himself into committing inhuman acts. He had been as much a victim as had Tartan.

And both had been victimized by Wood.

The entire world had been victimized by Wood.

I suddenly sensed Colin Junior standing behind me. I still couldn't touch the Nanomechanoids, what I felt was beyond that. I simply knew that he was there, could feel him staring at the back of my head. It was as if he were my shadow.

"How'd you get that loon to smoke himself?" he asked.

I didn't turn. He didn't deserve an answer, hadn't earned the right to know. He hadn't lived what I'd lived for the past four days. I doubted that even if I *did* explain what had taken place he'd be able to understand. He didn't have the tools to understand. *His* answer to conflict was a railgun and Nanomechanoid manipulation. He wouldn't be able to understand how much power there was in simply showing someone his true self.

"When that wacko checked out, I was able to get ahold of that dragon he'd made. I saw no sense in you wasting a shot and taking the risk of getting crushed by dragon chunks, so I reduced it to primary bits."

I still didn't answer, but stared across the quad to where Tartan had stood. The tidal wave of green slime had pinned her up against the ruby cross, only her hand protruding from the green sea. I waded forward, moving toward her. I didn't hurry. I knew there was no need to hurry.

"Sorry about the wife!" Colin Junior shouted at me.

I cringed. Had I ever really been like him, so insensitive, so unfeeling? How could he not know when to simply shut up? He might look like me, but he wasn't me. I don't think he ever had been.

I bent down and reached out.

But I couldn't touch her fingers.

She was dead, had been dead from the moment she'd hit the ground, her brain tearing itself apart. I knew that, the rational part of me knowing beyond any doubt that there wasn't even the slightest chance that she was still alive. But the emotional part couldn't accept it, absolutely refused to believe it. I'd seen miracles since arriving here, and wanted to offer up a prayer for just one more.

But there was no one to pray to. There were no gods here.

So I touched her fingers. They were cool and limp, the drying slime that caked them the only thing holding them up. I reached down for her wrist, pressing it tightly.

There was no pulse.

And that was because there was no brain to drive her heart.

"One down, one to go!"

I gently pushed her hand beneath the slime, then stood and turned toward Colin Junior. He held the railgun high, aiming it toward the pyramid. Who *was* he?

"The constraints are gone!" he shouted. "I can feel it. He knows that he's lost, and that there's absolutely nothing he can do to stop us."

Turning, I looked toward the pyramid. Without the binoculars Wood was just a miniscule blur, but I could sense him quietly sitting there, having watched what had happened, having watched me surmount the last obstacle that he'd placed between us.

"Don't waste the shot," I said, certain that the railgun simply wouldn't fire. Wood wouldn't let it end like that. Never.

He didn't lower the gun.

"I can take the top of that pyramid off and blow that old man into orbit."

"No you can't," I said. "He'd never let you. Weapons can't stop him, nothing *you* can do can stop him."

He lowered the railgun.

That I hadn't expected. He should have taken the shot. Had I still been twenty-one, I would have taken the shot. Hell, I would have taken the shot four days ago. This was just one more indication that he wasn't who he appeared to be.

"Why not?" he asked.

I'd answer *this* question. This time he deserved an answer. Lowering the gun had proved that. I waved my hand around the quad, and out over the sea of green slime. "That's what *this* was all about. It was a lesson that old man wanted me to learn, the last lesson, but the most important. I had seen Napoleon killed, having taken a spear through the heart. But he came back, stronger than before. Then I ripped his head from his body, leaving him totally helpless." I actually laughed. Tartan lay dead at my feet, but still I managed a laugh. Tears ran down my face. "But the old man saw that Napoleon wouldn't remain helpless for long. He gave him back his body, and then gave him all the powers I'd had." I pointed at him. "All the powers that you have. The old man was trying to tell me something but I just couldn't see it, was too damn stubborn and too damn egotistical to see the obvious: Napoleon was an enemy I could *not* defeat. No matter what I might do, the old man would see that Napoleon not only survived but actually grew stronger. He wanted me to realize that there was only one person that could stop Napoleon, and that would be Napoleon himself. He was his own worst enemy. All I had to do was force him into looking at himself."

Colin Junior looked puzzled. There was no mistaking the meaning behind those scrunched-up eyebrows and narrow-slit eyes. He wasn't me, but he knew my mannerisms better than I knew them myself.

"Superiority doesn't come with railguns, or even total control of the environment," I said, "but with the understanding of people. And that includes yourself. Understand yourself, and the people around you, and you can do anything."

I looked around.

"You can even create Heaven and Hell," I said.

"And you understand that old man?" he asked as he waved his gun up toward the pyramid.

I smiled. "Not yet, not completely, but I think I'm starting to understand myself, understand what I might do if I was in his place."

"That still doesn't tell me why I can't stop him." Again he raised up his railgun toward the pyramid.

"The only person who can stop that old man is himself," I said. "And he *wants* to be stopped. That's why I'm here. That's what all this is really about."

Colin Junior, or whoever he really was, lowered his railgun.

I marched across Dickson Plaza, beating at palm fronds and vines. Ugly green-and-black bugs, the size and shape of cigarettes, chewed at my arms and face.

"I don't understand," said Colin Junior. "If he wants to be stopped, if he wants to let us go, then why doesn't he simply do it?"

And that *was* the question.

He was all-powerful, could apparently do anything he pleased, except for one thing: He couldn't let go, couldn't give up the world. He'd called me back, created me, so I could—supposedly—take it from him. But no one could really *take it*. He would have to willingly *give it*. The same way that Napoleon had willingly given up his life, Wood would have to do the same. And somehow I held the key to all of this happening. Wood had tortured me for four days, killing everyone around me, running me through a maze, forcing me into making decisions that I would have thought myself incapable of making. I'd killed to stay alive. I'd watched those around me die so that I could live.

Why had he done this to me?

If he wanted out, and no longer wanted to live as the egomaniac that had killed billions and even now was killing millions more, then why not just pull his own plug, and be done with it?

What did he really need me for?

I stopped. I felt the barrel of Colin Junior's railgun nudge me in the back as he stopped.

"What is it?" he asked. "What do you see?"

What do I see? An excellent question. A highly relevant question. I turned around and stared at him. As I continued to swat at the bugs that crawled over me, I noticed that none of them was chewing at him. Even here, in this slice of insanity generated by Wood, Colin Junior seemed to have control. I knew that meant something, but something that I couldn't quite see.

"Do you ever get bored with what you're doing?" I asked him, wondering if Wood was being driven not by guilt or insanity but by boredom. Had he simply lived too many years, and now wanted to die, to put everything behind him?

Once again Colin Junior's brow twisted. "All the time."

I remembered back. When I'd been his age, my attention span probably could have been measured in milliseconds. That was what had made school such a grind. Back then the world had seemed too big, too strange, and just too wonderfully bizarre, to keep my head buried in books and myself locked away for years pounding out a thesis. But I'd done it. I'd managed to complete it.

"What kept you going when you were in school? Why didn't you just chuck it all and wander the world?"

He smiled, almost laughed, as if I had told him a joke. "I had a goal," he said. "There were things I wanted to do with my life, but all those things required that little piece of paper."

The Ph.D.

"Without that, no one would let me in and let me play with the toys that would let me see the things that had never been seen before. I knew what I wanted, and where I was going, *and* that nothing would stand in my way." He waved his free hand over his head, not indicating this Mexican jungle but the UCLA campus that surrounded it. "I had made a promise to myself, and that meant I had a responsibility to myself."

I nodded. I knew what he meant. Life is goals, and the commitment to those goals is what drives life, what keeps you alive and keeps you working, even when you think you can't get through another day. That's how I saw life. But did Wood still see it that way? Was all this insanity and destruction just the result of an egomaniac running wild?

I turned, batting aside a fern.

A body lay, face-up.

The face was mine. A hole, the size of a fist, had been punched through its chest, just where its heart should have been. But the heart was gone. I stepped over the body, and then over another exactly like it. By the time we reached the base of the pyramid the bodies were strewn waist-high, all with hearts ripped out and all having my face.

"What does it mean?" asked Colin Junior.

I didn't answer him.

We'd find out soon enough. Possibly too soon.

* * *

The view was majestic, spanning the distance from the azure Pacific all the way up to the Hollywood Hills. I didn't care. I certainly hadn't come all this way for the view.

Wood still sat perched on the edge of the stone altar—an altar filled with the still-beating hearts of the hundreds of lookalikes that he'd dumped down the pyramid's steps. They all beat in unison, the gentle *thump-thump* pulsing into the stone and then pounding up through the soles of my boots. Wood tugged and fussed with several blood-streaked cockatoo feathers in his headdress, then adjusted his jaguar shawl.

"Do you like my temple?" he asked.

I looked first at the altar full of beating hearts, then down the blood-streaked steps, to the pile of bodies below. In the Mexican jungle heat the bodies were already bloating, and the overripe scent of a stockyard was drifting up toward us.

"An appropriate enough place, I guess, for a psychotic like yourself," I said.

But even as I said it the words didn't quite ring true. He'd destroyed a sick world, then created an even worse one. On the surface it was an act of insanity. How could killing billions be anything else *but* an act of insanity? And here he sat, dressed as some blood-crazed Aztec priest, before an altar of still-beating hearts, obviously insane, obviously having blown every rational part of his brain.

Too obvious.

Wood was subtle.

The past four days had shown me that. Nothing in his world was obvious, nothing was written in black and white. I had come into this world viewing people as good or bad, right or wrong, and that's how I'd tried to label the ones I met here. But they hadn't been good or bad, right or wrong. They'd simply been people—people who were confused and hurt, doing the best they could, muddling through life based on what was often incomplete information, or just flat-out lies. In this world nothing was obvious, nothing was as it seemed. There were no black and whites.

I smiled.

There never *had* been any black and whites—they'd only been in my *head.* The world had always been a gray, conflicting, confusing place, but I had filtered it, always assuming that I knew what was right and wrong, that I could judge. I couldn't. I'd never really been able to, but until now I hadn't realized that.

From over the edge of my shoulder I saw the barrel of Colin Junior's railgun being leveled at Wood. Half turning, I grabbed it, and was about to raise it up, but then stopped and removed my hand.

"What do you think you're going to do?" I asked.

"Blow this psycho's head to the moon," said Colin Junior.

I looked back at Wood's rust-red face. I looked into the face of this demented, withered-up old man. It was too obvious, too black and white. The world wasn't built that way.

Pieces came together.

"Be my guest," I said. "But he's not real, he's just like those bodies that he's dumped down the temple. And you should know that."

"Why?" he asked, as he lowered his railgun.

I should have known when he had first taken me into his lab. I should have known when I'd seen the railgun, and O'Neil's book. I should have known the instant I'd seen him sitting on the curb.

"Because *you* made him. You've made this entire place."

His eyes grew large.

"Because you're Colin Wood, the *real* Colin Wood."

He then smiled, and began to unfasten his railgun's power pack. "An interesting theory," he said. The smile vanished as quickly as it had materialized, and his face turned dark. He pushed the railgun into my hands, wrapping my fingers around the trigger and tugging the gun up. One end pointed at his head and the other at what I was certain was just another Colin Wood simulation.

"I'll make it easy on you then. Even if you're

wrong, you'll be right. Squeeze that trigger, and we'll both be gone."

He stepped forward, pushing his forehead against the barrel of the gun. Wrinkles and creases suddenly filled his young face.

"This is a no-lose scenario, boy. Take the shot, and it's all over. But I'm warning you, this is your only chance. Either the both of us die, or you die. You've gotten this far, and earned the *right* to choose."

My finger tensed against the trigger.

Too obvious.

And far too easy.

"The choice is yours, boy. You've run through my little game, kept your skin intact, figured out what was what, and who was who. I'm declaring you the winner. Take the prize."

He pushed against the railgun's barrel.

"Choose!" he screamed.

He said the game was over, but it wasn't. This was the last hand. He was still testing me, still poking and prodding at me. He hadn't put me through the past four days simply to get his head vaporized like this.

There had to be another way.

"Choose!"

And I knew. One moment I hadn't, then an instant later I did. It was the only thing that made sense. The insane pieces suddenly seemed to fit together into a logical whole.

"I choose that no one dies," I said.

"That was not one of the choices given!" he screeched.

"If I've won the game as you've said, then I can redefine the choices. The winner always makes the rules. That's always true. It may be the only true thing in the world."

He stepped back.

"You think you can change the rules here, change the very nature of reality? You think you know enough to call the shots?"

I took a step toward him. I suddenly felt that I knew him, just as well as I knew myself. There'd be no backing down. The slightest sign of weakness would get me killed.

"Yes!"

He stepped further back, actually staggered back.

"Good," he said. "I was starting to have my doubts." He clicked his fingers.

Behind me, I heard something wet splash against stone.

I turned.

Just like Napoleon, the Aztec priest incarnation of Wood was disintegrating, melting into a greasy-looking puddle that was being sucked down into the pyramid.

"You've almost gone the distance, boy. But it's not quite over yet."

He walked past me, stepping over the puddle that was all that remained of the Aztec Colin Wood. Again he snapped his fingers, and a slab of stone in front of him swirled molten, flowed back on itself, and then revealed a staircase.

It wasn't a stone staircase, something in keeping with this insane Aztec motif, but one made of chrome-and-glass steps that led down into the dark.

"We've got to talk," he said as he stepped down. "There's a few things you don't yet understand."

A few things I don't yet understand.

In my four days here that was without a doubt the stupidest, most inane thing I had yet heard. It was only after his head had completely disappeared that I was even able to move toward the staircase. My eyelids were twitching uncontrollably.

Full Circle.

I stood in a bay window and stared down the California coast. It was early morning, and the sea glimmered orange. Beyond the houses, and beyond the sea wall, a surfer paddled out. It was an illusion, a projection on the backside of this Nanomechanoid-created bay window, but that really didn't seem to matter.

Reality was no longer something cold and fixed, something filled with absolutes and bounded with hard and fast rules. Reality was subjective. Reality was in the eye of the beholder. The scene I saw now was no less real than the one I had seen four days ago—or actually, eighty-six years ago.

I felt myself slipping.

"Smith."

I turned.

It *was* the Walnut Conference Room, complete with cheaply stained paneled walls and that twenty-seat black lacquer conference table. Wood, still in the guise of Colin Junior, sat at the far end, leaning back in his seat, feet propped up onto the table.

I felt something squirm on my wrist.

Ting! Ting! Ting!

Reflexes guided my hands and fingers, silencing the alarm of the watch, which had not been on my arm until only seconds ago. I glanced down at it, knowing what it would read, but some morbid streak deep within me forced me to look down just to make certain.

"Eight-thirty," I whispered.

"I'd like to start this meeting on time," said Wood.

Suddenly feeling mechanical, like some sort of automaton, I watched my hand jerk out, grab for the back of a chair, miss it, then grab for it again, this time getting it and pulling it out. Sitting, I stared at my reflection in the black tabletop.

"I killed over ten billion people," he said.

I blinked.

"Ten billion people."

I looked up. His feet were still propped up. He had one hand around the back of his neck, and in the other he held a Fudge Pop. He took a large bite from it and swallowed without even chewing. His eyelids fluttered, and I could see the pain flash across his face.

Ice cream headache.

I knew that feeling. It felt like a chisel being driven right between the eyes. If I ate ice cream too quickly the result was inevitable—an ice cream headache was guaranteed. He should have known better. How could he be so stupid? Why would he willingly subject himself to such pain?

"Ten billion people," he said once again.

He should have known better.

My hands were against the tabletop, palms down. The lacquered wood felt cool and hard, but most of all, undeniably real. It *was* real.

"I could never have done that," I said in a whisper. "Never."

He jerked his boots down from the table, and bent forward. "Don't be so sure," he said. "You have to remember the ones I rescued, the ones who lived, the ones who *will* live."

"No one has the right to make those choices," I said.

"I did not have the right," he said. He nodded, and for just a moment he glanced past me, looking out through the bay window. Then he quickly looked back at me. "I had the responsibility."

"No one can be given that type of responsibility," I said. There was no way that anyone, no matter what the circumstances, could justify the murder of ten billion people. Never. Absolutely never.

"Responsibility is not given. Circumstance thrusts it on you, demands that you respond. I was the right person at the right time at the right place. The responsibility was mine because I recognized its existence."

He was rambling. He was insane. Nothing could justify what he'd done.

"The world was at the brink. If it hadn't been my viroid that was let loose, it would have been someone else's. Every day that passed increased the odds that some madman would unleash something that would destroy the *entire* world."

That's exactly what *had* happened.

"But I was in the position to stop it, to make certain that it wouldn't happen. When I recognized the inevitable destruction, it was my responsibility to act. I could do nothing else. What would you have done if you truly believed, without any doubt, that the world was coming to an end? What would you do if you believed that nothing would survive, that man would cease to exist?''

''No one could be certain of that,'' I said, but as I said it I wondered. What if I was certain? What if I knew beyond any doubt that the world was going to destroy itself? How much of it would I be willing to kill, so that something might survive?

Smack!

He'd smashed an open palm against the table, and now stood.

''I was.'' His jaw was clenched, and the muscles in his cheeks twitched. ''I did what I felt I had to. I nearly destroyed the world so that it could be born again. I created this asylum so that mankind could have a chance. I wiped the slate clean, locking mankind into two hundred new Edens. I made the viroid, created the egomaniacal Loki, built the John Smith constructs, implemented Thor, and then *I* destroyed the world with them!''

He slumped down, practically crumpling into his chair.

''I took responsibility,'' he said.

I looked into his eyes. There was no uncertainty, no doubt, absolutely no question. But there was pain—more pain than any pair of eyes was ever meant to hold.

''And I killed them.''

Now I stood. For days now I had wanted nothing more than to kill this man. He'd destroyed a world, and I was certain that anyone who had done that deserved to die.

I *had* been certain.

Now I didn't know. What I did know, however, was that I was thankful that I hadn't faced what he had, that I hadn't been there to make the decision he had. I was thankful that the responsibility hadn't been mine.

''And are you so different?'' he asked.

''Yes!'' I said, spitting the word out without thinking about it, not having to think about it.

''But you've killed. You've made decisions that resulted in *innocent* people dying. You've manipulated and lied, done any and everything to achieve your goal."

"You were killing *millions*!" I screamed. "You still are killing millions." With every breath I took, countless Mushies probably were being vaporized.

He nodded. "I see then. It's all a numbers game. You can kill a handful in order to stop some madman who's killing millions."

The answer didn't come this time.

"No quick answers for that one, are there?"

What could I say? Was I any better, or for that matter any worse than him? Was a man who killed a million worse than a man who killed one?

"I created this place, this world, but I'm not a part of it. My world is gone and dead," he said.

Sweat dripped down my face.

I suddenly knew what he was going to say.

I knew what all this insanity had been about.

I understood it all.

I would have given anything not to have understood.

"I did my best to purge the worst of my world, but it isn't complete, isn't total. Some of the seeds still exist, hiding, buried deep. But I won't root them out, I can't. And that's because I'm part of it. I can see the world that will come, and I know that there's no place for me in it. I can't be."

I couldn't break away from his gaze. I wanted to, wanted it more than anything else I'd *ever* wanted in my life, but I couldn't.

"I needed someone to replace me, to shoulder my responsibility, to see that this new world has a chance to survive and to grow into something new. That's why I called you. But I couldn't bring you here and simply tell you what had happened, and then expect you to take over. You had to experience this world, come to know its people, see its strengths and its weaknesses. But most of all, you had to see yourself."

"You killed my friends," I said in a whisper. I could feel them all around me, as if they were seated at this table, packed tightly into this small room.

He nodded. "The person you were four days ago

would never be able to do the job you will *have* to do. I sacrificed them for those who are still to come. You had to learn what it is to see those close to you die, to feel that pain, to feel the waste and the tragedy. You had to feel that so that in the future, when faced with similar choices, you'll know what it is to take a life. You'll never be able to take a life without remembering those that were taken from you."

"How could you do this!"

Tears ran down my face.

"Because I was able to. Your memories come from a time and a place where no one person could really change the world, not even presidents or dictators. They'd claim they could change things but they couldn't, and that made them safe, it protected them from making the decisions that *no one* should be faced with. But I *had* the power. The world was going to be destroyed, totally destroyed. Everyone recognized that, but no one could do anything about it. But I could. And once I realized that I couldn't turn my back to it. It became my *responsibility*. Not to act would have murdered every unborn generation of mankind to come."

"But what if you were wrong?"

I had my answer before he even spoke. The pain that filled his eyes was his real answer.

"But what if I wasn't?" he said.

And that would be the only answer I would ever get. There'd be no black and white, no right and wrong. He'd been presented a choice and had made his decision.

That was all there was.

That was all there ever was.

"I'll give you all my powers. You'll control the last Laser Facility, the orbital Thor nodes, and have total global Nanomechanoid control. But you won't be alone. There are three thousand other John Smith constructs spread throughout the world, waiting to help you. You've proven to me you can do this job. Your responses and actions of the past four days have proven that. You've proven to me that you can make the types of decisions that no one should be asked to make."

"I don't want that responsibility. I don't want to have the power of life and death over millions of people. No one should have that kind of power! I don't know what to do, or even how to do it. Everyone I've so much as touched since coming here has been killed. I won't take the responsibility for anyone else's life!"

He smiled. The pain was still in his eyes, but he smiled.

"You've condemned yourself to that responsibility with your own words. This *was* the last test. I offered you the world, but you didn't want to take it. The only man who stands even the slightest chance of successfully guiding this new world is the man who believes he has *no right* to do that."

"No," I said, pleading with him.

Quickly standing, he walked back to the walnut paneling. "Yours is the last life I tamper with, the last life I uproot and destroy." He melded into the paneling, then vanished altogether.

"I'm sorry." His voice echoed throughout the room.

CHAPTER 20

Next Day

Clouds rolled in from the north.

I hoped it would rain and put out the fires. It was early morning but the sky was still dark, full of soot and embers. In the distance, looking like some ugly red sore, Palmdale burned.

But Thor was silent.

I'd removed the Speed Limit.

I sat on the same rocky crag that I'd sat on only a few days earlier. But now I sat here alone. The Laser Facility spread out beneath me, no longer white, nor even gray, but black, coated with the ashes from a burning world. My first impulse was to destroy it, bounce a beam from Thor and blast it to rubble. I could have, I knew the destruct codes.

I knew all the codes.

But I didn't destroy it.

Colin Wood had killed ten billion people to create this world. I could neither agree nor disagree with what he had done. I wasn't there, hadn't seen his world, so I couldn't pass judgment. But one thing that I did know was that this world had been bought with those ten billion lives. As insane, crazy, and twisted as this world was, they'd paid for it. And because of that, I wouldn't change it. I wouldn't drop the Quad Walls, or tamper with Thor or the Laser Facility.

Not yet.

Most likely, never.

There were two hundred worldlets out there, each with a chance to start over. But they wouldn't be starting clean. Again I looked up at the red glow that hovered over Palmdale. They definitely wouldn't be starting clean. Each and every survivor would carry scars of the old world, and it was my job, *my responsibility,* to see that those new worlds had a chance to grow into something new, something good.

I stood and adjusted the straps of my pack, redistributing the weight. I'd first head east, on foot, going out across the Mojave, moving toward Arizona or Nevada.

It would be slow going, and the terrain desolate.

But that's what I needed for now.

I needed the loneliness, the isolation.

I needed the time to heal.

So did the world.

About the Author

Robert A. Metzger has spent his entire life in the Los Angeles area, including his stint at UCLA where he received a Ph.D. in Electrical Engineering, and his current stint at the Hughes Research Laboratories in Malibu where he grows thin film materials for high speed transistors by a process called Molecular Beam Epitaxy. His short stories have appeared in *Aboriginal SF* and *Weird Tales*, and he writes a science column called "What If?" which appears in *Aboriginal SF*.

He lives with no cute pets, has no endearing hobbies, and hates yogurt with a passion that most people reserve for ax-murderers. He reads supermarket tabloids, refuses to wash his car, and has managed to convince several people that lettuce is his favorite food.

He is currently working on the sequel to *Quad World*.